Collier's *Junior* Classics

Series Editor
Margaret E. Martignoni

Series Titles	*Volume Editors*
A, B, C: GO!	**Rosemary E. Livsey**
ONCE UPON A TIME	**Elizabeth H. Gross**
MAGIC IN THE AIR	**Mary V. Gaver**
JUST AROUND THE CORNER	**Alice Brooks McGuire**
IN YOUR OWN BACKYARD	**Marian C. Young**
GIFTS FROM THE PAST	**Elenora Alexander**
LEGENDS OF LONG AGO	**Jane Darrah**
ROADS TO GREATNESS	**Louise Galloway**
CALL OF ADVENTURE	**Charlemae Rollins**
HARVEST OF HOLIDAYS	**Ruth Weeden Stewart**

LEGENDS
of long ago

A completely new selection of outstanding children's stories and poems compiled for enrichment reading by a distinguished editorial board of children's librarians.

Series Editor
MARGARET E. MARTIGNONI
Former Superintendent
Work with Children
Brooklyn Public Library

Editor-in-Chief
DR. LOUIS SHORES
Dean, Library School
Florida State University

Managing Editor
HARRY R. SNOWDEN, JR.

Volume Editor
JANE DARRAH
Superintendent
Work with Children
Seattle Public Library

Collier's *Junior* Classics Series

THE CROWELL-COLLIER PUBLISHING COMPANY • NEW YORK

Legends of Long Ago

Introduction

Collier's Junior Classics Series

We are children only once, and then only for a few brief years. But these are the most impressionable years of a lifetime. Never again will the world and everything in it be so eternally new, so filled with wonder. Never again will physical, mental, spiritual growth be so natural and unavoidable. During these years, habits become ingrained, tastes are developed, personality takes form. The child's whole being is geared toward learning. He instinctively reaches out for truth and, having no prejudices, seizes upon that which is good, just, beautiful. For these reasons, a child deserves what Walter de la Mare has called "only the rarest kind of best."

What do we mean by "best" in a book for children? Best books reflect universal truths with clarity and artistry. Such books reveal that man is essentially good and that life is infinitely worth living. They do not deny the existence of evil, but rather emphasize man's thrilling struggle against evil through faith, courage, and perseverance. They awaken the young reader's imagination, call forth his laughter as well as his tears, help him to understand and to love his fellow man. The reading of such books constitutes a rich heritage of experience which is every child's birthright.

The librarian-editors of *Collier's Junior Classics* have combed the best children's books of the past and present to assemble in a single series a sampling of the finest literature for boys and girls. High standards have been maintained for the art work also, which in most instances has been taken from the original book. No attempt has been made to cover all fields of knowledge or to include factual material for its own sake. The emphasis here is on good literature, chiefly fiction and biography, folk lore and legend, and some poetry. Special attention is given to the American scene and American democratic ideals, but many selections cover other cultures, geographical areas, and historical periods.

The purpose of *Collier's Junior Classics* is to introduce boys and girls to some of the best books ever written for children, to stimulate young readers to seek for themselves the books from which the selections have been drawn as well as other good books of similar appeal, and to encourage children to become discriminating, thoughtful, life-time readers. Author, title, and publisher are given at the foot of the page on which each selection opens. This enables readers to ask for the complete book at a library or bookstore. When necessary, brief introductions set the scene for the selection, while follow-up recommendations, complete with publishers' names, appear at the end of most stories.

Collier's Junior Classics is a series of ten individually indexed volumes. A, B, C: GO! has been lovingly compiled for the youngest, and consists of nursery rhymes, favorite folk tales, best-loved poems, and stories for reading aloud. Four volumes have been assembled for the intermediate group: ONCE UPON A TIME, a wonderous collection of fables, world folk tales, and modern fairy tales; MAGIC IN THE AIR, selections from great masterpieces of fantasy; JUST AROUND THE CORNER, excerpts from warm-hearted stories of other lands; and IN YOUR OWN BACKYARD, selections from stirring books about our own country. Four additional volumes cater to the interests of more mature boys and girls: GIFTS FROM THE PAST, memorable selections from world classics; LEGENDS OF LONG AGO, selections from great myths, epics, and American tall tales; ROADS TO GREATNESS, excerpts from biographies of some of the greatest men and women of the world; and CALL OF ADVENTURE, selections from action and suspense stories of today and yesterday. Finally, and most unusual of all, is the volume entitled HARVEST OF HOLIDAYS, a feast of stories, poems, documents, and factual material about twenty-two American national and religious holidays. Although perhaps of greatest interest to the intermediate group, HARVEST OF HOLIDAYS will intrigue and delight all ages.

The tables of contents for the ten volumes read like an all-time Who's Who of distinguished writers. A brief mention of only a few of these authors would include such names as Lewis Carroll, Kenneth Grahame, Charles Dickens, Mark Twain, Louisa May Alcott, Pearl Buck, Laura Ingalls Wilder, Eleanor Estes, Genevieve Foster, Robert Louis Stevenson, Robert McCloskey, Valenti Angelo, Carl Sandburg, A. A. Milne, Eleanor Farjeon, Elizabeth Enright, and Margaret Wise Brown. Among the illustrators, many of whom are also authors, are to be found the Petershams, the d'Aulaires, Wanda Gág, Louis Slobodkin, Helen Sewell, Lois Lenski, Roger Duvoisin, Maurice Sendak, Kurt Wiese, Marguerite de Angeli, Steele Savage, Howard Pyle, Lynd Ward, James Daugherty, Arthur Rackham, Fritz Kredel, and Gustave Dore.

Collier's Junior Classics is intended primarily for the home, although libraries will find the series valuable for browsing as well as for introducing children to many different books. Because each book is an individual volume, complete with its own index, it can be shelved where the librarian believes it will be most useful to the children.

No pains have been spared to make the individual volumes a series of stepping stones to all that is best in the magic world of children's books.

Margaret E. Martignoni
SERIES EDITOR

Contents

The Arabian Nights

Mythology

Epics and Hero Tales

American Tall Tales

Legends of Long Ago

Legends are stories from the past—with no known authors and no exact dates. They are the accumulated wisdom and imagination of the simple folk of every land—a mixture of fact and fiction.

The story of people, their hopes and their fears, is mirrored in their tales. They created heroes whose qualities they, themselves, most wanted in life. People suffering from social injustices created Robin Hood, who stole from the rich and gave to the poor. People with consummate faith in God and their King told about Arthur and his Round Table. And pioneers, carving out a wilderness and building a nation, created giant heroes with Bunyanesque strength.

Myths, too, are a reflection of the people's ideas. In their myths, the people tried to explain the unknown. They created gods to replace their doubts and fears. They incorporated in myths their ideas of right and wrong, of good and evil. The morals of the myths were the morals of the people.

The legends and myths that we read today have been written and rewritten in thousands of versions and in many languages. They are more than just studies of people—they are literature as well. "Ali Baba" and "Aladdin" not only tell about a people of long ago but also provide exciting entertainment. The myths are not merely moral studies, they are thrilling stories of contests in strength and wit. American tall tales are filled with fun and robust humor, and the hero tales and epics abound with adventure.

LEGENDS OF LONG AGO transports you by chariot, horseback, and magic to other places and other times. On lofty Olympus, at Sherwood Forest, and in the many other lands of the legends, you will experience the enchantment and excitement, the adventure and intrigue that has fascinated the world for centuries.

JANE DARRAH
Superintendent, Work with Children,
Seattle Public Library

THE ARABIAN NIGHTS

"Ali Baba and the Forty Thieves" and "Aladdin; or, "The Wonderful Lamp," are part of a huge collection of folk tales called *The Thousand and One Nights*, popularly known as *The Arabian Nights*. The origin of these tales has been lost in antiquity— some seem to have come from North Africa, others from Persia and ancient India. They were circulated in the marketplaces of the Moslem world and reflect the manners and customs of Medievel Moslem society.

It was a Frenchman, Antoine Galland, who introduced a French translation of these stories to the Western world in 1704. They have since been translated into many different languages and have become a part of the literary heritage of the western world.

Aladdin; or, The Wonderful Lamp

EDITED BY PADRAIC COLUM

Illustrations by William Colrus

IN a large and rich city of China, there once lived a tailor, named Mustapha. He was very poor. He could hardly, by his daily labour, maintain himself and his family, which consisted only of his wife and a son.

His son, who was called Aladdin, was a very careless and lazy fellow. He was disobedient to his father and mother, and would go out early in the morning and stay out all day, playing in the streets and public places with idle children of his own age.

When he was old enough to learn a trade, his father took him into his shop and taught him how to use a needle; but all Mustapha's endeavours to keep his son to work were vain, for no sooner was his back turned than the boy was gone for the day. Mustapha chastised him, but Aladdin clung to the habits he had formed and his father was forced to abandon him to his idleness; and this was such a grief to Mustapha that he fell sick and died in a few months.

Aladdin, who was now no longer restrained by the fear of a father, gave himself entirely over to his idle habits, and was never out of the streets. This course he followed till he was fifteen years old, without giving his mind to any useful pursuit or the least reflection on what would become of him. As he was one day playing, according to custom, in the street, with his bad companions, a stranger passing by stopped to observe him.

This stranger was a sorcerer, known as the African magician. He had but two days before arrived from Africa, his native country.

From *The Arabian Nights*, selected and edited by Padraic Colum. Copyright 1923, 1951, 1953 by The Macmillan Company.

The African magician, seeing in Aladdin's countenance some thing which assured him that he was a fit boy for his purpose, inquired his name and history of his companions, and when he had learnt all he desired to know, went up to him, and, taking him aside from the other lads, said, "Child, was not your father called Mustapha the tailor?"

"Yes, sir," answered the boy; "but he has been dead for many years."

At these words the African magician threw his arms about Aladdin's neck and kissed him several times, with tears in his eyes, and said: "I am your uncle. Your worthy father was my own brother. I knew you at first sight, you are so like him."

Then he gave Aladdin a handful of small money, saying, "Go, my son, to your mother, give my love to her, and tell her I will visit her to-morrow, that I may see where my good brother lived so long, and ended his days."

Aladdin ran to his mother, overjoyed at the money his uncle had given him. "Mother," said he, "have I an uncle?"

"No, Child," replied his mother, "you have no uncle by your father's side or mine."

"I am just now come," said Aladdin, "from a man who says he is my uncle and my father's brother. He cried and kissed me when I told him my father was dead, and gave me money, send-ing his love to you, and promising to come and pay you a visit, that he may see the house my father lived and died in."

"Indeed, child," replied the mother, "your father had no broth-er, nor have you an uncle."

The next day the magician found Aladdin playing in another part of town, and, embracing him as before, put two pieces of gold into his hand and said to him: "Carry this, child, to your mother. Tell her that I will come and see her to-night, and bid her get us something for supper; but first show me the house where you live."

Aladdin showed the African magician the house and carried the two pieces of gold to his mother, who went out and bought provisions; and considering she wanted various utensils, bor-rowed them of her neighbours. She spent the whole day in preparing the supper; and at night, when it was ready, said to her son: "Perhaps the stranger knows not how to find our house. Go and bring him, if you meet him."

Aladdin was just ready to go when the magician knocked at the door and came in loaded with all sorts of fruits, which he brought for a dessert. After he had given what he brought into Aladdin's hands, he saluted the boy's mother and began to talk with her.

"My good sister," said he, "do not be surprised at your never having seen me all the time you have been married to my brother Mustapha of happy memory. I have been forty years absent from this country, and during that time have travelled into the Indies, Persia, Arabia, and Syria, and afterwards crossed over into Africa, where I took up my abode. At last, as is natural, I was desirous to see my native country again, and to embrace my dear brother; and finding I had strength enough to undertake so long a journey, I made the necessary preparations, and set out. Nothing ever afflicted me so much as hearing of my brother's death. But God be praised for all things! It is a comfort for me to find, as it were, my brother in a son, who has almost the same features."

The African magician, perceiving that the widow wept at the remembrance of her husband, changed the conversation, and turning towards her son, asked him: "What business do you follow? Are you in any trade?"

At this question the youth hung his head, and was not a little abashed when his mother answered: "Aladdin is a lazy fellow. His father, when alive, strove all he could to teach him his trade, but could not succeed; and since his death, notwithstanding all I can say to him, he does nothing but idle away his time in the streets, as you saw him, without considering he is no longer a child; and if you do not make him ashamed of it, I despair of his ever coming to any good. For my part I am resolved, one of these days, to turn him out of doors and let him provide for himself."

After these words, Aladdin's mother burst into tears, and the magician said: "This is not well, nephew. You must think of helping yourself and getting your livelihood. There are many sorts of trades. Perhaps you do not like your father's, and would

prefer another. I will endeavour to help you. If you have no
mind to learn any handicraft, I will take a shop for you, and
furnish it with all sorts of fine stuffs and linens. Tell me freely
what you think of my proposal. You shall always find me ready
to keep my word."

This plan just suited Aladdin, who hated work. He told the
magician he had a greater inclination to the business suggested
than to any other, and that he should be much obliged to him
for his kindness.

"Well, then," said the African magician, "I will take you with
me to-morrow, clothe you as handsomely as the best merchants
in the city, and afterwards we will open a shop as I mentioned."

The widow, after his promises of kindness to her son, no
longer doubted that the magician was her husband's brother.
She thanked him for his good intentions; and after having exhorted Aladdin to render himself worthy of his uncle's favour,
served up supper, at which they talked of several indifferent
matters; and then the magician went away.

He came again the next day and took Aladdin with him to a
merchant, who sold all sorts of clothes for different ages and

ranks ready made, and a variety of fine stuffs, and bade Aladdin chose those he preferred, which he paid for.

When Aladdin found himself so handsomely equipped, he returned his uncle thanks, who thus addressed him, "As you are soon to be a merchant, it is proper you should frequent these shops and be acquainted with them."

He then showed him the largest and finest mosques, went with him to the khans where the merchants and travellers lodged, and afterwards to the Sultan's palace, and at last brought him to his own khan, where, meeting with some merchants he had become friendly with since his arrival, he gave them a treat, to make them and his pretended nephew acquainted.

This entertainment lasted till night, when Aladdin would have taken leave of his uncle to go home. The magician would not let him go by himself, but conducted him to his mother, who, as soon as she saw him so well dressed, was transported with joy, and bestowed a thousand blessings on the magician.

Early the next morning the magician called again for Aladdin and said he would take him to spend that day in the country, and on the next he would purchase the shop. He then led him out at one of the gates of the city, past some magnificent palaces, to each of which belonged beautiful gardens, into which anybody might enter. At every building he came to he asked Aladdin if he did not think it fine.

By this artifice the cunning magician led Aladdin some way into the country; and as he meant to carry him farther, to execute his design, he pretended to be tired, and took an opportunity to sit down in one of the gardens, on the brink of a fountain of clear water, which discharged itself by the mouth of a bronze lion into a basin. "Come, nephew," said he, "you must be weary as well as I. Let us rest ourselves, and we shall be better able to pursue our walk."

The magician pulled from his girdle a handkerchief in which were cakes and fruit, and while they ate he exhorted his nephew to leave off bad company, and to seek that of wise and prudent men to improve by their conversation. "For," said he, "you will soon be at man's estate, and you cannot too early begin to imitate their example."

When they had eaten as much as they wanted, they got up and pursued their walk beyond the gardens and across the country.

At last they arrived between two mountains of moderate height and equal size, divided by a narrow valley. This was the place where the magician intended to execute the design that had brought him from Africa to China.

"We will go no farther now," said he to Aladdin; "I will show you here some extraordinary things, which, when you have seen, you will thank me for; but while I prepare to strike a light, gather up all the loose dry sticks you can see to kindle a fire with."

Aladdin found so many dry sticks that he soon collected a great heap. The magician presently set them on fire; and when they were in a blaze, threw in some incense, pronouncing several magical words which Aladdin did not understand.

He had scarcely done so when the earth opened just before the magician, and exposed a stone with a brass ring fixed in it. Aladdin was so frightened that he would have run away, but the magician caught hold of him and gave him such a box on the ear that he knocked him down. Aladdin got up trembling, and with tears in his eyes said to the magician, "What have I done, uncle, to be treated in this severe manner?"

"I supply the place of your father," answered the magician; "and you ought to make no reply. But, child," added he, softening, "do not be afraid, for I shall not ask anything of you except that you obey me punctually. Only thus can you reap the advantages I intend for you. Know, then, that under this stone there is hidden a treasure, destined to be yours, and which will make you richer than the greatest monarch in the world. No person but yourself is permitted to lift this stone or enter the cave, and you must do exactly what I may command, for it is a matter of great consequence both to you and to me."

Aladdin, amazed at all he saw and heard, forgot what was past, and rising, said: "Well, uncle, what is to be done? Command me, I am ready to obey."

"I am overjoyed, child," said the African magician, embracing him. "Take hold of the ring and lift up that stone." "Indeed, uncle," replied Aladdin, "I am not strong enough. You must help me."

"You have no occasion for my assistance," answered the magician; "if I help you, we shall be able to do nothing. Take hold of the ring and lift up the stone. You will find it will come easily."

Aladdin did as the magician bade him, raised the stone with ease, and laid it at one side.

When the stone was pulled up, there appeared a staircase about three or four feet in length, leading to a door. "Descend those steps, my son," said the African magician, "and open that door. It will let you into a palace divided into three great halls. In each of the halls you will see four large brass cisterns full of gold and silver; but take care you do not meddle with them. Before you enter the first hall, be sure to tuck up your robe, wrap it about you, and then pass through the second into the third without stopping. Above all things, have a care that you do not touch the walls even with your clothes; for if you do, you will die instantly. At the end of the third hall, you will find a door which opens into a garden planted with fine trees loaded with fruit. Walk directly across the garden to a terrace, where you will see a niche before you, and in that niche a lighted

lamp. Take the lamp down and blow out the light. When you have thrown away the wick and poured out the liquid the lamp contains, put it in your waistband and bring it to me. Do not be afraid that the liquid will soil your clothes, for it is not oil, and as soon as it is poured out the lamp will be dry."

After these words the magician drew a ring off his finger and put it on one of Aladdin's, saying, "It is a talisman against all evil so long as you obey me. Go, therefore, boldly, and we shall both be rich all our lives."

Aladdin descended the steps, and, opening the door, found the three halls just as the African magician had described. He went through them with all the precaution the fear of death could inspire, crossed the garden without stopping, took down the lamp from the niche, threw out the wick and the liquid,

and put it in his waistband. But as he came down from the
terrace, he stopped in the garden to observe the trees, which
were loaded with extraordinary fruit of different colours. Some
trees bore fruit entirely white, and some clear and transparent
as crystal; some red, some green, blue, and purple, and others
yellow; in short, there was fruit of all colours. The white fruit
were pearls; the clear and transparent, diamonds; the red,
rubies; the green, emeralds; the blue, turquoises; the purple,
amethysts; and the yellow, sapphires. Aladdin, ignorant of their
value, would have preferred figs, or grapes, or pomegranates;
but he resolved to gather some of every sort. Having filled two
new purses, he wrapped some up in his robe and crammed his
bosom as full as it could hold.

Aladdin, having thus loaded himself with riches of which he

knew not the value, returned through the three halls and soon arrived at the mouth of the cave, where the African magician awaited him with the utmost impatience. As soon as Aladdin saw him, he cried out, "Pray, uncle, lend me your hand, to help me out."

"Give me the lamp first," replied the magician; "it will be troublesome to you."

"Indeed, uncle," answered Aladdin, "I cannot now, but I will as soon as I am up."

The African magician was determined that he would have the lamp before he would help him up; and Aladdin, who had encumbered himself so much with his fruit that he could not well get at it, refused to give it to him till he was out of the cave. The African magician, provoked at this obstinate refusal, flew into a passion, threw a little of his incense into the fire, and pronounced two magical words, when the stone which had closed the mouth of the staircase moved into its place, with the earth over it in the same manner as it lay at the arrival of the magician and Aladdin.

This action of the magician plainly revealed to Aladdin that he was no uncle of his, but one who designed him evil. The truth was that he had learnt from his magic books the secret and the value of this wonderful lamp, the owner of which would be made richer than any earthly ruler, and hence his journey to China. His art had also told him that he was not permitted to take it himself, but must receive it as a voluntary gift from the hands of another person. Hence he employed young Aladdin, and hoped by a mixture of kindness and authority to make him obedient to his word and will. When he found that his attempt had failed, he set out to return to Africa, but avoided the town, lest any person who had seen him leave in company with Aladdin should make inquiries after the youth. Aladdin, being suddenly enveloped in darkness, cried, and called out to his uncle to tell him he was ready to give him the lamp; but in vain, since his cries could not be heard. He descended to the bottom of the steps, with a design to get into the palace, but the door, which was opened before by enchantment, was now shut by the same means. He then redoubled his cries and tears, sat down on the steps without any hopes of ever seeing light again,

and in expectation of a speedy death. In this great emergency
he said, "There is no strength or power but in the great and
high God; and in joining his hands to pray he rubbed the ring
which the magician had put on his finger."

Immediately a Jinni of frightful aspect appeared, and said,
"What wouldst thou have? I am ready to obey thee. I serve
him who possesses the ring on thy finger, I and the other slaves
of that ring."

At another time Aladdin would have been frightened at the
sight of so extraordinary a figure, but the danger he was in
made him answer without hesitation, "Whoever thou art, deliver me from this place."

He had no sooner spoken these words than he found himself
on the very spot where the magician had last left him, and no
sign of cave or opening, nor disturbance of the earth. Returning
God thanks to find himself once more in the world, he made the
best of his way home. When he got within his mother's door,
the joy to see her and his weakness for want of food made him
so faint that he fell down and remained for a long time as dead.
As soon as he recovered, he related to his mother all that had
happened to him, and they were both very vehement in de-
nouncing the cruel magician. Aladdin slept soundly till late
the next morning, when the first thing he said to his mother
was, that he wanted something to eat, and wished she would
give him his breakfast.

"Alas! child," said she, "I have not a bit of bread to give you.
You ate up all the provisions I had in the house yesterday; but
I have a little cotton which I have spun. I will go and sell it,
and buy something for our dinner."

"Mother," replied Aladdin, "keep your cotton for another
time, and give me the lamp I brought home with me yesterday.
I will sell it, and the money I shall get will serve both for
breakfast and dinner, and perhaps supper too."

Aladdin's mother took the lamp, and said to her son: "Here
it is, but it is very dirty. If it was a little cleaner, I believe it
would bring something more."

She took some fine sand and water to clean it; but had no
sooner begun to rub it than in an instant a hideous Jinni of
gigantic size appeared before her, and said to her in a voice

of thunder: "What wouldst thou have? I am ready to obey thee as thy slave, and the slave of all those who have that lamp in their hands; I and the other slaves of the lamp."

Aladdin's mother, terrified at the sight of the Jinni, fainted. Aladdin, who had seen such a phantom in the cavern, snatched the lamp out of his mother's hand and said to the Jinni boldly, "I am hungry, bring me something to eat."

The Jinni disappeared immediately, but promptly returned with a large silver tray, on which were twelve covered dishes of the same metal, containing the most delicious viands. He set down the tray and disappeared. This was done before Aladdin's mother recovered from her swoon.

Aladdin fetched some water and sprinkled it in her face to revive her. Whether that or the smell of the meat effected her cure, it was not long before she came to herself.

"Mother," said Aladdin, "be not afraid. Get up and eat. Here is what will put you in heart, and at the same time satisfy my extreme hunger."

His mother was much surprised to see the great tray and twelve dishes, and to smell the savoury odour which exhaled from the food. "Child," said she, "to whom are we obliged for this great plenty and liberality? Has the Sultan been made acquainted with our poverty and had compassion on us?"

"It is no matter, mother," said Aladdin, "let us sit down and eat, for you have almost as much need for a good breakfast as myself. When we have done I will answer your questions."

Accordingly, both mother and son sat down, and ate with the better relish as the table was so well furnished. But all the time Aladdin's mother could not forbear looking at and admiring the tray and dishes, though she could not judge whether they were silver or some other metal.

The mother and son sat at breakfast till it was noon, and then they thought it would be best to eat dinner; yet, after this they found they should have enough left for supper, and two meals for the next day.

When Aladdin's mother had taken away what was left, she went and sat down by her son on the sofa, saying, "I expect now that you will satisfy my impatience, and tell me exactly what passed between the Jinni and you while I was in a swoon."

She was as greatly amazed at what her son told her as at the appearance of the Jinni, and said to him, "But, son, what have we to do with the Jinn? I never heard that any of my acquaintances had ever seen one. How came that vile Jinni to address himself to me, and not to you, to whom he had appeared before in the cave?"

"Mother," answered Aladdin, "the Jinni you saw is not the one who appeared to me. If you remember, he that I first saw called himself the slave of the ring on my finger; and this you saw called himself the slave of the lamp you had in your hand; but I believe you did not hear him, for I think you fainted as soon as he began to speak."

"What!" cried the mother, "was your lamp then the occasion of that cursed Jinni addressing himself rather to me than to you? Ah! my son, take it out of my sight, and put it where you please. I had rather you would sell it than run the hazard of being frightened to death again by touching it; and if you would take my advice, you would part also with the ring, and not have anything to do with the Jinn, who, as our prophet has told us, are only devils."

"With your leave, mother," replied Aladdin, "I shall now take care how I sell a lamp which may be so serviceable both to you and me. That false and wicked magician would not have undertaken so long a journey to secure this wonderful lamp if he had not known its value exceeded that of gold and silver. And since we have honestly come by it, let us make a profitable use of it, though without any great show to excite the envy and jealousy of our neighbours. However, since the Jinni frightens you so much, I will take it out of your sight, and put it where I may find it when I want it. The ring I cannot resolve to part with, for without that you had never seen me again; and though I am alive now, perhaps, if it was gone, I might not be so some moments hence. Therefore, I hope you will give me leave to keep it, and to wear it always on my finger."

Aladdin's mother replied that he might do what he pleased; but for her part, she would have nothing to do with the Jinn, and ordered him never to say anything more about them.

By the next night they had eaten all the provisions the Jinni had brought; and the following day Aladdin put one of the silver dishes under his vest, and went out early to sell it. He addressed himself to a pedlar whom he met in the streets, took him aside, and pulling out the plate, asked him if he would buy it. The cunning pedlar took the dish, examined it, and as soon as he found it was good silver, asked Aladdin at how much he valued it. Aladdin, who had never been used to such traffic, told him he would trust to his judgment and honour. The pedlar was somewhat confounded at this plain dealing; and doubting whether Aladdin understood the material or the full value of what he offered to sell, took a piece of gold out of his purse and gave it to him, though it was but the sixtieth part of the worth of the plate. Aladdin received the money very eagerly and retired with so much haste that the pedlar, not content with his great profit, was vexed he had not penetrated into Aladdin's ignorance. He was going to run after him, to endeavour to get some change out of the piece of gold; but Aladdin ran so fast, and had got so far, that it was impossible for the pedlar to overtake him.

Before Aladdin went home, he called at a baker's, bought some cakes of bread, changed his money, and on his return gave the rest to his mother, who went and purchased provisions enough to last them some time. After this manner they lived, till Aladdin had sold the twelve dishes one by one, as necessity pressed, to the pedlar, who paid each time the same money as for the first, because he durst not offer less, in fear of losing so good a bargain. When he had sold the last dish, he still had the tray, which weighed ten times as much as the dishes, and he would have carried it to his old purchaser, but it was too large and cumbersome. Therefore he was obliged to bring him home to his mother's, where, after the pedlar had estimated the weight of the tray, he laid down ten pieces of gold, with which Aladdin was very well satisfied.

When all the money was spent, Aladdin had recourse again to the lamp. He took it in his hand and looked for the part where his mother had rubbed it with the sand and water. There he rubbed it also, when the Jinni immediately appeared and said: "What wouldst thou have? I am ready to obey thee as thy slave, and the slave of all those who have that lamp in their hands; I, and the other slaves of the lamp."

"I am hungry," said Aladdin, "bring me something to eat."

The Jinni disappeared, and presently returned with a tray, containing the same number of covered dishes as before, set them down, and vanished.

As soon as Aladdin found that their provisions were again gone, he took one of the dishes, and went to look for his pedlar; but passing by a goldsmith's shop, the goldsmith perceiving him, called to him and said: "My lad, I imagine that you have something to sell to the pedlar, whom I often see you visit; but perhaps you do not know that he is a great rogue. I will give you the full worth of what you have to sell, or I will direct you to other merchants who will not cheat you."

This offer induced Aladdin to pull his plate from under his vest and show it to the goldsmith, who at first sight saw that it was made of the finest silver, and asked him if he had sold such as that to the pedlar. Aladdin told him that he had sold the pedlar twelve such, for a piece of gold each.

What a villain! cried the goldsmith. But, added he, my son, what is past cannot be recalled. By showing you the value of this plate, which is of the finest silver we use in our shops, I will let you see how much the pedlar has cheated you.

The goldsmith took a pair of scales, weighed the dish, and assured Aladdin that his plate would fetch by weight sixty pieces of gold, which he offered to pay immediately.

Aladdin thanked him for his fair dealing, and never after went to any other person.

Though Aladdin and his mother had a boundless treasure in their lamp, and might have had whatever they wished for, yet they lived with the same frugality as before, and it may easily be supposed that the money for which Aladdin had sold the dishes and tray was sufficient to maintain them some time.

During this interval, Aladdin frequented the shops of the principal merchants, where they sold cloth of gold and silver, linens, silk stuffs, and jewellery, and oftentimes joining in their conversation, acquired a knowledge of the world and a desire to improve himself. By his acquaintance among the jewellers he came to know that the fruits which he had gathered when he took the lamp were, instead of coloured glass, stones of immense value; but he had the prudence not to mention this to anyone, not even to his mother.

One day as Aladdin was walking about the town, he heard an order proclaimed, commanding the people to shut up their shops and houses, and keep within doors, while the Princess Bedr-el-Budur, the Sultan's daughter, went to the bath and returned.

This proclamation inspired Aladdin with eager desire to see the princess's face, and he determined to gratify this desire by placing himself behind the door of the bath, so that he could not fail to see her face as she went in.

Aladdin had not long concealed himself before the princess came. She was attended by a great crowd of ladies and slaves, who walked on each side and behind her. When she came within three or four paces of the door of the bath, she took off her veil, and gave Aladdin a chance for a full view of her features.

The princess was a noted beauty. Her eyes were large, lively, and sparkling; her smile bewitching; her nose faultless; her mouth small; her lips vermilion. It is not therefore surprising that Aladdin, who had never before seen such a blaze of charms, was dazzled and enchanted.

After the princess had passed by, and entered the bath, Aladdin quitted his hiding-place and went home. His mother perceived him to be more thoughtful and melancholy than usual, and asked what had happened to make him so, or if he was ill. He then told his mother all his adventure, and concluded by declaring, "I love the princess more than I can express, and am resolved that I will ask her in marriage of the Sultan."

Aladdin's mother listened with surprise to what her son told her; but when he talked of asking the princess in marriage, she laughed aloud. "Alas! child," said she, "what are you thinking of? You must be mad to talk thus."

"I assure you, mother," replied Aladdin, "that I am not mad, but in my right senses. I foresaw that you would reproach me with folly and extravagance; but I must tell you once more, that I am resolved to demand the princess of the Sultan in marriage; nor do I despair of success. I have the slaves of the lamp and of the ring to help me, and you know how powerful their aid is. And I have another secret to tell you: those pieces of glass, which I got from the trees in the garden of the underground palace, are jewels of inestimable value, and fit for the greatest monarchs. All the precious stones the jewellers have in Baghdad are not to be compared to mine for size or beauty; and I am sure that the offer of them will secure the favour of the Sultan. You have a large porcelain dish fit to hold them. Fetch it, and let us see how they will look, when we have arranged them according to their different colours."

Aladdin's mother brought the china dish, and he took the jewels and placed them in order, according to his fancy. But the brightness and lustre they emitted, and the variety of the colours, so dazzled the eyes both of mother and son that they were astonished beyond measure. Aladdin's mother, embold-

ened by the sight of these rich jewels, promised to carry them
the next morning to the Sultan. Aladdin rose before daybreak
and awakened his mother, urging her to get admittance to the
Sultan's palace, if possible, before the Grand Wezir and the
great officers of state went in to take their seats in the assembly,
where the Sultan always attended in person.

Aladdin's mother took the china dish in which they had put
the jewels the day before, wrapped it in two fine napkins, and
set forward for the Sultan's palace. When she came to the gates,
the Grand Wezir and most distinguished lords of the court
were just gone in; but not withstanding the crowd of people
was great, she got into a spacious hall, the entrance to which
was very magnificent. She placed herself just before the Sultan,
who sat in council with the Grand Wezir, and the great lords,
on his right and left hand. Several cases were called, according
to their order, pleaded and adjudged, until the time the assembly generally broke up, when the Sultan, rising, returned to
his apartment, attended by the grand Wezir. The other Wezirs
and ministers of state then retired, as did all those whose business had called them thither.

Aladdin's mother, seeing all the people depart, concluded
that the Sultan would not appear again that day, and resolved
to go home; and on her arrival said, with much simplicity: "Son,
I have seen the Sultan, and am very well persuaded he has
seen me too, for I placed myself just before him; but he was
so much taken up with those who attended on all sides of him
that I pitied him, and wondered at his patience. At last I believe
he was heartily tired, for he rose suddenly, and would not hear
a great many who were ready prepared to speak to him, but
went away, at which I was well pleased, for indeed I began to
lose all patience, and was extremely fatigued with staying so
long. But there is no harm done. I will go again to-morrow.
Perhaps the Sultan may not be so busy."

The next morning she repaired to the Sultan's palace with
the present, as early as the day before; and she went six times
afterwards on the days appointed, placing herself always directly before the Sultan, but with as little success as the first
morning.

On the sixth day, however, when the Sultan returned to his

own apartment, he said to his Grand Wezir: "I have for some time observed a certain woman, who attends constantly every day that I give audience, with something wrapped up in a napkin. She always stands from the beginning to the breaking up of the audience, and places herself just before me. If this woman comes to our next assembly, do not fail to call her, that I may hear what she has to say."

On the next audience day, when Aladdin's mother went to the assembly, and placed herself in front of the Sultan as usual, the Grand Wezir immediately called an officer, and pointing to her, bade him bring her before the Sultan. The old woman at once followed the officer, and when she reached the Sultan, bowed her head down to the carpet which covered the platform of the throne, and remained in that posture till he bade her rise, which she had no sooner done than he said to her: "Good woman, I have observed you standing many days, from the beginning to the end of the assembly. What business brings you here?"

After these words, Aladdin's mother prostrated herself a second time; and when she arose, said, "Monarch of monarchs, I beg you to pardon the boldness of my petition, and to assure me of your pardon and forgiveness."

"Well," replied the Sultan: "I will forgive you, be it what it may, and no hurt shall come to you. Speak boldly."

When Aladdin's mother had taken all these precautions, for fear of the Sultan's anger, she told him faithfully the errand on which her son had sent her.

The Sultan hearkened to this discourse without showing the least anger; but before he gave her any answer, asked her what she had brought tied up in the napkin. She took the china dish which she had set down at the foot of the throne, untied it, and presented it to the Sultan.

The Sultan's amazement and surprise were inexpressible when he saw so many large, beautiful, and valuable jewels collected in the dish. He remained for some time lost in admiration. At last, when he had recovered himself, he received the present from the hand of Aladdin's mother, saying, "How rich, how beautiful!"

After he had admired and handled all the jewels one after

another, he turned to his Grand Wezir, and showing him the
dish, said, "Behold, admire, wonder! and confess that your
eyes never saw jewels so rich and beautiful before."

The Wezir was charmed. "Well," continued the Sultan, "what
sayest thou to such a present? Is it not worthy of the princess
my daughter? And ought I not bestow her on one who values
her at so great a price?"

"I cannot but own," replied the Grand Wezir, "that the present
is worthy of the princess; but I beg of your majesty to grant me
three months before you come to a final resolution. I hope

before that time my son, whom you have regarded with your favour, will be able to make a nobler present than this Aladdin, who is an entire stranger to your majesty."

The Sultan granted his request, and he said to the old woman, "Good woman, go home, and tell your son that I agree to the proposal you have made me; but I cannot let him marry the princess my daughter for three months. At the expiration of that time come again."

Aladdin's mother returned home much more gratified than she had expected, and told her son the condescending answer she had received from the Sultan's own mouth; and that she was to come to the assembly again in three months.

Aladdin thought himself the most happy of all men at hearing this news, and thanked his mother for the pains she had taken in the affair, the success of which was of so great importance to his peace, that he counted every day, week, and even hour as it passed. When two of the three months were gone, his mother one evening having no oil in the house, went out to buy some, and found there was a general rejoicing. The houses were decorated with flowers, silks, and carpeting, and the people were all striving to show their joy. The streets were crowded with officers in costumes of ceremony, mounted on horses richly caparisoned, each attended by a great many footmen. Aladdin's mother asked the oil merchant what was the meaning of all this public festivity.

"Whence came you, good woman," said he, "that you don't know the Grand Wezir's son is to marry the Princess Bedr-el-Budur, the Sultan's daughter, to-night? She will presently return from the bath; and these officers are to assist at the cavalcade to the palace, where the ceremony is to be solemnized."

Aladdin's mother, on hearing this news, ran home very quickly. "My son," cried she, "you are undone! the Sultan's fine promises will come to naught. This night the Grand Wezir's son is to marry the Princess Bedr-el-Budur."

At this account, Aladdin was thunderstruck, and he bethought himself of the lamp, and of the Jinni who had promised to obey him; and without indulging in idle words against the Sultan, the Wezir, or his son, he determined, if possible, to prevent the marriage.

When Aladdin had got into his chamber, he took the lamp, and rubbed it. Immediately the Jinni appeared, and said to him: "What wouldst thou have? I am ready to obey thee as thy slave, I and the other slaves of the lamp."

"Hear me," said Aladdin; "thou hast hitherto done everything I ordered, but now I am about to impose on thee a harder task. The Sultan's daughter, who was promised me as my bride, is this night to marry the son of the Grand Wezir. Bring them both hither to me as soon after the ceremony as they are alone."

"Master," replied the Jinni, "I obey you."

Aladdin supped with his mother as was their habit, and then went to his own apartment, to await the return of the Jinni.

In the meantime the festivities in honour of the princess' marriage were conducted in the Sultan's palace with great magnificence. The ceremonies were at last brought to a conclusion, and the princess and the son of the Wezir retired to the apartment prepared for them. No sooner had they entered it, and dismissed their attendants, than the Jinni, the faithful slave of the lamp, to the great amazement and alarm of the bride and bridegroom, took them up and by an agency invisible to them transported them in an instant into Aladdin's room, where he set them down.

"Remove the bridegroom," said Aladdin to the Jinni, "and keep him a prisoner till to-morrow at dawn, and then return with him here."

On Aladdin's being left alone with the princess he endeavoured to calm her fears, and explained to her the treachery practised on him by the Sultan her father. He then went outside the door and laid himself down and there stayed till morning. At break of day, the Jinni appeared bringing back the bridegroom, and by Aladdin's command transported the bride and bridegroom into the palace of the Sultan.

At the instant that the Jinni had set them down in their own apartment, the Sultan came to offer his good wishes to his daughter.

Having been admitted, he kissed the princess on the forehead, but was extremely surprised to see her look so melancholy. She only cast at him a sorrowful look, expressive of great affliction. He suspected there was something extraordinary in this silence, and thereupon went immediately to his wife's apartment, told her in what state he found the princess, and how she had received him.

"I will go see her," said the princess' mother.

The princess greeted her with sighs and tears, and signs of deep dejection. Her mother urged her to tell her thoughts, and at last she gave a precise description of all that happened to her during the night; on which her mother enjoined the necessity of silence and discretion, as no one would give credence to so strange a tale. The Grand Wezir's son, elated with the honour of being the Sultan's son-in-law, kept silence on his part, and the events of the night were not allowed to cast the least gloom on the festivities of the following day, in continued celebration of the royal marriage.

When night came, the bride and bridegroom were again attended to their apartment with the same ceremonies as on the preceding evening. Aladdin, knowing that this would be so, had already given his commands to the Jinni of the lamp; and no sooner were they alone than they were removed in the same mysterious manner as on the preceding evening; and having passed the night in the same unpleasant way, they were in the morning conveyed to the palace of the Sultan. Scarcely had they been replaced in their apartment when the Sultan came to make his compliments to his daughter. The princess could no longer conceal from him the unhappy treatment she had suffered, and told him all that had happened, as she had already related it to her mother. The Sultan, on hearing these strange tidings, consulted with the Grand Wezir; and finding from him that his son had been subjected to even worse treatment by an invisible agency, he determined to declare the marriage cancelled, and to order all the festivities, which were yet to last for several days, ended.

This sudden change in the mind of the Sultan gave rise to various reports. Nobody but Aladdin knew the secret, and he kept it with the most perfect silence; and neither the Sultan nor the Grand Wezir, who had forgotten Aladdin and his request, had the least thought that he had any hand in the strange adventures that befell the bride and bridegroom.

On the very day that the three months contained in the

Sultan's promise expired, the mother of Aladdin again went to the palace and stood in the same place in the assembly. The Sultan knew her and directed his Wezir to have her brought before him.

After having prostrated herself, she made answer, in reply to the Sultan, "Sire, I come at the end of three months to ask of you the fulfillment of the promise you made to my son."

The Sultan little thought the request of Aladdin's mother was made to him in earnest, or that he would hear any more of the matter. He therefore took counsel with his Wezir, who suggested that the Sultan should attach such conditions to the marriage that no one could possibly fulfil them. In accordance with this suggestion of the Wezir, the Sultan replied to the mother of Aladdin: "Good woman, it is true sultans ought to abide by their word, and I am ready to keep mine by making your son happy in marriage with the princess my daughter. But as I cannot let her marry without some further proof of your son's ability to support her in royal state, tell him I will fulfil my promise as soon as he shall send me forty trays of massy gold, full of the same sort of jewels you have already made me a present of, and carried by the like number of black slaves, who shall be led by as many young and handsome white slaves, all dressed magnificently. On these conditions I am ready to bestow the princess my daughter upon him. Therefore, good woman, go and tell him so, and I will wait till you bring me his answer."

Aladdin's mother prostrated herself a second time before the Sultan's throne and retired. On her way home she laughed within herself at her son's foolish imagination. "Where," said she, "can he get so many large gold trays and such precious stones to fill them? It is altogether out of his power, and I believe he will not be much pleased with my visit this time."

When she came home, full of these thoughts, she told Aladdin all the circumstances of her interview with the Sultan, and the conditions on which he consented to the marriage. "The Sultan expects your answer immediately," said she; and then added, laughing, "I believe he may wait long enough!"

"Not so long, mother, as you think," replied Aladdin. "This demand is a mere trifle, and will prove no bar to my marriage with the princess. I will prepare at once to satisfy his request."

Aladdin retired to his own apartment and summoned the Jinni of the lamp, and required him to immediately prepare and present the gift, before the Sultan closed his morning audience, according to the terms in which it had been prescribed. The Jinni professed his obedience to the owner of the lamp and disappeared. Within a very short time a train of forty black slaves, led by the same number of white slaves, appeared opposite the house in which Aladdin lived. Each black slave carried on his head a basin of massy gold, full of pearls, diamonds, rubies, and emeralds. Aladdin then addressed his mother: "Mother, pray lose no time. Before the Sultan and the assembly rise, I would have you return to the palace with this present as the dowry demanded for the princess, that he may judge by my diligence and exactness of the ardent and sincere desire I have to procure myself the honour of this alliance."

As soon as this magnificent procession, with Aladdin's mother at its head, had begun to march from Aladdin's house, the whole city was filled with the crowds of people desirous to see so grand a sight. The graceful bearing and elegant form of each slave, their grave walk at an equal distance from each other, the lustre of their jewelled girdles, and the brilliancy of the precious stones in their turbans excited the greatest admiration. As they had to pass through several streets to the palace, the whole length of the way was lined with files of spectators. Nothing, indeed, was ever seen so beautiful and brilliant in the Sultan's palace, and the richest robes of the officers of his court were not to be compared to the costly dresses of these slaves.

As the Sultan, who had been informed of their approach, had given orders for them to be admitted, they met with no obstacle, but went into the assembly in regular order, one part turning to the right and the other to the left. After they were all entered, and had formed a semicircle before the Sultan's throne, the black slaves laid the golden trays on the carpet, prostrated themselves, touching the carpet with their foreheads, and the white slaves did the same. When they rose, the black slaves uncovered the trays, and then all stood with their arms crossed over their breasts.

In the meantime Aladdin's mother advanced to the foot of

the throne, and having prostrated herself, said to the Sultan, "Sire, my son knows this present is much below the notice of Princess Bedr-el-Budur; but hopes, nevertheless, that your majesty will accept it, and make it agreeable to the princess, and with the greater confidence since he has endeavoured to conform to the conditions you were pleased to impose."

The Sultan, overpowered at the sight of such more than royal splendour, replied without hesitation to the words of Aladdin's mother, "Go and tell your son that I wait with open arms to embrace him; and the more haste he makes to come and receive the princess my daughter from my hands, the greater pleasure he will do me."

As soon as Aladdin's mother had retired, the Sultan put an end to the audience; and rising from his throne, ordered that the princess' attendants should come and carry the trays into their mistress' apartment, whither he went himself to examine them with her at his leisure. The fourscore slaves were conducted into the palace; and the Sultan, telling the princess of their magnificent apparel, ordered them to be brought before her apartment, that she might see through the lattices he had not exaggerated in his account of them.

In the meantime Aladdin's mother reached home and showed
by her demeanour and countenance the good news she brought
her son. "My son," said she, "you may rejoice you are arrived
at the height of your desires. The Sultan has declared that you
shall marry the Princess Bedr-el-Budur. He waits for you with
impatience."

Aladdin, enraptured with this news, made his mother very
little reply, but retired to his chamber. There he rubbed his
lamp, and the obedient Jinni appeared.

"Jinni," said Aladdin, "convey me at once to a bath, and supply
me with the richest and most magnificent robe ever worn by
a monarch."

No sooner were the words out of his mouth than the Jinni
rendered Aladdin, as well as himself, invisible, and transported
him into a bath of the finest marble, where he was washed with
various scented waters, and when he returned into the hall he
found, instead of his own poor raiment, a robe, the magnificence
of which astonished him. The Jinni helped him to dress, and
when he had done, transported him back to his own chamber,
where he asked him if he had any other commands.

"Yes," answered Aladdin, "bring me a charger that surpasses

in beauty and goodness the best in the Sultan's stables, with a
saddle, bridle, and other caparisons to correspond with his
value. Furnish also twenty slaves, as richly clothed as those who
carried the present to the Sultan, to walk by my side and follow
me, and twenty more to go before me in two ranks. Besides
these, bring my mother six women slaves to attend her, as richly
dressed at least as any of the Princess Bedr-el-Budur's, each
carrying a complete dress fit for any princess. I want also ten
thousand pieces of gold in each of ten purses. Go and make
haste."

As soon as Aladdin had given these orders, the Jinni disappeared, but presently returned with the horse, the forty slaves,
ten of whom carried each a purse containing ten thousand
pieces of gold, and six women slaves, each bearing on her head
a different dress for Aladdin's mother, wrapped up in a piece
of silver tissue, and gave them all to Aladdin.

He presented the six women slaves to his mother, telling her
they were hers, and that the dresses they had brought were
for her use. Of the ten purses Aladdin took four, which he gave
to his mother, telling her those were to supply her with necessa-
ries; the other six he left in the hands of the slaves who brought
them, with an order to throw the gold by handfuls among the
people as they went to the Sultan's palace. The six slaves who
carried the purses he ordered to march before him, three on
the right hand and three on the left.

When Aladdin had thus prepared himself for his first interview with the Sultan, he dismissed the Jinni, and immediately
mounting his charger began his march, and though he never
was on horseback before, appeared with a grace the most ex-
perienced horseman might envy. The innumerable concourse of
people through whom he passed made the air echo with their
acclamations, especially every time the six slaves who carried
the purses threw handfuls of gold among the populace.

On Aladdin's arrival at the palace, the Sultan was surprised
to find him more richly and magnificently robed than he had
ever been himself, and was impressed with his good looks and
dignity of manner, which were so different from what he expected in the son of one so humble as Aladdin's mother. He
embraced him with demonstrations of joy, and when Aladdin

would have fallen at his feet, held him by the hand and made him sit near his throne. He shortly after led him, amidst the sounds of trumpets and all kinds of music, to a magnificent entertainment, at which the Sultan and Aladdin ate by themselves, and the great lords of the court, according to their rank and dignity, sat at different tables. After the feast the Sultan sent for the chief Kadi, and commanded him to draw up a contract of marriage between the Princess Bedr-el-Budur and Aladdin. When the contract had been drawn, the Sultan asked Aladdin if he would stay in the palace and complete the ceremonies of the marriage that day.

"Sire," said Aladdin, "though great is my impatience to enter on the honour granted me by your majesty, yet I beg you to permit me first to build a palace worthy to receive the princess your daughter. I pray you to grant me sufficient ground near your palace, and I will have it completed with the utmost ex·pedition."

The Sultan granted this request, and again embraced him, after which Aladdin took his leave with as much politeness as if he had always lived at court.

Aladdin returned home in the manner in which he had come, amidst the rejoicings of the people, who wished him all happiness and prosperity. As soon as he dismounted, he retired to his own chamber, took the lamp, and summoned the Jinni as usual.

"Jinni," said Aladdin, "build me a palace fit to receive the Princess Bedr-el-Budur. Let its materials be made of nothing less than porphyry, jasper, agate, and the finest marble. Let its walls be massive gold and silver bricks laid alternately. Let each front contain six windows, and let the lattices of these (except one, which I want left unfinished) be enriched with diamonds, rubies, and emeralds, so that they shall exceed anything of the kind ever seen in the world. Let there be an inner and outer court in front of the palace and a spacious garden; but above all things, provide a safe treasure-house, and fill it with gold and silver. Let there also be kitchens and storehouses, stables full of the finest horses and hunting equipage, officers, attendants, and slaves to form a retinue for the princess and myself. Go and execute my wishes."

When Aladdin gave these commands to the Jinni, the sun was set. The next morning at daybreak the Jinni presented himself, and having obtained Aladdin's consent, transported him in a moment to the palace he had made. The Jinni led him through all the apartments, where he found officers and slaves, habited according to their rank and the services to which they were appointed. The Jinni then showed him the treasury, which was opened by a treasurer, where Aladdin saw large vases of different sizes, piled up to the top with money, ranged all round the chamber. The Jinni thence led him to the stables, where were some of the finest horses in the world, and grooms busy in caring for them. Thence they went to the storehouses, which were filled with all things necessary both for food and ornament.

When Aladdin had examined every portion of the palace, and particularly the hall with the four-and-twenty windows, and found it to far exceed his fondest expectations, he said, "Jinni, there is one thing wanting, a fine carpet for the princess to walk on from the Sultan's palace to mine. Lay one down immediately."

The Jinni disappeared, and Aladdin saw what he desired executed in an instant. The Jinni then returned and carried him to his own home.

When the Sultan's porters came to open the gates, they were amazed to find what had been an unoccupied garden filled up with a magnificent palace, and a splendid carpet extending to it all the way from the Sultan's palace. They told the strange tidings to the Grand Wezir, and he informed the Sultan, who exclaimed: "It must be Aladdin's palace, which I gave him leave to build for my daughter. He has wished to surprise us, and let us see what wonders can be done in only one night."

Aladdin, on being conveyed by the Jinni to his own home, requested his mother to go to the Princess Bedr-el-Budur and tell her that the palace would be ready for her reception in the evening. She went, attended by her women slaves, in the same order as on the preceding day. Shortly after her arrival at the princess' apartment, the Sultan himself came in and was surprised to find her, whom he knew as a suppliant at his assembly in such humble guise, to be now more richly and sumptuously attired than his own daughter. This gave him a higher opinion of Aladdin, who took such care of his mother and made her share his wealth and honours. A little while after her departure, Aladdin, mounting his horse and accompanied by his retinue of attendants, left his old home forever, and went to the palace in the same pomp as on the day before. Nor did he forget to take with him the wonderful lamp, to which he owed all his good fortune, nor to wear the ring which was given him as a talisman.

The Sultan entertained Aladdin with the utmost magnificence. At night, on the conclusion of the marriage ceremonies, the princess took leave of the Sultan her father. Bands of music led the procession. Four hundred of the Sultan's young pages carried torches on each side, which together with the illuminations of the Sultan's and Aladdin's palaces, made all the vicinity as light as day. The princess, conveyed in a superb litter and attended by her women slaves, proceeded on the carpet which was spread from the Sultan's palace to that of Aladdin's. On her arrival Aladdin was ready to receive her at the entrance and led her into a large hall, illuminated with an infinite number of wax candles, where a noble feast was served. The dishes were of massy gold and contained the most delicate viands. The vases, basins, and goblets were gold, also, and of exquisite workmanship, and all the other ornaments of the hall were equal to this display. The princess, dazzled to see so much riches collected in one place, said to Aladdin, "I thought, prince, that nothing in the world was so beautiful as the Sultan my father's palace, but the sight of this hall alone is sufficient to show I was deceived."

When the supper was ended, there entered a company of female dancers, who performed according to the custom of the country, singing at the same time verses in praise of the bride and bridegroom. About midnight Aladdin and his bride retired.

The next morning the attendants of Aladdin presented themselves to dress him, and brought him another costume, as rich and magnificent as that worn the day before. He then ordered one of the horses to be got ready, mounted him, and went in the midst of a large troop of slaves to the Sultan's palace to entreat him to take a repast in the princess' palace. The Sultan consented with pleasure and, preceded by the principal officers of his palace and followed by all the great lords of his court, accompanied Aladdin.

The nearer the Sultan approached Aladdin's palace the more he was struck with its beauty; but when he entered it, came into the hall, and saw the windows enriched with diamonds, rubies, and emeralds, he was completely surprised and said to his son-in-law: This palace is one of the wonders of the world; for where in all the world besides shall we find walls built of gold and silver, and diamonds, rubies, and emeralds composing the windows? Yet what most surprises me is, that a hall of this magnificence should be left with one of its windows incomplete.

"Sire," answered Aladdin, "the omission was by design, since I wished that you should have the glory of finishing this hall."

"I take your intention kindly," said the Sultan, "and will give orders about it immediately."

At the close of the magnificent entertainment provided by Aladdin, the Sultan was informed that the jewellers and gold-smiths attended, upon which he returned to the hall and showed them the window which was unfinished.

"I sent for you," said he, "to fit up this window in as great perfection as the rest. Examine them well, and make all the despatch you can."

The jewellers and goldsmiths examined the three-and-twenty windows with great attention, and after they had consulted together to know what each could furnish, they returned and presented themselves before the Sultan. The principal jeweller, undertaking to speak for the rest, said, "Sire, we are willing to exert our utmost care and industry to obey you; but among us all we cannot furnish jewels enough for so great a work."

"I have more than are necessary," said the Sultan; "come to my palace, and you shall choose what may answer your purpose."

When the Sultan returned to his palace, he ordered his jewels to be brought out, and the jewellers took a great quantity, particularly those Aladdin had presented to him, which they soon used, without making any great advance in their work. They came again several times for more, and in a month's time had not finished half their work. In short, they used all the jewels the Sultan had, and borrowed of the Wezir, but yet the window was not half done.

Aladdin, who knew that all the Sultan's endeavours to make this window like the rest were in vain, sent for the jewellers and goldsmiths, and not only commanded them to desist from their work, but ordered them to undo what they had begun, and to carry all the jewels back to the Sultan and to the Wezir. They undid in a few hours what they had been six weeks about and retired, leaving Aladdin alone in the hall. He took the lamp, rubbed it, and presently the Jinni appeared.

"Jinni," said Aladdin, "I ordered thee to leave one of the four-and-twenty windows of this hall imperfect, and thou hast executed my commands. Now I would have thee make it like the rest."

The Jinni immediately disappeared. Aladdin went out of the hall, and returning soon after found the window, as he wished it to be, like the others.

In the meantime the jewellers and goldsmiths repaired to the palace, and were introduced into the Sultan's presence, where the chief jeweller presented the precious stones, which he had brought back. The Sultan asked them if Aladdin had given them any reason for so doing, and they answering that he had not, he ordered a horse to be brought, which he mounted, and rode to his son-in-law's palace, with some few attendants on foot, to inquire why he had ordered the completion of the window to be stopped. Aladdin met him at the gate, and without giving any reply to his inquiries conducted him to the grand reception hall, where the Sultan, to his great surprise, found that the window which was left imperfect was now exactly like the others. He fancied at first that he was mistaken, and examined the two windows on each side, and afterwards all the four-and-twenty; but when he was convinced that the window which several workmen had been so long about was finished in so short a time, he embraced Aladdin and kissed him.

"My son," said he, "what a man you are to do such surprising things always in the twinkling of an eye! There is not your fellow in the world. The more I know you, the more I admire you."

Aladdin did not confine himself in his palace, but went with much state, sometimes to one mosque, and sometimes to another, to prayers, or to visit the Grand Wezir, or the principal lords of the court. Every time he went out, he caused two slaves, who walked by the side of his horse, to throw handfuls of money among the people as he passed through the streets and squares. This generosity gained him the love and blessings of the people. Thus Aladdin, while he paid all respect to the Sultan, won by his affable behavior and liberality the affections of the people.

Aladdin had conducted himself in this manner several years, when the African magician, who had never doubted but that he had destroyed him, determined to inform himself with certainty whether he perished, as he supposed, in the underground cave or not. After he had resorted to a long course of magic ceremonies to ascertain Aladdin's fate, what was his surprise to find that Aladdin, instead of dying in the cave, had made his escape, and was living in royal splendour by the aid of the wonderful lamp!

On the very next day the magician set out and travelled with the utmost haste to the capital of China, where, on his arrival, he took up his lodging in a khan.

He then quickly learnt about the wealth, charities, happiness, and splendid palace of Prince Aladdin. As soon as he saw the gold and silver walls and bejewelled windows of the palace, he knew that none but the Jinn, the slaves of the lamp, could have performed such wonders; and envious at Aladdin's high estate, he returned to the khan, with the purpose to find out where the

lamp was—whether Aladdin carried it about with him, or where he left it. His magic art soon informed him, to his great joy, that the lamp was in the palace. "Well," said he, rubbing his hands in glee, "I shall have the lamp, and I shall make Aladdin return to his original poverty."

The next day the magician was told by the chief superintendent of the khan where he lodged that Aladdin had gone on a hunting trip that was to last for eight days, of which only three had expired. The magician wanted to know no more. He resolved at once on his plans. He went to a coppersmith and asked for a dozen copper lamps. The master of the shop told him he had not so many then, but if he would have patience till the next day, he would have them ready. The magician agreed to wait, and desired him to take care that they should be handsome and well polished.

The next day the magician called for the twelve lamps, paid the man his full price, put them into a basket hanging on his arm, and went directly to Aladdin's palace. As he approached, he began crying, "Who will change old lamps for new ones?"

As he went along a crowd of children collected, who hooted at him and thought he was a madman or a fool, as did all who chanced to be passing by, to offer to change new lamps for old ones.

The African magician regarded not their scoffs, hootings, or all they could say to him, but still continued crying, "Who will change old lamps for new ones?"

He repeated this so often, walking backwards and forwards in front of the palace, that the princess, who was then in the hall of the four-and-twenty windows, hearing a man shout something, and seeing a great mob crowding about him, sent one of her women slaves to learn what he had to sell.

The slave returned laughing so heartily that the princess rebuked her.

"Princess," answered the slave, "who can forbear laughing to see an old man with a basket on his arm, full of fine new lamps, asking to change them for old ones? The children and mob crowd about him so that he can hardly stir, and they make all the noise they can in derision."

Another female slave, hearing this, said: "Now you speak of

lamps, I know not whether the princess may have observed it, but there is an old one on a shelf of the Prince Aladdin's robing-room, and whoever owns it will not be sorry to find a new one in its stead. If the princess chooses, she may have the pleasure of trying if this old man is so silly as to give a new lamp for an old one, without taking anything for the exchange."

The princess, who knew not the value of this lamp and the interest that Aladdin had to keep it safe, entered into the pleas-antry and commanded a slave to take it and make the exchange. The slave obeyed, went out of the hall, and no sooner got to the palace gates than he saw the African magician, called to him, and showing him the old lamp, said, "Give me a new lamp for this."

The magician never doubted but this was the lamp he wanted. There could be no other such in the place, where every utensil was gold or silver. He snatched it eagerly out of the slave's hand, and thrusting it as far as he could into his breast, held out his basket, and bade the slave choose which lamp he liked best. The slave picked out one, and carried it to the princess; and the change was no sooner made than the place rung with the shouts of the children, deriding the magician's folly.

The African magician stayed no longer near the palace, nor cried any more, "New lamps for old ones," but made the best of his way to his khan. He had succeeded in his purpose, and by his silence he got rid of the children and the mob.

As soon as he was out of sight of the two palaces, he hastened down the least-frequented streets; and having no more occasion for his lamps or basket, set all down in a spot where nobody saw him. Then going down another street or two, he walked till he came to one of the city gates, and pursuing his way through the suburbs, which were very extensive, at length reached a lonely spot, where he stopped till the darkness of the night, as the most suitable time for the design he had in comtemplation. When it became quite dark, he pulled the lamp out of his breast, and rubbed it.

At that summons the Jinni appeared and said: "What wouldst thou have? I am ready to obey thee as thy slave, and the slave of all those who have that lamp in their hands; both I and the other slaves of the lamp."

"I command thee," replied the magician, "to transport me immediately, and the palace which thou and the other slaves of the lamp have built in this city, with all the people in it, to Africa."

The Jinni made no reply, but with the assistance of the other Jinn, the slaves of the lamp, immediately transported him and the entire palace to the spot whither he had been desired to convey them.

Early the next morning, when the Sultan, according to custom, went to contemplate and admire Aladdin's palace, his amazement was unbounded to find that it was nowhere in sight. He could not comprehend how so large a palace, which he had seen plainly every day for some years, should vanish so soon and not leave the least remains behind. In his perplexity he ordered the Grand Wezir to be sent for with haste.

The Grand Wezir, who, in secret, bore no good will to Aladdin, intimated his suspicion that the palace was built by magic, and that Aladdin had made his hunting excursion an excuse for the removal of his palace with the same suddenness with which it had been erected. He induced the Sultan to send a detachment of his guards to seize Aladdin as a prisoner of state. When his son-in-law was brought before him, he would not hear a word from him, but ordered him to be put to death. The decree caused so much discontent among the people, whose affection Aladdin had secured by his largesses and charities, that the Sultan, fearful of an insurrection, was obliged to grant him his life.

As soon as Aladdin found himself at liberty, he addressed the Sultan, and said, "Sire, I pray you to let me know the crime by which I have lost thy favour."

"Your crime!" answered the Sultan, "wretched man! do you not know it? Follow me, and I will show you."

The Sultan then took Aladdin into the apartment whence it was his habit to look at and admire his palace, and said, "You ought to know where your palace stood; look, consider, and tell me what has become of it."

Aladdin looked, and being utterly amazed at the loss of his palace, was speechless. At last recovering himself, he said: "It is true, I do not see the palace. It is vanished; but I had no concern in its removal. I beg you to give me forty days, and if in that time I cannot restore it, I will offer my head to be disposed of at your pleasure."

"I give you the time you ask," responded the Sultan, "but at the end of the forty days forget not to present yourself before me."

Aladdin went out of the Sultan's palace in a condition of exceeding humiliation. The lords who had courted him in the days of his splendour, now declined to have any words with him. For three days he wandered about the city, exciting the wonder and compassion of the multitude by asking everybody he met if they had seen his palace, or could tell him anything of it. On the third day he wandered into the country, and as he was approaching a river, he fell down the bank and rubbed the ring which the magician had given him. Immediately the

same Jinni appeared whom he had seen in the cave where the
magician had left him.

"What wouldst thou have?" said the Jinni. "I am ready to obey
thee as thy slave, and the slave of all those who have that ring
on their finger, both I and the other slaves of the ring."

Aladdin, agreeably surprised at an offer of help so little expected, replied, "Jinni, show me where the palace I caused to
be built now stands, and transport it back where it first stood."

"Your command," answered the Jinni, "is not wholly in my
power; I am only the slave of the ring, and not of the lamp."

"I command thee, then," replied Aladdin, "by the power of
the ring, to transport me to the spot where my palace stands,
in whatsoever part of the world it may be."

These words were no sooner out of his mouth than the Jinni
transported him into Africa, to the midst of a large plain, where
his palace stood at no great distance from a city, and placing
him under the window of the princess' apartment left him.

Now it so happened that shortly after Aladdin had been
transported by the slave of the ring to the neighbourhood of
of his palace, that one of the attendants of the Princess Bedr-el-
Budur looking through the window perceived him and instantly
told her mistress. The princess, who could not believe the joy-
ful tidings, hastened to the window, and seeing Aladdin, immediately opened it. The noise of opening the window made
Aladdin turn his head that way, and perceiving the princess,
he saluted her with an air that expressed his joy.

"I have sent to have the private door unlocked for you," said
she. "Enter, and come up."

The private door which was just under the princess' apartment was soon opened, and Aladdin was conducted up into the
chamber. It is impossible to express the joy of both at seeing
each other after so cruel a separation. They embraced and shed
tears of joy. Then they sat down, and Aladdin said, "I beg of
you princess, to tell me what is become of an old lamp which
stood on a shelf in my robing-chamber."

"Alas!" answered the princess, "I was afraid our misfortunes
might be owing to that lamp; and what grieves me most is, that
I have been the cause of them. I was foolish enough to change

the old lamp for a new one, and the next morning I found myself in this unknown country, which I am told is Africa."

"Princess," said Aladdin, interrupting her, "you have explained all by telling me we are in Africa. I desire you only to inform me if you know where the old lamp now is."

"The African magician carries it carefully wrapped up in his bosom," said the princess; "and this I can assure you, because he pulled it out before me and showed it to me in triumph."

"Princess," said Aladdin, "I think I have found the means to deliver you and to regain possession of the lamp on which all my prosperity depends. To execute this design, it is necessary for me to go to the town. I shall return by noon, and will tell you what must be done by you to insure success. In the meantime, I shall disguise myself, and I beg that the private door may be opened at the first knock."

When Aladdin was out of the palace, he looked round him on all sides, and perceiving a peasant going into the country, hastened after him; and when he had overtaken him, made a proposal to him to change clothes, which the man agreed to. When they had made the exchange, the countryman went about his business, and Aladdin entered the city. After traversing several streets, he came to that part of the town where the merchants and artisans had their particular streets according to their trades. He went into that of the druggists; and entering one of the largest and best furnished shops, asked the druggist if he had a certain powder which he named.

The druggist, judging by his habit to be very poor, told him he had it, but that it was expensive, on which Aladdin pulled out his purse, and showing him some gold asked for half a dram of the powder, which the druggist weighed and gave him, telling him the price was a piece of gold. Aladdin put the money into his hand and hastened to the palace, which he entered at once by the private door. When he came into the princess' apartment, he said to her: "Princess, you must take your part in the scheme which I propose for our deliverance. You must overcome your dislike of the magician and assume a most friendly manner towards him, and ask him to oblige you by partaking of a feast in your apartments. Before he leaves, ask him to exchange cups with you, which he, gratified at the honour you do him, will gladly do, when you must give him the cup containing this powder. On drinking it he will instantly fall dead, and we will obtain the lamp whose slaves will do all our bidding and restore us and the palace to the capital of China."

The princess obeyed to the utmost her husband's instructions. She assumed a look of pleasure on the next visit of the magician and asked him to a feast. He most willingly accepted the invitation, and at the close of the evening, during which the princess had tried all she could to please him, she asked him to exchange cups with her. Then she had the drugged cup brought to her, and gave it to the magician. He drank it contents, out of compliment to the princess, to the very last drop, when he fell back lifeless on the sofa.

The princess, expecting the success of her scheme, had so placed her women from the great hall to the foot of the staircase that the word was no sooner given that the African magician was fallen backwards than the door was opened, and Aladdin admitted to the hall. The princess rose from her seat and ran overjoyed to embrace him; but he stopped her and said, "Princess, retire to your apartment, and let me be left alone while I endeavour to transport you back to China as speedily as you were brought thence."

When the princess, her women, and slaves were gone out of the hall, Aladdin shut the door, and going directly to the dead body of the magician opened his vest, and took out the lamp which was carefully wrapped up. He rubbed it, and the Jinni immediately appeared. "Jinni," said Aladdin, "I command thee to transport this palace instantly to the place whence it was brought hither."

The Jinni bowed his head in token of obedience and disappeared. Immediately the palace was transported into China, and its removal was only felt by two little shocks, the one when it was lifted up, the other when it was set down, and both in a very short interval of time.

On the morning after the restoration of Aladdin's palace the Sultan was looking out of his window and mourning over the fate of his daughter, when he thought he saw that the vacancy created by the disappearance of the palace was filled up. On looking more attentively, he was convinced beyond the power of doubt that he saw his son-in-law's palace. Joy and gladness succeeded to sorrow and grief. He at once ordered a horse to be saddled, which he mounted that instant, thinking he could not make haste enough to the place.

Aladdin rose that morning by daybreak, put on one of the most magnificent habits his wardrobe afforded, and went up into the hall of twenty-four windows. Thence he perceived the Sultan approaching, and received him at the foot of the great staircase and helped him to dismount.

He led the Sultan into the princess' apartment. The happy father embraced her with tears of joy; and the princess, on her side, afforded similar proofs of her extreme pleasure. After a short interval devoted to explanations of all that had happened, the Sultan restored Aladdin to his favour and expressed his regret for the apparent harshness with which he had treated him. "My son," said he, "be not displeased at my proceedings against you. They arose from my paternal love, and therefore you ought to forgive them."

"Sire," replied Aladdin, "I have not the least reason to complain of your conduct, since you did nothing but what your duty required. This wicked magician, the basest of men, was the sole cause of my misfortune."

The African magician, who was thus twice foiled in his endeavour to ruin Aladdin, had a younger brother, who was as skilful a magician as himself, and exceeded him in wickedness and hatred of mankind. By mutual agreement they communicated with each other once a year, however widely separate might be their place of residence from each other. The younger brother not having received as usual his annual message, prepared to ascertain what the trouble was. By his magic art he found that his brother was no longer living, but had been poisoned; and that his body was in the capital of the kingdom of China; also that the person who had poisoned him was of humble birth, though married to a princess, a Sultan's daughter.

As soon as the magician had informed himself of his brother's fate, he resolved immediately to revenge his death and at once departed for China, where, after crossing plains, rivers, mountains, and deserts, he arrived, having endured many fatigues. When he came to the capital of China, he took a lodging at a

khan. His magic art promptly revealed to him that Aladdin was the person who had been the cause of the death of his brother. He had not been long in the city before he noticed that every one was talking of a woman called Fatimeh, who was retired from the world, and who wrought many miracles. As he fancied that this woman might be useful to him in the project he had conceived, he made minute inquiries, and requested to be informed more particularly who that holy woman was, and as to the sort of miracles she performed.

"What!" said the person whom he addressed, "have you never seen her? She is the admiration of the whole town for her fasting and her exemplary life. Except Mondays and Fridays she never stirs out of her little cell, but on those days she comes into the town and does an infinite deal of good; for there is not a person who is diseased whom she does not put her hand on and cure."

Having ascertained the place where the hermitage of this holy woman was, the magician went at night and killed the good woman. In the morning he dyed his face the same hue as hers, arrayed himself in her garb, and taking her veil, the large necklace she wore round her waist, and her staff, went straight to the palace of Aladdin.

No sooner did the people see the holy woman, as they imagined him to be, than they gathered about him in a great crowd. Some begged his blessing, others kissed his hand, and others, more reserved, only the hem of his garment; while others, suffering from disease, stooped for him to lay his hands on them, which he did, muttering some words in form of prayer, and, in short, he pretended so well that everybody took him for the holy woman. He came at last to the square before Aladdin's palace. The crowd was so great and so noisy that the princess, who was in the hall of four-and-twenty windows, heard it and asked what was the matter. One of her women told her a vast number of people had collected about the holy woman to be cured of diseases by the laying on of her hands.

The princess, who had long heard of Fatimeh, but had never seen her, was very desirous to have some conversation with her. The chief officer perceiving this, told the princess it was an easy matter to bring the holy woman into the palace, if she desired and commanded it; and the princess expressing her wishes, he immediately sent four slaves for the pretended Fatimeh.

As soon as the crowd saw the attendants from the palace, it made way; and the magician, perceiving that they were coming for him, advanced to meet them, overjoyed to find his plot was succeeding so well.

"Holy woman," said one of the slaves, "the princess wants to see you and has sent for you."

"The princess does me great honour," replied the false Fatimeh; "I am ready to obey her command," and he followed the slaves to the palace.

When the pretended Fatimeh had bowed, the princess said: "My good mother, I have one thing to request which you must not refuse. It is to stay with me, that you may edify me with your way of living, and that I may learn from your good example."

"Princess," said the false Fatimeh, "I beg of you not to ask what I cannot consent to without neglecting my prayers and devotions."

"That shall be no hindrance to you," answered the princess. "I have a great many apartments unoccupied; you shall choose which you like best, and have as much liberty to perform your devotions as if you were in your own cell."

The magician, who really desired nothing more than to introduce himself into the palace, where it would be a much easier matter for him to work his designs, did not long excuse himself from accepting the obliging offer which the princess made him. "Princess," said he, "whatever resolution a poor wretched woman as I am may have made to renounce the pomp and grandeur of this world, I dare not presume to oppose the will and commands of so pious and charitable a princess."

On this the princess, rising, said, "Come with me; I will show you what vacant apartments I have, that you may make choice of the one you like best."

The magician followed the princess, and of all the apartments she showed him, he chose that which was the worst, saying it was too good for him, and he only accepted it to please her.

Afterwards the princess would have brought him back into the great hall to make him dine with her; but he, considering that he should then be obliged to show his face, which he had always taken care to conceal with Fatimeh's veil, and fearing that the princess would find out that he was not Fatimeh, begged of her earnestly to excuse him, telling her that he never ate anything but bread and dried fruits, and desired to eat that slight repast in his own apartment. The princess granted his request, saying: "You may be as free here, good mother, as if you were in your own cell. I will order you a dinner, but remember I want to talk with you as soon as you have finished your repast."

After the princess had dined, and the false Fatimeh had been sent for by one of the attendants, he again waited on her.

"My good mother," said the princess, "I am overjoyed to see so holy a woman as yourself, who will confer a blessing on this palace. But now I am speaking of the palace, pray how do you like it? And before I show it all to you, tell me first what you think of this hall."

The false Fatimeh surveyed the hall from one end to the other. When he had examined it well, he said to the princess: "So far as such a solitary being as I, who am unacquainted with what the world calls beautiful, can judge, this hall is truly admirable. There wants but one thing."

"What is that, good mother?" demanded the princess. "Tell me, I conjure you. For my part, I always believed and have heard say it wanted nothing; but if it does, it shall be supplied."

"Princess," said the false Fatimeh, with great deceit, "forgive me the liberty I have taken; but my opinion is, that if a rukh's egg were hung up in the middle of the dome, this hall would have no equal in the four quarters of the world, and your palace would be the wonder of the universe."

"My good mother," said the princess, "what is a rukh, and where may one get an egg?"

"Princess," replied the pretended Fatimeh, "it is a bird of prodigious size, which inhabits the summit of Mount Caucasus. The architect who built your palace can get you one of its eggs."

After the princess had thanked the false Fatimeh for what she believed her good advice, she conversed with her on other matters; but could not forget the rukh's egg, which she resolved to request of Aladdin when next he should visit her apartments. He returned in the course of the evening, and shortly after he entered, the princess thus addressed him: "I always believed that our palace was the most superb, magnificent, and complete in the world; but I will tell you now what it wants, and that is a rukh's egg hung up in the midst of the dome."

"Princess," replied Aladdin, "it is enough that you think it wants such an ornament; you shall see by the diligence I use in obtaining it that there is nothing which I would not do for your sake."

Aladdin left the Princess Bedr-el-Budur that moment, and went up into the hall of four-and-twenty windows, where, pulling out of his bosom the lamp, which after the danger he had been exposed to he always carried about him, he rubbed it, and the Jinni immediately appeared. "Jinni," said Aladdin, "I command thee, in the name of this lamp, bring a rukh's egg to be hung up in the middle of the dome of the hall of the palace."

Aladdin had no sooner pronounced these words than the hall shook as if ready to fall, and the Jinni said in a loud and terrible voice: "Is it not enough that I and the other slaves of the lamp have done everything for you; and yet you, by an unheard-of ingratitude, command me to bring my master and hang him up in the midst of this dome? This attempt deserves that you, the princess, and the palace should be immediately reduced to ashes; but you are spared because this request does not come from yourself. Its true author is the brother of the African magician. He is now in your palace, disguised in the habit of the holy woman Fatimeh, whom he has murdered. At his suggestion your wife makes this wicked demand. His design is to kill you. Therefore take care of yourself."

After these words the Jinni disappeared.

Aladdin resolved at once what to do. He returned to the princess' apartment, and without mentioning a word of what had happened sat down and complained of a great pain which had suddenly seized his head. On hearing this, the princess told him how she had invited the holy Fatimeh to stay with her, and that she was now in the palace, and could no doubt cure him. At Aladdin's request the princess ordered Fatimeh to be summoned at once.

When the pretended Fatimeh entered, Aladdin said: "Come hither, good mother. I am glad to see you here at so fortunate a time. I am tormented with a violent pain in my head, and request your assistance and hope you will not refuse me that cure which you impart to afflicted persons."

So saying, he rose, but held down his head. The counterfeit Fatimeh advanced towards him with his hand all the time on a dagger concealed in his girdle under his gown. Aladdin observed this, and snatched the weapon from the magician's hand and pierced him to the heart with his own dagger.

"My dear prince, what have you done?" cried the princess, in surprise. "You have killed the holy woman!"

"No my princess," answered Aladdin, with emotion, "I have not killed Fatimeh, but a villain, who would have assassinated me if I had not prevented him. This wicked man, added he, uncovering his face, is the brother of the magician who attempted our ruin. He has strangled the true Fatimeh and disguised himself in her clothes with intent to murder me."

Aladdin then informed her how the Jinni had told him these facts, and how narrowly she and the palace had escaped destruction through the treacherous suggestion which had led to her request.

Thus was Aladdin delivered from the persecution of the two brothers who were magicians. Within a few years afterwards the Sultan died in a good old age, and as he left no sons, the Princess Bedr-el-Budur succeeded him, and she and Aladdin reigned together many years.

'Ali Baba and the Forty Thieves

EDITED BY PADRAIC COLUM

Illustrations by William Colrus

THERE once lived in a town of Persia two brothers, one named Kasim and the other 'Ali Baba. Their father divided a small inheritance equally between them. Kasim married a very rich wife and became a wealthy merchant. 'Ali Baba married a woman as poor as himself and lived by cutting wood and bringing it on three asses into the town to sell.

One day when 'Ali Baba was in the forest, and had just cut wood enough to load his asses, he saw at a distance a great cloud of dust which seemed to approach him. He observed it with attention and soon distinguished a body of horsemen, whom he suspected might be robbers. To save himself, he determined to leave his asses, and after driving them into a thicket out of sight he climbed a large tree, growing on a high rock. Its branches were thick enough to conceal him and yet enabled him to see all that passed.

The horsemen numbered forty, and were all well mounted and armed. They came to the foot of the rock on which the tree stood and there dismounted. Every man unbridled his horse, tied it to a shrub, and gave it a feed of corn from a bag he had brought behind him. Then each of them removed his saddle-bag, which seemed to 'Ali Baba to be full of gold and silver from its weight. One, whom he took to be the captain, came under the tree in which 'Ali Baba was hidden, and making his way

through some bushes, pronounced the words, "Open Simsim!"*

As soon as the captain of the robbers had thus spoken, a door opened in the rock; and after he had made all his troop enter before him, he followed them, when the door shut of itself.

The robbers stayed some time within the rock, during which time 'Ali Baba, fearful of being caught, remained in the tree.

At last the door opened again, and the captain came out first and stood to see the troop all pass by him, when 'Ali Baba heard him make the door close by pronouncing these words, "Shut, Simsim!"

Every man at once bridled his horse and mounted. When the captain saw them all ready, he put himself at their head, and they returned the way they had come.

* Simsim, or sesame, is an East Indian herb which bears small, edible seeds. This password is commonly written, "Open Sesame!"

'Ali Baba followed them with his eyes as far as he could see them, and afterwards stayed a considerable time before he descended. Remembering the words the captain of the robbers used to cause the door to open and shut, he had the curiosity to try if his pronouncing them would have the same effect. Accordingly he went among the bushes, and perceiving the door concealed behind them, stood before it and said, "Open, Simsim!"

The door instantly flew wide open. 'Ali Baba, who expected a dark, dismal cavern, was surprised to see a well-lighted and spacious chamber, which received the light from an opening at the top of the rock. In the chamber were all sorts of provisions, rich bales of silk, brocade, and valuable carpeting piled on one another, gold and silver ingots in great heaps, and money in bags. The sight of all these riches made him suppose that this cave must have been occupied for ages by robbers who had succeeded one another.

'Ali Baba went boldly into the cave and collected as much of the gold coin as he thought his three asses could carry. The gold was in bags, and when he had loaded the asses, he laid wood over the bags in such a manner that they could not be seen. When he had passed in and out as often as he wished, he stood before the door, and pronouncing the words, "Shut, Simsim!" the door closed itself. He then made the best of his way to town.

When 'Ali Baba got home, he drove his asses into his little yard, shut the gates very carefully, threw off the wood that covered the panniers, carried the bags into his house, and ranged them in order before his wife. He then emptied the bags, which raised such a great heap of gold as dazzled his wife's eyes, and he told her the whole adventure from beginning to end, and, above all, recommended her to keep it secret.

The wife rejoiced greatly at their good fortune and wanted to count all the gold, piece by piece. "Wife," said 'Ali Baba, "you do not know what you undertake when you speak of counting the money. You will never get done. I will dig a hole and bury it. There is no time to be lost."

"You are in the right, husband," replied she; "but let us know, as nigh as possible, how much we have. I will borrow a measure and measure it while you dig the hole."

Away the wife ran to the house of her brother-in-law, Kasim, who lived just by, and addressing herself to his wife, desired the loan of a measure for a little while. Her sister-in-law asked her whether she would have a great or a small one, and she asked for a small one.

The sister-in-law fetched it, but as she knew 'Ali Baba's poverty, she was curious to learn what his wife wanted to measure, and artfully putting some suet at the bottom of the measure, brought it to her, with an excuse that she was sorry she had made her stay so long, but that she could not find it sooner.

'Ali Baba's wife went home, set the measure on the heap of gold, filled it, and emptied it, till she had done. She was very well satisfied to find the number of measures amounted to so many as they did, as was also her husband, who had now finished digging the hole. While 'Ali Baba was burying the gold, his wife, to show her exactness and diligence to her sister-in-law, carried the measure back, but without taking notice that a piece of gold had stuck to the bottom. "Sister," said she, giving it to her, "you see that I have not kept your measure long. I am obliged to you for it and return it with thanks."

As soon as 'Ali Baba's wife was gone, Kasim's wife looked at the bottom of the measure and was surprised to find a piece of gold sticking to it. Envy immediately possessed her breast. "What!" said she, "has 'Ali Baba gold so plentiful as to measure it? Whence has he all this wealth?"

Kasim her husband was at his counting-house. When he came home, his wife said to him: "Kasim, I know you think yourself rich, but 'Ali Baba is infinitely richer than you. He does not count his money, but measures it."

Kasim desired her to explain the riddle, which she did by telling him the stratagem she had used to make the discovery, and showed him the piece of money, which was so old that they could not tell when it was coined.

Kasim after he had married the rich widow had never treated 'Ali Baba as a brother, but neglected him; and now, instead of being pleased, he conceived a base envy at his brother's prosperity. He could not sleep all that night and went to him in the morning before sunrise. "'Ali Baba," said he, "I am surprised at you; you pretend to be miserably poor, and yet you measure gold. My wife found this at the bottom of the measure you borrowed yesterday."

By this discourse, 'Ali Baba perceived that Kasim and his wife knew what he had so much reason to conceal; but what was done could not be undone. Therefore, without showing the least surprise or trouble, he confessed all, and offered his brother part of the treasure to keep the secret.

"I must know exactly where this treasure is," replied Kasim haughtily; "and how I may visit it myself when I choose. Otherwise I will go and inform against you, and then you will not only get no more, but will lose all you have, and I shall receive a share for my information."

'Ali Baba told him all he desired to know, even to the very words he was to use to gain admission into the cave.

Kasim rose the next morning long before the sun and set out

for the forest with ten mules bearing great chests, which he designed to fill with gold. He followed the road 'Ali Baba had pointed out to him, and it was not long before he reached the rock and found the place by the tree and other marks of which his brother had told him. When he reached the entrance of the cavern, he pronounced the words, "Open, Simsim!"

The door immediately opened, and when he was in, closed on him. In examining the cave, he was greatly astonished to find much more riches than he had expected from 'Ali Baba's relation. He quickly laid at the door of the cavern as many bags of gold as his ten mules could carry; but his thoughts were now so full of the great riches he should possess, that he could not think of the necessary word to make the door open. Instead of "Open, Simsim!" he said "Open, Barley!" and was much amazed to find that the door remained fast shut. He named several sorts of grain, but still the door would not open.

Kasim had never expected such an incident, and was so alarmed at the danger he was in that the more he endeavored to remember the word Simsim the more his memory was confounded, and he had as much forgotten it as if he had never heard it mentioned. He threw down the bags he had loaded himself with and walked distractedly up and down the cave, without having the least regard to the riches that were around him.

About noon the robbers visited their cave. As they approached they saw Kasim's mules straggling near the rock, with great chests on their backs. Alarmed at this, they galloped full speed to the cave. They drove away the mules, who strayed through the forest so far that they were soon out of sight. Then the robbers, with their naked sabres in their hands, went directly to the door, which, when their captain pronounced the proper words, immediately opened.

Kasim, who heard the noise of the horses' feet, at once guessed the arrival of the robbers and resolved to make one effort for his life. He rushed to the door, and no sooner saw it open than he ran out and threw the robber captain down, but he could not escape the other robbers, who, with their swords, cut off his head.

The first care of the robbers after this was to examine the

cave. They found all the bags which Kasim had brought to the door, ready to load on his mules, and carried them to their places, but they did not miss what 'Ali Baba had taken away before. Then holding a council, and deliberating on the occurrence, they guessed that Kasim, when he was in, had not been able to get out, but could not imagine how he had learned the secret words by which alone he could enter. They could not deny the fact of his being there; and to terrify any person or accomplice who should attempt the same thing, they agreed to cut Kasim's body into four quarters and hang two on one side and two on the other, within the door of the cave. They had no sooner taken this resolution than they put it in execution; and when they had nothing more to detain them, left the place of their hoards well closed. They mounted their horses, and went to beat the roads again and attack the caravans they might meet.

In the meantime Kasim's wife was very uneasy when night came and her husband had not returned. She ran to 'Ali Baba in great alarm and said: "I believe, brother-in-law, that you know Kasim has gone to the forest and on what account. It is now night, and he has not come back. I am afraid some misfortune has happened to him."

'Ali Baba told her that she need not frighten herself, for Kasim would certainly not think it proper to come into the town till the night was pretty far advanced.

Kasim's wife, considering how much it concerned her husband to keep the business secret, was easily persuaded to believe her brother-in-law. She went home and waited patiently till midnight. Then her fear redoubled, and her grief was the more marked because she was forced to keep it to herself. She repented her foolish curiosity and cursed her desire to pry into the affairs of other people. She spent all the night in weeping; and as soon as it was day, went to her brother- and sister-in-law, telling them by her tears the cause of her coming.

'Ali Baba did not wait for his sister-in-law to ask him to go to see what was become of Kasim, but begging her to moderate her affliction, departed immediately with his three asses. He went to the forest, and when he came to the rock, having seen neither his brother nor the mules on the way, was seriously alarmed at finding some blood near the door. He took this for an ill omen; but when he had pronounced the proper words, and the door had opened, he was struck with horror at the dismal sight of his brother's body. He was not long in determining how he should pay the last dues to his brother, and having loaded one of his asses with the body, covered it over with wood. The other two asses he loaded with bags of gold, covering them with wood also as before. Then he bid the door shut and came away; but was so cautious as to stop some time at the end of the forest, that he might not go into the town before night. When he reached home he drove the two asses loaded with gold into his little yard and left the care of unloading them to his wife, while he led the other to his sister-in-law's house.

'Ali Baba knocked at the door, which was opened by Marjaneh, a clever, intelligent slave, who was fruitful in inventions to meet the most difficult circumstances. When he came into the court, he unloaded the ass, and taking Marjaneh aside said to her: "You must observe close secrecy. I have brought your master's body. We must bury him as if he had died a natural death. Go now and tell your mistress. I leave the matter to your wit and skilful devices."

'Ali Baba helped to place the body in Kasim's house and then returned with his ass.

Marjaneh went out early the next morning to a druggist, and asked for a sort of lozenge which was considered efficacious in the most dangerous disorders. The apothecary inquired who was ill. She replied with a sigh, "My good master Kasim himself, and he can neither eat nor speak."

In the evening Marjaneh went to the same druggist again, and with tears in her eyes asked for an essence which they used to give to sick people only when at the last extremity. "Alas!" said she, taking it from the apothecary, "I am afraid that this remedy will have no better effect than the lozenges, and that I shall lose my good master."

Moreover, as 'Ali Baba and his wife were often seen going between Kasim's and their own house that day, and seemed melancholy, nobody was surprised in the evening to hear the lamentable shrieks and cries of Kasim's wife and of Marjaneh, who gave out everywhere that Kasim was dead. The next morn-

ing at daybreak, Marjaneh went to an old cobbler whom she knew to be always early at his stall, and bidding him good morrow, put a piece of gold into his hand, saying, "Baba Mustapha, bring with you your sewing tackle and come with me; but I must tell you, I shall blindfold you when you come to a certain place."

Baba Mustapha hesitated a little at these words. "Oh! oh!" replied he, "you would have me do something against my conscience or against my honour?"

"God forbid that I should ask anything contrary to your honour!" said Marjaneh, putting another piece of gold into his hand. "Only come along with me and fear nothing."

Baba Mustapha went with Marjaneh, who, after she had bound his eyes with a handkerchief at the place she had mentioned, guided him to her deceased master's house, and never unloosed his eyes till he had entered the room where she had the corpse. "Baba Mustapha," said she, "you must make haste and sew the parts of this body together; and when you have finished, I will give you another piece of gold."

When Baba Mustapha had finished his task, she blindfolded him again, gave him the third piece of gold as she had promised, and recommending secrecy to him, led him back to the place where she first bound his eyes. There she pulled off the bandage, and let him go home, but watched him till he was quite out of sight to make sure that he returned towards his stall. The next day four neighbours carried the corpse to the burying-ground, following the priest, who recited some prayers. 'Ali Baba came after with some neighbours. Marjaneh, who had been a slave to

the deceased, came last in the procession, weeping, beating her breast, and tearing her hair. Kasim's wife stayed at home mourning, uttering woeful cries with the women of the neighbourhood, who came, according to custom, during the funeral, and joining their wailings with hers, filled the quarter far and near with sounds of sorrow.

The manner of Kasim's melancholy death was concealed and hushed up between his widow, Marjaneh, and 'Ali Baba, with so much contrivance that nobody in the city had the least knowledge or suspicion of the cause of it. Three or four days after the funeral, 'Ali Baba removed his few goods openly to his sister-in-law's house, where it was agreed that he should in future live; but the money he had taken from the robbers he conveyed thither by night. Lastly, he intrusted his eldest son with the entire management of Kasim's warehouse.

While these things were being done, the forty robbers again visited their retreat in the forest. Great, then, was their surprise to find Kasim's body taken away, with some of their bags of gold. "We are certainly discovered," said the captain. "The removal of the body and the loss of more of our money plainly shows that the man whom we killed had an accomplice; and for our own lives' sake, we must try to find him. What say you, my lads?"

All the robbers approved of the captain's proposal.

"Well," said the captain, "one of the boldest and most skilful among you must go into the town, disguised as a traveller and a stranger, and try if he can hear any talk of the man whom we have killed, and endeavour to find out who he was and where he lived. This is a matter of the first importance, and for fear of treachery, I propose that whoever undertakes this business without success, even though the failure arises only from an error of judgment, shall suffer death."

Without waiting for the sentiments of his companions, one of the robbers started up and said, "I submit to this condition and think it an honour to expose my life to serve the troop."

After this robber had received great commendations from the captain and his comrades, he disguised himself; and taking his leave of the troop that night, went into the town just at day-break, and walked up and down, till accidentally he came to

Baba Mustapha's stall, which was always open before any of the shops.

Baba Mustapha was seated with an awl in his hand, just going to work. The robber saluted him, bidding him good morrow; and perceiving that he was old, said: "Honest man, you begin to work very early. Is it possible that one of your age can see so well? I question, even if it were somewhat lighter, whether you could see to stitch."

"You do not know me," replied Baba Mustapha; "for old as I am I have extraordinary good eyes; and you will not doubt it when I tell you that I sewed the body of a dead man together in a place where I had not so much light as I have now."

"Where was that?" asked the robber.

"You shall know no more," answered Baba Mustapha.

The robber felt sure that he had discovered what he sought. He pulled out a piece of gold, and putting it into Baba Mustapha's hand, said to him: "I do not want to learn your secret, though I can assure you that you might safely trust me with it. The only thing I desire of you is to show me the house where you did this work."

"If I were disposed to do you that favour," replied Baba Mustapha, "I assure you I cannot. I was taken to a certain place, whence I was led blindfold to the house, and afterwards brought back in the same manner. You see, therefore, the impossibility of my doing what you desire."

"Well," replied the robber, "you may, however, have some remembrance of the way that you were led blindfold. Come, let me blind your eyes at the same place. We will walk together; perhaps you may be able to go where you did before, and as everybody ought to be paid for their trouble, there is another piece of gold for you. Gratify me in what I ask you."

So saying, he put another piece of gold into the shoemaker's hand.

The two pieces of gold were great temptations to Baba Mustapha. He looked at them a long time in his hand, without saying a word, but at last he pulled out his purse and put them in it. "I am not sure that I can remember the way exactly," said he to the robber; "but since you desire, I will try what I can do."

At these words Baba Mustapha rose, to the great joy of the

robber, and led him to the place where Marjaneh had bound his eyes. "It was here that I was blindfolded," said Baba Mustapha; "and afterwards I turned this way."

The robber tied his handkerchief over the shoemaker's eyes and walked by him till he stopped directly before Kasim's house, where 'Ali Baba then lived. The thief marked the door with a piece of chalk, which he had ready in his hand, and then he pulled off the bandage from Baba Mustapha's eyes and asked him if he knew whose house that was. Baba Mustapha replied he did not live in the neighbourhood, and he could not tell.

The robber, finding he could discover no more from Baba Mustapha, thanked him for the trouble he had taken and left him to go back to his stall, while he returned to the forest, persuaded that he should be very well received.

A little after the robber and Baba Mustapha had parted, Marjaneh went out of 'Ali Baba's house on some errand, and on her return, seeing the mark the robber had made, stopped to observe it. "What can be the meaning of this mark?" she said to herself. "Somebody intends my master no good. However, with whatever intention it was done, it is advisable to guard against the worst."

Accordingly, she fetched a piece of chalk and marked two or three doors on each side, in the same manner, without saying a word to her master or mistress.

By this time the robber had rejoined his troop in the forest. He told the others of his success, rejoicing over his good fortune, in meeting so soon with the only person who could inform him of what he wanted to know. The robbers listened to him with the utmost satisfaction; and the captain, after commending his diligence, addressed himself to them all, and said: "Comrades, we have no time to lose. Let us set off well armed; but that we may not excite any suspicion, let only one or two go into the town together and we will meet at the great square. In the meantime our comrade who brought us the good news and I will go and find the house he has marked, that we may consult what had best be done."

This speech and plan were approved by all. They were soon ready, and filed off in parties of two each, and got into the town without being in the least suspected. The captain and he who had visited the town in the morning as a spy came in last. The spy led the captain into the street where he had marked 'Ali Baba's residence; and when they came to the first of the houses which Marjaneh had marked, he pointed it out. But the captain observed that the next door was chalked in the same manner and in the same place; and showing it to his guide, asked him which house it was, that or the first. The guide was so confounded that he knew not what answer to make, and he was still more puzzled when he and the captain saw five or six houses similarly marked. He assured the captain, with an oath, that he had marked but one, and could not tell who had chalked the rest, so that he could not distinguish the house which the cobbler had stopped at.

The captain, finding that their design had proved abortive, went directly to the great square where the robbers were to meet and told his troop that they had lost their labour and must return to their cave. He himself set them the example, and they separated in parties of two and returned as they had come.

When the troop were all got together, the captain told them the reason of their returning; and presently the robber who had acted as spy was declared deserving of death and was killed.

But as the safety of the troop required the discovery of the second intruder into the cave, another of the gang offered to go and seek out the intruder's dwelling. He promised himself that he should succeed better than his unlucky predecessor, and his offer being accepted, he went and corrupted Baba Mustapha, as the other had done; and being shown the house, marked it in a place more remote from sight with red chalk.

Not long afterward, Marjaneh, whose eyes nothing could escape, went out, and seeing the red chalk mark, and arguing that some evil was planned against her master, marked the neighbouring houses in the same place and manner.

The robber, at his return to his company, prided himself much on the care he had taken. He believed he had adopted a sure way of distinguishing 'Ali Baba's house from the others, and the captain and all of them thought now they must succeed. They conveyed themselves into the town with the same caution as before; but when the robber spy and his captain came to the street where 'Ali Baba lived they found several doors marked instead of one, at which the captain was enraged, and the spy was in as great confusion as the former guide.

Thus the captain and his troop were forced to retire a second time, and much more dissatisfied; and the robber, who had been the author of the mistake, underwent the same punishment as the other spy.

The captain, having lost two brave fellows of his troop, was afraid of diminishing it too much by pursuing this plan to get information of the residence of their plunderer. It was evident that their heads were not so good as their hands on such occasions, and he therefore resolved to take on himself the important commission.

Accordingly, he went and addressed himself to Baba Mustapha, who did him the same service he had done the other robbers. The captain did not set any particular mark on the house, but examined and observed it so carefully that it was impossible for him to mistake it. Well satisfied with his attempt, and informed of what he wanted to know, he returned to the forest; and when he came into the cave, where the troop waited for him, said, "Now, comrades, nothing can prevent our full revenge, as I am certain of the house; and on my way hither I have thought how to put the revenge into execution; but if any one can form a better plan, let him communicate it."

He then told his plan, and as they approved of it, ordered them to go into the villages about and buy nineteen mules, with thirty-eight large leather jars, one full of oil and the others empty.

In two or three days' time the robbers had purchased the mules and jars, and the captain after having put one of his men into each jar with the weapons which he thought fit, leaving open the seam which had been undone to allow them a chance to breathe, he rubbed the jars on the outside with oil from the full vessel.

Things being thus prepared, the nineteen mules were loaded with thirty-seven robbers in jars and the jar of oil. Then the captain, as their driver, set out with them, and reached the town by the dusk of the evening, as he had intended. He led them through the streets till he came to 'Ali Baba's, at whose door he designed to knock; but 'Ali Baba was sitting in the doorway

after supper to take a little fresh air. The robber stopped his
mules, addressed 'Ali Baba, and said: "I have brought some oil
a great way to sell at to-morrow's market, and it is now so late
that I do not know where to lodge. If I should not be troublesome to you, do me the favour to let me pass the night with you,
and I shall be very much obliged by your hospitality."

Though 'Ali Baba had seen the captain of the robbers in the
forest and had heard him speak, it was impossible to know him
in the disguise of an oil merchant. He told him he was welcome,
and immediately opened his gates for the mules to go into the
yard. At the same time he called to a slave and ordered him,
when the mules were unloaded, to put them into the stable and
feed them; and then went to Marjaneh to bid her get a good
supper for his guest. After they had finished supper, 'Ali Baba
charged Marjaneh afresh to take care of his guest.

In the meantime the captain of the robbers went into the yard, and took off the lid of each jar, and gave his comrades orders what to do. Beginning at the first jar and so on to the last, he said to each man, "As soon as I throw some pebbles from the chamber window where I lie, do not fail to come out, and I will immediately join you."

After this he returned into the house, and Marjaneh taking up a light conducted him to his chambers. There she left him; and he, to avoid any suspicion, put the light out soon after and lay down in his clothes, that he might be the more ready to rise.

Marjaneh began preparations for the morrow's breakfast; but while she was doing this, the oil burned out of the lamp she was using, and there was no more oil in the house, nor any candles. What to do she did not know. A fellow-servant, seeing her very uneasy, said, "Do not fret yourself, but go into the back yard, and take some oil out of one of the jars."

Marjaneh thanked him for his advice, took the oil-pot, and went into the yard; when as she came nigh the first jar, the robber within said softly, "Is it time?"

Though naturally much surprised at finding a man in the jar instead of the oil she wanted she immediately felt the importance of keeping silence, as 'Ali Baba, his family, and herself might be in great danger; and collecting herself, without showing the least emotion, she answered, "Not yet, but presently."

She went quietly in this manner to all the jars, giving the same answer till she came to the jar of oil.

By this means Marjaneh found that her master 'Ali Baba had admitted thirty-eight robbers into his house, and that this pretended oil merchant was their captain. She made what haste she could to fill her oil-pot and returned to her kitchen, where, as soon as she had lighted her lamp, she took a great kettle, went again to the oil-jar, filled the kettle, set it on a large wood fire, and as soon as it boiled, went and poured enough in every jar to stifle and destroy the robber within.

When this action was executed without any noise, as she had intended, she returned to the kitchen with the empty kettle; and having put out the fire she had made to boil the oil, and the lamp also, she remained silent, resolving not to go to rest till she had observed through a window of the kitchen, which opened into the yard, what might follow.

She had not waited long before the captain of the robbers got up, opened the window, and finding no light and hearing no noise, or any one stirring in the house, gave the appointed signal by throwing little stones, several of which hit the jars, as he doubted not by the sound they gave. He then listened, but not hearing or perceiving anything whereby he could judge that his companions stirred, he began to grow very uneasy, and threw stones a second and also a third time. He could not comprehend the reason that none of his men should answer his signal. Much alarmed he went softly down into the yard, and going to the first jar, asked the robber, whom he thought alive, if he was in readiness. Then he smelt the hot boiled oil, and suspected that his plot to murder 'Ali Baba and plunder his house was discovered. Examining all the jars, one after another, he found that all his gang were dead; and, enraged to despair at having failed in his design, he forced the lock of a door that led from the yard to the garden, and climbing over the garden wall made his escape.

When Marjaneh saw him depart, she went to bed, satisfied and pleased to have succeeded so well in saving her master and family.

'Ali Baba rose before day, and, followed by a slave, went to the baths, entirely ignorant of the important events which had happened at home.

When he returned, he was very much surprised to see the oil-jars, and wondered that the merchant was not gone with them and the mules. He asked Marjaneh, who opened the door, the reason. "My good master," answered she, "God preserve you and all your family. You will be better informed of what you wish to know when you have seen what I have to show you."

As soon as Marjaneh had shut the door, 'Ali Baba followed her, and she requested him to look into the first jar and see if there was any oil. 'Ali Baba did so, and seeing a man started back in alarm and cried out. "Do not be afraid," said Marjaneh, "the man you see there is dead."

"Ah, Marjaneh," said 'Ali Baba, "explain yourself."

"I will," replied Marjaneh. "Moderate your astonishment and do not excite the curiosity of your neighbours, for it is of great importance to keep this affair secret. Look into the other jars."

'Ali Baba examined all the other jars, one after another; and when he came to that which contained oil, found the oil nearly gone. He stood for some time motionless, looking at the jars, without saying a word, so great was his surprise. At last, when he had recovered himself, he asked, "And what is become of the merchant?"

"Merchant!" answered Marjaneh; "he is as much one as I am. I will tell you who he is and what is become of him; but you had better hear the story in your own room, for it is time that you had your broth after your bathing."

They went indoors and Marjaneh told all she had done, from first observing the mark on the house to the destruction of the robbers and the flight of their captain.

On hearing of these brave deeds from the lips of Marjaneh, 'Ali Baba said to her: "God, by your means, has delivered me from the snares these robbers laid for my destruction. I therefore owe my life to you; and, for a token of my acknowledgment, I will give you your liberty from this moment. I will complete your recompense later."

'Ali Baba's garden was very long and shaded at the farther end by a great number of large trees. Near these he and the slave dug a trench, long and wide enough to hold the bodies of the robbers; and as the earth was light, they were not long in doing it. When the burial was finished, 'Ali Baba hid the jars and weapons; and as he had no occasion for the mules, he sent them at different times to be sold in the market by his slave.

While 'Ali Baba took these measures, the captain of the forty robbers returned to the forest with inconceivable mortification. He did not stay long. The loneliness of the gloomy cavern became frightful to him. He determined, however, to avenge the fate of his companions and to accomplish the death of 'Ali Baba. For this purpose he returned to the town and took a lodging in a khan, and disguised himself as a merchant selling silks. Under this assumed character he gradually conveyed a great many sorts of rich stuffs and fine linen from the cavern to his lodging, but with all the necessary precautions to conceal the place whence he brought them. In order to dispose of the merchandise, he rented a warehouse, and it happened to be opposite Kasim's, which 'Ali Baba's son had occupied since the death of his uncle.

The robber took the name of Khoja Hoseyn. 'Ali Baba's son was, from his vicinity, one of the first to converse with Khoja Hoseyn, and the robber strove to cultivate his friendship. Two or three days after Khoja Hoseyn was settled, 'Ali Baba came to see his son and the captain of the robbers recognized him at once. After this he became more attentive than ever to 'Ali Baba's son, made him some small presents, and often asked him to dine and sup with him, when he treated him very handsomely.

'Ali Baba's son did not choose to continue under such obligation to Khoja Hoseyn; but was so much straitened for want of room in his house that he could not entertain him. He therefore acquainted his father, 'Ali Baba, with his wish to invite Khoja Hoseyn in return.

'Ali Baba with great pleasure took the treat on himself. "Son," said he, "to-morrow get Khoja Hoseyn to accompany you, and as you pass by my door, call in. I will go and order Marjaneh to provide a supper."

The next day 'Ali Baba's son and Khoja Hoseyn met by appointment, took their walk, and as they returned, 'Ali Baba's son led Khoja Hoseyn through the street where his father lived, and when they came to the house, stopped and knocked at the door. "This, sir," said he, "is the home of my father. From the account I have given him of your friendship, he has charged me to procure him the honour of your acquaintance, and I desire you to add this pleasure to those for which I am already indebted to you."

'Ali Baba received Khoja Hoseyn with a smiling countenance and in the most obliging manner one could wish. He thanked him for all the favours he had done his son; adding withal, the obligation was the greater as his son was a young man, not much acquainted with the world, and that he might contribute to his information.

Khoja Hoseyn returned the compliment by assuring 'Ali Baba that though his son might not have acquired the experience of older men, he had good sense equal to the experience of many others. After a little more conversation on different subjects, he offered to take his leave, when 'Ali Baba, stopping him, said: "Where are you going, sir, in so much haste? I beg you would do me the honour to sup with me. Though my entertainment may not be worthy your acceptance, such as it is, I heartily offer it."

"Sir," replied Khoja Hoseyn, "I am thoroughly persuaded of your good-will; but the truth is, I can eat no victuals that have any salt in them. Therefore judge how I should feel at your table."*

"If that is the only reason," said 'Ali Baba, "it ought not to deprive me of the honour of your company; for, in the first place, there is no salt ever put into my bread, and as to the meat we shall have to-night, I promise you there shall be none in that. Therefore you must do me the favour to stay."

'Ali Baba went into the kitchen and ordered Marjaneh to put no salt to the meat which was to be served that night.

Marjaneh, who was always ready to obey her master, could not help being surprised at his strange order. "Who is this man," said she, "who eats no salt with his meat? Your supper will be spoiled."

"Do not be angry, Marjaneh," replied 'Ali Baba. "He is an honest man. Therefore do as I bid you."

Marjaneh obeyed, though with no little reluctance, and had a curiosity to see this man who ate no salt. To this end, when she had finished what she had to do in the kitchen, she helped the servant to carry up the dishes; and looking at Khoja Hoseyn, knew him at first sight, notwithstanding his disguise, to be the captain of the robbers, and examining him very carefully perceived that he had a dagger under his garment.

When the servant came for the dessert of fruit and had put it with the wine and glasses before 'Ali Baba, Marjaneh retired, dressed herself neatly, girded her waist with a silver-gilt girdle, to which there hung a poniard with a hilt of the same metal, and put a handsome mask on her face. When she had thus arrayed herself she said to the servant, "Take your tambourine, and let us go and divert our master and his son's friend."

He took his tambourine and played all the way into the hall before Marjaneh, who, when she came to the door, made a low obeisance by way of asking leave to exhibit her skill. "Come in, Marjaneh," said 'Ali Baba, "and let Khoja Hoseyn see what you can do, that he may tell us what he thinks of your performance."

Khoja Hoseyn, who did not expect this diversion after supper, began to fear he should not be able to take advantage of the opportunity he thought he had found; but hoped, if he now

* By middle-eastern custom, the bond created by eating salt together is sacred and would have prevented Khoja Hoseyn from doing his host harm.

missed his purpose, to secure it another time, by keeping up a friendly intercourse with the father and son. Therefore, though he could have wished 'Ali Baba would have declined the dance, he pretended to be obliged to him for it, and expressed his satisfaction at what he saw.

As soon as 'Ali Baba and Khoja Hoseyn had done talking, the servant commenced to play on the tambourine and at the same time sung an air, to which Marjaneh, who was an excellent performer, danced in such a manner as would have created admiration in any company.

After she had danced several dances with much grace, she drew the poniard, and holding it in her hand, began a dance, in which she outdid herself by the many different figures, light movements, and the surprising leaps and wonderful exertions with which she accomplished it. At last she snatched the tambourine from the servant with her left hand, and holding the dagger in her right, presented the other side of the tambourine, after the manner of those who get a livelihood by dancing and solicit the liberality of the spectators.

'Ali Baba put a piece of gold into the tambourine, as did also his son; and Khoja Hoseyn seeing that she was coming to him, had pulled his purse out of his bosom to make her a present. But while he was putting his hand in the purse, Marjaneh plunged the poniard into his heart.

'Ali Baba and his son, shocked at this action, cried out aloud. "Unhappy woman!" exclaimed 'Ali Baba, "what have you done to ruin me and my family?"

"It was to preserve, not to ruin you," answered Marjaneh; "for see here," continued she, opening the pretended Khoja Hoseyn's garment and showing the dagger, "what an enemy you had entertained! Look well at him and you will find him to be both the false oil merchant and the captain of the gang of forty robbers. Before I saw him, I suspected him as soon as you told me you had such a guest. You now find that my suspicion was not groundless."

'Ali Baba, who immediately felt the new obligation he had to Marjaneh for saving his life a second time, embraced her. "Marjaneh," said he, "I gave you your liberty and then promised you that my gratitude should not stop there, but that I would soon give you higher proofs of its sincerity, which I now do by making you my daughter-in-law."

Then addressing himself to his son, he said: "I believe you, son, to be so dutiful a child that you will not refuse Marjaneh for your wife. You see that Khoja Hoseyn sought your friendship with a design to take away my life; and if he had succeeded, there is no doubt but he would have sacrificed you also to his revenge. Consider that by marrying Marjaneh you marry the preserver of my family and your own."

The son, far from showing any dislike, readily consented to the marriage, not only because he would not disobey his father, but also because it was agreeable to his inclination. After this they buried the captain of the robbers with his comrades. A few days later, 'Ali Baba celebrated the wedding of his son and Marjaneh with a great feast and the usual dancing, and had the satisfaction to see that his friends and neighbours whom he invited had no knowledge of the true motives of this marriage.

'Ali Baba did not visit the robbers' cave for a whole year, as he supposed the other two members of the troop, whom he could get no account of, might be alive. At the year's end, when he found they had not made any attempt to disturb him, he had the curiosity to make another journey to the place where the treasure was concealed in the forest. He mounted his horse, and when he came to the cave he alighted and tied his horse to a tree. Then approaching the entrance he pronounced the words, "Open, Simsim!" and the door opened.

He entered the cavern, and by the condition he found things in judged that nobody had been there since the captain had fetched the goods for his shop. It was quite evident that all the robbers who knew of the cave were dead, and 'Ali Baba believed he was the only person in the world who had the secret of opening it, and that all the treasure was at his sole disposal. He put as much gold into his saddle-bags as his horse would carry, and returned to town. Some years later he carried his son to the cave and taught him the secret of opening and shutting the door. The son handed the secret down to his posterity, who, using their good fortune with moderation, lived in great honour and splendour.

MYTHOLOGY

Myths are grown up fairy tales where dazzling gods drive through the heavens in winged chariots and play games with the helpless humans below. In mythology gods are the reasons for rain and the causes of thunder. Angry gods send storms at sea, playful gods cause loves and wars. To meet the gods of mythology is to share the dreams of the ancients, to understand their ideas, their fears, and their fun.

No one knows how myths began. They were probably created when people began to wonder. Who makes rain? What is sun? Why is thunder? There were no scientists to answer these questions, so the people answered them in their own way ... the gods. For the Greeks, Poseidon ruled the sea and Apollo was in charge of the sun. The Norse god Thor caused thunder.

Whenever something horrible happened, it was the fault of the gods. And when good times came, the gods were thanked. People created gods when something seemed strange or unexplainable. Every time a new god was created, he was given a personality. Some gods were good, some were bad, some were jealous. The stories of the gods were told over and over again. The more they were told, the more complicated and numerous they becaame.

As the years passed, mythology became more

than just answers to questions. It became literature and thought. Not only do we have stories about what is caused by the gods, but we also have tales of what happens in the world of the gods, tales that tell what happens when the gods visit our world, and myths that were created not to explain, but simply to entertain.

The most popular of all mythology is that of ancient Greece and Rome. Greek and Roman gods had their home on Mount Olympus. They romped on the mountain, fought among themselves, and meddled in the affairs of earth-people—sometimes for fun, sometimes for effect, and sometimes for vengeance.

The Romans created some gods of their own, but they also took as theirs most of the Greek gods. It is often confusing to read about the King of the gods as Jupiter one minute and Zeus the next. Or to discover that both Neptune and Poseidon are called God of the Sea. This list of the Greek and Roman names of the gods should help you in the stories that follow.

	Roman Name	Greek Name
King of the Gods	JUPITER	ZEUS
God of the Sun and Youth	APOLLO	APOLLO
God of War	MARS	ARES
God of the Sea	NEPTUNE	POSEIDON
Messenger of the Gods	MERCURY	HERMES
Blacksmith of the Gods	VULCAN	HEPHAESTUS
God of Wine	BACCHUS	DIONYSUS
God of Love	CUPID	EROS
God of the Underworld	PLUTO	PLUTO
God of Time	SATURN	KRONOS
Queen of the Gods	JUNO	HERA
Goddess of Agriculture	CERES	DEMETER
Goddess of the Moon and Hunting	DIANA	ARTEMIS
Goddess of Wisdom	MINERVA	ATHENA
Goddess of Love and Beauty	VENUS	APHRODITE
Goddess of the Home	VESTA	HESTIA

Stories of the Gods and Heroes

BY SALLY BENSON

Illustrations by Steele Savage

Pandora, the First Woman

ALTHOUGH Jupiter had punished Prometheus for stealing the divine fire from the chariot of the sun, he was not satisfied. He felt the gods should seek retaliation against Man for accepting the stolen gift. Summoning all the gods to the great hall, he asked them what they thought would plague and torment Man the most. It was decided, after many suggestions and arguments, that a woman might harry him and plant seeds of ambition and dissatisfaction in his breast. So, in much the same way as Prometheus had made Man, they brought clay from the earth and created a woman whom they named Pandora.

When she was given life, she was endowed by the gods with every gift; Venus bestowed beauty on her, Mercury gave her the art of persuasion, Apollo donated the love of music, and the Graces trained her in the social arts. Then, Vulcan fashioned an exquisite box of pure gold into which were put all the evils that have plagued mankind ever since— disease, famine, pestilence, fever, envy, greediness, gluttony, hatred and intolerance. It did not seem possible that a thing as lovely as the golden box could contain so many ills.

As they were about to close the box, the gods and goddesses regretted their hasty decision. And, although they were too proud to abandon the idea altogether, they added one beautiful gift that would lessen the pain caused by all the other disasters. The gift was called hope. The gods tucked it down into the bottom and cautioned Pandora not to open the box which was intended as an offering to the man who took her in marriage.

Then, bidding her goodbye, they gave her to Mercury, Jupiter's messenger, who bore her away with him to the earth. Mercury left her with Epimetheus, who was so struck by her unusual beauty and grace that he gladly took her into his home.

Seeing the golden box under her arm, he asked her what it contained, and she answered that she did not know, exactly, but that she had been told to give it to the man she married. She placed it on a table and its brilliance lighted the entire room. Leaving Pandora alone, after cautioning her not to look at the contents of the chest until he asked the advice of his brother, Epimetheus traveled a whole day until he reached Mount Caucasus where Prometheus lay in chains. He related to him all that had happened, and Prometheus, suspecting a trick, told Epimetheus to hasten back and hide the box in a place so remote that no one could ever find it.

In the meantime, Pandora explored her new home. She picked flowers and scattered their petals which were soft and fragrant under foot; she brought cold, sparkling water from the brook that roared over clean stones at the foot of the hill; she took honey from the bees and fruit from the trees. Each time she entered the house, the shining box caught her eye, and, more than once, she stopped to touch it, shake it, and wonder what it might hold. All day long she kept busy, until, as night drew near, she could find nothing else to do. Drawing a chair up to the table on which the box lay, she sat down, hypnotized by its beauty and glitter. Occasionally, she went to the door and looked in the distance to see if either Epimetheus or Man were approaching.

Finally, she took the box from the table and held it, turning it over and over, admiring its exquisite design. It was almost dark and she was all alone.

"Surely," she thought, "it can do no harm to open this lovely thing a mere crack and see what it contains. Is it a crown? A precious jewel? A magic cloak? A gift from the gods must be something both beautiful and rare."

The Furies who were hovering about robed in invisibility, read her thoughts and stung her conscience with tiny pricks. She fumbled with the clasp on the box and loosened it. "Perhaps," she said to herself, "it is a robe of purest gold thread, embroidered with diamonds, rubies and sapphires. And if it is, it would be better if I opened the cask and wore the robe so that I will look more beautiful in Man's eyes."

As she thought this, the Furies stung her madly, but her curiosity was so great that she scarcely felt them. She opened the box a little, and peering in, saw nothing. Angry and emboldened, she opened it wider and saw what at first looked to be a brown, ugly cloud. The cloud moved and separated, and then, with a loud buzzing sound, hundreds of things resembling small insects escaped into the room. Terrified, she tried to close the box, but her hands shook and she could not manage the catch. It was almost empty when she finally slammed the lid, and only one thing remained. This was hope which had lain on the bottom.

She hurriedly placed the box on the table again and ran to the door to see if Epimetheus or Man were in sight. She looked around the room to make sure that none of the evils remained to be seen. She shook her robe in fear that some might lurk in its folds and she combed her hair free of them. Then, she set the table for supper, selecting the ripest fruits, the most delicious berries and the loveliest scented flowers. Pulling her chair far away from the table, she sat down to await. Epimetheus and Man.

When they returned, they found her innocently busy mending their clothes. And she looked so beautiful sitting there, that Epimetheus almost forgot to ask her whether or not she had looked in the box. When he asked her, she pretended for a moment to have no idea what he meant. "The box?" she queried. "Oh, *that* one! It had slipped my mind entirely. Yes, I did open it a little, and there is a lovely, iridescent thing lying in it. It is more beautiful than the rarest jewel, and it is called hope."

"We will keep it there," Epimetheus told her.

She made no mention of the ugly, brown cloud composed of hundreds of ills that had flown out into the world, and it was some time before Epimetheus and Man knew that the box had contained anything but hope. When they did learn, Pandora had so endeared herself to them that they could not punish her. They looked at her sadly, unable to speak. Seeing the disapproval in their eyes, she tried to defend her disobedience. "It is true that I opened the box," she argued. "But it is also true that I allowed the evils to escape into the world. I brushed them from the room. They are not here and cannot harm us. And our house harbors only hope."

The Golden Touch of King Midas

There was a time when the people of Phrygia had no king. They appealed to the oracle to send them a man to rule over their country, and the oracle answered that the man who would be their sovereign would be of humble birth and arrive in the city in a wagon drawn by oxen. While the people were deliberating over what to do, a poor countryman named Gordius drove to town in his wagon with his wife and his little son, Midas. The crowds, seeing him approach and believing him

to be the man destined to rule them, acclaimed him and
made him king. He dedicated his wagon to the deity of the
oracle and tied it up in its place with a fast knot. This was
the celebrated Gordian knot, of which it was said that whoever
should untie it should become lord of all Asia. Many tried
to untie it, but none succeeded till Alexander the Great, in
his career of conquest, came to Phrygia. He tried his skill
with as ill success as the others, and finally, growing impatient,
he drew his sword and cut the knot. When he later conquered
all Asia, people thought that he had fulfilled the oracle's
prophecy.

Gordius ruled over his country wisely and when he died,
his son Midas succeeded to the throne. Now, in the neighboring country of Caria, there lived a king named Silenus.
He had introduced the worship of Bacchus into his kingdom
and consequently had been named foster father to the god.
He was a very old man and a very merry one, and he liked
to give large banquets, sometimes eating and drinking more
than was good for him. One day, after a tremendous feast,
he wandered away by himself, and was unable to find his
way home again. He lay down in a wheat field, where he
was found by some peasants who carried him to their king,
Midas. Midas recognized him and treated him hospitably,
entertaining him for ten days and ten nights with an unceasing
round of jollity. On the eleventh day, he brought Silenus back
and restored him safely to Bacchus. Bacchus was so grateful
that his foster father had been returned to him unharmed
that he offered Midas his choice of a reward, whatever he
might wish.

As a child, some ants had put grains of wheat into the
mouth of Midas which made him prudent and thrifty almost
to a fault. He considered wealth the most important thing
in the world. When Bacchus asked him what he wished, he
requested that whatever he might touch should be changed into
gold. Bacchus consented, warning Midas that he had not made
a wise choice.

Midas went his way, rejoicing in his newly acquired power,
which he hastened to put to the test. He could not believe
his eyes when he found that a twig of an oak, which he

plucked from the branch, became gold in his hand. He took up a stone; it changed to gold. He touched a piece of sod; it did the same. He took an apple from the tree, and it turned hard and shiny in his hands. His joy knew no bounds, and as soon as he got home he ordered the servants to set a splendid repast on the table. Hungry from his journey, he sat down to eat. But to his dismay, the bread he crumbled changed to gold and broke his teeth when he tried to bite it; the wine in his goblet poured down his throat like molten metal.

In anger he wished to divest himself of the power he had longed for. He hated the gift he had craved. But all in vain. Starvation seemed to await him. He raised his arms, all shining in gold, in prayer to Bacchus, begging to be delivered from his glittering destruction.

Bacchus felt that the greedy king had learned his lesson and took pity on him. "Go," he said, "to the river Pactolus, trace the stream to its fountainhead. There plunge your head and body in, and wash away your fault and its punishment."

Midas hurriedly prepared himself for the trip, and hungry and weak made his way to the source of the river. Obeying the god's instructions, he plunged his head and body in the waters. He had scarcely touched them before the gold-creating power passed into them, and the river sands changed into gold, as they remain to this day.

Midas returned home a changed man. He hated wealth and splendor and dwelt in the country, worshipping Pan, the god of the fields. Pan, who was a rather boastful fellow, one day dared to compare the music of his piping with that of Apollo, and he challenged the god of the lyre to a trial of skill. Apollo accepted the challenge, and Tmolus, the mountain god, was chosen umpire. He took his seat and cleared the trees away from his ears to listen. At a given signal, Pan blew on his pipes, and with his rustic melody charmed his own ears and those of his faithful follower, Midas. Then Tmolus turned his head toward Apollo, and all his trees turned with him. The sun god arose, his brow wreathed with Parnassian laurel in memory of Daphne, his robe of Tyrolean purple sweeping the ground. In his left hand he held the lyre, and with his right hand struck the strings.

Enchanted with the harmony, Tmolus at once awarded the victory to the god of the lyre, and all but Midas acquiesced in the judgment. He made a great fuss and questioned the justice of the award. Apollo announced that he would not suffer such a depraved set of ears to wear the human form any longer, and with a word, he caused them to grow long and hairy, and movable on their roots. In short, to be on the same pattern as the ears of an ass.

Midas was mortified at the change in his appearance and to hide his misfortune, he covered his head with a large turban. His hairdresser knew his secret, but Midas had cautioned him not to mention it, and threatened him with dire punishment if he dared disobey. The hairdresser found it too much for his discretion to keep the hilarious secret. He went out into the meadow, dug a hole in the ground, and, stooping down, whispered the story and covered it up. Before long a thick bed of reeds sprang up in the meadow, and as soon as it had gained its growth began whispering the story. From that day to this, every time a breeze passes over the place, the reeds laughingly tell the story of the ears of King Midas.

Perseus Slays the Gorgon

Perseus was the son of Jupiter and Danae. When he was born, his grandfather, Acrisius, consulted an oracle and prayed to know what the infant's fate would be. To his horror, the oracle answered that the child would one day slay him. Acrisius was terrified over this prophecy. He wanted to murder Perseus, but was too tender-hearted to do the deed himself. He finally decided to shut up Danae and her baby in a chest and set them adrift on the sea. He secretly hoped they would be dashed to pieces on the rocks. Clinging to her baby in the dark, hot chest, Danae huddled in terror while the box whirled and dipped in the waves. It seemed days before they were washed upon the shores of Seriphus, where they were found by a fisherman. He took the mother and her baby to Polydectes, the king of the country, who took them into his own home and treated them with kindness. Here Perseus grew to manhood.

Not far from Seriphus, there lived a horrible monster named Medusa the Gorgon. She had once been a beautiful maiden whose hair was her chief glory, but, like Psyche who was also punished for her charms, Medusa had dared to vie in beauty with Minerva. Minerva in a rage turned her into a horrible figure, and changed her beautiful ringlets into hissing serpents. She became cruel and of so frightful an aspect that no living thing could behold her without being turned to stone. She dwelt in a foul, dank cavern and all around lay the stony figures of men and animals that had unfortunately chanced to catch a glimpse of her and had been petrified with the sight.

When Perseus became of age, Polydectes told him the story of the monster and begged him to attempt her conquest. Although Minerva had been the cause of Medusa's downfall, she favored Perseus and lent him her shield to take on his journey, while Mercury gave him his winged shoes so that he might travel with the speed of the wind.

As he neared the mouth of the cave where the dreadful maiden lived, Perseus turned his back lest he see Medusa and share the fate of others who had tried to kill her. Slowly and stealthily, he walked backwards, holding his shield before his eyes and guiding himself by the reflections in it. He entered the cave and beholding Medusa's head mirrored in the shining metal, he stopped in horror. Medusa lay asleep. Fastened securely to her scalp by the tips of their tails, noisome snakes writhed and twisted about her face and neck. Their breaths were fetid and their eyes winked evilly. Water dropped from the roof of the cave and the air was dank. In the half-light, Perseus saw hundreds of lizards and giant toads crawling over her body. The sight was so dreadful that he almost ran from it in terror, but remembering his vow to Polydectes who had raised him, he advanced slowly, keeping Medusa's image reflected in the shield. Closer and closer he crept until he stood within reach of the pestilential serpents of her hair. And then he struck. Her head fell to the ground.

After the slaughter of Medusa, Perseus, bearing with him the head of the Gorgon, flew far and wide, over land and sea. As night came on, he reached the western limit of the earth, where the sun goes down. He was tired and would have gladly rested here until morning. It was the realm of King Atlas, brother of Prometheus, who was more tremendous than any man on earth. Atlas was rich and had no neighbor or rival to dispute his supremacy of the land. His gardens were his chief pride. Here golden fruit hung from golden branches, half hid with golden leaves. Perseus presented himself to Atlas and said, "I come as a guest. If you honor illustrious descent. I claim Jupiter for my father. If you honor mighty deeds, I plead the conquest of the Gorgon. I seek rest and food."

Atlas was about to welcome him to his castle when he remembered an ancient prophecy which had warned him that a son of Jupiter would one day rob him of his golden apples. So, turning away, he answered, "Begone! Neither your false claims of glory nor parentage shall protect you!"

When Perseus did not move, Atlas turned on him and attempted to thrust him from the door. Perseus, finding the giant too strong for him, said, "Since you value my friendship so little, deign to accept a present!" And, turning his own

face away, he held up the Gorgon's head. Atlas changed into
stone. His beard and hair became forests, his arms and
shoulders became cliffs; his head became a summit and his
bones turned into rocks. Each part increased in bulk until
he became a mountain and the gods willed that heaven with
all its stars should rest upon his shoulders.

Perseus continued his flight and eventually arrived at the
country of the Aethiopians, of which Cepheus was king. His
queen, Cassiopea, had been so proud of her beauty that she
had dared to compare herself to the sea-nymphs, which roused
their indignation to such a degree that they sent a prodigious
sea-monster to ravage the coast. Fishermen and ships were
destroyed by the dreadful monster, and Cepheus in dismay
consulted the oracle who directed him to sacrifice his daughter, Andromeda, to appease the deities. Weeping and sad,
Cepheus ordered his beautiful daughter to be chained to a
rock where the monster could find her and devour her. He
kissed her tenderly and hastened away, fearing to look back.

At this moment, Perseus, flying far overhead, glanced down
and saw the maiden. She was so pale and motionless, that
if it had not been for her flowing tears and her hair that
moved in the breeze, he would have taken her for a marble
statue. He was startled at the sight and almost forgot to
wave his wings. As he hovered over her, he said, "O maiden,
undeserving of those chains, tell me, I beseech you, your
name and the name of your country. Tell me why you are
thus bound."

At first she was silent, half-frightened at the sight of the
hero who floated in the wind above her. But seeing that he
was not going to harm her, she told him her name and that
of her country, and the punishment that had fallen on the
land because of her mother's pride of beauty. Before she had
finished speaking, a sound was heard far off on the water,
and the sea-monster appeared with his head raised above the
surface, cleaving the waves with his broad breast. Andromeda
shrieked in terror, and her father and mother who were hiding
not far away, rushed back to the rock. They stood near,
wretched and helpless.

Perseus flew close to them and said, "There will be time

enough for tears. This hour is all we have for rescue. My
rank as the son of Jupiter and my renown as the slayer of
Medusa might make me acceptable as a suitor. I will try to
win her, if the gods will only favor me. If she be rescued by
my valor, I demand that she be my reward."

The parents eagerly consented.

The monster was now within a stone's throw of Andromeda,
when, with a sudden bound, Perseus soared high into the

air. As an eagle in flight sees a serpent basking in the sun and pounces on him, so the youth darted down upon the back of the monster and plunged his sword into its shoulder. Irritated by the wound the monster raised himself up and then plunged into the depths. Like a wild boar surrounded by a pack of barking dogs, it turned swiftly from side to side. Perseus stuck to its back and stuck it time and again with his sword, piercing its sides, its flanks and its tail. The brute spouted water and blood from its nostrils, and the wings of the hero were wet with them. He no longer dared trust them to carry his weight and he alighted on a rock which rose above the waves. As the monster floated near, he gave it a death stroke.

The people who had gathered on the shore shouted so that the hills re-echoed the sound. The parents, wild with joy, embraced their future son-in-law, and Andromeda was unchained and descended from the rock.

At the palace a banquet was spread for them, and joy and festivity ruled the land. But, suddenly, a noise was heard and Phineus, the betrothed of Andromeda, burst in and demanded the maiden as his own. It was in vain that Cepheus reasoned, "You should have claimed her when she lay bound to the rock, the monster's victim. The sentence of the gods dooming her to such a fate dissolved the engagement, as death itself would have done."

Phineus made no reply and hurled his javelin at Perseus. It missed its mark and fell to the floor. Perseus would have thrown his in turn, but the cowardly assailant ran and took shelter behind the altar. His act was a signal to his band who set upon the guests of Cepheus. They defended themselves and a general conflict ensued. The old king retreated from the scene after fruitless arguments and called the gods to witness that he was guiltless of this outrage on the rights of hospitality.

Perseus and his friends fought on, but the numbers of their assailants were too great for them. Then Perseus thought once more of the Gorgon's head. "I will make my enemy defend me," he said to himself. He called out, "If I have any friend here, let him turn away his eyes!"

He held Medusa's head high. "Seek not to frighten us with

your tricks," a man cried, and raised his javelin to throw it. He was instantly turned to stone. Another was about to plunge his sword into the prostrate body of his foe when his arm stiffened and he could neither thrust it forward nor withdraw it. Men were petrified with their mouths open as they shouted in anger, and the swords of those still alive hit against the bodies of their enemies and broke.

Phineus, behind the altar, beheld the dreadful result of his injustice. He called aloud to his friends, but got no answer. He touched them and found them stone. Falling on his knees, he stretched out his hands to Perseus. "Take all," he begged. "Give me but my life!"

"Base coward," Perseus cried, "this much I will grant you. No weapon shall touch you. You shall be preserved in my house as a memorial of these events."

So saying, he held the Gorgon's head in front of Phineus, and in the very form in which he knelt with his hands outstretched and face half averted, he became fixed, a mass of stone!

The Golden Fleece

In very ancient times there lived in Thessaly a king and queen named Athamas and Nephele. They had two children, a boy and a girl. After a time Athamas grew tired of his wife, divorced her and married another. Nephele worried about her children and, not wishing to leave them with a stepmother, took measures to send them away. Mercury came to her aid and gave her a ram with golden fleece on which she put the two children, trusting that the ram would carry them to a place of safety. The ram vaulted into the air with the children on his back and crossed the straits that divide Europe and Asia. Here the girl, whose name was Helle, slipped from the ram's back and fell into the sea. And thereafter the straits were called the Hellespont. In modern times, they are called the Dardanelles. The ram continued his course until he reached the kingdom of Colchis, on the eastern shore of the Black Sea, where he safely landed the boy Phrixus. The king of the country, Aeetes, gladly welcomed the boy, and Phrixus asked that the ram be sacrificed to Jupiter. Its golden fleece was preserved and given to Aeetes. He placed it reverently in a consecrated grove under the care of a dragon who never slept.

There was another kingdom in Thessaly ruled over by a relative of King Athamas. The king, whose name was Aeson, grew tired of the cares of government and surrendered his crown to his brother Pelias, on the condition that he should reign only until Aeson's son, Jason, became of age. When Jason was grown up and came to demand the crown from his uncle, Pelias pretended to be willing to yield it, but suggested that Jason go on some glorious adventure before settling down to the worries of ruling a kingdom. He reminded him that the golden fleece was still in Colchis and that as it was the rightful property of their family, Jason should go in quest of it. The idea excited Jason and he made grand preparations for the expedition. At that time, the only way of navigation known to the Greeks was travel in small boats or canoes hollowed out from the trunks of trees. Jason, realizing that such boats would be too light for the long, hazardous trip, employed Argos to build him a vessel which would carry fifty men. It was considered a gigantic undertaking and took many months. When it was completed, Jason named the ship Argo in honor of the builder, and sent out an invitation to all the adventurous young men in Greece to join him on the expedition. He soon found himself the head of a band of bold youths, many of whom afterward were renowned among the heroes and demigods of Greece; Hercules, Orpheus and Nestor were among them. They called themselves the Argonauts.

The Argo with her crew of heroes left the shores of Thessaly and having stopped for supplies at the island of Lemnos, crossed over to Mysia and then to Thrace. Here they consulted a wise old man who gave them instructions as to what course to follow. The entrance to the Euxine Sea was impeded by two small rocky islands. These islands were tossed and heaved about by the sea and occasionally came together, crushing and grinding to atoms any object that might be caught between them. They were called the Symplegades, or Clashing Islands. The old man told the Argonauts how to pass this dangerous strait; when they reached the islands they released a dove from her cage and watched her as she passed between the rocks in safety. She lost only a few feathers from her tail. Then Jason and his men seized the favorable moment of the rebound, threw all their strength into the oars, and passed swiftly through, though the islands closed behind them and actually grazed their stern. They rowed close to the shore until they landed at the kingdom of Colchis.

Jason went before the king, Aeetes, who consented to give up the golden fleece, if Jason would yoke two fire-breathing bulls to the plough and sow more of the teeth of the dragon which Cadmus had slain. Aeetes knew very well that a crop of armed men would spring up who would turn against Jason. The young man agreed to sow the teeth and a time was set for making the experiment. Meanwhile, the Argonauts feasted and reveled.

As preparations were being made for the task, Jason met and fell in love with Medea, daughter of the king, and asked her to marry him as they stood before the altar of Hecate, who witnessed their oaths. Then Medea, who was skilled in the art of sorcery, gave him a charm which would protect him against the fire-breathing bulls and the weapons of the armed men.

At the appointed time, the people assembled at the grove of Mars and the king assumed his royal seat, while multitudes covered the nearby hillside. The brazen-foot bulls rushed onto the field, breathing fire from their nostrils that burned up grass and bushes as they passed. The sound of their breathing was like the roar of a furnace, and the smoke like that of water upon quicklime. Everybody shrank back at their approach, but Jason walked forth boldly to meet them. His friends turned away in fear for his life. He went near the beasts and soothed them with his voice, patted their necks and adroitly slipped on the yoke. When they were harnessed, he gently guided the plough. The Colchians were amazed. The Greeks shouted for joy. Jason next sowed the dragon's teeth and ploughed them in. And soon the crop of armed

men sprang up, but no sooner had they reached the surface than they began to brandish their weapons and rush about Jason. The Argonauts trembled for their leader and even Medea feared her charm might not protect him. For a time Jason kept his assailants at bay with his sword and shield. Then, finding that their numbers were overwhelming, he resorted to the charm which Medea had taught him. He seized a stone and threw it into the midst of his foes. They immediately turned their arms against one another and soon there was not one of the dragon's brood left alive. The Greeks cheered their hero and Medea sat proud and happy at her father's side.

Jason, having won the right to the golden fleece, had to pass by the huge dragon to get it. Once more, Medea came to his aid. She gave him a powerful oil which Jason scattered near the monster. At the smell, he stood motionless for a moment, then shut his great eyes that had never been known to close before, turned over on his side, and went fast to sleep.

Jason seized the fleece and with his friends and Medea hastened to the Argo before Aeetes could dispute their departure. They sailed back to Thessaly and Jason delivered the fleece to Pelias and dedicated the Argo to Jupiter.

There was great rejoicing at the recovery of the golden fleece, and Jason longed for his father, Aeson, to share in the festivities. But Aeson was old and infirm and could not take part in them. Jason turned to Medea for help. "My spouse," he said, "would that your arts, whose powers have aided me, could do me one more service. Take some of the years from my life and add them to my father's."

Medea replied, "I shall not do it at such a cost, but if my art serves me, his life shall be lengthened without shortening yours."

The next full moon, she went forth all alone, while everyone slept. Not a breath stirred the foliage and all was still. She addressed her incantations to the stars and to the moon; she called on Hecate who represented the darkness and its terrors, and on Tellus, the goddess of the earth, who produced plants potent for enchantments. She invoked the gods of the woods and caverns, of mountains and valleys, of lakes and rivers, of winds and vapors. As she spoke, the stars shone brighter, and presently a chariot descended through the air, drawn by flying serpents. She stepped into it and was borne aloft to distant regions where strange plants grew. She spent nine days and nine nights selecting a few from the thousands that she saw, and during this time, she did not enter a door, nor did she sleep under a roof, nor speak to any mortal.

She next erected two altars, one to Hecate and the other to Hebe, goddess of youth, and sacrificed a black sheep to the goddesses, pouring them libations of milk and wine. She begged Pluto and his stolen bride, Proserpina, not to take the old man's life. Then she directed that Aeson should be led forth and she put him to sleep with a potent charm. She laid him on a bed of herbs, like one dead. Throughout these ceremonies, Jason and all the others were kept away so that no profane eyes should look upon her mysteries. With her hair streaming, she moved around the altars three times, dipped flaming twigs in the blood of the sheep and laid them on the altars to burn. She prepared a huge cauldron and in it she put magic herbs, with seeds and flowers of acrid juices, stones from the distant East and sand from the shore of the all-surrounding ocean. She put in hoarfrost, gathered by moonlight, a screech owl's head and wings, and the entrails of a wolf. She added fragments of the shells of tortoises, and the liver of stags, the head and beak of a crow that outlives nine generations of men. These with many other things so weird that they had no name she boiled together, stirring them up with a wild olive branch. And when the branch was taken out of the mixture, it instantly became green! Before long it was covered with leaves and a plentiful growth of young olives. As the liquor boiled and bubbled, grass sprouted on the ground where the liquid fell.

When all was ready, Medea cut the old man's throat and let out all his blood and poured into his mouth and into the wound the juices of her cauldron. Slowly his hair and beard changed from white to a rich dark black; he lost his paleness and his body grew vigorous and robust. Aeson was amazed when he awoke to find that he looked as he had forty years ago.

When Pelias's daughters saw what Medea had done for Aeson, they begged her to restore youth to their own father. But, Medea, remembering that Pelias had kept Jason from ruling his kingdom while he sent him on the dangerous quest for the golden fleece, only pretended to agree. She prepared her cauldron as before, and at her request an old sheep was brought and plunged into it. Very soon a bleating was heard in the kettle, and a lamb jumped forth and ran frisking away to the meadows. The daughters of Pelias saw this experiment and were delighted, and appointed a time for their father to undergo the same operation. But Medea put water and a few simple herbs in it, instead. And in the night, she and the daughters entered the bedchamber of the old king while he and his guards slept soundly. The daughters stood by the bedside, but hesitated to cut their father's throat until Medea jeered at them for their irresolution. Turning away their heads, they struck random blows. Pelias, starting from his sleep, cried out, "My daughters, what are you doing? Will you kill your father?"

Their hearts failed them and the weapons fell from their hands, but Medea struck him a final blow. His daughters carried him to the altar and placed him in the cauldron, and Medea hastened to depart in her serpent-drawn chariot. She escaped, but was to live to repent her evil deed. Jason turned away from her in disgust and desired to marry Creusa, princess of Corinth. Medea, enraged at his ingratitude after the help she had given him, sent a poisoned robe as a gift to the princess and then set fire to the palace. She escaped once more in her serpent-drawn chariot and fled to Athens, where she married King Aegeus, the father of Theseus.

The Flight of Icarus

When Theseus escaped from the labyrinth, King Minos flew into a rage with its builder, Daedalus, and ordered him shut up in a high tower that faced the lonely sea. In time, with the help of his young son, Icarus, Daedalus managed to escape from the tower, only to find himself a prisoner on the island. Several times he tried by bribery to stow away on one of the vessels sailing from Crete, but King Minos kept strict watch over them and no ships were allowed to sail without being carefully searched.

Daedalus was an ingenious artist and was not discouraged by his failures. "Minos may control the land and sea," he said, "but he does not control the air. I will try that way."

He called his son Icarus to him and told the boy to gather up all the feathers he could find on the rocky shore. As thousands of gulls soared over the island, Icarus soon collected a huge pile of feathers. Daedalus then melted some wax and made a skeleton in the shape of a bird's wing. The smallest feathers he pressed into the soft wax and the large ones he tied on with thread. Icarus played about on the beach happily while his father worked, chasing the feathers that blew away in the strong wind that swept the island and sometimes taking bits of the wax and working it into strange shapes with his fingers.

It was fun making the wings. The sun shone on the bright feathers, the breezes ruffled them. When they were finished Daedalus fastened them to his shoulders and found himself lifted upwards where he hung poised in the air. Filled with excitement, he made another pair for his son. They were smaller than his own, but strong and beautiful.

Finally, one clear, wind-swept morning, the wings were finished and Daedalus fastened them to Icarus's shoulders and taught him how to fly. He bade him watch the movements of the birds, how they soared and glided overhead. He pointed out the slow, graceful sweep of their wings as they beat the air steadily, without fluttering. Soon Icarus was sure that he, too, could fly and, raising his arms up and down, skirted over the white sand and even out over the waves, letting his feet touch the snowy foam as the water thundered and broke over the sharp rocks. Daedalus watched him proudly but with misgivings. He called Icarus to his side, and putting his arm round the boy's shoulders, said, "Icarus, my son, we are about to make our flight. No human being has ever traveled through the air before, and I want you to listen carefully to my instructions. Keep at a moderate height, for if you fly too low the fog and spray will clog your wings, and if you fly too high the heat will melt the wax that holds them together. Keep near me and you will be safe."

He kissed Icarus and fastened the wings more securely to his son's shoulders. Icarus, standing in the bright sun, the shining wings drooping gracefully from his shoulders, his golden hair wet with spray and his eyes bright and dark with excitement, looked like a lovely bird. Daedalus's eyes filled with tears and turning away he soared into the sky, calling to Icarus to follow. From time to time, he looked back to see that the boy was safe and to note how he managed his wings in his flight. As they flew across the land to test their prowess before setting out across the dark wild sea, ploughmen below stopped their work and shepherds gazed in wonder, thinking Daedalus and Icarus were gods.

Father and son flew over Samos and Delos which lay to their left, and Lebinthus, which lay on their right. Icarus, beating his wings in joy, felt the thrill of the cool wind on his face and the clear air above and below him. He flew higher and higher up into the blue sky until he reached the clouds. His father saw him and called out in alarm. He tried

to follow him, but he was heavier and his wings would not
carry him. Up and up Icarus soared, through the soft moist
clouds and out again toward the glorious sun. He was bewitched by a sense of freedom and beat his wings frantically
so that they would carry him higher and higher to heaven
itself. The blazing sun beat down on the wings and softened
the wax. Small feathers fell from the wings and floated softly

down, warning Icarus to stay his flight and glide to earth. But the enchanted boy did not notice them until the sun became so hot that the largest feathers dropped off and he began to sink. Frantically he fluttered his arms, but no feathers remained to hold the air. He cried out to his father but his voice was submerged in the blue waters of the sea, which has forever after been called by his name.

Daedalus, crazed by anxiety, called back to him, "Icarus! Icarus, my son, where are you?" At last he saw the feathers floating from the sky and soon his son plunged through the clouds into the sea. Daedalus hurried to save him, but it was too late. He gathered the boy in his arms and flew to land, the tips of his wings dragging in the water from the double burden they bore. Weeping bitterly, he buried his small son and called the land Icaria in his memory.

Then, with a flutter of wings, he once more took to the air, but the joy of his flight was gone and his victory over the air was bitter to him. He arrived safely in Sicily where he built a temple to Apollo and hung up his wings as an offering to the god, and in the wings he pressed a few bright feathers he had found floating on the water where Icarus fell. And he mourned for the bird-like son who had thrown caution to the winds in the exaltation of his freedom from the earth.

Tales of Love

BY EDITH HAMILTON

Illustrations by Steele Savage

Pyramus and Thisbe

ONCE upon a time the deep red berries of the mulberry tree were white as snow. The change in color came about strangely and sadly. The death of two young lovers was the cause.

Pyramus and Thisbe, he the most beautiful youth and she the loveliest maiden of all the East, lived in Babylon, the city of Queen Semiramis, in houses so close together that one wall was common to both. Growing up thus side by side they learned to love each other. They longed to marry, but their parents forbade. Love, however, cannot be forbidden. The more that flame is covered up, the hotter it burns. Also love can always find a way. It was impossible that these two whose hearts were on fire should be kept apart.

In the wall both houses shared there was a little chink. No one before had noticed it, but there is nothing a lover does not notice. Our two young people discovered it and through it they were able to whisper sweetly back and forth, Thisbe on one side, Pyramus on the other. The hateful wall that separated them had become their means of reaching each other. "But for you we could touch, kiss," they would say. "But at least you let us speak together. You give a passage for loving words to reach loving ears. We are not ungrateful." So they would talk, and as night came on and they must part, each would press on the wall kisses that could not go through to the lips on the other side.

Every morning when the dawn had put out the stars, and the sun's rays had dried the hoarfrost on the grass, they

would steal to the crack and, standing there, now utter words
of burning love and now lament their hard fate, but always
in softest whispers. Finally a day came when they could
endure no longer. They decided that that very night they
would try to slip away and steal out through the city into
the open country where at last they could be together in
freedom. They agreed to meet at a well-known place, the
Tomb of Ninus, under a tree there, a tall mulberry full of
snow-white berries, near which a cool spring bubbled up.
The plan pleased them and it seemed to them the day would
never end.

At last the sun sank into the sea and night arose. In the
darkness Thisbe crept out and made her way in all secrecy
to the tomb. Pyramus had not come; still she waited for him,
her love making her bold. But of a sudden she saw by the
light of the moon a lioness. The fierce beast had made a kill;
her jaws were bloody and she was coming to slake her thirst
in the spring. She was still far enough away for Thisbe to
escape, but as she fled she dropped her cloak. The lioness
came upon it on her way back to her lair and she mouthed
it and tore it before disappearing into the woods. That is what
Pyramus saw when he appeared a few minutes later. Before
him lay the bloodstained shreds of the cloak and clear in the
dust were the tracks of the lioness. The conclusion was in-
evitable. He never doubted that he knew all. Thisbe was
dead. He had let his love, a tender maiden, come alone to a
place full of danger, and not been there first to protect her.
"It is I who killed you," he said. He lifted up from the trampled
dust what was left of the cloak and kissing it again and again
carried it to the mulberry tree. "Now," he said, "you shall

drink my blood too." He drew his sword and plunged it into his side. The blood spurted up over the berries and dyed them a dark red.

Thisbe, although terrified of the lioness, was still more afraid to fail her lover. She ventured to go back to the tree of the tryst, the mulberry with the shining white fruit. She could not find it. A tree was there, but not one gleam of white was on the branches. As she stared at it, something moved on the ground beneath. She started back shuddering. But in a moment, peering through the shadows, she saw what was there. It was Pyramus, bathed in blood and dying. She flew to him and threw her arms around him. She kissed his cold lips and begged him to look at her, to speak to her. "It is I, your Thisbe, your dearest," she cried to him. At the sound of her name he opened his heavy eyes for one look. Then death closed them.

She saw his sword fallen from his hand and beside it her cloak stained and torn. She understood all. "Your own hand killed you," she said, "and your love for me. I too can be brave. I too can love. Only death would have had the power to separate us. It shall not have that power now." She plunged into her heart the sword that was still wet with his life's blood.

The gods were pitiful at the end, and the lovers' parents too. The deep red fruit of the mulberry is the everlasting memorial of these true lovers, and one urn holds the ashes of the two whom not even death could part.

Orpheus and Eurydice

The very earliest musicians were the gods. Athena was not distinguished in that line, but she invented the flute although she never played upon it. Hermes made the lyre and gave it to Apollo who drew from it sounds so melodious that when he played in Olympus the gods forgot all else. Hermes also made the shepherd-pipe for himself and drew enchanting music from it. Pan made the pipe of reeds which can sing as sweetly as the nightingale in spring. The Muses had no instrument peculiar to them, but their voices were lovely beyond compare.

Next in order came a few mortals so excellent in their art that they almost equaled the divine performers. Of these by far the greatest was Orpheus. On his mother's side he was more than mortal. He was the son of one of the Muses and a Thracian prince. His mother gave him the gift of music and Thrace where he grew up fostered it. The Thracians were the most musical of the peoples of Greece. But Orpheus had no rival there or anywhere except the gods alone. There was no limit to his power when he played and sang. No one and nothing could resist him.

> In the deep still woods upon the Thracian mountains
> Orpheus with his singing lyre led the trees,
> Led the wild beasts of the wilderness.

Everything animate and inanimate followed him. He moved the rocks on the hillside and turned the courses of the rivers.

Little is told about his life before his ill-fated marriage, for which he is even better known than for his music, but he went on one famous expedition and proved himself a most useful member of it. He sailed with Jason on the *Argo*, and when the heroes were weary or the rowing was especially difficult he would strike his lyre and they would be aroused to fresh zeal and their oars would smite the sea together in time to the melody. Or if a quarrel threatened he would play so tenderly and soothingly that the fiercest spirits would grow calm and forget their anger. He saved the heroes, too, from the Sirens. When they heard far over the sea singing so enchantingly sweet that it drove out all other thoughts except a desperate longing to hear more, and they turned the ship to the shore where the Sirens sat, Orpheus snatched up his lyre and played a tune so clear and ringing that it drowned the sound of those lovely fatal voices. The ship was put back on her course and the winds sped her away from the dangerous place. If Orpheus had not been there the Argonauts, too, would have left their bones on the Sirens' island.

Where he first met and how he wooed the maiden he loved, Eurydice, we are not told, but it is clear that no maiden he

wanted could have resisted the power of his song. They were
married, but their joy was brief. Directly after the wedding,
as the bride walked in a meadow with her bridesmaids, a
viper stung her and she died. Orpheus' grief was overwhelming. He could not endure it. He determined to go down to
the world of death and try to bring Eurydice back. He said
to himself,

> With my song
> I will charm Demeter's daughter,
> I will charm the Lord of the Dead,
> Moving their hearts with my melody.
> I will bear her away from Hades.

He dared more than any other man ever dared for his
love. He took the fearsome journey to the underworld. There
he struck his lyre, and at the sound all that vast multitude
were charmed to stillness. The dog Cerberus relaxed his
guard; the wheel of Ixion stood motionless; Sisiphus sat at
rest upon his stone; Tantalus forgot his thirst; for the first
time the faces of the dread goddesses, the Furies, were wet
with tears. The ruler of Hades drew near to listen with his
queen. Orpheus sang,

> O Gods who rule the dark and silent world,
> To you all born of woman needs must come.
> All lovely things at last go down to you.
> You are the debtor who is always paid.
> A little while we tarry up on earth.
> Then we are yours forever and forever.
> But I seek one who came to you too soon.
> The bud was plucked before the flower bloomed.
> I tried to bear my loss. I could not bear it.
> Love was too strong a god. O King, you know
> If that old tale men tell is true, how once
> The flowers saw the rape of Proserpine.
> Then weave again for sweet Eurydice
> Life's pattern that was taken from the loom
> Too quickly. See, I ask a little thing,
> Only that you will lend, not give, her to me.
> She shall be yours when her years' span is full.

No one under the spell of his voice could refuse him anything. He

> Drew iron tears down Pluto's cheek.
> And made Hell grant what Love did seek.

They summoned Eurydice and gave her to him, but upon
one condition: that he would not look back at her as she
followed him, until they had reached the upper world. So
the two passed through the great doors of Hades to the path
which would take them out of the darkness, climbing up
and up. He knew that she must be just behind him, but
he longed unutterably to give one glance to make sure. But
now they were almost there, the blackness was turning gray;
now he had stepped out joyfully into the daylight. Then
he turned to her. It was too soon; she was still in the cavern.
He saw her in the dim light, and he held out his arms to clasp
her; but on the instant she was gone. She had slipped back
into the darkness. All he heard was one faint word, "Farewell."
Desperately he tried to rush after her and follow her down,
but he was not allowed. The gods would not consent to his
entering the world of the dead a second time, while he was
still alive. He was forced to return to the earth alone, in utter
desolation. Then he forsook the company of men. He wandered through the wild solitudes of Thrace, comfortless except
for his lyre, playing, always playing, and the rocks and the
rivers and the trees heard him gladly, his only companions.
But at last a band of Maenads came upon him. They were
as frenzied as those who killed Pentheus so horribly. They
slew the gentle musician, tearing him limb from limb, and
flung the severed head into the swift river Hebrus. It was
borne along past the river's mouth on to the Lesbian shore,
nor had it suffered any change from the sea when the Muses
found it and buried it in the sanctuary of the island. His
limbs they gathered and placed in a tomb at the foot of
Mount Olympus, and there to this day the nightingales sing
more sweetly than anywhere else.

Pygmalion and Galatea

A gifted young sculptor of Cyprus, named Pygmalion, was a woman-hater.

> Detesting the faults beyond measure which nature
> has given to women,

he resolved never to marry. His art, he told himself, was enough for him. Nevertheless, the statue he made and devoted all his genius to was that of a woman. Either he could not dismiss what he so disapproved of from his mind as easily as from his life, or else he was bent on forming a perfect woman and showing men the deficiencies of the kind they had to put up with.

However that was, he labored long and devotedly on the statue and produced a most exquisite work of art. But lovely as it was he could not rest content. He kept on working at it and daily under his skillful fingers it grew more beautiful. No woman ever born, no statue ever made, could approach it. When nothing could be added to its perfections, a strange fate had befallen its creator: he had fallen in love, deeply, passionately in love, with the thing he had made. It must be said in explanation that the statue did not look like a statue; no one would have thought it was ivory or stone, but warm human flesh, motionless for a moment only. Such was the wondrous power of this disdainful young man. The supreme achievement of art was his, the art of concealing art.

But from that time on, the sex he scorned had their revenge. No hopeless lover of a living maiden was ever so desperately unhappy as Pygmalion. He kissed those enticing lips—they could not kiss him back; he caressed her hands, her face—they were unresponsive; he took her in his arms —she remained a cold and passive form. For a time he tried to pretend, as children do with their toys. He would dress her in rich robes, trying the effect of one delicate or glowing color after another, and imagine she was pleased. He would bring her the gifts real maidens love, little birds and gay flowers and the shining tears of amber Phaëthon's sisters weep,

and then dream she thanked him with eager affection. He put her to bed at night, and tucked her in all soft and warm, as little girls do their dolls. But he was not a child; he could not keep on pretending. In the end he gave up. He loved a lifeless thing and he was utterly and hopelessly wretched.

This singular passion did not long remain concealed from the Goddess of Passionate Love. Venus was interested in something that seldom came her way, a new kind of lover, and she determined to help a young man who could be enamored and yet original.

The feast of Venus was, of course, especially honored in Cyprus, the island which first received the goddess after she rose from the foam. Snow-white heifers whose horns had been gilded were offered in numbers to her; the heavenly odor of incense was spread through the island from her many altars; crowds thronged her temples; not an unhappy lover but was there with his gift, praying that his love might turn kind. There too, of course, was Pygmalion. He dared to ask the goddess only that he might find a maiden like his statue, but Venus knew what he really wanted and as a sign that she favored his prayer the flame on the altar he stood before leaped up three times, blazing into the air.

Very thoughtful at this good omen Pygmalion sought his house and his love, the thing he had created and given his heart to. There she stood on her pedestal, entrancingly beautiful. He caressed her and then he started back. Was it self-deception or did she really feel warm to his touch? He kissed her lips, a long lingering kiss, and felt them grow soft beneath his. He touched her arms, her shoulders; their hardness vanished. It was like watching wax soften in the sun. He clasped her wrist; blood was pulsing there. Venus, he thought. This is the goddess's doing. And with unutterable gratitude and joy he put his arms around his love and saw her smile into his eyes and blush.

Venus herself graced their marriage with her presence, but what happened after that we do not know, except that Pygmalion named the maiden Galatea, and that their son, Paphos, gave his name to Venus' favorite city.

The Miraculous Pitcher

BY NATHANIEL HAWTHORNE

Illustrations by Walter Crane and Hammatt Billings

ONE evening, in times long ago, old Philemon and his old wife Baucis sat at their cottage door, enjoying the calm and beautiful sunset. They had already eaten their frugal supper, and intended now to spend a quiet hour or two before bed-time. So they talked together about their garden, and their cow, and their bees, and their grapevine, which clambered over the cottage wall, and on which the grapes were beginning to turn purple. But the rude shouts of children and the fierce barking of dogs, in the village near at hand, grew louder and louder, until, at last, it was hardly possible for Baucis and Philemon to hear each other speak.

"Ah, wife," cried Philemon, "I fear some poor traveler is seeking hospitality among our neighbors yonder, and, instead of giving him food and lodging, they have set their dogs at him, as their custom is!"

"Well-a-day!" answered old Baucis, "I do wish our neighbors felt a little more kindness for their fellow creatures. And only think of bringing up their children in this naughty way, and patting them on the head when they fling stones at strangers!"

"Those children will never come to any good," said Philemon, shaking his white head. "To tell you the truth, wife, I should not wonder if some terrible thing were to happen to all the people in the village unless they mend their manners. But, as for you and me, so long as Providence affords us a crust of bread, let us be ready to give half to any poor, homeless stranger that may come along and need it."

"That's right, husband!" said Baucis. "So we will!"

These old folk, you must know, were quite poor, and had to work pretty hard for a living. Old Philemon toiled diligently in

From *The Wonder Book for Boys and Girls,* by Nathaniel Hawthorne. Published by Houghton Mifflin Company.

his garden, while Baucis was always busy with her distaff, or making a little butter and cheese with their cow's milk, or doing one thing and another about the cottage. Their food was seldom anything but bread, milk, and vegetables, with sometimes a portion of honey from their beehive, and now and then a bunch of grapes, that had ripened against the cottage wall. But they were two of the kindest old people in the world, and would cheerfully have gone without their dinners any day rather than refuse a slice of their brown loaf, a cup of new milk, and a spoonful of honey, to the weary traveler who might pause before their door. They felt as if such guests had a sort of holiness, and that they ought, therefore, to treat them better and more bountifully than their own selves.

Their cottage stood on a rising ground, at some short distance from a village, which lay in a hollow valley, that was about half a mile in breadth. This valley, in past ages, when the world was new, had probably been the bed of a lake. There, fishes had glided to and fro in the depths, and waterweeds had grown along the margin, and trees and hills had seen their reflected images in the broad and peaceful mirror. But, as the waters subsided, men had cultivated the soil, and built houses on it, so that it was now a fertile spot, and bore no traces of the ancient lake, except a very small brook which meandered through the midst of the village and supplied the inhabitants with water. The valley had been dry land so long, that oaks had sprung up and grown great and high, and perished with old age and been succeeded by others, as tall and stately as the first. Never was there a prettier or more fruitful valley. The very sight of the plenty around them should have made the inhabitants kind and gentle, and ready to show their gratitude to Providence by doing good to their fellow creatures.

But, we are sorry to say, the people of this lovely village were not worthy to dwell in a spot on which Heaven had smiled so beneficently. They were a very selfish and hardhearted people, and had no pity for the poor, nor sympathy with the homeless. They would only have laughed had anybody told them that human beings owe a debt of love to one another, because there is no other method of paying the debt of love and care which all of us owe to Providence. You will hardly believe what I am going to tell you. These naughty people taught their children to be no better than themselves, and used to clap their hands, by way of encouragement, when they saw the little boys and girls run after some poor stranger, shouting at his heels and pelting him with stones. They kept large and fierce dogs, and whenever a traveler ventured to show himself in the village street, this pack of disagreeable curs scampered to meet him, barking, snarling, and showing their teeth. Then they would seize him by his leg, or by his clothes, just as it happened; and if he were ragged when he came, he was generally a pitiable object before he had time to run away. This was a very terrible thing to poor travelers, as you may suppose, especially when they chanced to be sick, or feeble, or lame, or old. Such persons (if they once knew how badly these unkind people, and their unkind children and curs, were in the habit of behaving) would go miles and miles out of their way, rather than try to pass through the village again.

What made the matter seem worse, if possible, was that when rich persons came in their chariots, or riding on beautiful horses, with their servants in rich liveries attending on them, nobody could be more civil and obsequious than the inhabitants of the village. They would take off their hats and make the humblest bows you ever saw. If the children were rude, they were pretty certain to get their ears boxed; and as for the dogs, if a single cur in the pack presumed to yelp, his master instantly beat him with a club, and tied him up without any supper. This would have been all very well, only it proved that the villagers cared much about the money that a stranger had in his pocket, and nothing whatever for the human soul which lives equally in the beggar and the prince.

So now you can understand why old Philemon spoke so sorrowfully, when he heard the shouts of the children and the barking of the dogs, at the farther extremity of the village street. There was a confused din, which lasted a good while, and seemed to pass quite through the breadth of the valley.

"I never heard the dogs so loud!" observed the good old man.

"Nor the children so rude!" answered his good old wife.

They sat shaking their heads, one to another, while the noise came nearer and nearer; until, at the foot of the little eminence on which their cottage stood, they saw two travelers approaching on foot. Close behind them came the fierce dogs, snarling at their very heels. A little farther off, ran a crowd of children, who sent up shrill cries, and flung stones at the two strangers, with all their might. Once or twice, the younger of the two men (he was a slender and very active figure) turned about and drove back the dogs with a staff which he carried in his hand. His companion, who was a very tall person, walked calmly along, as if disdaining to notice either the naughty children or the pack of curs whose manners the children seemed to imitate.

Both of the travelers were very humbly clad, and looked as if they might not have money enough in their pockets to pay for a night's lodging. And this, I am afraid, was the reason why the villagers had allowed their children and dogs to treat them so rudely.

"Come, wife," said Philemon to Baucis, "let us go and meet these poor people. No doubt, they feel almost too heavy-hearted to climb the hill."

"Go you and meet them," answered Baucis, "while I make haste within doors, and see whether we can get them anything for suppor. A comfortable bowl of bread and milk would do wonders toward raising their spirits."

Accordingly, she hastened into the cottage. Philemon, on his part, went forward, and extended his hand with so hospitable an aspect that there was no need of saying what nevertheless he did say, in the heartiest tone imaginable, "Welcome, strangers! Welcome!"

"Thank you!" replied the younger of the two, in a lively kind of way, notwithstanding his weariness and trouble. "This is quite another greeting than we have met with yonder in the village. Pray, why do you live in such a bad neighborhood?"

"Ah!" observed old Philemon, with a quiet and benign smile, "Providence put me here, I hope, among other reasons, in order that I may make you what amends I can for the inhospitality of my neighbors."

"Well said, old father!" cried the traveler, laughing; "and if the truth must be told, my companion and myself need some amends. Those children (the little rascals!) have bespattered us finely with their mud balls; and one of the curs has torn my cloak, which was ragged enough already. But I took him across the muzzle with my staff; and I think you may have heard him yelp, even thus far off."

Philemon was glad to see him in such good spirits; nor, indeed, would you have fancied, by the traveler's look and manner, that he was weary with a long day's journey, besides being disheartened by rough treatment at the end of it. He was dressed in rather an odd way, with a sort of cap on his head, the brim of which stuck out over both ears. Though it was a summer evening, he wore a cloak which he kept wrapt closely about him, perhaps because his under garments were shabby. Philemon perceived, too, that he had on a singular pair of shoes; but, as it was now growing dusk, and as the old man's eyesight was none the sharpest, he could not precisely tell in what the strangeness consisted. One thing, certainly, seemed queer. The traveler was so wonderfully light and active, that it appeared as if his feet sometimes rose from the ground of their own accord, or could only be kept down by an effort.

"I used to be light-footed, in my youth," said Philemon to the traveler. "But I always found my feet grow heavier toward nightfall."

"There is nothing like a good staff to help one along," answered the stranger; "and I happen to have an excellent one, as you see."

This staff, in fact, was the oddest-looking staff that Philemon had ever beheld. It was made of olive wood, and had something like a little pair of wings near the top. Two snakes, carved in the wood, were represented as twining themselves about the staff, and were so very skillfully executed that old Philemon (whose eyes, you know, were getting rather dim) almost thought them alive, and that he could see them wriggling and twisting.

"A curious piece of work, sure enough!" said he. "A staff with wings! It would be an excellent kind of stick for a little boy to ride astride of!" By this time, Philemon and his two guests had reached the cottage door.

"Friends," said the old man, "sit down and rest yourselves here on this bench. My good wife Baucis has gone to see what you

can have for supper. We are poor folks; but you shall be welcome to whatever we have in the cupboard."

The younger stranger threw himself carelessly on the bench,
letting his staff fall, as he did so. And here happened something
rather marvelous, though trifling enough, too. The staff seemed
to get up from the ground of its own accord, and, spreading its
little pair of wings, it half hopped, half flew, and leaned itself
against the wall of the cottage. There it stood quite still, except
that the snakes continued to wriggle. But, in my private opinion,
old Philemon's eyesight had been playing him tricks again.

Before he could ask any questions, the elder stranger drew
his attention from the wonderful staff, by speaking to him.

"Was there not," asked the stranger, in a remarkably deep
tone of voice, "a lake, in very ancient times, covering the spot
where now stands yonder village?"

"Not in my day, friend," answered Philemon; "and yet I am
an old man, as you see. There were always the fields and
meadows, just as they are now, and the old trees, and the little
stream murmuring through the midst of the valley. My father,
nor his father before him, ever saw it otherwise, so far as I
know; and doubtless it will still be the same, when old Philemon shall be gone and forgotten!"

"That is more than can be safely foretold," observed the
stranger; and there was something very stern in his deep voice.
He shook his head, too, so that his dark and heavy curls were
shaken with the movement. "Since the inhabitants of yonder
village have forgotten the affections and sympathies of their
nature, it were better that the lake should be rippling over their
dwellings again!"

The traveler looked so stern that Philemon was really almost
frightened; the more so, that, at his frown, the twilight seemed
suddenly to grow darker, and that, when he shook his head,
there was a roll of thunder in the air.

But, in a moment afterwards, the stranger's face became so
kindly and mild that the old man quite forgot his terror. Nevertheless, he could not help feeling that this elder traveler must
be no ordinary personage, although he happened now to be
attired so humbly and to be journeying on foot. Not that Philemon fancied him a prince in disguise, or any character of that

sort; but rather some exceedingly wise man, who went about the world in this poor garb, despising wealth and all worldly objects, and seeking everywhere to add a mite to his wisdom. This idea appeared the more probable, because, when Philemon raised his eyes to the stranger's face, he seemed to see more thought there in one look than he could have studied out in a lifetime.

While Baucis was getting the supper, the travelers both began to talk very sociably with Philemon. The younger, indeed, was extremely loquacious, and made such shrewd and witty remarks that the good old man continually burst out a-laughing, and pronounced him the merriest fellow whom he had seen for many a day.

"Pray, my young friend," said he, as they grew familiar together, "what may I call your name?"

"Why, I am very nimble, as you see," answered the traveler. "So, if you call me Quicksilver, the name will fit tolerably well."

"Quicksilver? Quicksilver?" repeated Philemon, looking in the traveler's face, to see if he were making fun of him. "It is a very odd name! And your companion there? Has he as strange a one?"

"You must ask the thunder to tell it you!" replied Quicksilver, putting on a mysterious look. "No other voice is loud enough."

This remark, whether it were serious or in jest, might have caused Philemon to conceive a very great awe of the elder stranger, if, on venturing to gaze at him, he had not beheld so much beneficence in his visage. But, undoubtedly, here was the grandest figure that ever sat so humbly beside a cottage door. When the stranger conversed, it was with gravity, and in such a way that Philemon felt irresistibly moved to tell him everything which he had most at heart. This is always the feeling that people have when they meet with anyone wise enough to comprehend all their good and evil, and to despise not a tittle of it.

But Philemon, simple and kindhearted old man that he was, had not many secrets to disclose. He talked, however, quite garrulously, about the events of his past life, in the whole course of which he had never been a score of miles from this very spot. His wife Baucis and himself had dwelt in the cottage from

their youth upward, earning their bread by honest labor, always poor, but still contented. He told what excellent butter and cheese Baucis made, and how nice were the vegetables which he raised in his garden. He said, too, that, because they loved one another so very much, it was the wish of both that death might not separate them, but that they should die, as they had lived, together.

As the stranger listened, a smile beamed over his countenance, and made its expression as sweet as it was grand.

"You are a good old man," said he to Philemon, "and you have a good old wife to be your helpmeet. It is fit that your wish be granted."

And it seemed to Philemon just then as if the sunset clouds threw up a bright flash from the west, and kindled a sudden light in the sky.

Baucis had now got supper ready, and, coming to the door, began to make apologies for the poor fare which she was forced to set before her guests.

"Had we known you were coming," said she, "my good man and myself would have gone without a morsel, rather than you should lack a better supper. But I took the most part of today's milk to make cheese; and our last loaf is already half eaten. Ah me! I never feel the sorrow of being poor, save when a poor traveler knocks at our door."

"All will be very well; do not trouble yourself, my good dame," replied the elder stranger, kindly. "An honest, hearty welcome to a guest works miracles with the fare, and is capable of turning the coarsest food to nectar and ambrosia."

"A welcome you shall have," cried Baucis, "and likewise a little honey that we happen to have left, and a bunch of purple grapes besides."

"Why, Mother Baucis, it is a feast!" exclaimed Quicksilver, laughing, "an absolute feast! and you shall see how bravely I will play my part at it! I think I never felt hungrier in my life."

"Mercy on us!" whispered Baucis to her husband. "If the young man has such a terrible appetite, I am afraid there will not be half enough supper!"

They all went into the cottage.

And now, my little auditors, shall I tell you something that will make you open your eyes very wide? It is really one of the oddest circumstances in the whole story. Quicksilver's staff, you recollect, had set itself up against the wall of the cottage. Well; when its master entered the door, leaving this wonderful staff behind, what should it do but immediately spread its little wings, and go hopping and fluttering up the doorsteps! Tap, tap, went the staff, on the kitchen floor; nor did it rest until it had stood itself on end, with the greatest gravity and decorum, beside Quicksilver's chair. Old Philemon, however, as well as his wife, was so taken up in attending to their guests, that no notice was given to what the staff had been about.

As Baucis had said, there was but a scanty supper for two hungry travelers. In the middle of the table was the remnant of a brown loaf, with a piece of cheese on one side of it, and a dish of honeycomb on the other. There was a pretty good bunch of grapes for each of the guests. A moderately sized earthen pitcher, nearly full of milk, stood at a corner of the board; and when Baucis had filled two bowls, and set them before the strangers, only a little milk remained in the bottom of the pitcher. Alas! it is a very sad business when a bountiful heart finds itself pinched and squeezed among narrow circumstances. Poor Baucis kept wishing that she might starve for a week to come, if it were possible by so doing to provide these hungry folk a more plentiful supper.

And, since the supper was so exceedingly small, she could not help wishing that their appetites had not been quite so large. Why, at their very first sitting down, the travelers both drank off all the milk in their two bowls, at a draught.

"A little more milk, kind Mother Baucis, if you please," said Quicksilver. "The day has been hot, and I am very much a-thirst."

"Now, my dear people," answered Baucis, in great confusion, "I am so sorry and ashamed! But the truth is, there is hardly a drop more milk in the pitcher. O husband! husband! why didn't we go without our supper?"

"Why, it appears to me," cried Quicksilver, starting up from table and taking the pitcher by the handle, "it really appears to me that matters are not quite so bad as you represent them. Here is certainly more milk in the pitcher."

So saying, and to the vast astonishment of Baucis, he proceeded to fill not only his own bowl but his companion's likewise, from the pitcher that was supposed to be almost empty. The good woman could scarcely believe her eyes. She had certainly poured out nearly all the milk, and had peeped in afterwards and seen the bottom of the pitcher as she set it down upon the table.

"But I am old," thought Baucis to herself, "and apt to be forgetful. I suppose I must have made a mistake. At all events, the pitcher cannot help being empty now, after filling the bowls twice over."

"What excellent milk!" observed Quicksilver, after quaffing the contents of the second bowl. "Excuse me, my kind hostess, but I must really ask you for a little more."

Now Baucis had seen, as plainly as she could see anything, that Quicksilver had turned the pitcher upside down, and consequently had poured out every drop of milk in filling the last bowl. Of course, there could not possibly be any left. However, in order to let him know precisely how the case was, she lifted the pitcher and made a gesture as if pouring milk into Quicksilver's bowl, but without the remotest idea that any milk would stream forth. What was her surprise, therefore, when such an abundant cascade fell bubbling into the bowl, that it was immediately filled to the brim and overflowed upon the table! The two snakes that were twisted about Quicksilver's staff (but neither Baucis nor Philemon happened to observe this circumstance) stretched out their heads, and began to lap the spilt milk.

And then what a delicious fragrance the milk had! It seemed as if Philemon's only cow must have pastured, that day, on the richest herbage that could be found anywhere in the world. I only wish that each of you, my beloved little souls, could have a bowl of such nice milk at supper time!

"And now a slice of your brown loaf, Mother Baucis," said Quicksilver, "and a little of that honey!"

Baucis cut him a slice, accordingly; and though the loaf, when she and her husband ate of it, had been rather too dry and crusty to be palatable, it was now as light and moist as if but a few hours out of the oven. Tasting a crumb, which had fallen on the table, she found it more delicious than bread ever was before, and could hardly believe that it was a loaf of her own kneading and baking. Yet, what other loaf could it possibly be?

But, oh, the honey! I may just as well let it alone, without trying to describe how exquisitely it smelt and looked. Its color was that of the purest and most transparent gold; and it had the odor of a thousand flowers; but of such flowers as never grew in an earthly garden, and to seek which the bees must have flown high above the clouds. The wonder is, that, after alighting on a flower bed of so delicious fragrance and immortal bloom, they should have been content to fly down again to their hive in Philemon's garden. Never was such honey tasted, seen, or smelt. The perfume floated around the kitchen, and made it so delightful, that, had you closed your eyes you would instantly have forgotten the low ceiling and smoky walls, and have fancied yourself in an arbor, with celestial honeysuckles creeping over it.

Although good Mother Baucis was a simple old dame, she could not but think that there was something rather out of the common way in all that had been going on. So, after helping the guests to bread and honey, and laying a bunch of grapes by each of their plates, she sat down by Philemon, and told him what she had seen, in a whisper.

"Did you ever hear the like?" asked she.

"No, I never did," answered Philemon, with a smile. "And I rather think, my dear old wife, you have been walking about in a sort of a dream. If I had poured out the milk, I should have seen through the business at once. There happened to be a little more in the pitcher than you thought—that is all."

"Ah, husband," said Baucis, "say what you will, these are very uncommon people."

"Well, well," replied Philemon, still smiling, "perhaps they are. They certainly do look as if they had seen better days; and I am heartily glad to see them making so comfortable a supper."

Each of the guests had now taken his bunch of grapes upon his plate. Baucis (who rubbed her eyes in order to see the more clearly) was of opinion that the clusters had grown larger and richer and that each separate grape seemed to be on the point of bursting with ripe juice. It was entirely a mystery to her how such grapes could ever have been produced from the old stunted vine that climbed against the cottage wall.

"Very admirable grapes these!" observed Quicksilver, as he swallowed one after another, without apparently diminishing his cluster. "Pray, my good host, whence did you gather them?"

"From my own vine," answered Philemon. "You may see one

of its branches twisting across the window, yonder. But wife and I never thought the grapes very fine ones."

"I never tasted better," said the guest. "Another cup of this delicious milk, if you please, and I shall then have supped better than a prince."

This time, old Philemon bestirred himself and took up the pitcher; for he was curious to discover whether there was any reality in the marvels which Baucis had whispered to him. He knew that his good old wife was incapable of falsehood, and that she was seldom mistaken in what she supposed to be true; but this was so very singular a case that he wanted to see into it with his own eyes. On taking up the pitcher, therefore, he slyly peeped into it, and was fully satisfied that it contained not so much as a single drop. All at once, however, he beheld a little white fountain which gushed up from the bottom of the pitcher, and speedily filled it to the brim with foaming and deliciously fragrant milk. It was lucky that Philemon, in his surprise, did not drop the miraculous pitcher from his hand.

"Who are ye, wonder-working strangers?" cried he, even more bewildered than his wife had been.

"Your guests, my good Philemon, and your friends," replied the elder traveler, in his mild, deep voice, that had something at once sweet and awe-inspiring in it. "Give me likewise a cup of the milk; and may your pitcher never be empty for kind Baucis and yourself, any more than for the needy wayfarer!"

The supper being now over, the strangers requested to be shown to their place of repose. The old people would gladly have talked with them a little longer, and have expressed the wonder which they felt, and their delight at finding the poor and meager supper prove so much better and more abundant than they hoped. But the elder traveler had inspired them with such reverence that they dared not ask him any questions. And when Philemon drew Quicksilver aside, and inquired how under the sun a fountain of milk could have got into an old earthen pitcher, this latter personage pointed to his staff.

"There is the whole mystery of the affair," quoth Quicksilver; "and if you can make it out, I'll thank you to let me know. I can't tell what to make of my staff. It is always playing such odd tricks as this; sometimes getting me a supper, and, quite as often, stealing it away. If I had any faith in such nonsense, I should say the stick was bewitched!"

He said no more, but looked so slyly in their faces that they rather fancied he was laughing at them. The magic staff went hopping at his heels as Quicksilver quitted the room. When left alone, the good old couple spent some little time in conversation about the events of the evening, and then lay down on the floor and fell fast asleep. They had given up their sleeping room to the guests, and had no other bed for themselves save these planks, which I wish had been as soft as their own hearts.

The old man and his wife were stirring betimes in the morning, and the strangers likewise arose with the sun, and made their preparations to depart. Philemon hospitably entreated them to remain a little longer, until Baucis could milk the cow, and bake a cake upon the hearth, and, perhaps, find them a few fresh eggs for breakfast. The guests, however, seemed to think it better to accomplish a good part of their journey before the heat of the day should come on. They therefore persisted in setting out immediately, but asked Philemon and Baucis to walk forth with them a short distance, and show them the road which they were to take.

So they all four issued from the cottage, chatting together like old friends. It was very remarkable, indeed, how familiar the old couple insensibly grew with the elder traveler, and how their good and simple spirits melted into his, even as two drops of water would melt into the illimitable ocean. And as for Quicksilver, with his keen, quick, laughing wits, he appeared to discover every little thought that but peeped into their minds, before they suspected it themselves. They sometimes wished, it is true, that he had not been quite so quick-witted, and also that he would fling away his staff, which looked so mysteriously mischievous with the snakes always writhing about it. But then, again, Quicksilver showed himself so very good-humored, that they would have been rejoiced to keep him in their cottage, staff, snakes, and all, every day, and the whole day long.

"Ah me! Well-a-day!" exclaimed Philemon, when they had walked a little way from their door. "If our neighbors only knew what a blessed thing it is to show hospitality to strangers, they would tie up all their dogs and never allow their children to fling another stone."

"It is a sin and shame for them to behave so—that it is!" cried good old Baucis, vehemently. "And I mean to go this very day, and tell some of them what naughty people they are!"

"I fear," remarked Quicksilver, slyly smiling, "that you will find none of them at home."

The elder traveler's brow just then assumed such a grave, stern, and awful grandeur, yet serene withal, that neither Baucis nor Philemon dared to speak a word. They gazed reverently into his face, as if they had been gazing at the sky.

"When men do not feel toward the humblest stranger as if he were a brother," said the traveler in tones so deep that they sounded like those of an organ, "they are unworthy to exist on earth, which was created as the abode of a great human brotherhood!"

"And, by the by, my dear old people," cried Quicksilver, with the liveliest look of fun and mischief in his eyes, "where is this same village that you talk about? On which side of us does it lie? Methinks I do not see it hereabouts."

Philemon and his wife turned toward the valley, where, at sunset, only the day before, they had seen the meadows, the houses, the gardens, the clumps of trees, the wide, green-margined street, with children playing in it, and all the tokens of business, enjoyment, and prosperity. But what was their astonishment! There was no longer any appearance of a village! Even the fertile vale in the hollow of which it lay had ceased to have existence. In its stead, they beheld the broad, blue surface of a lake, which filled the great basin of the valley from brim to brim, and reflected the surrounding hills in its bosom with as tranquil an image as if it had been there ever since the creation of the world. For an instant, the lake remained perfectly smooth. Then a little breeze sprang up, and caused the water to dance, glitter, and sparkle in the early sunbeams, and to dash with a pleasant rippling murmur against the hither shore.

The lake seemed so strangely familiar that the old couple were greatly perplexed, and felt as if they could only have been dreaming about a village having lain there. But, the next mo-

ment, they remembered the vanished dwellings and the faces
and characters of the inhabitants far too distinctly for a dream.
The village had been there yesterday, and now was gone!

"Alas!" cried these kindhearted old people, "what has become
of our poor neighbors?"

"They exist no longer as men and women," said the elder
traveler, in his grand and deep voice, while a roll of thunder
seemed to echo it at a distance. "There was neither use nor
beauty in such a life as theirs; for they never softened or
sweetened the hard lot of mortality by the exercise of kindly
affections between man and man. They retained no image of
the better life in their bosoms; therefore, the lake that was of
old has spread itself forth again, to reflect the sky!"

"And as for those foolish people," said Quicksilver, with his
mischievous smile, "they are all transformed to fishes. There
needed but little change, for they were already a scaly set of
rascals and the coldest-blooded beings in existence. So, kind
Mother Baucis, whenever you or your husband have an appetite for a dish of broiled trout, he can throw in a line, and pull
out half a dozen of your old neighbors!"

"Ah," cried Baucis, shuddering, "I would not, for the world,
put one of them on the gridiron!"

"No," added Philemon, making a wry face, "we could never
relish them!"

"As for you, good Philemon," continued the elder traveler—
"and you, kind Baucis—you, with your scanty means, have
mingled so much heartfelt hospitality with your entertainment
of the homeless stranger, that the milk became an inexhaustible
fount of nectar and the brown loaf and the honey were ambrosia. Thus, the divinities have feasted, at your board, off the
same viands that supply their banquets on Olympus. You have
done well, my dear old friends. Wherefore, request whatever
favor you have most at heart and it is granted."

Philemon and Baucis looked at one another, and then—I know
not which of the two it was who spoke, but that one uttered
the desire of both their hearts.

"Let us live together while we live, and leave the world at the
same instant when we die! For we have always loved one
another!"

"Be it so!" replied the stranger, with majestic kindness. "Now, look toward your cottage!"

They did so. But what was their surprise on beholding a tall edifice of white marble, with a wide-open portal, occupying the spot where their humble residence had so lately stood!

"There is your home," said the stranger, beneficently smiling on them both. "Exercise your hospitality in yonder palace as freely as in the poor hovel to which you welcomed us last evening."

The old folk fell on their knees to thank him; but, behold! neither he nor Quicksilver was there.

So Philemon and Baucis took up their residence in the marble palace and spent their time, with vast satisfaction to themselves, in making everybody jolly and comfortable who happened to pass that way. The milk pitcher, I must not forget to say, retained its marvelous quality of being never empty when it was desirable to have it full. Whenever an honest, good-humored, and freehearted guest took a draught from this pitcher, he invariably found it the sweetest and most invigorating fluid that ever ran down his throat. But, if a cross and disagreeable curmudgeon happened to sip, he was pretty certain to twist his visage into a hard knot and pronounce it a pitcher of sour milk!

Thus the old couple lived in their palace a great, great while, and grew older and older, and very old indeed. At length, however, there came a summer morning when Philemon and Baucis failed to make their appearance as on other mornings, with one hospitable smile overspreading both their pleasant faces, to invite the guests of overnight to breakfast. The guests searched everywhere from top to bottom of the spacious palace, and all to no purpose. But, after a great deal of perplexity, they espied, in front of the portal, two venerable trees, which nobody could remember to have seen there the day before. Yet there they stood, with their roots fastened deep into the soil, and a huge breadth of foliage overshadowing the whole front of the edifice. One was an oak, and the other a linden tree. Their boughs— it was strange and beautiful to see—were intertwined together, and embraced one another, so that each tree seemed to live in the other tree's bosom much more than in its own.

While the guests were marveling how these trees that must

have required at least a century to grow could have come to be so tall and venerable in a single night, a breeze sprang up, and set their intermingled boughs astir. And then there was a deep, broad murmur in the air, as if the two mysterious trees were speaking.

"I am old Philemon!" murmured the oak.

"I am old Baucis!" murmured the linden tree.

But, as the breeze grew stronger, the trees both spoke at once—"Philemon! Baucis! Baucis! Philemon!"—as if one were both and both were one, and talking together in the depths of their mutual heart. It was plain enough to perceive that the good old couple had renewed their age and were now to spend a quiet and delightful hundred years or so, Philemon as an oak, and Baucis as a linden tree. And oh, what a hospitable shade did they fling around them! Whenever a wayfarer paused beneath it, he heard a pleasant whisper of the leaves above his head, and wondered how the sound should so much resemble words like these:

"Welcome, welcome, dear traveler, welcome!"

And some kind soul, that knew what would have pleased old Baucis and old Philemon best, built a circular seat around both their trunks, where, for a great while afterwards, the weary, and the hungry, and the thirsty used to repose themselves, and quaff milk abundantly out of the miraculous pitcher.

And I wish, for all our sakes, that we had the pitcher here now!

The Chimaera

BY NATHANIEL HAWTHORNE

Illustrations by Walter Crane and Hammatt Billings

ONCE, in the old, old times (for all the strange things which I tell you about happened long before anybody can remember), a fountain gushed out of a hillside, in the marvelous land of Greece. And, for aught I know, after so many thousand years, it is still gushing out of the very selfsame spot. At any rate, there was the pleasant fountain, welling freshly forth and sparkling a-down the hillside, in the golden sunset, when a handsome young man named Bellerophon drew near its margin. In his hand he held a bridle, studded with brilliant gems, and adorned with a golden bit. Seeing an old man, and another of middle age, and a little boy, near the fountain, and likewise a maiden, who was dipping up some of the water in a pitcher, he paused, and begged that he might refresh himself with a draught.

"This is very delicious water," he said to the maiden as he rinsed and filled her pitcher, after drinking out of it. "Will you be kind enough to tell me whether the fountain has any name?"

"Yes; it is called the Fountain of Pirene," answered the maiden; and then she added, "My grandmother has told me that this clear fountain was once a beautiful woman; and when her son was killed by the arrows of the huntress Diana, she melted all away into tears. And so the water, which you find so cool and sweet, is the sorrow of that poor mother's heart!"

"I should not have dreamed," observed the young stranger, "that so clear a well spring, with its gush and gurgle, and its cheery dance out of the shade into the sunlight, had so much as one teardrop in its bosom! And this, then, is Pirene? I thank you, pretty maiden, for telling me its name. I have come from a far-away country to find this very spot."

From *The Wonder Book for Boys and Girls*, by Nathaniel Hawthorne. Published by Houghton Mifflin Company.

A middle-aged country fellow (he had driven his cow to drink out of the spring) stared hard at young Bellerophon, and at the handsome bridle which he carried in his hand.

"The watercourses must be getting low, friend, in your part of the world," remarked he, "if you come so far only to find the Fountain of Pirene. But, pray, have you lost a horse? I see you carry the bridle in your hand; and a very pretty one it is with that double row of bright stones upon it. If the horse was as fine as the bridle, you are much to be pitied for losing him."

"I have lost no horse," said Bellerophon, with a smile. "But I happen to be seeking a very famous one, which, as wise people have informed me, must be found hereabouts, if anywhere. Do you know whether the winged horse Pegasus still haunts the Fountain of Pirene, as he used to do in your forefathers' days?"

But then the country fellow laughed.

Some of you, my little friends, have probably heard that this Pegasus was a snow-white steed, with beautiful silvery wings, who spent most of his time on the summit of Mount Helicon. He was as wild, and as swift, and as buoyant, in his flight through the air, as any eagle that ever soared into the clouds. There was nothing else like him in the world. He had no mate; he never had been backed or bridled by a master; and, for many a long year, he led a solitary and a happy life.

Oh, how fine a thing it is to be a winged horse! Sleeping at night, as he did, on a lofty mountain-top, and passing the greater part of the day in the air, Pegasus seemed hardly to be a creature of the earth. Whenever he was seen, up very high above people's heads, with the sunshine on his silvery wings, you would have thought that he belonged to the sky, and that, skimming a little too low, he had got astray among our mists and vapors, and was seeking his way back again. It was very pretty to behold him plunge into the fleecy bosom of a bright cloud, and be lost in it, for a moment or two, and then break forth from the other side. Or, in a sullen rainstorm, when there was a gray pavement of clouds over the whole sky, it would sometimes happen that the winged horse descended right through it, and the glad light of the upper region would gleam after him. In another instant, it is true, both Pegasus and the pleasant light would be gone away together. But anyone that was fortunate enough to see this wondrous spectacle felt cheerful the whole day afterwards, and as much longer as the storm lasted.

In the summertime, and in the beautifullest of weather, Pegasus often alighted on the solid earth, and, closing his silvery wings, would gallop over hill and dale for pastime, as fleetly as the wind. Oftener than in any other place, he had been seen near the Fountain of Pirene, drinking the delicious water, or rolling himself upon the soft grass of the margin. Sometimes, too (but Pegasus was very dainty in his food), he would crop a few of the clover blossoms that happened to be sweetest.

To the Fountain of Pirene, therefore, people's great-grand-fathers had been in the habit of going (as long as they were youthful, and retained their faith in winged horses), in hopes of getting a glimpse of the beautiful Pegasus. But, of late years, he had been very seldom seen. Indeed, there were many of the country folk, dwelling within half an hour's walk of the fountain, who had never beheld Pegasus, and did not believe that there was any such creature in existence. The country fellow to whom Bellerophon was speaking chanced to be one of those incredulous persons.

And that was the reason why he laughed.

"Pegasus, indeed!" cried he, turning up his nose as high as such a flat nose could be turned up—"Pegasus, indeed! A winged horse, truly! Why, friend, are you in your senses? Of what use would wings be to a horse? Could he drag the plow so well, think you? To be sure, there might be a little saving in the expense of shoes; but then, how would a man like to see his horse flying out of the stable window?—yes, or whisking him up above the clouds, when he only wanted to ride to mill? No, no! I don't believe in Pegasus. There never was such a ridiculous kind of a horse-fowl made!"

"I have some reason to think otherwise," said Bellerophon, quietly.

And then he turned to an old, gray man, who was leaning on a staff, and listening very attentively, with his head stretched forward, and one hand at his ear, because, for the last twenty years, he had been getting rather deaf.

"And what say you, venerable sir?" inquired he. "In your younger days, I should imagine, you must frequently have seen the winged steed!"

"Ah, young stranger, my memory is very poor!" said the aged man. "When I was a lad, if I remember rightly, I used to believe there was such a horse, and so did everybody else. But, nowadays, I hardly know what to think, and very seldom think about the winged horse at all. If I ever saw the creature, it was a long, long while ago; and, to tell you the truth, I doubt whether I ever did see him. One day, to be sure, when I was quite a youth, I remember seeing some hoof-tramps round about the brink of the fountain. Pegasus might have made those hoof-marks; and so might some other horse."

"And have you never seen him, my fair maiden?" asked Bellerophon of the girl, who stood with the pitcher on her head, while this talk went on. "You certainly could see Pegasus, if anybody can, for your eyes are very bright."

"Once I thought I saw him," replied the maiden, with a smile and a blush. "It was either Pegasus, or a large white bird, a very great way up in the air. And one other time, as I was coming to the fountain with my pitcher, I heard a neigh. Oh, such a brisk and melodious neigh as that was! My very heart leaped with delight at the sound. But it startled me, nevertheless; so that I ran home without filling my pitcher."

"That was truly a pity!" said Bellerophon.

And he turned to the child, whom I mentioned at the beginning of the story, and who was gazing at him, as children are apt to gaze at strangers, with his rosy mouth wide open.

"Well, my little fellow," cried Bellerophon, playfully pulling one of his curls, "I suppose you have often seen the winged horse."

"That I have," answered the child, very readily. "I saw him yesterday, and many times before."

"You are a fine little man!" said Bellerophon, drawing the child closer to him. "Come, tell me all about it."

"Why," replied the child, "I often come here to sail little boats in the fountain, and gather pretty pebbles out of its basin. And sometimes, when I look down into the water, I see the image of the winged horse, in the picture of the sky that is there. I wish he would come down, and take me on his back, and let me ride him up to the moon! But, if I so much as stir to look at him, he flies far away out of sight."

And Bellerophon put his faith in the child, who had seen the image of Pegasus in the water, and in the maiden, who had heard him neigh so melodiously, rather than in the middle-aged clown, who believed only in cart horses, or in the old man who had forgotten the beautiful things of his youth.

Therefore, he haunted about the Fountain of Pirene for a great many days afterwards. He kept continually on the watch, looking upward at the sky, or else down into the water, hoping forever that he should see either the reflected image of the winged horse, or the marvelous reality. He held the bridle, with its bright gems and golden bit, always ready in his hand. The rustic people, who dwelt in the neighborhood, and drove their cattle to the fountain to drink, would often laugh at poor Bellerophon, and sometimes take him pretty severely to task. They told him that an able-bodied young man, like himself, ought to have better business than to be wasting his time in such an idle pursuit. They offered to sell him a horse, if he wanted one; and when Bellerophon declined the purchase, they tried to drive a bargain with him for his fine bridle.

Even the country boys thought him so very foolish, that they used to have a great deal of sport about him, and were rude enough not to care a fig, although Bellerophon saw and heard it. One little urchin, for example, would play Pegasus, and cut the oddest imaginable capers, by way of flying; while one of his schoolfellows would scamper after him, holding forth a twist of bulrushes, which was intended to represent Bellerophon's ornamental bridle. But the gentle child, who had seen the picture of Pegasus in the water, comforted the young stranger more than all the naughty boys could torment him. The dear little fellow, in his play-hours, often sat down beside him, and, without speaking a word, would look down into the fountain and up toward the sky, with so innocent a faith, that Bellerophon could not help feeling encouraged.

Now you will, perhaps, wish to be told why it was that Bellerophon had undertaken to catch the winged horse. And we shall find no better opportunity to speak about this matter than while he is waiting for Pegasus to appear.

If I were to relate the whole of Bellerophon's previous adventures, they might easily grow into a very long story. It will be quite enough to say, that, in a certain country of Asia, a terrible monster, called a Chimaera, had made its appearance, and was doing more mischief than could be talked about between now and sunset. According to the best accounts which I have been able to obtain, this Chimaera was nearly, if not quite, the ugliest and most poisonous creature, and the strangest and unaccountablest, and the hardest to fight with, and the most difficult to run away from, that ever came out of the earth's inside. It had a tail like a boa constrictor; its body was like I do not care what; and it had three separate heads, one of which was a lion's, the second a goat's, and the third an abominably great snake's. And a hot blast of fire came flaming out of each of its three mouths! Being an earthly monster, I doubt whether it had any wings; but, wings or no, it ran like a goat and a lion, and wriggled along like a serpent, and thus contrived to make about as much speed as all the three together.

Oh, the mischief, and mischief, and mischief that this naughty creature did! With its flaming breath, it could set a forest on fire, or burn up a field of grain, or, for that matter, a village, with all its fences and houses. It laid waste the whole country round about, and used to eat up people and animals alive, and cook them afterwards in the burning oven of its stomach. Mercy on us, little children, I hope neither you nor I will ever happen to meet a Chimaera!

While the hateful beast (if a beast we can anywise call it) was doing all these horrible things, it so chanced that Bellerophon came to that part of the world, on a visit to the king. The king's name was Iobates, and Lycia was the country which he ruled over. Bellerophon was one of the bravest youths in the world, and desired nothing so much as to do some valiant and beneficent deed, such as would make all mankind admire and love him. In those days, the only way for a young man to distinguish himself was by fighting battles, either with the enemies of his country, or with wicked giants, or with troublesome dragons, or with wild beasts, when he could find nothing more dangerous to encounter. King Iobates, perceiving the courage of his youthful visitor, proposed to him to go and fight the Chimaera, which everybody else was afraid of, and which, unless it should be soon killed, was likely to convert Lycia into a desert. Bellerophon hesitated not a moment, but assured the king that he would either slay this dreaded Chimaera, or perish in the attempt.

But, in the first place, as the monster was so prodigiously swift, he bethought himself that he should never win the victory by fighting on foot. The wisest thing he could do, therefore, was to get the very best and fleetest horse that could anywhere be found. And what other horse, in all the world, was half so fleet as the marvelous horse Pegasus, who had wings as well as legs, and was even more active in the air than on the earth? To be sure, a great many people denied that there was any such horse with wings, and said that the stories about him were all poetry and nonsense. But, wonderful as it appeared, Bellerophon believed that Pegasus was a real steed, and hoped that he himself might be fortunate enough to find him; and, once fairly mounted on his back, he would be able to fight the Chimaera at better advantage.

And this was the purpose with which he had traveled from Lycia to Greece, and had brought the beautifully ornamented bridle in his hand. It was an enchanted bridle. If he could only succeed in putting the golden bit into the mouth of Pegasus, the winged horse would be submissive, and would own Bellerophon for his master, and fly whithersoever he might choose to turn the rein.

But, indeed, it was a weary and anxious time, while Bellerophon waited and waited for Pegasus, in hopes that he would come and drink at the Fountain of Pirene. He was afraid lest King Iobates should imagine that he had fled from the Chimaera. It pained him, too, to think how much mischief the monster was doing, while he himself, instead of fighting with it, was compelled to sit idly poring over the bright waters of Pirene, as they gushed out of the sparkling sand. And as Pegasus came thither so seldom in these latter years, and scarcely alighted there more than once in a lifetime, Bellerophon feared that he might grow an old man, and have no strength left in his arms nor courage in his heart, before the winged horse would appear. Oh, how heavily passes the time, while an adventurous youth is yearning to do his part in life, and to gather in the harvest of his renown! How hard a lesson it is to wait! Our life is brief, and how much of it is spent in teaching us only this!

Well was it for Bellerophon that the gentle child had grown so fond of him, and was never weary of keeping him company. Every morning the child gave him a new hope to put in his bosom, instead of yesterday's withered one.

"Dear Bellerophon," he would cry, looking up hopefully into his face, "I think we shall see Pegasus today!"

And, at length, if it had not been for the little boy's unwavering faith, Bellerophon would have given up all hope, and would have gone back to Lycia, and have done his best to slay the Chimaera without the help of the winged horse. And in that case poor Bellerophon would at least have been terribly scorched by the creature's breath, and would most probably have been killed and devoured. Nobody should ever try to fight an earthborn Chimaera, unless he can first get upon the back of an aerial steed.

One morning the child spoke to Bellerophon even more hopefully than usual.

"Dear, dear Bellerophon," cried he, "I know not why it is, but I feel as if we should certainly see Pegasus today!"

And all that day he would not stir a step from Bellerophon's side; so they ate a crust of bread together, and drank some of the water of the fountain. In the afternoon, there they sat, and Bellerophon had thrown his arm around the child, who likewise had put one of his little hands into Bellerophon's. The latter was lost in his own thoughts, and was fixing his eyes vacantly on the trunks of the trees that overshadowed the fountain, and on the grapevines that clambered up among the branches. But the gentle child was gazing down into the water; he was grieved, for Bellerophon's sake, that the hope of another day should be deceived, like so many before it; and two or three quiet teardrops fell from his eyes, and mingled with what were said to be the many tears of Pirene, when she wept for her slain children.

But, when he least thought of it, Bellerophon felt the pressure of the child's little hand, and heard a soft, almost breathless, whisper.

"See there, dear Bellerophon! There is an image in the water!"

The young man looked down into the dimpling mirror of the fountain, and saw what he took to be the reflection of a bird which seemed to be flying at a great height in the air, with a gleam of sunshine on its snowy or silvery wings.

"What a splendid bird it must be!" said he. "And how very large it looks, though it must really be flying higher than the clouds!"

"It makes me tremble!" whispered the child. "I am afraid to look up into the air! It is very beautiful, and yet I dare only look at its image in the water. Dear Bellerophon, do you not see that it is no bird? It is the winged horse Pegasus!"

Bellerophon's heart began to throb! He gazed keenly upward, but could not see the winged creature, whether bird or horse; because, just then, it had plunged into the fleecy depths of a summer cloud. It was but a moment, however, before the object reappeared, sinking lightly down out of the cloud, although still at a vast distance from the earth. Bellerophon caught the child in his arms, and shrank back with him, so that they were both hidden among the thick shrubbery which grew all around the fountain. Not that he was afraid of any harm, but he dreaded lest, if Pegasus caught a glimpse of them, he would fly far away, and alight in some inaccessible mountain-top. For it was really the winged horse. After they had expected him so long, he was coming to quench his thirst with the water of Pirene.

Nearer and nearer came the aerial wonder, flying in great circles, as you may have seen a dove when about to alight. Downward came Pegasus, in those wide, sweeping circles, which grew narrower, and narrower still, as he gradually approached the earth. The nigher the view of him, the more beautiful he was, and the more marvelous the sweep of his silvery wings. At last, with so light a pressure as hardly to bend the grass about the fountain, or imprint a hoof-tramp in the sand of its margin, he alighted, and, stooping his wild head, began to drink. He drew in the water, with long and pleasant sighs, and tranquil pauses of enjoyment; and then another draught, and another, and another. For, nowhere in the world, or up among the clouds, did Pegasus love any water as he loved this of Pirene. And when his thirst was slaked, he cropped a few of the honey blossoms of the clover, delicately tasting them, but not caring to make a hearty meal, because the herbage, just beneath the clouds, on the lofty sides of Mount Helicon, suited his palate better than this ordinary grass.

After thus drinking to his heart's content, and, in his dainty fashion, condescending to take a little food, the winged horse began to caper to and fro, and dance as it were, out of mere idleness and sport. There never was a more playful creature made than this very Pegasus. So there he frisked, in a way that it delights me to think about, fluttering his great wings as lightly as ever did a linnet, and running little races, half on earth and half in air, and which I know not whether to call a flight or a gallop. When a creature is perfectly able to fly, he sometimes chooses to run, just for the pastime of the thing; and so did Pegasus, although it cost him some little trouble to keep his hoofs so near the ground. Bellerophon, meanwhile, holding the child's hand, peeped forth from the shrubbery, and thought that never was any sight so beautiful as this, nor ever a horse's eyes so wild and spirited as those of Pegasus. It seemed a sin to think of bridling him and riding on his back.

Once or twice, Pegasus stopped, and snuffed the air, pricking up his ears, tossing his head, and turning it on all sides, as if he partly suspected some mischief or other. Seeing nothing, however, and hearing no sound, he soon began his antics again.

At length—not that he was weary, but only idle and luxurious—Pegasus folded his wings, and lay down on the soft green turf. But, being too full of aerial life to remain quiet for many moments together, he soon rolled over on his back, with his four slender legs in the air. It was beautiful to see him, this one solitary creature, whose mate had never been created, but who needed no companion, and, living a great many hundred years, was as happy as the centuries were long. The more he did such things as mortal horses are accustomed to do, the less earthly and the more wonderful he seemed. Bellerophon and the child almost held their breath, partly from a delightful awe, but still more because they dreaded lest the slightest stir or murmur should send him up, with the speed of an arrow flight, into the farthest blue of the sky.

Finally, when he had had enough of rolling over and over, Pegasus turned himself about, and, indolently, like any other horse, put out his forelegs, in order to rise from the ground; and Bellerophon, who had guessed that he would do so, darted suddenly from the thicket, and leaped astride of his back.

Yes, there he sat, on the back of the winged horse!

But what a bound did Pegasus make, when, for the first time, he felt the weight of a mortal man upon his loins! A bound, indeed! Before he had time to draw a breath, Bellerophon found himself five hundred feet aloft, and still shooting upward, while the winged horse snorted and trembled with terror and anger. Upward he went, up, up, up, until he plunged into the cold misty bosom of a cloud, at which, only a little while before, Bellerophon had been gazing, and fancying it a very pleasant spot. Then again, out of the heart of the cloud, Pegasus shot down like a thunderbolt, as if he meant to dash both himself and his rider headlong against a rock. Then he went through about a thousand of the wildest caprioles that had ever been performed either by a bird or a horse.

I cannot tell you half that he did. He skimmed straight forward, and sideways, and backward. He reared himself erect, with his forelegs on a wreath of mist, and his hind legs on nothing at all. He flung out his heels behind, and put down his head between his legs, with his wings pointing right upward. At about two miles' height above the earth, he turned a somerset, so that Bellerophon's heels were where his head should have been, and he seemed to look down into the sky, instead of up. He twisted his head about, and, looking Bellerophon in the face, with fire flashing from his eyes, made a terrible attempt to bite him. He fluttered his pinions so wildly that one of the silver feathers was shaken out, and, floating earthward, was picked up by the child, who kept it as long as he lived, in memory of Pegasus and Bellerophon.

But the latter (who, as you may judge, was as good a horseman as ever galloped) had been watching his opportunity, and at last clapped the golden bit of the enchanted bridle between the winged steed's jaws. No sooner was this done, than Pegasus became as manageable as if he had taken food, all his life, out of Bellerophon's hand. To speak what I really feel, it was almost a sadness to see so wild a creature grow suddenly so tame. And Pegasus seemed to feel it so, likewise. He looked round to Bellerophon, with the tears in his beautiful eyes, instead of the fire that so recently flashed from them. But when Bellerophon patted his head, and spoke a few authoritative, yet kind and soothing words, another look came into the eyes of Pegasus; for he was glad at heart, after so many lonely centuries, to have found a companion and a master.

Thus it always is with winged horses, and with all such wild and solitary creatures. If you can catch and overcome them, it is the surest way to win their love.

While Pegasus had been doing his utmost to shake Bellerophon off his back, he had flown a very long distance; and they had come within sight of a lofty mountain by the time the bit was in his mouth. Bellerophon had seen this mountain before, and knew it to be Helicon, on the summit of which was the winged horse's abode. Thither (after looking gently into his rider's face, as if to ask leave) Pegasus now flew, and alighting, waited patiently until Bellerophon should please to dismount. The young man, accordingly, leaped from his steed's back, but still held him fast by the bridle. Meeting his eyes, however, he was so affected by the gentleness of his aspect, and by the thought of the free life which Pegasus had heretofore lived, that he could not bear to keep him a prisoner, if he really desired his liberty.

Obeying this generous impulse he slipped the enchanted bridle off the head of Pegasus, and took the bit from his mouth. "Leave me, Pegasus!" said he. "Either leave me, or love me."

In an instant, the winged horse shot almost out of sight, soaring straight upward from the summit of Mount Helicon.

Being long after sunset, it was now twilight on the mountain-
top, and dusky evening over all the country round about. But
Pegasus flew so high that he overtook the departed day, and
was bathed in the upper radiance of the sun. Ascending higher
and higher, he looked like a bright speck, and, at last, could
no longer be seen in the hollow waste of the sky. And Bellerophon was afraid that he should never behold him more. But,
while he was lamenting his own folly, the bright speck reappeared, and drew nearer and nearer, until it descended lower
than the sunshine; and, behold, Pegasus had come back! After
this trial there was no more fear of the winged horse's making
his escape. He and Bellerophon were friends, and put loving
faith in one another.

That night they lay down and slept together, with Bellerophon's arm about the neck of Pegasus, not as a caution, but for
kindness. And they awoke at peep of day, and bade one another good morning, each in his own language.

In this manner, Bellerophon and the wondrous steed spent
several days, and grew better acquainted and fonder of each
other all the time. They went on long aerial journeys, and sometimes ascended so high that the earth looked hardly bigger
than—the moon. They visited distant countries, and amazed the
inhabitants, who thought that the beautiful young man, on the
back of the winged horse, must have come down out of the
sky. A thousand miles a day was no more than an easy space
for the fleet Pegasus to pass over. Bellerophon was delighted
with this kind of life, and would have liked nothing better than
to live always in the same way, aloft in the clear atmosphere;
for it was always sunny weather up there, however cheerless
and rainy it might be in the lower region. But he could not
forget the horrible Chimaera, which he had promised King
Iobates to slay. So, at last, when he had become well accustomed to feats of horsemanship in the air, and could manage
Pegasus with the least motion of his hand, and had taught him
to obey his voice, he determined to attempt the performance
of this perilous adventure.

At daybreak, therefore, as soon as he unclosed his eyes, he
gently pinched the winged horse's ear, in order to arouse him.
Pegasus immediately started from the ground and pranced

about a quarter of a mile aloft, and made a grand sweep around the mountain-top, by way of showing that he was wide awake, and ready for any kind of an excursion. During the whole of this little flight, he uttered a loud, brisk, and melodious neigh, and finally came down at Bellerophon's side, as lightly as ever you saw a sparrow hop upon a twig.

"Well done, dear Pegasus! well done, my sky-skimmer!" cried Bellerophon, stroking the horse's neck. "Now, my fleet, beautiful friend, we must break our fast. Today we fight the terrible Chimaera."

As soon as they had eaten their morning meal, and drunk some sparkling water from a spring called Hippocrene, Pegasus held out his head, of his own accord, so that his master might put on the bridle. Then, with a great many playful leaps and airy caperings, he showed his impatience to be gone; while Bellerophon was girding on his sword, and hanging his shield about his neck, and preparing himself for battle. When everything was ready, the rider mounted, and (as was his custom, when going a long distance) ascended five miles perpendicularly, so as the better to see whither he was directing his course. He then turned the head of Pegasus toward the east, and set out for Lycia. In their flight they overtook an eagle, and came so nigh him, before he could get out of their way, that Bellerophon might easily have caught him by the leg. Hastening onward at this rate, it was still early in the forenoon when they beheld the lofty mountains of Lycia, with their deep and shaggy valleys. If Bellerophon had been told truly, it was in one of those dismal valleys that the hideous Chimaera had taken up its abode.

Being now so near their journey's end, the winged horse gradually descended with his rider; and they took advantage of some clouds that were floating over the mountain-tops, in order to conceal themselves. Hovering on the upper surface of a cloud, and peeping over its edge, Bellerophon had a pretty distinct view of the mountainous part of Lycia, and could look into all its shadowy vales at once. At first there appeared to be nothing remarkable. It was a wild, savage, and rocky tract of high and precipitous hills. In the more level part of the country, there were the ruins of houses that had been burnt, and, here and there, the carcasses of dead cattle, strewn about the pastures where they had been feeding.

"The Chimaera must have done this mischief," thought Bellerophon. "But where can the monster be?"

As I have already said, there was nothing remarkable to be detected, at first sight, in any of the valleys and dells that lay among the precipitous heights of the mountains. Nothing at all; unless, indeed, it were three spires of black smoke, which issued from what seemed to be the mouth of a cavern, and clambered sullenly into the atmosphere. Before reaching the mountain-top, these three black smoke wreaths mingled themselves into one. The cavern was almost directly beneath the winged horse and his rider, at the distance of about a thousand feet. The smoke, as it crept heavily upward, had an ugly, sulphurous, stifling scent, which caused Pegasus to snort and Bellerophon to sneeze. So disagreeable was it to the marvelous steed, accustomed to breathe only the purest air, that he waved his wings, and shot half a mile out of range of this offensive vapor.

But, on looking behind him, Bellerophon saw something that induced him first to draw the bridle, and then to turn Pegasus about. He made a sign, which the winged horse understood, and sunk slowly through the air, until his hoofs were scarcely more than a man's height above the rocky bottom of the valley. In front, as far off as you could throw a stone, was the cavern's mouth, with the three smoke wreaths oozing out. And what else did he behold?

There seemed to be a heap of strange and terrible creatures curled up within the cavern. Their bodies lay so close together, that Bellerophon could not distinguish them apart; but, judging by their heads, one of these creatures was a huge snake, the second a fierce lion, and the third an ugly goat. The lion and the goat were asleep; the snake was broad awake, and kept staring around him with a great pair of fiery eyes. But—and this was the most wonderful part of the matter—the three spires of smoke evidently issued from the nostrils of these three heads! So strange was the spectacle, that, though Bellerophon had been all along expecting it, the truth did not immediately occur to him, that here was the terrible three-headed Chimaera. He had found out the Chimaera's cavern. The snake, the lion, and the goat, as he supposed them to be, were not three separate creatures, but one monster.

The wicked, hateful thing! Slumbering as two thirds of it were, it still held, in its abominable claws, the remnant of an unfortunate lamb—or possibly (but I hate to think so) it was a dear little boy—which its mouths had been gnawing, before two of them fell asleep!

All at once, Bellerophon started as from a dream, and knew it to be the Chimaera. Pegasus seemed to know it, at the same instant, and sent forth a neigh, that sounded like the call of a trumpet to battle. At this sound the three heads reared themselves erect, and belched out great flashes of flame. Before Bellerophon had time to consider what to do next, the monster flung itself out of the cavern and sprung straight toward him, with its immense claws extended, and its snaky tail twisting itself venomously behind. If Pegasus had not been as nimble as a bird, both he and his rider would have been overthrown by the Chimaera's headlong rush, and thus the battle have been ended before it was well begun. But the winged horse was not to be caught so. In the twinkling of an eye he was up aloft, halfway to the clouds, snorting with anger. He shuddered, too, not with affright, but with utter disgust at the loathsomeness of this poisonous thing with three heads.

The Chimaera, on the other hand, raised itself up so as to stand absolutely on the tip-end of its tail, with its talons pawing fiercely in the air, and its three heads spluttering fire at Pegasus and his rider. How it roared, and hissed, and bellowed! Bellerophon, meanwhile, was fitting his shield on his arm, and drawing his sword.

"Now, my beloved Pegasus," he whispered in the winged horse's ear, "thou must help me to slay this insufferable monster; or else thou shalt fly back to thy solitary mountain-peak without thy friend Bellerophon. For either the Chimaera dies, or its three mouths shall gnaw this head of mine, which has slumbered upon thy neck!"

Pegasus whinnied, and, turning back his head, rubbed his nose tenderly against his rider's cheek. It was his way of telling him that, though he had wings and was an immortal horse, yet he would perish, if it were possible for immortality to perish, rather than leave Bellerophon behind.

"I thank thee, Pegasus," answered Bellerophon. "Now, then, let us make a dash at the monster!"

Uttering these words, he shook the bridle; and Pegasus darted down aslant, as swift as the flight of an arrow, right toward the Chimaera's three-fold head, which, all this time, was poking itself as high as it could into the air. As he came within arm's length, Bellerophon made a cut at the monster, but was carried onward by his steed, before he could see whether the blow had been successful. Pegasus continued his course, but soon wheeled round, at about the same distance from the Chimaera as before. Bellerophon then perceived that he had cut the goat's head of the monster almost off, so that it dangled downward by the skin, and seemed quite dead.

But, to make amends, the snake's head and the lion's head had taken all the fierceness of the dead one into themselves, and spit flame, and hissed, and roared, with more fury than before.

"Never mind, my brave Pegasus!" cried Bellerophon. "With another stroke like that, we will stop either its hissing or its roaring."

And again he shook the bridle. Dashing aslantwise, as before, the winged horse made another arrow flight toward the Chimaera, and Bellerophon aimed another downright stroke at one of the two remaining heads, as he shot by. But this time, neither he nor Pegasus escaped so well as at first. With one of its claws, the Chimaera had given the young man a deep scratch in his shoulder, and had slightly damaged the left wing of the flying steed with the other. On his part, Bellerophon had mortally wounded the lion's head of the monster, insomuch that it now hung downward, with its fire almost extinguished, and sending out gasps of thick black smoke. The snake's head, however (which was the only one now left), was twice as fierce and venomous as ever before. It belched forth shoots of fire five hundred yards long, and emitted hisses so loud, so harsh, and so ear-piercing, that King Iobates heard them, fifty miles off, and trembled till the throne shook under him.

"Well-a-day!" thought the poor king; "the Chimaera is certainly coming to devour me!"

Meanwhile Pegasus had again paused in the air, and neighed angrily, while sparkles of pure crystal flame darted out of his eyes. How unlike the lurid fire of the Chimaera! The aerial steed's spirit was all aroused, and so was that of Bellerophon.

"Dost thou bleed, my immortal horse?" cried the young man, caring less for his own hurt than for the anguish of this glorious creature, that ought never to have tasted pain. "The execrable Chimaera shall pay for this mischief with his last head!"

Then he shook the bridle, shouted loudly, and guided Pegasus, not aslantwise as before, but straight at the monster's hideous front. So rapid was the onset, that it seemed but a dazzle and a flash before Bellerophon was at close grips with his enemy.

The Chimaera, by this time, after losing its second head, had got into a red-hot passion of pain and rampant rage. It so flounced about, half on earth and partly in the air, that it was impossible to say which element it rested upon. It opened its snake jaws to such an abominable width, that Pegasus might almost, I was going to say, have flown right down its throat, wings outspread, rider and all! At their approach it shot out a tremendous blast of its fiery breath, and enveloped Bellerophon and his steed in a perfect atmosphere of flame, singeing the wings of Pegasus, scorching off one whole side of the young man's golden ringlets, and making them both far hotter than was comfortable, from head to foot.

But this was nothing to what followed.

When the airy rush of the winged horse had brought him within a distance of a hundred yards, the Chimaera gave a spring, and flung its huge, awkward, venomous, and utterly detestable carcass right upon poor Pegasus, clung round him with might and main, and tied up its snaky tail into a knot! Up flew the aerial steed, higher, higher, higher, above the mountain-peaks, above the clouds, and almost out of sight of the solid earth. But still the earthborn monster kept its hold, and was borne upward, along with the creature of light and air. Bellerophon, meanwhile, turning about, found himself face to face with the ugly grimness of the Chimaera's visage, and could only avoid being scorched to death, or bitten right in twain, by holding up his shield. Over the upper edge of the shield, he looked sternly into the savage eyes of the monster.

But the Chimaera was so mad and wild with pain, that it did not guard itself so well as might else have been the case. Perhaps, after all, the best way to fight a Chimaera is by getting as close to it as you can. In its efforts to stick its horrible iron claws into its enemy, the creature left its own breast quite exposed; and perceiving this, Bellerophon thrust his sword up to the hilt into its cruel heart. Immediately the snaky tail untied its knot. The monster let go its hold of Pegasus, and fell from the vast height, downward; while the fire within its bosom, instead of being put out, burned fiercer than ever, and quickly began to consume the dead carcass. Thus it fell out of the sky, all a-flame, and (it being nightfall before it reached the earth) was mistaken for a shooting star or a comet. But, at early sunrise, some cottagers were going to their day's labor, and saw, to their astonishment, that several acres of ground were strewn with black ashes. In the middle of a field, there was a heap of whitened bones, a great deal higher than a haystack. Nothing else was ever seen of the dreadful Chimaera!

And when Bellerophon had won the victory, he bent forward and kissed Pegasus, while the tears stood in his eyes. "Back now, my beloved steed!" said he. "Back to the Fountain of Pirene!"

Pegasus skimmed through the air, quicker than ever he did before, and reached the fountain in a very short time. And there he found the old man leaning on his staff, and the country fellow watering his cow, and the pretty maiden filling her pitcher.

"I remember now," quoth the old man, "I saw this winged horse once before, when I was quite a lad. But he was ten times handsomer in those days."

"I own a cart horse, worth three of him!" said the country fellow. "If this pony were mine, the first thing I should do would be to clip his wings!"

But the poor maiden said nothing, for she had always the luck to be afraid at the wrong time. So she ran away, and let her pitcher tumble down, and broke it.

"Where is the gentle child," asked Bellerophon, "who used to keep me company, and never lost his faith, and never was weary of gazing into the fountain?"

"Here am I, dear Bellerophon!" said the child, softly.

For the little boy had spent day after day, on the margin of Pirene, waiting for his friend to come back; but when he perceived Bellerophon descending through the clouds, mounted on the winged horse, he had shrunk back into the shrubbery. He was a delicate and tender child, and dreaded lest the old man and the country fellow should see the tears that were gushing from his eyes.

"Thou hast won the victory," said he, running to the knee of Bellerophon, who still sat on Pegasus. "I knew thou wouldst."

"Yes, dear child!" replied Bellerophon, alighting from the winged horse. "But if thy faith had not helped me, I should never have waited for Pegasus, and never have gone up above the clouds, and never have conquered the terrible Chimaera. Thou, my beloved little friend, hast done it all. And now let us give Pegasus his liberty."

So he slipped off the bridle from the head of the marvelous steed.

"Be free, forevermore, my Pegasus!" cried he, with a shade of sadness in his tone. "Be as free as thou art fleet!"

But Pegasus rested his head on Bellerophon's shoulder, and would not be persuaded to take flight.

"Well, then," said Bellerophon, caressing the airy horse, "thou shalt be with me, as long as thou wilt; and we will go together, forthwith, and tell King Iobates that the Chimaera is destroyed."

Then Bellerophon embraced the gentle child, and promised to come to him again, and departed. But, in after years, that child took higher flights upon the aerial steed than ever did Bellerophon, and achieved more honorable deeds than his friend's victory over the Chimaera. For, gentle and tender, he grew to be a mighty poet!

Phaeton

BY THOMAS BULFINCH

Illustrations by Boris Artzybasheff

PHAETON was the son of Apollo and the nymph Clymene. One day a schoolfellow laughed at the idea of his being the son of the god, and Phaeton went in rage and shame and reported it to his mother. "If," said he, "I am indeed of heavenly birth, give me, mother, some proof of it, and establish my claim to the honor." Clymene stretched forth her hands toward the skies, and said, "I call to witness the Sun which looks down upon us, that I have told you the truth. If I speak falsely, let this be the last time I behold his light. But it needs not much labor to go and inquire for yourself; the land whence the Sun rises lies next to ours. Go and demand of him whether he will own you as a son." Phaeton heard with delight. He traveled to India, which lies directly in the regions of sunrise; and, full of hope and pride, approached the goal whence his parent begins his course.

The palace of the Sun stood reared aloft on columns, glittering with gold and precious stones, while polished ivory formed the ceilings, and silver the doors. The workmanship surpassed the material, for upon the walls Vulcan had represented earth, sea, and skies, with their inhabitants. In the sea were the nymphs, some sporting in the waves, some riding on the backs of fishes, while others sat upon the rocks and dried their sea-green hair. Their faces were not all alike—but such as sisters' ought to be. The earth had its towns and forests and rivers and rustic

From *The Age of Fable,* by Thomas Bulfinch.

153

divinities. Over all was carved the likeness of the glorious heaven; and on the silver doors the twelve signs of the zodiac, six on each side.

> The sun's bright palace, on high columns rais'd,
> With burnish'd gold, and flaming jewels blaz'd,
> The folding gates diffus'd a silver light,
> And with a milder gleam refresh'd the sight.
> —ADDISON.

Clymene's son advanced up the steep ascent, and entered the halls of his disputed father. He approached the paternal presence, but stopped at a distance, for the light was more than he could bear. Phoebus, arrayed in a purple vesture, sat on a throne which glittered as with diamonds. On his right hand and his left stood the Day, the Month, and the Year, and, at regular intervals, the Hours. Spring stood with her head crowned with flowers, and Summer, with garment cast aside, and a garland formed of spears of ripened grain, and Autumn, with his feet stained with grape juice, and icy Winter, with his hair stiffened with hoarfrost.

Surrounded by these attendants, the Sun, with the eye that sees everything, beheld the youth dazzled with the novelty and splendor of the scene, and inquired the purpose of his errand. The youth replied, "O light of the boundless world, Phoebus, my father—if you permit me to use that name—give me some proof, I beseech you, by which I may be known as yours." He ceased; and his father, laying aside the beams that shone all around his head, bade him approach, and embracing him, said, "My son, you deserve not to be disowned, and I confirm what your mother has told you. To put an end to your doubts, ask what you will, the gift shall be yours. I call to witness that dreadful lake, which I never saw, but which we gods swear by in our most solemn engagements." Phaeton immediately asked to be permitted for one day to drive the chariot of the Sun. The father repented of his promise; thrice and four times he shook his radiant head in warning. "I have spoken rashly," said he; "this request only I would fain deny. I beg you to withdraw it.

It is not a safe boon, nor one, my Phaeton, suited to your youth
and strength. Your lot is mortal, and you ask what is beyond a
mortal's power. In your ignorance you aspire to do that which
not even the gods themselves may do. None but myself may
drive the flaming car of day. Not even Jupiter, whose terrible
right arm hurls the thunderbolts. The first part of the way is
steep, and such as the horses when fresh in the morning can
hardly climb; the middle is high up in the heavens, whence I
myself can scarcely, without alarm, look down and behold the
earth and sea stretched beneath me. The last part of the road
descends rapidly, and requires most careful driving. Tethys, who
is waiting to receive me, often trembles for me lest I should fall
headlong. Add to all this, the heaven is all the time turning
round and carrying the stars with it. I have to be perpetually
on my guard lest that movement, which sweeps everything else
along, should hurry me also away. Suppose I should lend you
the chariot, what would you do? Could you keep your course
while the earth was revolving under you? Perhaps you think
that there are forests and cities, the abodes of gods, and palaces
and temples on the way. On the contrary, the road is through
the midst of frightful monsters. You pass by the horns of the
Bull, in front of the Archer, and near the Lion's jaws, and where
the Scorpion stretches its arms in one direction and the Crab in
another. Nor will you find it easy to guide those horses, with
their breasts full of fire that they breathe forth from their
mouths and nostrils. I can scarcely govern them myself, when
they are unruly and resist the reins. Beware, my son, lest I be the
donor of a fatal gift, recall your request while yet you may. Do
you ask me for a proof that you are sprung from my blood? I
give you a proof in my fears for you. Look at my face—I would
that you could look into my breast, you would there see all a
father's anxiety. Finally," he continued, "look round the world
and choose whatever you will of what earth or sea contains most
precious—ask it and fear no refusal. This only I pray you not to
urge. It is not honor, but destruction you seek. Why do you
hang round my neck and still entreat me? You shall have it if
you persist—the oath is sworn and must be kept—but I beg you
to choose more wisely."

Choose out a gift from seas, or earth, or skies,
For open to your wish all nature lies;
Only decline this one unequal task,
For 'tis a mischief, not a gift, you ask.
—ADDISON.

He ended; but the youth rejected all admonition and held to his demand. So, having resisted as long as he could, Phoebus at last led the way to where stood the lofty chariot.

It was of gold, the gift of Vulcan; the axle was of gold, the pole and wheels of gold, the spokes of silver. Along the seat were rows of chrysolites and diamonds which reflected the brightness of the sun. While the daring youth gazed in admiration, the early Dawn threw open the purple doors of the east, and showed the pathway strewn with roses. The stars withdrew, marshaled by the Day star, which last of all retired also. The father, when he saw the earth beginning to glow, and the Moon preparing to retire, ordered the Hours to harness up the horses. They obeyed, and led forth from the lofty stalls the steeds full fed with ambrosia, and attached the reins. Then the father bathed the face of his son with a powerful ointment, and made him capable of enduring the brightness of the flame. He set the rays on his head, and, with a foreboding sigh, said, "If, my son, you will in this at least heed my advice, spare the whip and hold tight the reins. They go fast enough of their own accord; the labor is to hold them in. You are not to take the straight road directly between the five circles, but turn off to the left. Keep within the limit of the middle zone, and avoid the northern and the southern alike. You will see the marks of the wheels, and they will serve to guide you. And, that the skies

and the earth may each receive their due share of heat, go not too high, or you will burn the heavenly dwellings, nor too low, or you will set the earth on fire; the middle course is safest and best. And now I leave you to your chance, which I hope will plan better for you than you have done for yourself. Night is passing out of the western gates and we can delay no longer. Take the reins; but if at last your heart fails you, and you will benefit by my advice, stay where you are in safety, and suffer me to light and warm the earth." The agile youth sprang into the chariot, stood erect, and grasped the reins with delight, pouring out thanks to his reluctant parent.

Meanwhile the horses fill the air with their snortings and fiery breath, and stamp the ground impatiently. Now the bars are let down, and the boundless plain of the universe lies open before them. They dart forward and cleave the opposing clouds,

and outrun the morning breezes which started from the same
eastern goal. The steeds soon perceived that the load they drew
was lighter than usual; and as a ship without ballast is tossed
hither and thither on the sea, so the chariot, without its accustomed weight, was dashed about as if empty. They rush
headlong and leave the traveled road. Phaeton is alarmed, and
knows not how to guide them; nor, if he knew, has he the power.
Then, for the first time, the Great and Little Bear were scorched
with heat, and would fain, if it were possible, have plunged
into the water; and the Serpent which lies coiled up round the
north pole, torpid and harmless, grew warm, and with warmth
felt its rage revive. Boötes, they say, fled away, though encumbered with his plow, and all unused to rapid motion.

When hapless Phaeton looked down upon the earth, now
spreading in vast extent beneath him, he grew pale and his
knees shook with terror. In spite of the glare all around him,
the sight of his eyes grew dim. He wished he had never touched
his father's horses, never learned his parentage, never prevailed
in his request. He is borne along like a vessel that flies before a
tempest, when the pilot can do no more and betakes himself
to his prayers. What shall he do? Much of the heavenly road
is left behind, but more remains before. He turns his eyes from
one direction to the other; now to the goal whence he began
his course, now to the realms of sunset which he is not destined
to reach. He loses his self-command, and knows not what to do
—whether to draw tight the reins or throw them loose; he for-
gets the names of the horses. He sees with terror the monstrous
forms scattered over the surface of heaven. Here the Scorpion
extended his two great arms, with his tail and crooked claws
stretching over two signs of the zodiac. When the boy beheld
him, reeking with poison and menacing with his fangs, his
courage failed, and the reins fell from his hands. The horses,
when they felt them loose on their backs, dashed headlong, and
unrestrained went off into unknown regions of the sky, in among
the stars, hurling the chariot over pathless places, now up in
high heaven, now down almost to the earth. The Moon saw
with astonishment her brother's chariot running beneath her
own. The clouds begin to smoke, and the mountain tops take
fire; the fields are parched with heat, the plants wither, the

trees with their leafy branches burn, the harvest is ablaze! But these are small things. Great cities perished, with their walls and towers; whole nations with their people were consumed to ashes! The forest-clad mountains burned, Athos and Taurus and Tmolus and Oete; Ida, once celebrated for fountains, but now all are dry; the Muses' mountain Helicon, and Haemus; Aetna, with fires within and without, and Parnassus, with his two peaks, and Rhodope, forced, at last, to part with his snowy crown. Her cold climate was no protection to Scythia, Caucasus burned, and Ossa and Pindus, and, greater than both, Olympus; the Alps high in air, and the Apennines crowned with clouds.

Then Phaeton beheld the world on fire, and felt the heat intolerable. The air he breathed was like the air of a furnace and full of burning ashes, and the smoke was of a pitchy darkness. He dashed forward he knew not whither. Then, it is believed, the people of Aethiopia became black by the blood being forced so suddenly to the surface, and the Libyan desert was dried up to the condition in which it remains to this day. The Nymphs of the fountains, with disheveled hair, mourned their waters, nor were the rivers safe beneath their banks. Tanais smoked, and Caicus, Xanthus and Meander. Babylonian Euphrates and Ganges, Tagus with golden sands, and Cayster where the swans resort. Nile fled away and hid his head in the desert, and there it still remains concealed. Where he used to discharge his waters through seven mouths into the sea, there seven dry channels alone remained. The earth cracked open, and through the chinks light broke into Tartarus, and frightened the King of Shadows and his queen. The sea shrank up. Where before was water, it became a dry plain; and the mountains that lie beneath the waves lifted up their heads and became islands. The fishes sought the lowest depths, and the dolphins no longer ventured as usual to sport on the surface. Even Nereus, and his wife Doris, with the Nereids, their daughters, sought the deepest caves for refuge. Thrice Neptune essayed to raise his head above the surface, and thrice was driven back by the heat. Earth, surrounded as she was by waters, yet with head and shoulders bare, screening her face with her hand, looked up to heaven, and with a husky voice called on Jupiter:

"O ruler of the gods, if I have deserved this treatment, and it is your will that I perish with fire, why withhold your thunder-bolts? Let me at least fall by your hand. Is this the reward of my fertility, of my obedient service? Is it for this that I have supplied herbage for cattle, and fruits for men, and frankincense for your altars? But if I am unworthy of regard, what has my brother Ocean done to deserve such a fate? If neither of us can excite your pity, think, I pray you, of your own heaven, and behold how both the poles are smoking which sustain your palace, which must fall if they be destroyed. Atlas faints, and scarce holds up his burden. If sea, earth, and heaven perish, we fall into ancient Chaos. Save what yet remains to us from the devouring flame. Oh, take thought for our deliverance in this awful moment!"

Thus spoke Earth, and overcome with heat and thirst, could say no more. Then Jupiter omnipotent, calling to witness all the gods, including him who had lent the chariot, and showing them that all was lost unless some speedy remedy were applied, mounted the lofty tower from whence he diffuses clouds over the earth, and hurls the forked lightnings. But at that time not a cloud was to be found to interpose for a screen to earth, nor was a shower remaining unexhausted. He thundered, and brandishing a lightning bolt in his right hand launched it against the charioteer, and struck him at the same moment from his seat and from existence! Phaeton, with his hair on fire, fell headlong, like a shooting star which marks the heavens with its brightness as it falls, and Eridanus, the great river, received him and cooled his burning frame.

The Italian Naiades reared a tomb for him, and inscribed these words upon the stone:

> Driver of Phoebus' chariot, Phaeton,
> Struck by Jove's thunder, rests beneath this stone,
> He could not rule his father's car of fire,
> Yet was it much so nobly to aspire.

> —OVID.

His three sisters, the Heliades, as they were called, lamented his fate, and were turned into poplar trees on the banks of the river, while their tears, which continued to flow, became amber as they dropped into the stream.

Thunder of the Gods

BY DOROTHY HOSFORD

Illustrations by Claire and George Louden

Like the Greeks and Romans, the ancient Norsemen created a world of gods that explained nature. Odin, ruler of the gods, and his wife, Frigg, queen among goddesses, lived with the other gods in the beautiful city of Asgard on the top of a lofty mountain. The myths of the Norsemen tell of Thor, god of thunder, of Balder the Beautiful, and of the wicked Loki, son of evil giants.

Thor Gains His Hammer

LOKI made much trouble for the gods with his evil pranks and his malice. But there was one time his mischief worked for good in the end. Thor might never have owned his wonderful hammer had it not been for Loki. It came about in this way:

Thor had a beautiful wife whose name was Sif. Her hair was long and yellow and shone like gold in the sunlight. Thor was proud of her.

One day, while Sif lay sleeping under the trees where Iduna's apples grew, Loki cut off all her hair. He did it for a prank. When Sif woke and discovered the loss of her beautiful hair, she went weeping to Thor.

"This is the work of that rascal Loki," cried Thor angrily. "I'll break every bone in his body."

He rushed off to look for Loki. It was not long before he found him and seized him.

Loki was filled with terror when he saw Thor's anger. He begged for mercy, but Thor would not let him go.

161

"Wait, O mighty Thor," begged Loki. "Don't punish me and I will get new hair for Sif. I will find hair of real gold that will shine in the sunlight and will grow like other hair."

"How will you do that?" said Thor.

"I will go to the Dark Elves, to the Sons of Ivaldi, and ask them to make the hair for me," said Loki. "They can make every kind of wondrous thing."

Thor gave his consent.

"But remember," he cried, shaking Loki so that his teeth chattered in his head. "If you don't bring back hair that will grow like other hair, I will break every bone in your body. And it must be as long and beautiful as Sif's own hair. Now go."

Loki was only too glad to set out. The dwarfs lived deep within the mountains and he had a long journey to make.

When Loki came to the dwelling place of the Dark Elves they said that they could perform his task. They made the hair, and they made two other gifts as well. They made the spear Gungnir, which became Odin's possession, and they made the magic ship, Skidbladnir.

On his way home with the gifts Loki met another dwarf named Brock. Loki was feeling pleased with himself and proud of his success. At once he made a wager with Brock.

"See what I have," cried Loki. "I'll wager my head that your brother Sindri can't make three gifts as precious as these."

Sindri was famed among the dwarfs and Brock knew how great was his brother's skill.

"I'll take that wager," said Brock. "Come with me. We will go to the smithy and we will see what Sindri can make."

Brock explained the wager to his brother and Sindri started the fire in the forge. The flames lit up the far corners of the dwarfs' cave. When it was hot enough Sindri laid within the fire a pig's hide. He handed the bellows to Brock and told him to work them without ceasing until he should return. Then he left the cave.

As soon as Sindri had gone Loki changed himself into a huge fly. He lit upon Brock's hand and stung him. But Brock kept the bellows working and did not let go.

When Sindri returned he took the work out of the fire. It was a boar, a wild pig with mane and bristles of gold.

Then Sindri placed gold in the fire and bade Brock work the bellows as before. This time the fly settled on Brock's neck and stung twice as hard. But Brock did not let go of the bellows. When Sindri returned he took out of the fire the golden ring which is called Draupnir.

For the third gift Sindri placed iron in the fire. "Keep the bellows going, Brock, or all will be spoiled," said Sindri, as he left the smithy.

This was Loki's last chance and the fly settled between Brock's eyes and stung his eyelids so hard that the blood ran down. The pain and the blood blinded him. Brock had to pause to sweep the fly away. He let go of the bellows with one hand and only for an instant. But the fire died down.

At that moment Sindri returned and said that what was in the hearth had come near to being spoiled. He took the work out of the fire and it was a hammer.

Sindri gave the three gifts to Brock. "Take these to the gods," he said, "and see whose gifts will win the wager."

Loki and Brock set off for Asgard, the home of the gods, each bearing his gifts. The gods were called together and met in the great council hall named Gladsheim. They took their places on the high seats. It was agreed that Odin and Thor and Frey should decide whose gifts were best.

Loki presented his gifts first. He gave Thor the golden hair for Sif, to Odin he gave the spear Gungnir, and to Frey the ship Skidbladnir, telling the virtues of each. As soon as it was placed upon Sif's head the hair would grow like other hair. The spear Gungnir would never fall short of its mark; and the ship Skidbladnir would always find favoring winds, no matter in what direction it was set. Yet it could be folded like a napkin and placed in Frey's pocket, if he so wished.

Then Brock offered his gifts. He gave to Odin the golden ring which is called Draupnir.

"Every ninth night eight other rings like itself will drop from it," said Brock.

He gave the boar, which was called Gold-Mane, to Frey.

"No horse can run through the air or over the sea with such swiftness," said Brock. "And you can always find your way by the light which shines from its mane and bristles of gold, no matter how black and dark the night may be."

Brock gave the hammer to Thor.

"The name of the hammer is Mjollnir," he told Thor. "With it you can strike as hard a blow as you please at whatever comes in your way. You can hurl it as far as you like, and it will always find its mark and return to your hand. Yet, if you wish, you can make the hammer small and put it in your pocket."

The hammer had only one fault, though Brock did not mention that. The handle was a little short. That was because Loki had caused Brock to drop the bellows.

Odin and Thor and Frey held a council. They decided that Brock's gifts were best, for Thor's hammer was the most valuable gift of all. This was just the weapon the gods needed in their wars against the Frost-Giants. The giants had better beware. Now Thor could hurl his mighty hammer at them and catch it again in his hand.

Odin rose to his feet and announced to all that Brock had won the wager.

Brock immediately demanded Loki's head.

"What good is my head to you?" cried Loki. "I will give you a great sum of gold for a ransom. You will be the richest of all the dwarfs."

Dwarfs love gold, but Brock would have none of it, and said that Loki must keep to the terms of his bargain.

"Then catch me if you can!" cried Loki.

In an instant he was far off, for he had on the shoes which

would carry him through air and over water in the twinkling of an eye.

Brock begged Thor to catch Loki. Thor was still angry with Loki and willing enough to do so. Thor asked Frey to lend him the boar Gold-Mane. He leapt on the boar's back and away he went through the air. Before long he had brought Loki back to Asgard.

Brock was ready to cut off his head, but Loki cried: "My head, yes! But not an inch of my neck. I did not wager my neck."

How could Brock cut off Loki's head without touching his neck? Brock had to let it go at that.

"If I had my brother's awl I would sew your mischief-speaking lips together," he cried out in anger.

No sooner had he spoken than the awl was there and of itself pierced Loki's lips. Then Brock sewed them together with a thong. Not that it troubled Loki much, for when Brock was gone he ripped out the thongs.

Loki, as usual, got off with little punishment. But the gods were much richer for their new gifts.

How Odin Brought
the Mead to Asgard

In the early days of the world a dispute arose between the gods and the Vanir. A meeting was held to settle the quarrel and as a pledge of peace the gods created a man whom they called Kvasir. They gave him great wisdom, so that he knew the answer to all questions.

Kvasir traveled far and wide over the world sharing his wisdom with men. He taught men all manner of things. His words were gentle and beautiful and fell softly on the ear.

It came about that Kvasir was invited to the dwelling of certain dwarfs. Their names were Fjalar and Galarr. They were crafty and treacherous and loved to do evil. They killed Kvasir and let his blood run into two large crocks and a kettle. The dwarfs blended honey with the blood. They made a mead from this brew which had not only the richness and sweetness of honey, but the wisdom which ran in Kvasir's blood. The mead had this virtue: anyone who drank of it became a poet, bringing songs and beauty to men.

When the dwarfs had slain Kvasir they looked about for new mischief to do. They asked the giant Gilling to visit them and to bring his wife. When Gilling came they took him out upon the sea to fish. When they were well out from land, the dwarfs rowed into a reef and capsized the boat. Gilling was unable to swim and was drowned, but the dwarfs righted their boat and returned to land. They told Gilling's wife that the giant had fallen out of the boat and drowned. She took the news grievously and wept aloud.

"Would it ease your heart," said Fjalar craftily, "if you could look out upon the sea at the spot where Gilling perished?"

The giant's wife said that it would comfort her and prepared to go forth to the sea.

Then Fjalar whispered to his brother to go up over the doorway and when the giant's wife came out to let a millstone fall on her head.

"Her weeping grows wearisome to me," said Fjalar.

His brother did as he was told.

Now the giant Suttung, who was Gilling's son, learned of these things and set out to seek revenge. He was a great and powerful giant. He came to where the dwarfs lived and he carried them out to sea and set them on a reef, over which the sea swept at high tide. The dwarfs begged Suttung to spare their lives.

"Save us and we will give you the precious mead made from Kvasir's blood," cried the dwarfs. "Men and gods would give anything to possess it, for he who drinks of it becomes a poet."

The giant thought that would be a precious thing to own indeed. The ransom was agreed upon and he carried the dwarfs safely to land. Suttung took the mead home and concealed it. He put his daughter Gunlod to keep watch over it.

When all these events came to the knowledge of Odin, he determined to secure the mead for the gods. The gods had created Kvasir. The precious mead brewed from his blood belonged to the gods, not to the giants. Odin told the other gods the purpose of his journey and set forth from Asgard.

He had traveled a long way when he came to a certain field

where nine thralls were cutting hay. Odin watched the men working.

"Your scythes seem not oversharp," said he. "I have a good whetstone. Would you like them sharpened?"

"We would like them sharpened," said the thralls.

Odin took his whetstone from his belt and sharpened the scythes. When the thralls began mowing the field again it seemed that their scythes had never cut so well. They asked Odin if he would sell the whetstone.

"It is an excellent stone as you see," said Odin, "and worth a high price."

"We agree to any price," said the thralls. "Pray sell us the stone."

Odin was willing, but since each one clamored for the stone he tossed it into the air for them to catch. All wished to lay their hands upon it at once. They became so entangled that they cut each other's throats with their scythes. All were killed.

Odin then sought a night's lodging with the giant Baugi, who was Suttung's brother. He lived near by and the thralls belonged to him.

Baugi welcomed Odin for the night, and while they sat at supper Baugi lamented the loss of his thralls.

"They were stupid indeed to lose their lives in such fashion," he said, "but they were my only thralls. What will happen to my fields now? I know no way to find new laborers."

"I will do the work of your thralls this summer," said Odin. "I myself can do all that they did."

"Who are you that can do the work of nine men?" said Baugi.

"My name is Bolverk," said Odin. And that was all he said about himself. The name Bolverk means one who can perform the most difficult tasks.

"But if I do this work for you," continued Bolverk, "I must have one drink of Kvasir's mead. It is your brother Suttung who keeps it."

Baugi declared that Suttung guarded the mead jealously and let no one come near it.

"I have never seen it," said Baugi. "Nevertheless when the summer is over I will go with you to Suttung. We shall see if we can persuade him to let you drink of the mead."

And so the bargain was made. Through the summer Bolverk worked for Baugi and did the work of nine men.

When the summer was over they both set out for Suttung's dwelling.

Baugi told Suttung of his bargain with Bolverk, but Suttung flatly refused them a single drop of the mead. Then Bolverk suggested to Baugi that they try certain wiles and see whether they could find a way to get at the mead. Baugi readily agreed to this.

Suttung had hidden the mead in a huge rocky cave. Gunlod, Suttung's daughter, kept watch over it. Bolverk and Baugi went to the cave. They looked at it from every side and saw that there was no way to make an easy entrance to it.

"The mead is indeed well guarded," said Bolverk, "but I think we can find a means to get at it."

Then Bolverk drew forth from his pocket an auger.

"Take this," he said to Baugi, "and see if you can bore through the rock with it."

Baugi began to bore with the auger. It was hard work cutting through the rock and Baugi grew weary. At length Baugi said he had bored through the rock. But when Bolverk blew into the auger hole the chips flew up in his face.

"I see that you would deceive me, Baugi, if you could," said Bolverk. "The hole has not been bored through the rock or the chips would not fly in my face. Take the auger and bore again."

Baugi set to work once more, but he was angry that he had been unable to deceive Bolverk. After a while Baugi said that he was now through the rock. When Bolverk blew the second time the chips were blown through the hole and Bolverk knew an opening had been made at the other end.

Then Bolverk changed himself into a serpent and crawled into the hole. Baugi wished to be rid of Bolverk and of his bargain, and he tried to pierce the serpent with the auger. But the serpent was already beyond his reach.

Bolverk crawled through the hole to the inside of the cave. There he resumed his true shape. He approached the giant's daughter. Gunlod was lonely, sitting here by herself watching over the mead. She welcomed the guest who greeted her so pleasantly. And she surmised from his appearance and the strange fashion of his coming that he must be one of the gods.

Odin remained with Gunlod for three days and she was happy in his company. At the end of that time he persuaded her to give him leave to drink three times from the mead. In the first draught he drank every drop out of the kettle, and in the second drink he emptied the first crock, and in the third drink he emptied the last crock.

Then Odin flung open the door of the cave. Changing himself into an eagle he soared into the sky, flying with all speed in the direction of Asgard.

From his dwelling Suttung saw the flight of the eagle from the cave. He guessed what had happened. He also changed himself into an eagle and flew in pursuit of Odin.

Odin flew with such power that it was not long before the golden towers of Asgard came into view. But Suttung also had great strength and he was only a short distance behind Odin.

When the gods saw the two eagles flying they knew it was Odin with Suttung in pursuit. Quickly they set out large crocks. The moment Odin flew over the walls of Asgard he emptied the mead, which he had carried in his mouth, into the crocks.

But so great had been his hurry to escape Suttung that some of the mead had spilled to the ground in his flight. The gods were not concerned with this and let who would gather it up.

Suttung, when he saw Odin wheel across the walls of Asgard, knew he was safe. The precious mead was forever in the possession of the gods. Suttung, to save himself, whirled in the air and flew off speedily toward Jotunheim.

Thus Odin brought the magic gift of Kvasir to the gods. The gods kept it not for themselves, but bestowed it as a gift upon those among men who knew how to value it. They became poets. Gods and men loved to hear their words and the wondrous songs they sang. The drops of mead which spilled to the ground were left to comfort the would-be poets upon earth.

So Kvasir's mead, instead of lying useless in Suttung's cave, brought wonder and joy and beauty to the world.

The Death of Balder

Balder was the fairest and most beloved of all the gods. He was wise in judgment, gracious in speech, and all his deeds were pure and good. Wherever Balder went there was joy and warmth and gladness. He was beloved by gods and men, and so beautiful that the whitest flower which grew on the hillside was named "Balder's Brow."

It came about that Balder dreamed great and perilous dreams touching his life. Night after night they troubled his sleep. When Balder spoke of these dreams to the other gods they were filled with foreboding. They knew some danger threatened him and all the gods took counsel together as to how they might save Balder. They came to this decision: they would ask safety for Balder from every kind of danger.

Frigg, who was the mother of Balder, went to all things in the world to ask their help. Fire and water, stones, earth, and trees, iron and metal of all kinds, birds, beasts, and even serpents promised they would not harm Balder.

When the gods knew that Balder was safe they made up a game which they took delight in playing. Balder would stand in a circle of the gods and they would strike at him or hurl stones or cast missiles of one kind or another. But Balder stood unhurt in the midst of it all. And this seemed to the gods a wondrous thing, full of awe.

Loki alone was not pleased that Balder took no hurt. His evil, crafty mind began to plot against Balder the Good. Loki made himself appear like an old woman and in this likeness he went to the dwelling of Balder's mother. He greeted Frigg and she asked him if he knew what the gods were doing at their assembly.

"The gods have a new game. Balder stands before them and they hurl weapons of every kind at him," answered Loki, speaking with the voice of an old woman. "It is a strange thing that nothing harms him."

"Nothing will harm Balder, neither weapons nor rocks nor trees," said Frigg. "I have taken oaths of them all."

"Have all things taken oaths to spare Balder?" asked the old woman.

"All things save one," said Frigg. "A small tree-sprout grows west of Valhalla. It is called Mistletoe. I thought it too young a thing to be bound by an oath."

Immediately the old woman went away. Loki changed himself into his own shape and went west of Valhalla. He tore up the Mistletoe by the roots and carried it to where the gods were assembled.

Hod, the brother of Balder, took no part in the game because he was blind. He stood outside the ring of men.

Loki spoke to him. "Why do you not shoot at Balder?"

"I cannot see where Balder stands, nor have I any weapons," answered Hod.

Then Loki said: "You should do as the others do and show Balder honor. I will show you where he stands. Shoot at him with this wand."

Hod took the Mistletoe wand and shot at Balder, and Loki guided his hand.

The shaft flew through Balder and he fell dead to the earth. This was the greatest mischance that had ever befallen gods and men.

When Balder fell to the earth the gods could not speak a word for grief and anguish, nor could they move to lift him where he lay. Each looked at the other and they were all of one mind whose evil hand had done this deed. Yet they could take no revenge for they stood on hallowed ground.

When they tried to speak the tears came and the gods wept bitterly for the loss of Balder. They had no words with which to name their sorrow. Of them all Odin grieved most, for he understood best how great was the loss which had come to the gods.

The mother of Balder was the first to speak. "If any among you," said Frigg, "would win all my love and favor, let him ride the road to Hela's realm and seek Balder among the dead. Let him offer Hela a ransom if she will but let Balder come home to Asgard."

Hermod the Bold undertook the perilous journey. The great eight-footed horse of Odin, named Sleipnir, was brought forth. Hermod mounted and sped at once upon his way.

The gods took the body of Balder and brought it down to

the sea, where Balder's ship was drawn up upon the shore. The gods wished to launch the ship and build Balder's funeral pyre upon it, but they could not move it from its place.

Then Odin sent for the giantess Hyrrokin, famed for her strength. She thrust the boat into the waters with such might that fire burst from the rollers beneath it and the earth trembled.

When the funeral pyre had been built, the body of Balder was borne to the ship. When his wife, Nanna, saw it her heart broke with grief and she died. The gods, with sorrow, laid her body beside Balder. The fire was kindled. Thor stood near. With a sad heart he lifted his hammer above the blaze and hallowed the flames.

People of many races came to the burning. First of all was Odin. His two ravens flew above him and Frigg was by his side. The Valkyries were also with him. Frey rode in his chariot drawn by his boar called Gold-Mane and Freyja drove her cats. Then came the other gods and goddesses. Many from the lands of the Frost-Giants and the Hill-Giants were there also. All grieved for Balder.

Odin laid upon the fire his ring which was called Draupnir, from which every ninth night dropped eight gold rings like to itself. The flames from the funeral ship rose on high, shining in the air and on the waters. The hearts of the gods were heavy with grief as they watched the burning.

Meanwhile Hermod was on his way to Hela. He rode nine nights through valleys so dark and deep that he could see nothing. At length he came to the river Gjoll. He rode on to the bridge which is paved with glittering gold and guarded by the maiden Modgud. She asked Hermod his name and from what country and people he came.

"Only yesterday," she said, "five companies of dead men crossed this bridge. But today it thunders as much under you riding alone. Nor have you the pallor of death. Why come you this way?"

"I have been sent to seek Balder among the dead," Hermod answered. "Has Balder passed this road?"

The maiden answered that Balder had crossed the bridge. "The way lies downward and to the north," she said.

Hermod rode on until he came to the wall of Hela's realm.

He got down from his horse and made the girths of the saddle tight. Then he mounted again and pricked the horse with his spurs. In one great leap Sleipnir cleared the gates.

Hermod rode to the great hall where the dead were gathered. He dismounted and went inside. There he saw Balder sitting in the place of honor. Hermod stayed through the night. When morning came he begged Hela that Balder might ride home with him.

"The gods are desolate without him," said Hermod. "Every being in the world longs for his return."

Hela answered that it should be put to a test whether Balder were so greatly beloved.

"If all things in the world, living and dead, weep for him," said Hela, "he shall go back to Asgard and the gods. But if there is one thing which bears him no love and will not weep, Balder must remain with me."

When Hermod rose to leave, Balder went with him out of the hall. Balder gave the ring Draupnir to Hermod and asked that he take it to Odin for a remembrance. Nanna, Balder's wife, sent Frigg a linen smock and other gifts.

Hermod rode back and came to Asgard. He told all that he had seen and heard. Then the gods sent messengers all over the world to ask all things to weep for Balder, that he might return to them. All wept for Balder: men, and all living things; the earth and stones and trees, and every kind of metal. In the early morning you can still see their tears when the dew lies upon the grass.

As the messengers came home, their work well done, they found an old woman sitting by a cave. They asked her, as they had asked all others, to weep tears that Balder might come forth from the place of the dead. But she answered:

"I will weep no tears for Balder. I loved him not. Let Hela keep what she holds. Let her keep what she holds."

And because one out of all the world would not weep for the god, Balder must stay where he was. Gods and men knew that this again was Loki's evil work. This time he must pay the price for all that he had done. The gods revenged themselves on Loki. But Balder remained with Hela, and the earth was never again as fair to gods or men.

The Punishment of Loki

The gods did not forgive Loki. Deep in their hearts they knew who had brought about the death of Balder and whose evil had kept Balder within Hela's gates. But while Loki remained within the hallowed ground of Asgard he was safe from their revenge.

Loki pursued his old ways. He taunted and defied the gods until one day Thor could stand it no longer.

"Hold your tongue, Loki!" he cried, raising his hammer. "Hold your tongue, or I will strike you dead where you stand."

Then Loki grew fearful. He knew the gods scorned him and Thor longed to destroy him. He fled from Asgard and made himself a hiding place deep in the mountains. Here he built a house with four doors. Each side of the house had a door so that he might look out in all directions. Loki knew the gods would try to find where he was hidden and he would need all his wiles to escape them. Often he would change into the likeness of a salmon and swim in the great river that flowed near his door.

One day as he was swimming he wondered what sort of thing the gods could make to catch him in the river. When he went back to his house he amused himself by taking linen twine and tying it together in meshes, in the fashion in which a fisherman's net has been made ever since.

Meanwhile far off in Asgard the gods were plotting how they might take Loki. Odin sat down in his high seat from whence he could look out over all the world. He searched the valleys and the seas and the mountains. At last he saw where Loki had hidden himself. Then the gods went forth against Loki.

Loki was sitting before his fire making his net larger. When he saw the gods coming he threw the net into the fire and ran to the river. At once he dived into the water, changing into a salmon.

When the gods reached Loki's house Kvasir, who was known for his wisdom, was the first to enter. As soon as Kvasir saw in the fire the white ash where the net had burned he understood that this was something to be used for catching fish.

Then the gods knew that Loki must have changed himself into a fish and was hiding in the river.

"Ah," cried Thor, "we will catch him with his own tricks!"

So the gods took more cord and set to work to make a net. They tied the twine in meshes, following the pattern of the burnt-out ashes of Loki's net. When it was ready they went to the river and cast the net into the water. Thor took hold of one end and the other gods held up the other end. There was a mighty waterfall in the river and they cast the net near the foot of it and dragged it toward the sea. As they came near to him Loki lay quiet between two stones on the bottom of the river. The net passed over him. But the gods saw that something moved in front of the net.

A second time they went up to the waterfall and cast in the net. This time they tied stones in it so that it would sink and nothing could pass under it. Loki swam ahead of the net, until he saw that it was but a short distance to the sea. With a mighty leap he jumped out of the water and over the net and swam back to the waterfall.

This time the gods saw where Loki hid. They divided into two companies, each holding one end of the net. Thor plunged into midstream and waded behind the net as the gods drew it toward the sea. Loki saw that he had only two choices. It would be a great risk of his life to be carried out to sea . . . the one thing left was to leap over the net once more. With all his strength Loki gave a great leap into the air. But now Thor was waiting for him. Thor clutched at Loki as he jumped and his great hand closed on the salmon's back. The wet fish slipped in Thor's fingers but Thor squeezed hard and held on. This is the reason that the back of a salmon grows narrow toward the tail.

Thus Loki was taken captive outside the bounds of any hallowed place. He need expect no mercy On dry land he changed into his own shape and the gods carried him to a cavern deep within the mountains. They took three flat stones and bored a hole in each stone. They bound Loki over the stones with bonds that turned to iron. Then they took a serpent and fastened it up over him, so that the venom should drip from the serpent into Loki's face. And there the gods left him.

Only Loki's wife, Sigyn, remained faithful to him. She stood beside him and caught the drops of venom in a basin. But when the basin was full she must turn aside to empty it. Then the venom drops upon Loki. He writhes against it with such force that the whole earth trembles. But Loki must lie in these bonds till that last day when the gods shall be overcome in battle.

The New Day

Loki lay in his bonds until the day when the last battle of the gods drew near. The wise Odin, and Frigg, and all who understood the prophecies, knew that the world of the gods would not last forever. The death of Balder hastened the day of doom. Beauty and innocence were gone from the earth. Violence and all the ways of evil increased. Brother fought against brother, and son against father.

Sunlight and warmth grew less on the earth. There came three years like one long winter, when bitter winds blew from every quarter and snow piled in great drifts. The sun and the moon were darkened in the heavens and the stars were quenched. Earth and all the mountains trembled; trees were uprooted and all bonds were burst asunder.

Loki was free to work his evil will and Fenris Wolf escaped his shackles. The Midgard Serpent rose from the depths of the sea. The waters, lashed into turmoil, washed over the earth. Streams overflowed their banks, lakes had no shores,

and the sea spread through valleys and covered mountains.

Fire was abroad on the earth. The giant Surt rode forth from the south, all the sons of Muspellheim in his wake, with flame burning before him and behind him.

The Frost-Giants and Hill-Giants came forth in all their might. Together with Surt and Loki and all the evil forces of the world they hurled themselves on the bridge Bifrost. It broke beneath their weight; but they had crossed into Asgard.

Heimdal blew his Gjallar-Horn in warning, and its echoes rang through all the worlds. The gods' cock, with the golden comb, crowed to waken the heroes that they might fight by the side of Odin and the gods.

Gods and heroes donned their armor and marched to the fields of Vigrid. Odin rode foremost, his golden helmet and byrnie gleaming. Thor strode at his side. They hurled themselves against their foes and the turmoil of battle rose. On every hand were fierce encounters. But fate was against the gods.

Fenris Wolf destroyed Odin. Thor could give no help for he struggled against the Midgard Serpent. Thor killed the Serpent, but when he had walked eight paces he fell dead, slain by the Serpent's venom. Loki and Heimdal killed each other. Frey fought with Surt and was overcome. Then he could have used well that good sword which he gave to Skirnir.

The gods were doomed. The day of their last battle had come. Yggdrasil, the tree of the universe, trembled and all things in heaven and earth were filled with dread.

Yet, as was told in the prophecies, this was not the end. After darkness and silence, a new day came. Out of the sea arose a new earth, green and fair, whose fields bore harvest without the sowing of seed. A new sun, daughter of the old, shone in the heavens, even more beautiful than her mother. All the ancient evil was passed and gone. Balder was again among the living, and light and beauty returned to the earth.

Those gods who remained made their dwelling again where Asgard had stood. In the grass they found scattered the gold chessmen with which they once played, and they remembered together the vanished past and the days of Thor and Odin.

A new race of men walked the earth; goodness and happiness were their portion. Halls roofed with gold, more fair than the sun, rose among the clouds. And all awaited the coming of the Mighty One, he who should govern all things.

EPICS AND HERO TALES

For hundreds of years, epics and hero tales have been told around campfires, sung in village squares, and later, written in thousands of versions. For millions of rapt listeners, Robin Hood's arrows whiz through the air—the horn Oliphant heralds the death of Roland—Excalibur, King Arthur's sword, swishes its way to victory. The tales grew out of the many ballads and folk songs that were created about great warriors or leaders of the people. Early epics, like the *Odyssey* and the *Kalevala, Finland's Saga,* are filled with gods and men. But unlike the myths where gods are the heroes, in epics men are the main figures.

Epic heroes are great and noble figures who reflect the ideals of the people who created them. Odysseus represents the Greek love of manly courage, wisdom, and beauty. Robin Hood personifies the English sense of justice and fair play.

Hero tales are fun as well as fascinating. They are filled with bloody battles, and exaggerated action.

ILLUSTRATION BY ESTELLE HOLLINGWORTH

The Last Adventure

BY BABETTE DEUTSCH

Illustrations by Fritz Eichenberg

*In Kalevala, old Finland's Land of Heroes,
live the great magician Vainamoinen and
his brother Ilmarinen, mighty smith and forg-
er of the Sampo, a magic mill that will grind
corn, salt, and money. In a battle with Louhi,
Mistress of the North Country, the Sampo is
destroyed. Enraged when the heroes manage to save a few magic pieces, crafty Louhi
swears to have her vengeance.*

Now it happened that the blackest and ugliest of the
daughters of Tuoni, Lord of the Dead, had wandered to the
North Country and there given birth to nine hideous children.
And in the time of childbirth it was crafty old Louhi, the
Mistress of the North Country, who had helped her and cared
for her. The names of four of these children were Colic and
Itch and Gout and Plague, and there were four more as ugly,
but the ninth and the nastiest was Envy. It was these horrid
creatures that old Louhi sent forth to the Land of Heroes to
destroy its people.

Great then was the misery in that country. The singing was
changed to wailing and the laughter to tears. Lusty old Vainamoinen put aside his kantele and with fire and water he made
magic against the dread diseases. Then he took his sharp sword
and drove them to the Mount of Torments, where the stones
would not weep for pain nor the rocks complain of aching. With
eight soothing salves and nine magic drugs old Vainamoinen
rubbed and anointed the sick till all were sound and hale. The
diseases were sealed up in a barrel and locked fast in the Mount
of Torments. And Envy was banished with them.

The folk of the Land of Heroes were full of gratitude to the
oldest magician and to Ukko the Creator, who had helped him

to dispel all these evils. But the news that her sorcery was in vain was not pleasing to old Louhi, when it came at last to her ears, and she set to work to devise another way of injuring those who possessed the pieces of the magic Sampo. She awakened the great Bear of the heath from his slumbers, and drove him to the Land of Heroes to work ill among its people.

But old Vainamoinen called upon his brother the smith to forge him a new spear with a copper shaft and three cutting edges. Then with Ilmarinen's handiwork he went forth against the shaggy monster.

It was not long before the old huntsman returned victorious. Then great was the rejoicing. The honey-eater was stripped of his skin, and the flesh was cut up and placed in cauldrons of copper and gilded kettles. There it simmered away, till the meat was sweet, and then it was heaped on brimming platters and carried to the tables beside great mugs of red ale. There was enough bear-steak for an abundant feast and more than enough to be salted away. It was evening before the feast was over, and then the time was come for singing. So lusty old Vainamoinen took his kantele and played so sweetly that the moon came from his house and stood on a crooked birch-tree to listen and the sun came from his castle and sat on a fir-tree to hear.

But crafty old Louhi, the Mistress of the North Country, was ill content. Instead of destroying the folk of the Land of Heroes, the honey-eater had provided them with a fat feast. Still, she had not come to the end of her evil magic.

She set to work to capture the sun from the top of the fir-tree and to seize the moon from the birch-tree. She carried the lights of heaven home with her to the dark and misty regions of the North Country, and there she hid them in a mountain as hard as steel among rocks as strong as iron. The Land of Heroes was left in cold and darkness. The sky was filled with night, and the house of Ukko the Creator was as dismal as the lightless homes in Vainamoinen's country.

Ukko the Creator felt strange indeed without his moon or his sun, so he walked out in his blue stockings to the edge of the clouds and the borders of the heavens to seek them. But he could not find any sign of them. Then he took his sword and struck it against his finger-nail and a bright spark flew

forth. Ukko gave the spark to one of the Maidens of the Air to tend, hoping to fashion a new sun of this brightness. But the stupid Maiden of the Air dropped it and it fell flaming through the six spangled vaults of heaven and fell into a lake.

The waters of the lake boiled up. All the fishes rushed to seize the spark that was destroying their watery homes, and in the end it was swallowed by a herring. The unhappy creature swam up and down, tormented by the fiery spark, till a salmon-trout, tired of its complaints, gulped it down. Now it was the salmon-trout's turn to swim up and down in burning misery, until a great grey pike came forward and swallowed the salmon-trout who had swallowed the herring who had swallowed the fiery spark.

Old Vainamoinen had seen the spark fall from the sky and he was eager to get hold of it, for he too hoped it would replace the light of the stolen sun and moon. He went out onto the lake where it had fallen and there the fishes told him the story of what had happened. But try as he might, Vainamoinen could not capture the grey pike.

At last he returned home and prepared a linen net of the fairest flax, a net of a hundred meshes. He placed this in his boat, and taking along his brother Ilmarinen, he set forth once more. He cast the linen net into the water and drew it and dragged it, and many a perch and many a salmon-trout and many a bream came to his net, but never the grey pike with the spark of fire in his belly. All Vainamoinen's labors were in vain.

But he had a friend, a dwarf, a very small hero, and the dwarf came down to the shore of the lake and lifted a pine-tree from the bank and threshed the water with it till the fish swam by hundreds into Vainamoinen's net. The oldest magician urged his boat with its heavy load to the red bridge-end, and there he sorted out the fishes. Among them was the grey pike.

But Vainamoinen knew that it was a risky thing to take bare-handed a fish with a spark of fire in its belly. For such a task he needed iron gloves or gauntlets of stone or perhaps copper mittens. While he was reflecting what he had best do, the son of the Sun spoke to him and said:

"Do not fret, old Vainamoinen. I will venture to take the grey

pike in my own hands, for fire will not hurt me, and I will rip
him up with the knife my father gave me. It has a golden haft
and a silver blade."

With these words the son of the Sun dropped down beside
old Vainamoinen and took his knife from his belt and ripped
open the body of the grey pike. There was the salmon-trout
and within it lay the smooth-skinned herring. The son of the
Sun split open the herring and found a blue clew in the third
fold of its entrails. He unwound it and found a red clew. In
the middle of the red clew was the spark of fire itself.

"How shall I carry it to the cold dark dwellings of the Land
of Heroes?" Vainamoinen wondered.

But before he could think of a plan the spark flew up and
singed the hands of the son of the Sun and singed the beard
of lusty old Vainamoinen. His brother the smith was standing
beside him. The spark leaped up and singed the hands and
scorched the cheeks of Ilmarinen so terribly that he had to run
to the shore of the lake and cry to Ukko the Creator for ice
and hoar-frost with which to soothe his stinging burns.

But lusty old Vainamoinen was not to be daunted. He thrust
the fiery spark into a piece of tinder and carried it to the hearths
and kettles of his people to give light and heat for cooking.

Still, it was of no use as a substitute for the stolen sun and
moon. The crops were consumed by frost. The cattle suffered.
The birds of the air felt strange in this enduring night. And
the folk of the Land of Heroes mourned in darkness. They
never knew whether it was morning or evening. It was indeed
hard to live without the lights of the sky.

They came to Ilmarinen the smith and begged him to forge
them a new sun and a new moon out of silver and gold. He
labored long at the task, and when the false sun and moon
were finished, he lifted them and set them up, the one on the
tip of a birch-tree and the other on the summit of a fir. But
though they were very beautiful, they did not shine like sunlight and like moonlight.

Then the oldest magician took counsel with himself and
made magic with a handful of sticks from the boughs of the
alder. He questioned the sticks and they told him that the
real sun and moon were hidden deep in the stone mountain
in the dark and misty regions of the North Country.

So old Vainamoinen took ship and sailed for that place to demand the lights of heaven.

"You may have them," said old Louhi's warriors mockingly, "if you overcome us in open combat."

Now old Vainamoinen's sword was longer than theirs by only so much as a barley-grain or perhaps the width of a corn-stalk. But he sliced off their heads like turnip-tops and went forthwith to the stone mountain to fetch what he had come for.

There were nine doors and a hundred bolts to the stone mountain. There were dreadful serpents guarding the stolen treasures. It was a trifle for the oldest magician to destroy the serpents. But not all his spells were sufficient to break the bolts and move the heavy doors.

Very much annoyed, he went home, and sought out his brother the smith.

"You must forge me mighty spears and a dozen hatchets," he said. "You must give me a bunch of enormous keys to open the doors of the stone mountain. Otherwise I shall never be able to get at the sun and moon."

Ilmarinen set to work at once. He made a great bundle of spears and he forged twelve strong hatchets and then he began making a bunch of enormous keys. The noise in the smithy was so loud that it thundered far off in the cold and misty regions of the North Country. Old Louhi heard the clatter and the clamor. She was fearful of what it might mean. So she took the form of a hawk and came flying to the Land of Heroes.

She flew straight to Ilmarinen's smithy. She flew so fast that the smith thought a fierce wind was blowing. He went to the window of his smithy to see what he could see. But he found only the grey hawk that was old Louhi.

"What are you doing here outside my window, O bird of prey?" he inquired.

"I have come to watch you at work," answered crafty old Louhi. "You are indeed a marvelous smith. What skilful fingers you have and what mighty arms!" she said, flattering him. "You are truly a wonderful craftsman."

"It is no wonder," answered Ilmarinen. "It was I who forged the heavens and I who welded the arch of the air."

"But what are you making now, O smith?" asked the hawk. "What are you forging this time?"

"I am forging a collar," replied Ilmarinen. "I am making a ring
for the neck of the wicked Mistress of the North Country.
When this work is done she will be firmly fettered forever to
the side of a great mountain."

When old Louhi heard these words she felt her doom coming
upon her. Filled with fear she flew swiftly back to her own
country. She did not stop until she had come to the place
where she had hidden the lights of heaven. Quickly she freed
the sun and moon from hiding. Then, taking the shape of a
pigeon, she flew back to Ilmarinen's smithy.

"What are you doing here, O pigeon?" asked the smith. "Why
are you perched on my threshold?"

"I have come to bring you news," said old Louhi. "The moon
has risen out of the stone. The sun is freed from the rock."

Ilmarinen did not wait to see the bird depart for the North
Country, nevermore to return. He hurried out of the dark
smithy into the open, and gazed anxiously at the sky. There
he saw the moon was truly gleaming on high and the sun was
shining as before. At once he rushed to the house of his brother,
old Vainamoinen.

"Come, brother!" he cried. "Here is something for a singer to
see! The moon is shining and the sun is shining too. They have
been restored to their places in the heavens. Come and look!"

Lusty old Vainamoinen hurried out into the open and lifted
up his head, and there indeed he saw the moon risen and the
sun beaming freely.

"Hail, fair-cheeked Moon!" he cried. "You are a silver dove in
the heavens. And you, bright Sun, like a golden cuckoo! How
good it is to see you again! Now you may travel on your
accustomed ways, and bring us health and increase."

Now as never before was a time for singing. Lusty old Vainamoinen took his birch-wood kantele and sang sweetly and
surely. He sang of the lights of heaven and of the prospering
earth. He sang of the Land of Heroes and its people, their sor-
rows and their feasts and their great deeds. He sang the story
of the magic Sampo. He sang too of his own childhood and of
his strange birth in the beginning of the beginning.

For it came to pass that the Virgin of the Air, tiring of her
lonely life in the upper regions, descended to the surface of
the sea. There she mated with the wind, and became the Mother

of Waters, but it was long and long before she bore the child Vainamoinen. And as she swam restlessly back and forth, a teal came flying in search of a dwelling. Then the Mother of Waters lifted up her knee and on her knee the teal made its nest and laid a great egg. The egg was so heavy a burden that the Mother of Waters moved her knee, and the egg fell into the water and broke. But it was not lost. The under half of the shell turned to solid earth, and the upper half to the arch of heaven. The yolk became the sun and the white of the egg was the bright moon. Then the Mother of Waters, swimming amid the waves, pointed with her finger and produced the rocky headlands, and stepped over the depths of the sea and left in her footprints the caves of the fishes. She set all Creation in order. But the child Vainamoinen had not yet been born. Long and long he rested in his mother's body, but it was a narrow room he found there and he longed for freedom. He too wished to see the lights of heaven and the stars of the Great Bear. He begged them to help him come forth. But they could not help him to be born. At last by his own mighty efforts he issued forth and floated on the surface of the sea, admiring the sun and moon and the stars of the Great Bear. Thus was born the oldest magician and the wisest and sweetest of singers.

All this Vainamoinen sang anew, playing the while on his birch-wood kantele with his ten fingers, so that the folk rejoiced to hear him. There was no song too strange and no music too wonderful for him. And the old men listened and nodded, and the young men heard and applauded. The women laughed for pleasure and the young girls were dancing. And all the little children marveled.

But lusty old Vainamoinen could not remain forever in one place. He could not sing always. He felt the need for journeying further. So he boarded his ship, a splendid ship with a copper deck, and he took his birch-wood kantele on his arm, and bade the Land of Heroes farewell.

None knows where he sailed or whether he will return. None has heard since the pure strains of his kantele. But parts of his songs are remembered and sung even now, and most of them you have heard, and the few remaining, if you are eager for them, it may be that one day you shall yet hear.

Odysseus at the Palace Of King Alcinoüs

BY PADRAIC COLUM

Illustrations by John Flaxman

Perhaps the greatest of all epics, the Odyssey is generally attributed to the blind poet Homer, who lived in ancient Greece or Asia Minor about one thousand years before Christ. The twenty-four books of the poem tell of Odysseus' adventures during ten years of wanderings. The feats of Odysseus are heroic and his story has held generations spellbound.

I

EVER mindful was Pallas Athene of Odysseus although she might not help him openly because of a wrong he had done Poseidon, the god of the sea. But she spoke at the council of the gods, and she won from Zeus a pledge that Odysseus would now be permitted to return to his own land. On that day she went to Ithaca, and, appearing to Telemachus, moved him, as has been told, to go on the voyage in search of his father. And on that day, too, Hermes, by the will of Zeus, went to Ogygia—to that Island where, as the Ancient One of the Sea had shown Menelaus, Odysseus was held by the nymph Calypso.

Beautiful indeed was that Island. All round the cave where Calypso lived was a blossoming wood—alder, poplar and cypress trees were there, and on their branches roosted long-winged birds—falcons and owls and chattering sea crows. Be-

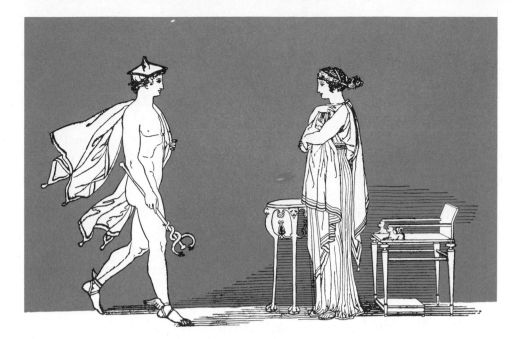

fore the cave was a soft meadow in which thousands of violets
bloomed, and with four fountains that gushed out of the ground
and made clear streams through the grass. Across the cave grew
a straggling vine, heavy with clusters of grapes. Calypso was
within the cave, and as Hermes came near, he heard her singing
one of her magic songs.

She was before a loom weaving the threads with a golden
shuttle. Now she knew Hermes and was pleased to see him on
her Island, but as soon as he spoke of Odysseus and how it was
the will of Zeus that he should be permitted to leave the Island,
her song ceased and the golden shuttle fell from her hand.

"Woe to me," she said, "and woe to any immortal who loves a
mortal, for the gods are always jealous of their love. I do not
hold him here because I hate Odysseus, but because I love him
greatly, and would have him dwell with me here—more than
this, Hermes, I would make him an immortal so that he would
know neither old age nor death."

"He does not desire to be freed from old age and death," said
Hermes, "he desires to return to his own land and to live with
his dear wife, Penelope, and his son, Telemachus. And Zeus, the
greatest of the gods, commands that you let him go upon his
way."

"I have no ship to give him," said Calypso, "and I have no company of men to help him to cross the sea."

"He must leave the Island and cross the sea—Zeus commands it," Hermes said.

"I must help him to make his way across the sea if it must be so," Calypso said. Then she bowed her head and Hermes went from her.

Straightway Calypso left her cave and went down to the sea. By the shore Odysseus stayed, looking across the wide sea with tears in his eyes.

She came to him and she said, "Be not sorrowful any more, Odysseus. The time has come when thou mayest depart from my Island. Come now. I will show how I can help thee on thy way."

She brought him to the side of the Island where great trees grew and she put in his hands a double-edged ax and an adze. Then Odysseus started to hew down the timber. Twenty trees he felled with his ax of bronze, and he smoothed them and made straight the line. Calypso came to him at the dawn of the next day; she brought augers for boring and he made the beams fast. He built a raft, making it very broad, and set a mast upon it and fixed a rudder to guide it. To make it more secure, he wove out of osier rods a fence that went from stem to stern as a bulwark against the waves, and he strengthened the bulwark with wood placed behind. Calypso wove him a web of cloth for sails, and these he made very skillfully. Then he fastened the braces and the halyards and sheets, and he pushed the raft with levers down to the sea.

That was on the fourth day. On the fifth Calypso gave him garments for the journey and brought provision down to the raft—two skins of wine and a great skin of water; corn and many dainties. She showed Odysseus how to guide his course by the star that some call the Bear and others the Wain, and she bade farewell to him. He took his place on the raft and set his sail to the breeze and he sailed away from Ogygia, the island where Calypso had held him for so long.

But not easily or safely did he make his way across the sea. The winds blew upon his raft and the waves dashed against it; a fierce blast came and broke the mast in the middle; the sail

and the yard arm fell into the deep. Then Odysseus was flung
down on the bottom of the raft. For a long time he lay there
overwhelmed by the water that broke over him. The winds
drove the raft to and fro—the South Wind tossed it to the North
to bear along, and the East Wind tossed it to the West to chase.

In the depths of the sea there was a Nymph who saw his toils
and his troubles and who had pity upon him. Ino was her name.
She rose from the waves in the likeness of a sea gull and she sat
upon the raft and she spoke to Odysseus in words.

"Hapless man," she said, "Poseidon, the god of the sea, is still
wroth with thee. It may be that the waters will destroy the raft
upon which thou sailest. Then there would be no hope for thee.
But do what I bid thee and thou shall yet escape. Strip off thy
garments and take this veil from me and wind it around thy
breast. As long as it is upon thee thou canst not drown. But
when thou reachest the mainland loose the veil and cast it into
the sea so that it may come back to me."

She gave him the veil, and then, in the likeness of a sea gull,
she dived into the sea and the waves closed over her. Odysseus
took the veil and wound it around his breast, but he would not
leave the raft as long as its timbers held together.

Then a great wave came and shattered the raft. He held himself on a single beam as one holds himself on a horse, and then,
with the veil bound across his breast, he threw himself into
the waves.

For two nights and two days he was tossed about on the
waters. When on the third day the dawn came and the winds
fell he saw land very near. He swam eagerly toward it. But when
he drew nearer he heard the crash of waves as they struck
against rocks that were all covered with foam. Then indeed was
Odysseus afraid.

A great wave took hold of him and flung him toward the shore.
Now would his bones have been broken upon the rocks if he had
not been ready-minded enough to rush toward a rock and to
cling to it with both hands until the wave dashed by. Its backward drag took him and carried him back to the deep with the
skin stripped from his hands. The waves closed over him. When
he rose again he swam round looking for a place where there
might be, not rocks, but some easy opening into the land.

At last he saw the mouth of a river. He swam toward it until
he felt its stream flowing through the water of the sea. Then in
his heart he prayed to the river. "Hear me, O River," was what
he said, "I am come to thee as a suppliant, fleeing from the
anger of Poseidon, god of the sea. Even by the gods is the man
pitied who comes to them as a wanderer and a hapless man. I
am thy suppliant, O River; pity me and help me in my need."

Now the river water was smooth for his swimming, and he
came safely to its mouth. He came to a place where he might
land, but with his flesh swollen and streams of salt water gushing from his mouth and nostrils. He lay on the ground without
breath or speech, swooning with the terrible weariness that was
upon him. But in a while his breath came back to him and his
courage rose. He remembered the veil that the Sea-nymph had
given him and he loosened it and let it fall back into the flowing
river. A wave came and bore it back to Ino who caught it in
her hands.

But Odysseus was still fearful, and he said in his heart, "Ah
me! what is to befall me now? Here am I, naked and forlorn,
and I know not amongst what people I am come. And what shall
I do with myself when night comes on? If I lie by the river in
the frost and dew I may perish of the cold. And if I climb up
yonder to the woods and seek refuge in the thickets I may
become the prey of wild beasts."

He went from the cold of the river up to the woods, and he
found two olive trees growing side by side, twining together
so that they made a shelter against the winds. He went and lay
between them upon a bed of leaves, and with leaves he covered
himself over. There in that shelter, and with that warmth he
lay, and sleep came on him, and at last he rested from perils
and toils.

II

And while he rested, the goddess, Pallas Athene, went to the
City of the Phaeacians, to whose land Odysseus had now come.

She came to the Palace of the King, and, passing through all
the doors, came to the chamber where the King's daughter,
Nausicaa slept. She entered into Nausicaa's dream, appearing to

her in it as one of her girl-comrades. And in the dream she spoke
to the Princess:

"Nausicaa," she said, "the garments of your household are all
uncared for, and the time is near when, more than ever, you
have need to have much and beautiful raiment. Your marriage
day will be soon. You will have to have many garments ready
by that time—garments to bring with you to your husband's
house, and garments to give to those who will attend you at your
wedding. There is much to be done, Nausicaa. Be ready at the
break of day, and take your maidens with you, and bring the
garments of your household to the river to be washed. I will be
your mate in the toil. Beg your father to give you a wagon with
mules to carry all the garments that we have need to wash."

So in her dream Pallas Athene spoke to the Princess in the
likeness of her girl-comrade. Having put the task of washing
into her mind, the goddess left the Palace of the King and the
country of the Phaeacians.

Nausicaa, when she rose, thought upon her dream, and she
went through the Palace and found her father. He was going
to the assembly of the Phaeacians. She came to him, but she
was shy about speaking of that which had been in her dream—
her marriage day—since her parents had not spoken to her about
such a thing. Saying that she was going to the river to wash the
garments of the household, she asked for a wagon and for mules.
"So many garments have I lying soiled," she said. "Yea, and

thou too, my father, would have fresh raiment when you go
forth to the assembly of the Phaeacians. And in our house are
the two unwedded youths, my brothers, who are always eager
for new washed garments wherein to go to dances."

Her father smiled on her and said, "The mules and wagon
thou mayst have, Nausicaa, and the servants shall get them
ready for thee now."

He called to the servants and bade them get ready the mules
and the wagon. Then Nausicaa gathered her maids together and
they brought the soiled garments of the household to the wagon.
And her mother, so that Nausicaa and her maids might eat while
they were from home, put in a basket filled with dainties and a
skin of wine. Also she gave them a jar of olive-oil so that they
might rub themselves with oil when bathing in the river.

Young Nausicaa herself drove the wagon. She mounted it and
took the whip in her hands and started the mules, and then
went through fields and by farms and came to the river bank.

The girls brought the garments to the stream, and leaving
them in the shallow parts trod them with their bare feet. The
wagon was unharnessed and the mules were left to graze along
the river side.

Now when they had washed the garments they took them to
the seashore and left them on the clean pebbles to dry in the
sun. Then Nausicaa and her companions went into the river
and bathed and sported in the water.

When they had bathed they sat down and ate the meal that
had been put on the wagon for them. The garments were not
yet dried and Nausicaa called on her companions to play.
Straightway they took a ball and threw it from one to the other,
each singing a song that went with the game. And as they
played on the meadow they made a lovely company, and the
Princess Nausicaa was the tallest and fairest and noblest of
them all.

Before they left the river side to load the wagon they played
a last game. The Princess threw the ball, and the girl whose
turn it was to catch missed it. The ball went into the river and
was carried down the stream. At that they all raised a cry. It
was this cry that woke up Odysseus who, covered over with
leaves, was then sleeping in the shelter of the two olive trees.

He crept out from under the thicket, covering his naked-
ness with leafy boughs that he broke off the trees. And when
he saw the girls in the meadow he wanted to go to them to beg
for their help. But when they looked at him they were terribly
frightened and they ran this way and that way and hid themselves. Only Nausicaa stood still, for Pallas Athene had taken
fear from her mind.

Odysseus stood a little way from her and spoke to her in a
beseeching voice. "I supplicate thee, lady, to help me in my
bitter need. I would kneel to thee and clasp thy knees only I
fear thine anger. Have pity upon me. Yesterday was the twen-
tieth day that I was upon the sea, driven hither and thither by
the waves and the winds."

And still Nausicaa stood, and Odysseus looking upon her was
filled with reverence for her, so noble she seemed. "I know not
as I look upon thee," he said, "whether thou art a goddess or
a mortal maiden. If thou art a mortal maiden, happy must thy
father be and thy mother and thy brothers. Surely they must be
proud and glad to see thee in the dance, for thou art the very
flower of maidens. And happy above all will he be who will lead
thee to his home as his bride. Never have my eyes beheld one
who had such beauty and such nobleness. I think thou art like
to the young palm tree I once saw springing up by the altar of
Apollo in Delos—a tree that many marveled to look at. O lady,
after many and sore trials, to thee, first of all the people, have
I come. I know that thou wilt be gracious to me. Show me the
way to the town. Give me an old garment to cast about me. And
may the gods grant thee thy wish and heart's desire—a noble
husband who will cherish thee."

She spoke to him as a Princess should, seeing that in spite
of the evil plight he was in, he was a man of worth. "Stranger,"
she said, "since thou hast come to our land, thou shalt not lack
for raiment nor aught else that is given to a suppliant. I will show
thee the way to the town also."

He asked what land he was in. "This, stranger," she said, "is
the land of the Phaeacians, and Alcinoüs is King over them. And
I am the King's daughter, Nausicaa."

Then she called to her companions. "Do not hide yourselves,"
she said. "This is not an enemy, but a helpless and an unfriended

man. We must befriend him, for it is well said that the stranger
and the beggar are from God."

The girls came back and they brought Odysseus to a sheltered
place and they made him sit down and laid a garment beside
him. One brought the jar of olive oil that he might clean himself when he bathed in the river. And Odysseus was very glad
to get this oil, for his back and shoulders were all crusted over
with flakes of brine. He went into the river and bathed and
rubbed himself with the oil. Then he put on the garment that
had been brought him. So well he looked that when he came
toward them again the Princess said to the maids:

"Look now on the man who a while ago seemed so terrifying!
He is most handsome and stately. Would that we might see
more of him. Now, my maidens, bring the stranger meat and
drink."

They came to him and they served him with meat and drink
and he ate and drank eagerly, for it was long since he had
tasted food. And while he ate, Nausicaa and her companions
went down to the seashore and gathered the garments that were
now dried, singing songs the while. They harnessed the mules
and folded the garments and left them on the wagon.

When they were ready to go Nausicaa went to Odysseus and
said to him, "Stranger, if thou wouldst make thy way into the
city, come with us now, so that we may guide thee. But first
listen to what I would say. While we are going through the
fields and by the farms walk thou behind, keeping near the
wagon. But when we enter the ways of the City, go no farther
with us. People might speak unkindly of me if they saw me
with a stranger such as thou. They might say, 'Whom does
Nausicaa bring to her father's house? Someone she would like
to make her husband most likely.' So that we may not meet with
such rudeness I would have thee come alone to my father's
house. Listen now and I will tell thee how thou mayst do this.

"There is a grove kept for the goddess Pallas Athene within a
man's shout of the city. In that grove is a spring, and when we
come near I would have thee go and rest thyself by it. Then
when thou dost think we have come to my father's house, enter
the City and ask thy way to the palace of the King. When thou
hast come to it, pass quickly through the court and through the

great chamber and come to where my mother sits weaving yarn by the light of the fire. My father will be sitting near, drinking his wine in the evening. Pass by his seat and come to my mother, and clasp your hands about her knees and ask for her aid. If she become friendly to thee thou wilt be helped by our people and wilt be given the means of returning to thine own land."

So Nausicaa bade him. Then she touched the mules with the whip and the wagon went on. Odysseus walked with the maids behind. As the sun set they came to the grove that was outside the City—the grove of Pallas Athene. Odysseus went into it and sat by the spring. And while he was in her grove he prayed to the goddess, "Hear me, Pallas Athene, and grant that I may come before the King of this land as one well worthy of his pity and his help."

III

About the time that the maiden Nausicaa had come to her father's house, Odysseus rose up from where he sat by the spring in the grove of Pallas Athene and went into the City. There he met one who showed him the way to the palace of King Alcinoüs. The doors of that place were golden and the doorposts were of silver. And there was a garden by the great door filled with fruitful trees—pear trees and pomegranates; apple trees and trees bearing figs and olives. Below it was a vineyard showing clusters of grapes. That orchard and that vineyard were marvels, for in them never fruit fell or was gathered but other fruit ripened to take its place; from season to season there was fruit for the gathering in the king's close.

Odysseus stood before the threshold of bronze and many thoughts were in his mind. But at last with a prayer to Zeus he crossed the threshold and went through the great hall. Now on that evening the Captains and the Councilors of the Phaeacians sat drinking wine with the King. Odysseus passed by them, and stayed not at the King's chair, but went where Arete, the Queen, sat. And he knelt before her and clasped her knees with his hands and spoke in supplication:

"Arete, Queen! After many toils and perils I am come to thee and to thy husband, and to these, thy guests! May the gods give all who are here a happy life and may each see his children in safe possession of his halls. I have come to beg that thou put me on my way to my own land, for long have I suffered far from my friends."

Then, having spoken, Odysseus went and sat down in the ashes of the hearth with his head bowed. No one spoke for long. Then an aged Councilor who was there spoke to the King.

"O Alcinoüs," he said, "it is not right that a stranger should sit in the ashes by thy hearth. Bid the stranger rise now and let a chair be given him and supper set before him."

Then Alcinoüs took Odysseus by the hand, and raised him from where he sat, and bade his son Laodamas give place to him. He sat on a chair inlaid with silver and the house-dame brought him bread and wine and dainties. He ate, and King Alcinoüs spoke to the company and said: "Tomorrow I shall call you together and we will entertain this stranger with a feast in our halls, and we shall take counsel to see in what way we can convoy him to his own land."

The Captains and Councilors assented to this, and then each one arose and went to his own house. Odysseus was left alone in the hall with the King and the Queen. Now Arete, looking closely at Odysseus, recognized the mantle he wore, for she herself had wrought it with her handmaids. And when all the company had gone she spoke to Odysseus and said: "Stranger, who art thou? Didst thou not speak of coming to us from across the deep? And if thou didst come that way, who gave thee the raiment that thou hast on?"

Said Odysseus, "Lady, for seven and ten days I sailed across the deep, and on the eighteenth day I sighted the hills of thy land. But my woes were not yet ended. The storm winds shattered my raft, and when I strove to land the waves overwhelmed me and dashed me against great rocks in a desolate place. At length I came to a river, and I swam through its mouth and I found a shelter from the wind. There I lay amongst the leaves all the night long and from dawn to midday. Then came thy daughter down to the river. I was aware of her playing with her friends, and to her I made my supplication. She gave me bread and wine, and she bestowed these garments upon me, and she showed an understanding far beyond her years."

Then said Alcinoüs the King, "Our daughter did not do well when she did not bring thee straight to our house."

Odysseus said, "My Lord, do not blame the maiden. She bade me follow with her company, and she was only careful that no one should have cause to make ill-judged remarks upon the stranger whom she found."

Then Alcinoüs, the King, praised Odysseus and said that he should like such a man to abide in his house and that he would give him land and wealth, in the country of the Phæacians. "But if it is not thy will to abide with us," he said, "I shall give thee a ship and a company of men to take thee to thy own land, even if that land be as far as Eubœa, which, our men say, is the farthest of all lands." As he said this Odysseus uttered a prayer in his heart, "O Father Zeus, grant that Alcinoüs the King may fulfill all that he has promised—and for that may his fame never be quenched—and that I may come to my own land."

Arete now bade the maids prepare a bed for Odysseus. This they did, casting warm coverlets and purple blankets upon it. And when Odysseus came to the bed and lay in it, after the tossing of the waves, rest in it seemed wonderfully good.

At dawn of day he went with the King to the assembly of the Phaeacians. When the Princes and Captains and Councilors were gathered together, Alcinoüs spoke to them saying:

"Princes and Captains and Councilors of the Phaeacians! This stranger has come to my house in his wanderings, and he desires

us to give him a ship and a company of men, so that he may cross
the sea and come to his own land. Let us, as in times past we
have done for others, help him in his journey. Nay, let us even
now draw down a black ship to the sea, and put two and fifty
of our noblest youths upon it, and let us make it ready for the
voyage. But before he departs from amongst us, come all of you
to a feast that I shall give to this stranger in my house. And
moreover, let us take with us the minstrel of our land, blind
Demodocus, that his songs may make us glad at the feast."

So the King spoke, and the Princes, Captains and Councilors
of the Phaeacians went with him to the palace. And at the same
time two and fifty youths went down to the shore of the sea,
and drew down a ship and placed the masts and sails upon it,
and left the oars in their leathern loops. Having done all this
they went to the palace where the feast was being given and
where many men had gathered.

The henchman led in the minstrel, blind Demodocus. To him
the gods had given a good and an evil fortune—the gift of song
with the lack of sight. The henchman led him through the company, and placed him on a seat inlaid with silver, and hung his
lyre on the pillar above his seat. When the guests and the minstrel had feasted, blind Demodocus took down the lyre and
sang of things that were already famous—of the deeds of Achil-
les and Odysseus.

Now when he heard the words that the minstrel uttered,
Odysseus caught up his purple cloak and drew it over his head.
Tears were falling down his cheeks and he was ashamed of their
being seen. No one marked his weeping except the King, and
the King wondered why his guest should be so moved by what
the minstrel related.

When they had feasted and the minstrel had sung to them,
Alcinoüs said, "Let us go forth now and engage in games and
sports so that our stranger guest may tell his friends when he
is amongst them what our young men can do."

All went out from the palace to the place where the games
were played. There was a foot race, and there was a boxing-
match, and there was wrestling and weight-throwing. All the
youths present went into the games. And when the sports were
ending Laodamas, the son of King Alcinoüs, said to his friends:

"Come, my friends, and let us ask the stranger whether he is skilled or practised in any sport." And saying this he went to Odysseus and said, "Friend and stranger, come now and try thy skill in the games. Cast care away from thee, for thy journey shall not be long delayed. Even now the ship is drawn down to the sea, and we have with us the company of youths that is ready to help thee to thine own land."

Said Odysseus, "Sorrow is nearer to my heart than sport, for much have I endured in times that are not far past."

Then a youth who was with Laodamas, Euryalus, who had won in the wrestling bout, said insolently, "Laodamas is surely mistaken in thinking that thou shouldst be proficient in sports. As I look at thee I think that thou art one who makes voyages for gain—a trader whose only thought is for his cargo and his gains."

Then said Odysseus with anger, "Thou hast not spoken well, young man. Thou hast beauty surely, but thou hast not grace of manner nor speech. And thou hast stirred the spirit in my breast by speaking to me in such words."

Thereupon, clad as he was in his mantle, Odysseus sprang up and took a weight that was larger than any yet lifted, and with one whirl he flung it from his hands. Beyond all marks it flew, and one who was standing far off cried out, "Even a blind man, stranger, might know that thy weight need not be confused with

the others, but lies far beyond them. In this bout none of the
Phaeacians can surpass thee."

And Odysseus, turning to the youths, said, "Let who will,
pass that throw. And if any of you would try with me in boxing
or wrestling or even in the foot race, let him stand forward—
anyone except Laodamas, for he is of the house that has be-
friended me. A rude man he would surely be who should strive
with his host."

All kept silence. Then Alcinoüs the King said, "So that thou
shalt have something to tell thy friends when thou art in thine
own land, we shall show thee the games in which we are most
skillful. For we Phaeacians are not perfect boxers or wrestlers,
but we excel all in running and in dancing and in pulling with
the oar. Lo, now, ye dancers! Come forward and show your
nimbleness, so that the stranger may tell his friends, when he
is amongst them, how far we surpass all men in dancing as well
as in seamanship and speed of foot."

A place was leveled for the dance, and the blind minstrel,
Demodocus, took the lyre in his hands and made music, while
youths skilled in the dance struck the ground with their feet.
Odysseus as he watched them marveled at their grace and their
spirit. When the dance was ended he said to the King, "My
Lord Alcinoüs, thou didst boast thy dancers to be the best in the
world, and thy word is not to be denied. I wonder as I look
upon them."

At the end of the day Alcinoüs spoke to his people and said,
"This stranger, in all that he does and says, shows himself to be
a wise and a mighty man. Let each of us now give him the
stranger's gift. Here there are twelve princes of the Phaeacians
and I am the thirteenth. Let each of us give him a worthy gift,
and then let us go back to my house and sit down to supper. As
for Euryalus, let him make amends to the stranger for his rudeness of speech as he offers him his gift."

All assented to the King's words, and Euryalus went to Odysseus and said, "Stranger, if I have spoken aught that offended
thee, may the storm winds snatch it and bear it away. May the
gods grant that thou shalt see thy wife and come to thine own
country. Too long hast thou endured afflictions away from thy
friends."

So saying, Euryalus gave Odysseus a sword of bronze with a silver hilt and a sheath of ivory. Odysseus took it and said, "And to you, my friend, may the gods grant all happiness, and mayst thou never miss the sword that thou hast given me. Thy gracious speech hath made full amends."

Each of the twelve princes gave gifts to Odysseus, and the gifts were brought to the palace and left by the side of the Queen. And Arete herself gave Odysseus a beautiful coffer with raiment and gold in it, and Alcinoüs, the King, gave him a beautiful cup, all of gold.

In the palace the bath was prepared for Odysseus, and he entered it and was glad of the warm water, for not since he had left the Island of Calypso did he have a warm bath. He came from the bath and put on the beautiful raiment that had been given him and he walked through the hall, looking a king amongst men.

Now the maiden, Nausicaa, stood by a pillar as he passed, and she knew that she had never looked upon a man who was more splendid. She had thought that the stranger whom she had saved would have stayed in her father's house, and that one day he would be her husband. But now she knew that by no means would he abide in the land of the Phaeacians. As he passed by, she spoke to him and said, "Farewell, O Stranger! And when thou art in thine own country, think sometimes of me, Nausicaa, who helped thee." Odysseus took her hand and said to her, "Farewell, daughter of King Alcinoüs! May Zeus grant that I may return to my own land. There every day shall I pay homage to my memory of thee, to whom I owe my life."

He passed on and he came to where the Princes and Captains and Councilors of the Phaeacians sat. His seat was beside the King's. Then the henchman brought in the minstrel, blind Demodocus, and placed him on a seat by a pillar. And when supper was served Odysseus sent to Demodocus a portion of his own meat. He spoke, too, in praise of the minstrel saying, "Right well dost thou sing of the Greeks and all they wrought and suffered —as well, methinks, as if thou hadst been present at the war of Troy. I would ask if thou canst sing of the Wooden Horse—that brought destruction to the Trojans. If thou canst, I shall be a

witness amongst all men how the gods have surely given thee
the gift of song."

Demodocus took down the lyre and sang. His song told how
one part of the Greeks sailed away in their ships and how others
with Odysseus to lead them were now in the center of Priam's
City all hidden in the great Wooden Horse which the Trojans
themselves had dragged across their broken wall. So the Wooden
Horse stood, and the people gathered around talked of what
should be done with so wonderful a thing—whether to break
open its timbers, or drag it to a steep hill and hurl it down on
the rocks, or leave it there as an offering to the gods. As an offering to the gods it was left at last. Then the minstrel sang how
Odysseus and his comrades poured forth from the hollow of
the horse and took the City.

As the minstrel sang, the heart of Odysseus melted within
him and tears fell down his cheeks. None of the company saw
him weeping except Alcinoüs the King. But the King cried out
to the company saying, "Let the minstrel cease, for there is one
amongst us to whom his song is not pleasing. Ever since it began
the stranger here has wept with tears flowing down his cheeks."

The minstrel ceased, and all the company looked in surprise
at Odysseus, who sat with his head bowed and his mantle
wrapped around his head. Why did he weep? each man asked.
No one had asked of him his name, for each thought it was more
noble to serve a stranger without knowing his name.

Said the King, speaking again, "In a brother's place stands
the stranger and the suppliant, and as a brother art thou to us,
O unknown guest. But wilt thou not be brotherly to us? Tell us
by what name they call thee in thine own land. Tell us, too, of
thy land and thy city. And tell us, too, where thou wert borne
on thy wanderings, and to what lands and peoples thou camest.
And as a brother tell us why thou dost weep and mourn in spirit
over the tale of the going forth of the Greeks to the war of Troy.
Didst thou have a kinsman who fell before Priam's City—a
daughter's husband, or a wife's father, or someone nearer by
blood? Or didst thou have a loving friend who fell there—one
with an understanding heart who was to thee as a brother?"

Such questions the King asked, and Odysseus taking the
mantle from around his head turned round to the company.

IV

Then Odysseus spoke before the company and said, "O Alcinoüs, famous King, it is good to listen to a minstrel such as Demodocus is. And as for me, I know of no greater delight than when men feast together with open hearts, when tables are plentifully spread, when wine-bearers pour out good wine into cups, and when a minstrel sings to them noble songs. This seems to me to be happiness indeed. But thou hast asked me to speak of my wanderings and my toils. Ah, where can I begin that tale? For the gods have given me more woes than a man can speak of!

"But first of all I will declare to you my name and my country. I am Odysseus, son of Laertes, and my land is Ithaca, an island around which many islands lie. Ithaca is a rugged isle, but a good nurse of hardy men, and I, for one, have found that there is no place fairer than a man's own land. But now I will tell thee, King, and tell the Princes and Captains and Councilors of the Phaeacians, the tale of my wanderings.

"The wind bore my ships from the coast of Troy, and with our white sails hoisted we came to the cape that is called Malea. Now if we had been able to double this cape we should soon have come to our own country, all unhurt, but the North Wind came and swept us from our course and drove us wandering past Cythera.

"Then for nine days we were borne onward by terrible winds, and away from all known lands. On the tenth day we came to a strange country. Many of my men landed there. The people of that land were harmless and friendly, but the land itself was most dangerous. For there grew there the honey-sweet fruit of the lotus that makes all men forgetful of their past and neglectful of their future. And those of my men who ate the lotus that the dwellers of that land offered them became forgetful of their country and of the way before them. They wanted to abide forever in the land of the lotus. They wept when they thought of all the toils before them and of all they had endured. I led them back to the ships, and I had to place them beneath the benches and leave them in bonds. And I commanded those who had not eaten of the lotus to go at once aboard the ships. Then, when I had got all my men upon the ships, we made haste to sail away.

"Later we came to the land of the Cyclopes, a giant people. There is a waste island outside the harbor of their land, and on it there is a well of bright water that has poplars growing round it. We came to that empty island, and we beached our ships and took down our sails.

"As soon as the dawn came we went through the empty island, starting the wild goats that were there in flocks, and shooting them with our arrows. We killed so many wild goats there that we had nine for each ship. Afterwards we looked across to the land of the Cyclopes, and we heard the sound of voices and saw the smoke of fires and heard the bleating of flocks of sheep and goats.

"I called my companions together and I said, 'It would be well for some of us to go to that other island. With my own ship and with the company that is on it I shall go there. The rest of you abide here. I will find out what manner of men live there, and whether they will treat us kindly and give us gifts that are due to strangers—gifts of provisions for our voyage.'

"We embarked and we came to the land. There was a cave near the sea, and round the cave there were mighty flocks of sheeps and goats. I took twelve men with me and I left the rest to guard the ship. We went into the cave and found no man there. There were baskets filled with cheeses, and vessels of whey, and pails and bowls of milk. My men wanted me to take some of the cheeses and drive off some of the lambs and kids and come away. But this I would not do, for I would rather that he who owned the stores would give us of his own free will the offerings that were due to strangers.

"While we were in the cave, he whose dwelling it was returned to it. He carried on his shoulder a great pile of wood for his fire. Never in our lives did we see a creature so frightful as this Cyclops was. He was a giant in size, and, what made him terrible to behold, he had but one eye, and that single eye was in his forehead. He cast down on the ground the pile of wood that he carried, making such a din that we fled in terror into the corners and recesses of the cave. Next he drove his flocks into the cave and began to milk his ewes and goats. And when he had the flocks within, he took up a stone that not all our strengths could move and set it as a door to the mouth of the cave.

"The Cyclops kindled his fire, and when it blazed up he saw us in the corners and recesses. He spoke to us. We knew not what he said, but our hearts were shaken with terror at the sound of his deep voice.

"I spoke to him saying that we were Agamemnon's men on our way home from the taking of Priam's City, and I begged him to deal with us kindly, for the sake of Zeus who is ever in the company of strangers and suppliants. But he answered me saying, 'We Cyclopes pay no heed to Zeus, nor to any of thy gods. In our strength and our power we deem that we are mightier than they. I will not spare thee, neither will I give thee aught for the sake of Zeus, but only as my own spirit bids me. And first I would have thee tell me how thou camest to our land.'

"I knew it would be better not to let the Cyclops know that my ship and my companions were at the harbor of the island. Therefore I spoke to him guilefully, telling him that my ship had been broken on the rocks, and that I and the men with me were the only ones who had escaped utter doom.

"I begged again that he would deal with us as just men deal with strangers and suppliants, but he, without saying a word, laid hands upon two of my men, and swinging them by the legs, dashed their brains out on the earth. He cut them to pieces and ate them before our very eyes. We wept and we prayed to Zeus as we witnessed a deed so terrible.

"Next the Cyclops stretched himself amongst his sheep and went to sleep beside the fire. Then I debated whether I should take my sharp sword in my hand, and feeling where his heart was, stab him there. But second thoughts held me back from doing this. I might be able to kill him as he slept, but not even with my companions could I roll away the great stone that closed the mouth of the cave.

"Dawn came, and the Cyclops awakened, kindled his fire and milked his flocks. Then he seized two others of my men and made ready for his midday meal. And now he rolled away the great stone and drove his flocks out of the cave.

"I had pondered on a way of escape, and I had thought of something that might be done to baffle the Cyclops. I had with me a great skin of sweet wine, and I thought that if I could make him drunken with wine I and my companions might be able for him. But there were other preparations to be made first. On the floor of the cave there was a great beam of olive wood which the Cyclops had cut to make a club when the wood should be seasoned. It was yet green. I and my companions went and cut off a fathom's length of the wood, and sharpened it to a point and took it to the fire and hardened it in the glow. Then I hid the beam in a recess of the cave.

"The Cyclops came back in the evening, and opening up the cave drove in his flocks. Then he closed the cave again with the stone and went and milked his ewes and his goats. Again he seized two of my companions. I went to the terrible creature with a bowl of wine in my hands. He took it and drank it and cried out, 'Give me another bowl of this, and tell me thy name that I may give thee gifts for bringing me this honey-tasting drink.'

"Again I spoke to him guilefully and said, 'No-man is my name. No-man my father and my mother call me.'

" 'Give me more of the drink, No-man,' he shouted. 'And the gift that I shall give to thee is that I shall make thee the last of thy fellows to be eaten.'

"I gave him wine again, and when he had taken the third bowl he sank backwards with his face upturned, and sleep came upon him. Then I, with four companions, took that beam of olive wood, now made into a hard and pointed stake, and thrust it into the ashes of the fire. When the pointed end began to glow we drew it out of the flame. Then I and my companions laid hold on the great stake and, dashing at the Cyclops, thrust it into his eye. He raised a terrible cry that made the rocks ring and we dashed away into the recesses of the cave.

"His cries brought other Cyclopes to the mouth of the cave, and they, naming him as Polyphemus, called out and asked him what ailed him to cry. 'No-man,' he shrieked out, 'No-man is slaying me by guile.' They answered him saying, 'If no man is slaying thee, there is nothing we can do for thee, Polyphemus. What ails thee has been sent to thee by the gods.' Saying this, they went away from the mouth of the cave without attempting to move away the stone.

"Polyphemus then, groaning with pain, rolled away the stone and sat before the mouth of the cave with his hands out-stretched, thinking that he would catch us as we dashed out. I showed my companions how we might pass by him. I laid hands on certain rams of the flock and I lashed three of them together with supple rods. Then on the middle ram I put a man of my company. Thus every three rams carried a man. As soon as the dawn had come the rams hastened out to the pasture, and, as they passed, Polyphemus laid hands on the first and the third of each three that went by. They passed out and Poly-phemus did not guess that a ram that he did not touch carried out a man.

"For myself, I took a ram that was the strongest and fleeciest of the whole flock and I placed myself under him, clinging to the wool of his belly. As this ram, the best of all his flock, went by, Polyphemus, laying his hands upon him, said, 'Would that you, the best of my flock, were endowed with speech, so that you might tell me where No-man, who has blinded me, has hidden himself.' The ram went by him, and when he had gone a little way from the cave I loosed myself from him and went and set my companions free.

"We gathered together many of Polyphemus' sheep and we drove them down to our ship. The men we had left behind would have wept when they heard what had happened to six of their companions. But I bade them take on board the sheep we had brought and pull the ship away from that land. Then when we had drawn a certain distance from the shore I could not forbear to shout my taunts into the cave of Polyphemus. 'Cyclops,' I cried, 'you thought that you had the company of a fool and a weakling to eat. But you have been worsted by me, and your evil deeds have been punished.'

"So I shouted, and Polyphemus came to the mouth of the cave with great anger in his heart. He took up rocks and cast them at the ship and they fell before the prow. The men bent to the oars and pulled the ship away or it would have been broken by the rocks he cast. And when we were farther away I shouted to him:

" 'Cyclops, if any man should ask who it was set his mark upon you, say that he was Odysseus, the son of Laertes.'

"Then I heard Polyphemus cry out, 'I call upon Poseidon, the god of the sea, whose son I am, to avenge me upon you, Odysseus. I call upon Poseidon to grant that you, Odysseus, may never come to your home, or if the gods have ordained your return, that you come to it after much toil and suffering, in an evil plight and in a stranger's ship, to find sorrow in your home.'

"So Polyphemus prayed, and, to my evil fortune, Poseidon heard his prayer. But we went on in our ship rejoicing at our escape. We came to the waste island where my other ships were. All the company rejoiced to see us, although they had to mourn for their six companions slain by Polyphemus. We divided amongst the ships the sheep we had taken from Polyphemus' flock and we sacrificed to the gods. At the dawn of the next day we raised the sails on each ship and we sailed away.

V

"We came to the Island where Aeolus, the Lord of the Winds, he who can give mariners a good or a bad wind, has his dwelling. With his six sons and his six daughters Aeolus lives on a floating island that has all around it a wall of bronze. And when we came to his island, the Lord of the Winds treated us kindly and kept us at his dwelling for a month. Now when the time came for us to leave, Aeolus did not try to hold us on the island. And to me, when I was going down to the ships, he gave a bag made from the hide of an ox, and in that bag were all the winds that blow. He made the mouth of the bag fast with a silver thong, so that no wind that might drive us from our course could escape. Then he sent the West Wind to blow on our sails that we might reach our own land as quickly as a ship might go.

"For nine days we sailed with the West Wind driving us, and on the tenth day we came in sight of Ithaca, our own land. We saw its coast and the beacon fires upon the coast and the people tending the fires. Then I thought that the curse of the Cyclops was vain and could bring no harm to us. Sleep that I had kept from me for long I let weigh me down, and I no longer kept watch.

"Then even as I slept, the misfortune that I had watched against fell upon me. For now my men spoke together and said, 'There is our native land, and we come back to it after ten years' struggles and toils, with empty hands. Different it is with our lord, Odysseus. He brings gold and silver from Priam's treasure-chamber in Troy. And Aeolus, too, has given him a treasure in an ox-hide bag. But let us take something out of that bag while he sleeps.'

"So they spoke, and they unloosed the mouth of the bag, and behold! all the winds that were tied in it burst out. Then the winds drove our ship toward the high seas and away from our land. What became of the other ships I know not. I awoke and I found that we were being driven here and there by the winds. I did not know whether I should spring into the sea and so end all my troubles, or whether I should endure this terrible misfortune. I muffled my head in my cloak and lay on the deck of my ship.

"The winds brought us back again to the floating Island. We landed and I went to the dwelling of the Lord of the Winds. I sat by the pillars of his threshold and he came out and spoke to me. 'How now, Odysseus?' said he. 'How is it thou hast returned so soon? Did I not give thee a fair wind to take thee to thine own country, and did I not tie up all the winds that might be contrary to thee?'

"'My evil companions,' I said, 'have been my bane. They have undone all the good that thou didst for me, O King of the Winds. They opened the bag and let all the winds fly out. And now help me, O Lord Aeolus, once again.'

"But Aeolus said to me, 'Far be it from me to help such a man as thou—a man surely accursed by the gods. Go from my Island, for nothing will I do for thee.' Then I went from his dwelling and took my way down to the ship.

"We sailed away from the Island of Aeolus with heavy hearts. Next we came to the Aeean Island, where we met with Circe, the Enchantress. For two days and two nights we were on that island without seeing the sign of a habitation. On the third day I saw smoke rising up from some hearth. I spoke of it to my men, and it seemed good to us that part of our company should go to see were there people there who might help us. We drew lots to find out who should go, and it fell to the lot of Eurylochus to go with part of the company, while I remained with the other part.

"So Eurylochus went with two and twenty men. In the forest glades they came upon a house built of polished stones. All around that house wild beasts roamed—wolves and lions. But these beasts were not fierce. As Eurylochus and his men went toward the house the lions and wolves fawned upon them like house dogs.

"But the men were affrighted and stood round the outer gate of the court. They heard a voice within the house singing, and it seemed to them to be the voice of a woman, singing as she went to and fro before a web she was weaving on a loom. The men shouted, and she who had been singing opened the polished doors and came out of the dwelling. She was very fair to see. As she opened the doors of the house she asked the men to come within and they went into her halls.

"But Eurylochus tarried behind. He watched the woman and he saw her give food to the men. But he saw that she mixed a drug with what she gave them to eat and with the wine she gave them to drink. No sooner had they eaten the food and drunk the wine than she struck them with a wand, and behold! the men turned into swine. Then the woman drove them out of the house and put them in the swine-pens and gave them acorns and mast and the fruit of the cornel tree to eat.

"Eurylochus, when he saw these happenings, ran back through the forest and told me all. Then I cast about my shoulder my good sword of bronze, and, bidding Eurylochus stay by the ship, I went through the forest and came to the house of the enchantress. I stood at the outer court and called out. Then Circe the Enchantress flung wide the shining doors, and called to me to come within. I entered her dwelling and she brought me to a chair and put a footstool under my feet. Then she brought me in a golden cup the wine into which she had cast a harmful drug.

"As she handed me the cup I drew my sword and sprang at her as one eager to slay her. She shrank back from me and cried out, 'Who art thou who art able to guess at my enchantments? Verily, thou art Odysseus, of whom Hermes told me. Nay, put up thy sword and let us two be friendly to each other. In all things I will treat thee kindly.'

"But I said to her, 'Nay, Circe, thou must swear to me first that thou wilt not treat me guilefully.'

"She swore by the gods that she would not treat me guilefully, and I put up my sword. Then the handmaidens of Circe prepared a bath, and I bathed and rubbed myself with olive oil, and Circe gave me a new mantle and doublet. The handmaidens brought out silver tables, and on them set golden baskets with bread and meat in them, and others brought cups of honey-tasting wine. I sat before a silver table but I had no pleasure in the food before me.

"When Circe saw me sitting silent and troubled she said, "Why, Odysseus, dost thou sit like a speechless man? Dost thou think there is a drug in this food? But I have sworn that I will not treat thee guilefully, and that oath I shall keep.'

"And I said to her, 'O Circe, Enchantress, what man of good heart could take meat and drink while his companions are as swine in swine-pens? If thou wouldst have me eat and drink, first let me see my companions in their own forms.'

"Circe, when she heard me say this, went to the swine-pen and anointed each of the swine that was there with a charm. As she did, the bristles dropped away and the limbs of the man were seen. My companions became men again, and were even taller and handsomer than they had been before.

"After that we lived on Circe's island in friendship with the enchantress. She did not treat us guilefully again and we feasted in her house for a year.

"But in all of us there was a longing to return to our own land. And my men came to me and craved that I should ask Circe to let us go on our homeward way. She gave us leave to go and she told us of the many dangers we should meet on our voyage.

VI

"When the sun sank and darkness came on, my men went to lie by the hawsers on the ship. Then Circe the Enchantress took my hand, and, making me sit down by her, told me of the voyage that was before us.

"'To the Sirens first you shall come,' said she, 'to the Sirens, who sit in their field of flowers and bewitch all men who come near them. He who comes near the Sirens without knowing their ways and hears the sound of their voices—never again shall that man see wife or child, or have joy of his home-coming. All round where the Sirens sit are great heaps of the bones of men. But I will tell thee, Odysseus, how thou mayst pass them.

"'When thou comest near put wax over the ears of thy company lest any of them hear the Sirens' song. But if thou thyself

art minded to hear, let thy company bind thee hand and foot to
the mast. And if thou shalt beseech them to loose thee, then must
they bind thee with tighter bonds. When thy companions have
driven the ship past where the Sirens sing then thou canst be un-
bound.

" 'Past where the Sirens sit there is a dangerous place indeed.
On one side there are great rocks which the gods call the Rocks
Wandering. No ship ever escapes that goes that way. And round
these rocks the planks of ships and the bodies of men are tossed
by waves of the sea and storms of fire. One ship only ever passed
that way, Jason's ship, the Argo, and that ship would have been
broken on the rocks if Hera the goddess had not helped it to
pass, because of her love for the hero Jason.

" 'On the other side of the Rocks Wandering are two peaks
through which thou wilt have to take thy ship. One peak is
smooth and sheer and goes up to the clouds of heaven. In the
middle of it there is a cave, and that cave is the den of a monster
named Scylla. This monster has six necks and on each neck there
is a hideous head. She holds her heads over the gulf, seeking for
prey and yelping horribly. No ship has ever passed that way
without Scylla seizing and carrying off in each mouth of her six
heads the body of a man.

" 'The other peak is near. Thou couldst send an arrow across to
it from Scylla's den. Out of the peak a fig tree grows, and below
that fig tree Charybdis has her den. She sits there sucking down
the water and spouting it forth. Mayst thou not be near when
she sucks the water down, for then nothing could save thee.
Keep nearer to Scylla's than to Charybdis' rock. It is better to
lose six of your company than to lose thy ship and all thy company. Keep near Scylla's rock and drive right on.

" 'If thou shouldst win past the deadly rocks guarded by Scylla
and Charybdis thou wilt come to the Island of Thrinacia. There
the Cattle of the Sun graze with immortal nymphs to guard
them. If thou comest to that Island, do no hurt to those herds.
If thou doest hurt to them I foresee ruin for thy ship and thy
men, even though thou thyself shouldst escape.'

"So Circe spoke to me, and having told me such things she took
her way up the island. Then I went to the ship and roused my
men. Speedily they went aboard, and, having taken their seats

upon the benches, struck the water with their oars. Then the sails were hoisted and a breeze came and we sailed away from the Isle of Circe, the Enchantress.

"I told my companions what Circe had told me about the Sirens in their field of flowers. I took a great piece of wax and broke it and kneaded it until it was soft. Then I covered the ears of my men, and they bound me upright to the mast of the ship. The wind dropped and the sea became calm as though a god had stilled the waters. My company took their oars and pulled away. When the ship was within a man's shout from the land we had come near, the Sirens espied us and raised their song.

" 'Come hither, come hither, O Odysseus,' the Sirens sang, 'stay thy bark and listen to our song. None hath ever gone this way in his ship until he hath heard from our own lips the voice sweet as a honeycomb, and hath joy of it, and gone on his way a wiser man. We know all things—all the travail the Greeks had in the war of Troy, and we know all that hereafter shall be upon the earth. Odysseus, Odysseus, come to our field of flowers, and hear the song that we shall sing to thee.'

"My heart was mad to listen to the Sirens. I nodded my head to the company commanding them to unloose me, but they bound me the tighter, and bent to their oars and rowed on. When we had gone past the place of the Sirens the men took the wax from off their ears and loosed me from the mast.

"But no sooner had we passed the Island than I saw smoke arising and heard the roaring of the sea. My company threw down their oars in terror. I went amongst them to hearten them, and I made them remember how, by my device, we had escaped from the Cave of the Cyclops. I told them nothing of the monster Scylla, lest the fear of her should break their hearts. And now we began to drive through the narrow strait. On one side was Scylla and on the other Charybdis. Fear gripped the men when they saw Charybdis gulping down the sea. But as we drove by, the monster Scylla seized six of my company—the hardiest of the men who were with me. As they were lifted up in the mouths of her six heads they called to me in their agony. But I could do nothing to aid them. They were carried up to be devoured in the monster's den. Of all the sights I have seen on the ways of the water, that sight was the most pitiful.

"Having passed the rocks of Scylla and Charybdis we came to the Island of Thrinacia. While we were yet on the ship I heard the lowing of the Cattle of the Sun. I spoke to my company and told them that we should drive past that Island and not venture to go upon it.

"The hearts of my men were broken within them at that sentence, and Eurylochus answered me, speaking sadly.

" 'It is easy for thee, O Odysseus, to speak like that, for thou art never weary, and thou hast strength beyond measure. But is thy heart, too, of iron that thou wilt not suffer thy companions to set foot upon shore where they may rest themselves from the sea and prepare their supper at their ease?'

"So Eurylochus spoke and the rest of the company joined in what he said. Their force was greater than mine. Then said I, 'Swear to me a mighty oath, one and all of you, that if we go upon this Island none of you will slay the cattle out of any herd.'

"They swore the oath that I gave them. We brought our ship to a harbor, and landed near a spring of fresh water, and the men got their supper ready. Having eaten their supper they fell to weeping, for they thought upon their comrades that Scylla had devoured. Then they slept.

"The dawn came, but we found that we could not take our ship out of the harbor, for the North Wind and the East Wind blew a hurricane. So we stayed upon the Island and the days and the weeks went by. When the corn we had brought in the ship was all eaten the men went through the island fishing and hunting. Little they got to stay their hunger.

"One day while I slept, Eurylochus gave the men a most evil counsel. 'Every death,' he said, 'is hateful to man, but death by hunger is by far the worst. Rather than die of hunger let us drive off the best cattle from the herds of the Sun. Then, if the gods would wreck us on the sea for the deed, let them do it. I would rather perish on the waves than die in the pangs of hunger.'

"So he spoke, and the rest of the men approved of what he said. They slaughtered them and roasted their flesh. It was then that I awakened from my sleep. As I came down to the ship the smell of the roasting flesh came to me. Then I knew that a terrible deed had been committed and that a dreadful thing would befall all of us.

"For six days my company feasted on the best of the cattle. On the seventh day the winds ceased to blow. Then we went to the ship and set up the mast and the sails and fared out again on the deep.

"But, having left that island, no other land appeared, and only sky and sea were to be seen. A cloud stayed always above our ship and beneath that cloud the sea was darkened. The West Wind came in a rush, and the mast broke, and, in breaking, struck off the head of the pilot, and he fell straight down into the sea. A thunderbolt struck the ship and the men were swept from the deck. Never a man of my company did I see again.

"The West Wind ceased to blow but the South Wind came and it drove the ship back on its course. It rushed toward the terrible rocks of Scylla and Charybdis. All night long I was borne on, and, at the rising of the sun, I found myself near Charybdis. My ship was sucked down. But I caught the branches of the fig tree that grew out of the rock and hung to it like a bat. There I stayed until the timbers of my ship were cast up again by Charybdis. I dropped down on them. Sitting on the boards I rowed with my hands and passed the rock of Scylla without the monster seeing me.

"Then for nine days I was borne along by the waves, and on the tenth day I came to Ogygia where the nymph Calypso dwells. She took me to her dwelling and treated me kindly. But why tell the remainder of my toils? To thee, O King, and to thy noble wife I told how I came from Calypso's Island, and I am not one to repeat a plain-told tale."

The Death of Roland

TRANSLATED BY MERRIAM SHERWOOD

Illustrations by Emil Weiss

> *Count Roland wielded his sword and lost his life many hundreds of years ago. He left behind him a story, "Chanson de Roland," half history and half legend. Through the treachery of Ganelon, Roland and his warriors were separated from their king and leader, Charlemagne, in a valley of the Pyrenees. They were utterly destroyed by their Saracen enemies.*

ROLAND looked over the mountains and the heath. Of those of France how many he saw lying dead! Like a gentle knight he wept for them:

"Noble Lords, may God have mercy on you! May He grant Paradise to all your souls! May he make them to lie among the holy flowers! Never saw I better vassals than you. How long and constantly have you served me! What great countries have you conquered for Charles! But woe the day that the Emperor took you into his household! Land of France, O most sweet country, today forlorn and ravaged! Barons of France, I see you dying for me. I cannot fight for you or save you. May God, Who never lied, help you! Oliver my Brother, I must not fail you. I shall die of grief, if I am slain by nothing else. Sir Comrade, let us go smite once more!"

Count Roland returned to the fight. Wielding Durendal, he struck like a knight. He cut through the middle Faldrun of Pui and twenty-four of the Pagans most renowned. Never will any man have such desire to avenge himself. As the stag flees before the hounds, so fled the Pagans before Roland. Said the Archbishop:

From *The Song of Roland*, translated by Merriam Sherwood. Copyright 1938 by Longmans, Green and Co.

"Bravo! Well done! Such valor as that befits a knight who bears
good arms and sits a good steed. In battle he should be fierce
and strong; otherwise, he is not worth fourpence, but should be
a monk in some monastery, praying without cease for our sins!"

Roland answered:

"Smite, nor spare them!"

At these words the French began to fight once more. Heavy
were the losses of the Christians. When a man knows that there
will be no quarter, he puts up a brave defense in such a battle.
That is why the French were as fierce as lions.

Lo! There came Marsile, riding in lordly wise on a horse that
he called Gaignon. He dug in his spurs and went to smite Be-
von, lord of Dijon and of Beaune. He pierced his shield and rent
his hauberk, striking him dead without doing him other hurt.
Then he slew Ivorie and Ivon, and along with them, Gerard of

Roussillon. Count Roland was not far away. He said to the Pagan:

"The Lord God give thee ill! Wickedly thou slayest my companions. Thou shalt feel a blow of mine before we part. This very day shalt thou learn the name of my sword!"

He rode in knightly wise to strike him. The Count cut off the King's right hand. Then he severed the head of Jurfaleu the Blond, King Marsile's son. The Pagans cried out:

"Help us, Mahound! Ye Gods of ours, avenge us on Charles! He has placed in our land scoundrels who, even at the risk of dying for it, will not flee the field!"

The one said to the other: "Well then, let us flee!"

At these words a hundred thousand took to their heels. No matter who might bid them, they would not return. Of what avail their flight? Marsile might flee, but his uncle remained, the Caliph, Lord of Carthage, Alferne, and Garmalie, and of Ethiopia—a cursed land; he held sway over the black race. They have big noses and large ears. More than fifty thousand of them were assembled there. They charged fierce and furiously, then shouted the Pagan battle cry. Said Roland:

"This is our martyrdom! Now I know well that we have not long to live; but he is a traitor who does not first sell himself dear. Strike, my Lords, with your furbished swords! Do battle for your dead and for your lives, that sweet France may not be dishonored by us! When Charles my Lord shall come to this field and, beholding the punishment we have wrought upon the Saracens, shall find for every one of our men fifteen Pagans slain he will not fail to bless us."

When Roland saw the accursed people, blacker than any ink, with no spot of white except their teeth, he said:

"Now I know for certain that we shall die today. Strike, Frenchmen, for I am starting the fight anew!"

Said Oliver:

"Cursed be the last to strike!"

At these words the French fell upon the Pagans, who, when they saw how few were the French, were filled with pride and comfort. Said one to the other:

"The Emperor is in the wrong!"

The Caliph bestrode a sorrel horse. He dug in his gilded

spurs, and struck Oliver from behind in the middle of his back. He rent the white hauberk, even to the body. He thrust the spear clean through his breast. Then he said:

"You have received a rude blow! Alas for you that Charlemagne left you at the pass! He has wronged us, nor is it right that he boast of it: for, in you alone, I have avenged my people!"

Oliver felt himself wounded to the death. He grasped Hauteclaire, whose steel was burnished, and smote the Caliph on his pointed gilt helmet, striking off its painted flowers and crystals. He split open his head down to the small front teeth, shook the sword, and struck him dead. Then he said:

"Pagan, curses on thee! I do not say that Charles has not lost, but thou wilt not be able to boast to wife or to any lady, in the kingdom whence thou art, that thou hast taken from me a penny'sworth, or hast done scathe to me or to any other."

Then he cried out to Roland to help him.

Oliver felt that he was wounded mortally. He would never have his fill of avenging himself. He hurled himself into the press, striking like a baron. He slashed through spear-shafts and bucklers, cut off feet and hands, cleft saddles and flanks. Whoever had seen him dismember the Saracens, flinging one dead upon the other, might indeed mind him of a doughty vassal! Nor did he forget the battle-cry of Charles. "Montjoie!" he shouted loud and clear. He called to Roland, his friend and peer:

"Sir Comrade, come to my side! With bitter sorrow we must part today!"

Roland looked into the face of Oliver. It was wan, discolored, livid, pale. The bright blood streaked his body, the clots falling to the ground.

"O Lord," said the Count, "now I know not what to do. Sir Comrade, alack for your prowess! Never will there be a man to equal thee! Ah, sweet France, how art thou pillaged today of good vassals! How art thou confounded and laid low! The Emperor will suffer great scathe."

With these words he swooned on his horse. Behold Roland swooned and Oliver wounded unto death. Oliver had lost so much blood that his vision was troubled. He could not see clearly enough to recognize mortal man, far or near. As he approached his comrade he struck him on his jeweled and gilded helmet, cleaving it as far as the nose-piece; but he did not reach the flesh. At that blow Roland looked at him, and asked him gently and softly:

"Sir Comrade, are you doing this of your own wish? This is Roland, who has always loved you well! You have struck me without challenging me first!"

Said Oliver:

"Now I know you, for I hear you speak. I cannot see you, but may the Lord God do so! I struck you. Forgive me, I pray!"

Roland answered:

"You did not hurt me. I forgive you here before God."

At these words the one bowed to the other. Thus, in great love, they parted.

Oliver felt the anguish of death approaching. Both his eyes turned in his head. He lost his sense of hearing and of sight. He dismounted and lay on the ground. He confessed his sins in a loud voice, both his hands clasped toward heaven, and prayed God to grant him Paradise and to bless Charles and sweet France, and, above all men, his comrade Roland. His heart failed, his helmet sank, his whole body fell upon the ground. Dead was the Count, no longer might he live. Roland the Brave wept for him and mourned. Never on earth will you hear of a man more sorrowful.

Roland saw that his friend was dead, saw him lying, face down, on the ground. Very gently he began to lament him:

"Sir Comrade, alas for your bold courage! We have been together for years and for days. You have never done me harm, nor I you. Since you are dead, it is my grief that I live!"

With these words the Marquis fainted on his horse Veillantif. He was held on by his stirrups of fine gold; thus, wheresoever he might go, he could not fall off.

Before Roland came to himself and recovered consciousness, a great disaster befell him: the French were slain; he had lost them all, except the Archbishop and Walter of l'Hum. Walter had come down from the mountains, whither Roland had sent him. He had fought hard against those of Spain. His men were slain; the Pagans had vanquished them. Willy-nilly he was fleeing down the valleys, calling on Roland to come to his aid:

"Ah, noble Count, brave Warrior, where art thou? I have never

known fear when thou wert with me. I am Walter, who conquered Maëlgut; Walter, the nephew of Droon the Old and
Hoary. For my prowess I have ever been a favorite with thee.
My lance is broken, and pierced my shield, my hauberk rent
and torn, my body transversed by a spear. I am on the point of
death, but I have sold myself dear."

Roland heard these words. He spurred his horse and rode
toward Walter. He was filled with grief and anger. In the thickest of the press he began to smite. Of those of Spain he struck
dead twenty; Walter, six; the Archbishop, five. Said the Pagans:

"Fell fighters these! See to it, my Lords, that they escape not
with their lives. A traitor he who does not attack them; a coward
he who allows them to survive!"

Then the hue and cry began anew. On every side they returned to the attack. Count Roland was a noble warrior; Walter
of l'Hum, a valiant knight; the Archbishop, a proven fighter. Not
one of them had wish to abandon the others. In the thick of the
press they struck the Pagans. A thousand Saracens dismounted,
to fight on foot; there were forty thousand others on horseback.
You may take my word for it, they dared not approach the three.
They cast lances and spears at them, and javelins and darts.
With the first blows they slew Walter. They pierced the shield
of Archbishop Turpin of Rheims, cleft his helmet and wounded
him in the head, rent and tore his hauberk. Four spears passed
through his body, and his horse was killed beneath him. Great
was the mourning when the Archbishop fell.

Turpin of Rheims, when he felt himself struck from his horse,
his body pierced by four spears, sprang quickly to his feet. He
looked at Roland, ran to him, and spoke these words:

"I am yet unvanquished! A good vassal is not taken alive!"

He drew Almace, his sword of burnished steel. In the thick of
the press he struck a thousand blows and more. Charles said
afterwards that it was clear he had spared no one; for the King
found him surrounded by four hundred Saracens, some wounded, some pierced through and through, and some without heads.
This is vouched for by the Annals and by him who was on the
field of battle: the Baron Saint Giles, for whom God performs
miracles, and who made the charter in the monastery of Laon.
He who knows not this knows not enough about it.

Count Roland fought nobly; but his body was very hot and drenched with sweat, and his head ached painfully, from the bursting of his temples when he blew his horn. But he wanted to know whether Charles was coming. He took his horn and blew it feebly. The Emperor stood still and listened.

"My Lords," said he, "it is going very ill with us! Roland my Nephew departs from us this day. I know from his blowing that he is near unto death. He who wishes to be with him must ride fast! Blow your clarions, as long as there are any left in this host!"

Sixty thousand trumpets gave voice so loud that the mountains resounded and the valleys answered. The Pagans heard it, and they thought it no jest. Said one to the other:

"We shall have Charles anon!"

Said the Pagans:

"The Emperor is coming back. Hark! The clarions of those of France are blowing! If Charles arrives, we shall suffer losses. If Roland lives, our war will start anew. We have lost Spain, our land!"

Four hundred assembled, helmeted, from among those who deemed themselves best in the field. Hard and heavy the attack they made on Roland. Now, as for the Count, he had enough to do! When Count Roland saw them advancing, how strong and fierce and eager he became! He would not yield to them so long as life remained. He sat his horse called Veillantif. He dug in his spurs of fine gold, and rode to attack them all in the thick of the press. Beside him was Archbishop Turpin. Said the one to the other:

"Come hither, Friend! We have heard the horns of those of France. Charles the mighty King is coming back!"

Count Roland never loved a coward, or a proud man, or a wicked, or a knight who was not a good fighter. He called to Archbishop Turpin:

"Sire, you are on foot and I on horseback. For love of you I will take my stand here. We shall receive together both the good and the evil; nor will any man of flesh and blood make me leave you. We will render to the Pagans their attack. The best of all blows are those of Durendal!"

Said the Archbishop:

"A traitor he who should fail to deal good blows! Charles is returning, and he will indeed avenge us."

The Pagans said:

"Alack that we were ever born! Dire for us the day that dawned this morning! We have lost our lords and our peers. Charles the Noble is returning with his great army. We hear the clear-voiced clarions of those of France. Loud is the noise as the Franks shout 'Montjoie!' So fierce and proud is Count Roland that he will never be vanquished by mortal man. Let us take aim at him, and then leave it at that!"

They cast at him a bevy of javelins, of spears and lances and feathered darts. Roland's shield was broken and pierced, and his hauberk rent and torn; yet his body was unscathed. But they wounded Veillantif in thirty places, striking him dead under the Count. Then the Pagans fled and left Roland there. Count Roland remained behind on foot.

The Pagans fled, angry and wrathful. They made every effort to return toward Spain. Count Roland had no means of pursuing them, for he had lost his charger Veillantif. Willy-nilly he was left standing there.

He went to succor Archbishop Turpin. He unlaced the gilded helmet from his head and took off his light white hauberk. He cut up all his tunic and stanched his deep wounds with the strips. Then he embraced him, clasping him to his breast, and laid him softly on the green grass. Very gently Roland besought him:

"Ah, noble Lord, pray grant my request! Our comrades, whom we held so dear, are now dead. We should not abandon them. I will go to look for and identify them, gather them together and lay them out before you."

Said the Archbishop:

"Go, and return! The field is yours, praise be to God, yours and mine!"

Roland turned away, and went all alone across the battlefield. He searched the valleys, he searched the mountains. There he found Ivorie and Ivon. There he found the Gascon Engelier. There he found Gerin and his comrade Gerier. And so he found

Berengier and Otto. There he found Anseïs and Samson. He
found Gerard the Old of Roussillon. One by one the Baron took
them and brought them to the Archbishop. He laid them in a
row before Turpin's knees. The Archbishop could not help but
weep. He raised his hand and gave his benediction. Then he
said:

"Alas for you, my Lords! May God the Glorious receive all
your souls! May He place them in Paradise among the holy
flowers! How woeful my own death is rendering me now! I shall
never more see the mighty Emperor."

Roland turned away, and went to search the field anew. He
found his comrade Oliver. He clasped him to his breast in a
close embrace. As well as he could he came back to the Archbishop. He laid Oliver on a shield beside the others, and the
Archbishop absolved him and made the sign of the Cross over
him. Then their grief and pity knew no bounds. Said Roland:

"Fair Comrade Oliver, you were the son of Duke Renier, who
held the march of the valley of Runers. For breaking a lance
and for shattering shields, for vanquishing and dismaying the
proud, for leading and counseling the brave, and for conquering and terrifying scoundrels: never in any land was there a
better knight."

Count Roland, when he saw his peers dead, and Oliver whom
he loved so well, was overcome with tenderness and began to
weep. His face lost its color. So great was his grief that he
could no longer stand but willy-nilly fell swooning to the ground.
Said the Archbishop:

"Baron, alack for you!"

The Archbishop, when he saw Roland faint, was filled with
such grief as he had never felt before. He stretched out his
hand and took Roland's horn. At Roncevaux there is a stream of
water. He wanted to go to it and fetch some for Roland. He
turned thither staggering, walking with short steps. So feeble
was he that he could not go on. He had not the strength. He
had lost too much blood. Sooner than one might take a hundred
paces, his heart gave out and he fell forward. The agony of
death came upon him.

Count Roland regained consciousness. He stood up, but he

suffered great pain. He looked up and down. On the green grass, beyond his companions, he beheld the noble baron lying, the Archbishop, God's delegate. He was confessing his sins, his eyes raised, both his hands clasped on high toward heaven, and he was praying God to grant him Paradise.

Dead was Turpin, the warrior of Charles. In mighty battles and in most beauteous sermons, he was ever the Emperor's champion against the Pagans. May God grant him His Holy benediction!

Count Roland saw the Archbishop on the ground. He saw his entrails spread outside his body, his brain seething from his forehead. High on his breast the Count crossed the fair white hands of Turpin. After the custom of his land, Roland lamented him aloud:

"Ah, noble Lord, highborn Knight, today I commend thee to the Glorious King of Heaven! Never will a man more willingly serve Him. Never, since the Apostles, hath there been such a prophet to keep the Law and to draw men after him. May your soul know no hardship! May the gates of Paradise be opened to it!"

Roland felt that death was near. His brain issued forth from his ears. He prayed God for his peers, that He would call them. Then, for himself, he prayed to the Angel Gabriel. He took his horn, that no one might reproach him; and, in his other hand, his sword Durendal. More than a bowshot toward Spain, into a fallow field, he went. He climbed upon a knoll, where, under two fair trees, there were four blocks of stone, cut from marble. He fell down on his back on the green grass. There he swooned, for death was near him.

High were the mountains and very high the trees. Four blocks of stone were there, of shining marble. On the green grass Count Roland had fainted. All the time a Saracen was watching him, and feigning death as he lay among the slain. He had smeared his body and his face with blood. He got to his feet and hastened to run forward. Handsome was he, and strong, and of great prowess. In his pride he was seized with a mortal madness. He laid hold of Roland, of his body and of his weapons, and he spoke these words:

"Vanquished is Charles's nephew! I will bear away this sword of his to Araby!"

As he pulled at it, the Count came a little to his senses. Roland was conscious that his sword was being taken from him. He opened his eyes and spoke these words:

"Methinks thou art not one of ours!"

He grasped his horn, which he had no wish to lose, and struck the Pagan on the helmet, jeweled and gold-adorned. He shattered the steel and his head and his bones. Both his eyes burst from their sockets and he fell dead at Roland's feet. Said the Count:

"Pagan lout, how hadst thou the presumption to lay hold of me, whether rightly or wrongly? No man shall hear of this without deeming thee a fool. The large end of my horn has been cracked; the crystal and the gold have been knocked off."

Roland felt that his sight was going. He got to his feet, exerting all his strength. All color had left his face. Before him there was a dark stone. In grief and anger he struck ten blows upon it. The steel grated, but did not break or nick.

"Ah!" said the Count. "Help me, Saint Mary! Ah, Durendal, good Sword, alas for thee! Since I am dying, I am no longer thy keeper. How many pitched battles have I won with thee! Conquered how many wide lands, which Charles of the Hoary Beard now holds! May no man have thee who would flee from another! A good vassal has long carried you. Never will there be such a one in France the Holy!"

Roland struck on the stone of sardonyx. The steel grated but it did not crack or chip. When he saw that he could not break it, he began to lament it to himself:

"Ah, Durendal, how fair and bright and white art thou! How thou dost sparkle and flame in the sun! Charles was in the vales of Maurienne, when God sent him word from heaven by His angel that he should give thee to a count and captain. Then was I girt with thee by the noble King, the great King. With thee I conquered for him Anjou and Brittany; with thee I conquered for him Poitou and Maine. For him I conquered with thee Normandy the Free. With thee I conquered for him Provence and Aquitaine and Lombardy and all Romagna. With thee I conquered for him Bavaria and all Flanders and Burgundy and all Apulia, Constantinople, whose homage he received, and Saxony, where he does what he will. With thee I conquered for him Scotland, Wales and Ireland; and England, which he considered crownland. With thee how many lands and countries have I conquered for Charles of the Hoary Beard to rule! For this sword I have dolor and grief. Rather would I die than leave it among Pagans. God! Father! Let not France be thus shamed!"

Roland smote a dark stone. He chipped off more of it than I can say. The sword crunched but did not break or shiver. Instead, it rebounded toward heaven. When the Count saw that he could not break it, he bewailed it very softly to himself:

"Ah, Durendal, how beautiful thou art, and holy! In thy golden hilt are relics a-plenty: a tooth of Saint Peter and some of Saint Basil's blood, and hair of my Lord Saint Denis; and there is a piece of Saint Mary's dress. It is not right for Pagans to have thee; thou shouldst be served by Christians. May coward never wield thee! Wide are the lands I shall have conquered with you, for Charles of the Hoary Beard to rule—lands which have brought the Emperor power and riches."

Roland felt that death was taking hold of him. From his head it was descending toward his heart. Beneath a pine tree he went running. He lay down on his face on the green grass. Under him he placed his sword and his horn. He turned his head toward the Pagan people. This he did because he wished that Charles and all his men should say that he, the gentle Count, died conquering. He confessed himself again and again. For his sins he offered God his glove.

Roland felt that his time was short. He lay on a sharp peak, facing Spain. With one hand he struck his breast:

"God, by Thy power forgive my sins, great and small, which I have committed from the hour that I was born until this day when I am slain!"

He held out his right glove toward God. The angels of heaven descended to him.

Count Roland lay beneath a pine tree. He had turned his face toward Spain. He began to mind him of many things: of how many lands he had conquered, of sweet France, of the men

of his kin, of Charlemagne his Lord, who had fostered him. He could not help but weep and sigh. Yet himself he would not forget. He confessed his sins and prayed God for mercy:

"True Father, Who never liest, Thou Who didst raise Lazarus from the dead, and save Daniel from the lions, keep, I pray Thee, my soul from all perils arising from the sins I have committed in my life!"

He offered his right glove to God. Saint Gabriel took it from his hand. On his arm his head was resting. With clasped hands he went to his death. God sent to him His angel Cherubin and Saint Michael of the Peril of the Sea. Saint Gabriel came with them. Together they bore the soul of the Count to Paradise.

The Merry Adventures of Robin Hood

BY HOWARD PYLE

Illustrations by Lewis Zacks

Although some claim that the Robin Hood legends may have originated with the exploits of a real person who lived during the last years of the twelfth century, most scholars feel that they are mythical. The archer-outlaw lived in Sherwood Forest near Nottingham, England. With his stalwart companions, Little John, Will Scarlet, Allan a Dale, and others, he robbed and fought the rich to help the poor.

NOW it was told before how two hundred pounds were set upon Robin Hood's head, and how the Sheriff of Nottingham swore that he himself would seize Robin, both because he would fain have the two hundred pounds and because the slain man was a kinsman of his own. Now the Sheriff did not yet know what a force Robin had about him in Sherwood, but thought that he might serve a warrant for his arrest as he could upon any other man that had broken the laws; therefore he offered fourscore golden angels to any one who would serve this warrant. But men of Nottingham Town knew more of Robin Hood and his doings than the Sheriff did, and many laughed to think of serving a warrant upon the bold outlaw, knowing well that all they would get for such service would be cracked crowns; so that no one came forward to take the matter in hand. Thus a fortnight passed, in which time none came forward to do the Sheriff's business. Then said he: "A

From *The Merry Adventures of Robin Hood*, by Howard Pyle.

right good reward have I offered to whomsoever would serve my warrant upon Robin Hood, and I marvel that no one has come to undertake the task."

Then one of his men who was near him said: "Good master, thou wottest not the force that Robin Hood has about him and how little he cares for warrant of king or sheriff. Truly, no one likes to go on this service, for fear of cracked crowns and broken bones."

"Then I hold all Nottingham men to be cowards," said the Sheriff. "And let me see the man in all Nottinghamshire that dare disobey the warrant of our sovereign lord, King Harry, for, by the shrine of Saint Edmund, I will hang him forty cubits high! But if no man in Nottingham dare win fourscore angels, I will send elsewhere, for there should be men of mettle somewhere in this land."

Then he called up a messenger in whom he placed great trust, and bade him saddle his horse and make ready to go to Lincoln Town to see whether he could find any one there that would do his bidding, and win the reward. So that same morning the messenger started forth upon his errand.

Bright shone the sun upon the dusty highway that led from Nottingham to Lincoln, stretching away all white over hill and dale. Dusty was the highway and dusty the throat of the messenger, so that his heart was glad when he saw before him the sign of the Blue Boar Inn, when somewhat more than half his journey was done. The inn looked fair to his eyes, and the shade of the oak trees that stood around it seemed cool and pleasant, so he alighted from his horse to rest himself for a time, calling for a pot of ale to refresh his thirsty throat.

There he saw a party of right jovial fellows seated beneath

the spreading oak that shaded the greensward in front of the door. There was a tinker, two barefoot friars, and a party of six of the King's foresters all clad in Lincoln green, and all of them were quaffing humming ale and singing merry ballads of the good old times. Loud laughed the foresters, as jests were bandied about between the singing, and louder laughed the friars, for they were lusty men with beards that curled like the wool of black rams; but loudest of all laughed the Tinker, and he sang more sweetly than any of the rest. His bag and his hammer hung upon a twig of the oak tree, and near by leaned his good stout cudgel, as thick as his wrist and knotted at the end.

"Come," cried one of the foresters to the tired messenger, "come join us for this shot. Ho, landlord! bring a fresh pot of ale for each man."

The messenger was glad enough to sit down along with the others who were there, for his limbs were weary and the ale was good.

"Now what news bearest thou so fast?" quoth one, "and whither ridest thou to-day?"

The messenger was a chatty soul and loved a bit of gossip dearly; beside, the pot of ale warmed his heart; so that, settling himself in an easy corner of the inn bench, while the host leaned upon the doorway and the hostess stood with her hands beneath her apron, he unfolded his budget of news with great comfort. He told all from the very first: how Robin Hood had slain the forester, and how he had hidden in the greenwood to escape the law; how that he lived therein, all against the law, God wot, slaying his Majesty's deer and levying toll on fat abbot, knight, and esquire, so that none dare travel even on broad Watling Street or the Foss Way for fear of him; how that the Sheriff, Heaven save his worship, who paid him, the messenger, sixpence every Saturday night, of good broad money stamped with the King's head, beside ale at Michaelmas and a fat goose at Christmas-tide, had a mind to serve the king's warrant upon this same rogue, though little would he mind warrant of either king or sheriff, for he was far from being a law-abiding man. Then he told how none could be found in all Nottingham Town to serve this warrant, for fear of cracked pates and broken bones, and how that he, the messenger, was now upon his way to Lincoln Town to find of what mettle the Lincoln men might be, and whether there were any there that dared serve this same warrant; wherefore was he now sitting among the prettiest lads he had ever known, and the ale was the best ale he had tasted in all his life.

To this discourse they listened with open mouths and eyes, for it was a fair piece of gossip to them. Then when the messenger had done the jolly Tinker broke silence.

"Now come I, forsooth, from good Banbury Town," said he, "and no one nigh Nottingham—nor Sherwood either, an that be the mark—can hold cudgel with my grip. Why lads, did I not meet that mad wag, Simon of Ely, even at the famous Fair at Hertford Town, and beat him in the ring at that place before Sir Robert of Leslie and his lady? This same Robin Hood, of whom, I wot, I never heard before, is a right merry blade, but gin he be strong, am not I stronger? and gin he be sly, am not I slyer? Now by the bright eyes of Nan o' the Mill, and by mine own name, and that's Wat o' the Crabstaff, and by mine own mother's son, and that's myself, will I, even I, Wat o' the Crabstaff, meet this same sturdy rogue, and gin he mind not the seal of our glorious sovereign, King Harry, and the warrant of the good Sheriff of Nottinghamshire, I will so bruise, beat, and bemaul his pate, that he shall never move finger or toe again! Hear ye that, bully boys? Come, let us have another bout."

"Now art thou the man for my farthing," cried the messenger. "And back thou goest with me to Nottingham Town."

"Nay," quoth the Tinker, shaking his head slowly from side to side. "Go I with no man gin it be not with mine own free will."

"Nay, nay," said the messenger, "no man is there in Nottinghamshire could make thee go against thy will, thou brave fellow."

"Ay, that be I brave," said the Tinker.

"Ay, marry," said the messenger, "thou art a brave lad; but our good Sheriff hath offered fourscore angels of bright gold to whosoever shall serve the warrant upon Robin Hood; though little good will it do."

"Then I will go with thee, lad. Do but wait till I get my bag, and hammer, and my cudgel. Ay, let me but meet this same Robin Hood, and let me see whether he will not mind the King's warrant." So, after having paid their score, the messenger, with the Tinker striding beside his nag, started back to Nottingham again.

One bright morning soon after this time, Robin Hood started off to Nottingham Town to find what was a-doing there, walking merrily along the roadside where the grass was sweet with daisies, his eyes wandering and his thoughts also. His buglehorn hung at his hip and his bow and arrows at his back, while in his hand he bore a good stout oaken staff, which he twirled with his fingers as he strolled along.

As thus he walked down a shady lane he saw a tinker coming, trolling a merry song as he drew nigh. On his back hung his bag and his hammer, and in his hand he carried a right stout crabstaff full six feet long, and thus sang he:—

> *"In peascod time, when hound to horn*
> *Gives ear till buck be killed,*
> *And little lads with pipes of corn*
> *Sit keeping beasts afield"*—

"Halloa, good friend!" cried Robin.

> *"I went to gather strawberries"*—

"Halloa!" cried Robin again.

> *"By woods and groves full fair"*—

"Halloa! art thou deaf, man? Good friend, say I!"

"And who art thou dost so boldly check a fair song?" quoth the Tinker, stopping in his singing. "Halloa, thine own self, whether thou be good friend or no. But let me tell thee, thou stout fellow, gin thou be a good friend it were well for us both; but gin thou be no good friend it were ill for thee."

"Then let us be good friends," quoth jolly Robin, "for ill

would it be to be ill, and ill like I thine oaken staff full well to make it but well, so friends let us be."

"Ay, marry, then let us be," said the Tinker. "But, good youth, thy tongue runneth so nimbly that my poor and heavy wits can but ill follow it, so talk more plainly, I pray, for I am a plain man, forsooth."

"And whence comest thou, my lusty blade?" quoth Robin.

"I come from Banbury," answered the Tinker.

"Alas!" quoth Robin, "I hear there is sad news this merry morn."

"Ha! is it indeed so?" cried the Tinker, eagerly. "Prythee tell it speedily, for I am a tinker by trade, as thou seest, and as I am in my trade I am greedy for news, even as a priest is greedy for farthings."

"Well then," quoth Robin, "list thou and I will tell, but bear thyself up bravely, for the news is sad, I wot. Thus it is: I hear that two tinkers are in the stocks for drinking ale and beer!"

"Now a murrain seize thee and thy news, thou scurvy dog," quoth the Tinker, "for thou speakest but ill of good men. But sad news it is indeed, gin there be two stout fellows in the stocks."

"Nay," said Robin, "thou hast missed the mark and dost but weep for the wrong sow. The sadness of the news lieth in that there be but two in the stocks, for the others do roam the country at large."

"Now by the pewter platter of Saint Dunstan," cried the Tinker, "I have a good part of a mind to baste thy hide for thine ill jest. But gin men be put in the stocks for drinking ale and beer, I trow thou wouldst not lose thy part."

Loud laughed Robin and cried: "Now well taken, Tinker, well taken! Why, thy wits are like beer, and do froth up most when they grow sour! But right art thou, man, for I love ale and beer right well. Therefore come straightway with me hard by the sign of the Blue Boar, and if thou drinkest as thou appearest,—and I wot thou wilt not belie thy looks,—I will drench thy throat with as good homebrewed as ever was tapped in all broad Nottinghamshire."

"Now by my faith," said the Tinker, "thou art a right good fellow in spite of thy scurvy jests. I love thee, my sweet chuck, and gin I go not with thee to that same Blue Boar thou mayst call me a heathen Jew."

"Tell me thy news, good friend, I prythee," quoth Robin as they trudged along together, "for tinkers, I ween, are all as full of news as an egg of meat."

"Now I love thee as my brother, my bully blade," said the Tinker, "else I would not tell thee my news; for sly am I, man, and I have in hand a grave undertaking that doth call for all my wits, for I come to seek a bold outlaw that men, hereabouts, call Robin Hood. Within my pouch I have a warrant, all fairly written out on parchment, forsooth, with a great red seal for to make it lawful. Could I but meet this same Robin Hood I would serve it upon his dainty body, and if he minded it not I would beat him till every one of his ribs would cry Amen. But thou livest hereabouts, mayhap thou knowest Robin Hood thyself, good fellow."

"Ay, marry, that I do somewhat," quoth Robin, "and I have seen him this very morn. But, Tinker, men say that he is but a sad, sly thief. Thou hadst better watch thy warrant, man, or else he may steal it out of thy very pouch."

"Let him but try!" cried the Tinker. "Sly may he be, but sly am I, too. I would I had him here now, man to man!" And he made his heavy cudgel to spin again. "But what manner of man is he, lad?"

"Much like myself," said Robin, laughing, "and in height and build and age nigh the same; and he hath blue eyes, too, like mine."

"Nay," quoth the Tinker, "thou art but a green youth. I thought him to be a great bearded man, Nottingham men feared him so."

"Truly, he is not so old nor so stout as thou art," said Robin. "But men do call him a right deft hand at quarterstaff."

"That may be," said the Tinker, right sturdily; "but I am more deft than he, for did I not overcome Simon of Ely in a fair bout in the ring at Hertford Town? But if thou knowest him, my jolly blade, wilt thou go with me and bring me to him? Fourscore bright angels hath the Sheriff promised me if I serve the warrant upon the knave's body, and ten of them will I give to thee if thou showest me him."

"Ay, that will I," quoth Robin; "but show me thy warrant, man, until I see whether it be good or no."

"That will I not do, even to mine own brother," answered the Tinker. "No man shall see my warrant till I serve it upon yon fellow's own body."

"So be it," quoth Robin. "An thou show it not to me I know not to whom thou wilt show it. But here we are at the sign of the Blue Boar, so let us in and taste his brown October."

No sweeter inn could be found in all Nottinghamshire than that of the Blue Boar. None had such lovely trees standing around, or was so covered with trailing clematis and sweet woodbine; none had such good beer and such humming ale; nor, in winter time, when the north wind howled and snow drifted around the hedges, was there to be found, elsewhere, such a roaring fire as blazed upon the hearth of the Blue Boar. At such times might be found a goodly company of yeomen or country folk seated around the blazing hearth, bandying

merry jests, while roasted crabs* bobbed in bowls of ale upon the hearthstone. Well known was the inn to Robin Hood and his band, for there had he and such merry companions as Little John or Will Stutely or young David of Doncaster often gathered when all the forest was filled with snow. As for mine host, he knew how to keep a still tongue in his head, and to swallow his words before they passed his teeth, for he knew very well which side of his bread was spread with butter, for Robin and his band were the best of customers, and paid their scores without having them chalked up behind the door. So now, when Robin Hood and the Tinker came thereto and called aloud for two great pots of ale, none would have known from look or speech that the host had ever set eyes upon the outlaw before.

"Bide thou here," quoth Robin to the Tinker, "while I go and see that mine host draweth ale from the right butt, for he hath

* Small sour apples.

good October, I know, and that brewed by Withold of Tamworth." So saying, he went within and whispered to the host to add a measure of Flemish strong waters to the good English ale; which the latter did and brought it to them.

"By Our Lady," said the Tinker, after a long draught of the ale, "yon same Withold of Tamworth—a right good Saxon name, too, I would have thee know—breweth the most humming ale that e'er passed the lips of Wat o' the Crabstaff."

"Drink, man, drink," cried Robin, only wetting his own lips meanwhile. "Ho, landlord! bring my friend another pot of the same. And now for a song, my jolly blade."

"Ay, that will I give thee a song, my lovely fellow," quoth the Tinker, "for I never tasted such ale in all my days before. By'r Lady, it doth make my head hum even now! Hey, Dame Hostess, come listen, an thou wouldst hear a song; and thou too, thou bonny lass, for never sing I so well as when bright eyes do look upon me the while."

Then he sang an ancient ballad of the time of good King Arthur, called the Marriage of Sir Gawaine, which you may some time read, yourself, in stout English of early times; and as he sang, all listened to that noble tale of noble knight and his sacrifice to his king. But long before the Tinker came to the last verse his tongue began to trip and his head to spin, because of the strong waters mixed with the ale. First his tongue tripped, then it grew thick of sound; then his head wagged from side to side, until at last he fell asleep as though he never would waken again.

Then Robin Hood laughed aloud, and quickly took the warrant from out the Tinker's pouch with his deft fingers. "Sly art thou, Tinker," quoth he, "but not yet, I trow, art thou as sly as that same sly thief, Robin Hood."

Then he called the host to him and said, "Here, good man, are ten broad shillings for the entertainment thou hast given us this day. See that thou takest good care of thy fair guest there, and when he wakes thou mayst again charge him ten shillings also, and if he hath it not, thou mayst take his bag and hammer, and even his coat, in payment. Thus do I punish those that come into the greenwood to deal dole to me. As for thine own self, never knew I landlord yet that would not charge twice an he could."

At this the host smiled slyly, as though saying to himself the rustic saw, "Teach a magpie to suck eggs."

Then Tinker slept until the afternoon drew to a close and the shadows grew long beside the woodland edge, then he awoke. First he looked up, then he looked down, then he looked east, then he looked west, for he was gathering his wits together, like barley-straws blown apart by the wind. First he thought of his merry companion, but he was gone. Then he thought of his stout crabstaff, and that he had within his hand. Then of his warrant, and of the fourscore angels he was to gain for serving it upon Robin Hood. He thrust his hand into his pouch, but not a scrap nor a farthing was there. Then he sprang to his feet in a rage.

"Ho, landlord!" cried he, "whither hath that knave gone that was with me but now?"

"What knave meaneth your worship?" quoth the landlord, calling the Tinker worship to soothe him, as a man would pour oil upon angry water; "I saw no knave with your worship, for I swear no man would dare call that man knave so nigh to Sherwood Forest. A right stout yeoman I saw with your worship, but I thought that your worship knew him, for few there be about here that pass him by and know him not."

"Now, how should I, that ne'er have squealed in your sty, know all the swine therein? Who was he, then, an thou knowest him so well?"

"Why, yon same is a right stout fellow whom men hereabouts do call Robin Hood; which same"—

"Now, by'r Lady!" cried the Tinker hastily, and in a deep voice like an angry bull, "thou didst see me come into thine inn, I, a staunch, honest craftsman, and never told me who my company was, well knowing thine own self who he was. Now, I have a right round piece of a mind to crack thy knave's pate for thee!" Then he took up his cudgel and looked at the landlord as though he would smite him where he stood.

"Nay," cried the host, throwing up his elbow, for he feared the blow, "how knew I that thou knewest him not?"

"Well and truly thankful mayst thou be," quoth the Tinker, "that I be a patient man, and so do spare thy bald crown, else wouldst thou ne'er cheat customer again. But as for this same knave, Robin Hood, I go straightway to seek him, and if I do not score his knave's pate, cut my staff into fagots and call me woman." So saying, he gathered himself together to depart.

"Nay," quoth the landlord, standing in front of him and holding out his arms like a gooseherd driving his flock, for money made him bold, "thou goest not till thou hast paid me my score."

"But did not he pay thee?"

"Not so much as one farthing; and ten good shillings' worth of ale have ye drunk this day. Nay, I say, thou goest not away without paying me, else shall our good sheriff know of it."

"But nought have I to pay thee with, good fellow," quoth the Tinker.

"'Good fellow' not me," said the landlord. "Good fellow am
I not when it cometh to lose ten shillings! Pay me that thou
owest me in broad money, or else leave thy coat and bag and
hammer; yet, I wot they are not worth ten shillings, and I shall
lose thereby. Nay, an thou stirrest, I have a great dog within
and I will loose him upon thee. Maken, open thou the door
and let forth Brian if this fellow stirs one step."

"Nay," quoth the Tinker,—for, by roaming the country, he had
learned what dogs were,—"take thou what thou wilt have, and
let me depart in peace, and may a murrain go with thee. But
oh, landlord! an I catch yon scurvy varlet, I swear he shall
pay full with usury for that he hath had!"

So saying, he strode away toward the forest, talking to himself, while the landlord and his worthy dame and Maken stood
looking after him, and laughed when he had fairly gone.

"Robin and I stripped yon ass of his pack main neatly," quoth the landlord.

Now it happened about this time that Robin Hood was going through the forest to Foss Way, to see what was to be seen there, for the moon was full and the night gave promise of being bright. In his hand he carried his stout oaken staff, and at his side hung his bugle horn. As thus he walked up a forest path, whistling, down another path came the Tinker, muttering to himself and shaking his head like an angry bull; and so, at a sudden bend, they met sharply face to face. Each stood still for a time, and then Robin spoke:—

"Halloa, my sweet bird," said he, laughing merrily, "how likest thou thine ale? Wilt not sing to me another song?"

The Tinker said nothing at first, but stood looking at Robin with a grim face. "Now," quoth he at last, "I am right glad I have met thee, and if I do not rattle thy bones within thy hide this day, I give thee leave to put thy foot upon my neck."

"With all my heart," cried merry Robin; "rattle my bones, an thou canst." So saying, he gripped his staff and threw himself upon his guard. Then the Tinker spat upon his hands, and, grasping his staff, came straight at the other. He struck two or three blows, but soon found that he had met his match, for Robin warded and parried all of them, and, before the Tinker thought, he gave him a rap upon the ribs in return. At this Robin laughed aloud, and the Tinker grew more angry than ever, and smote again with all his might and main. Again Robin warded two of the strokes, but at the third, his staff broke beneath the mighty blows of the Tinker. "Now, ill betide thee, traitor staff," cried Robin, as it fell from his hands; "a foul stick art thou to serve me thus in mine hour of need."

"Now yield thee," quoth the Tinker, "for thou art my captive; and if thou do not, I will beat thy pate to a pudding."

To this Robin Hood made no answer, but, clapping his horn to his lips, he blew three blasts, loud and clear.

"Ay," quoth the Tinker, "blow thou mayest, but go thou must with me to Nottingham Town, for the Sheriff would fain see thee there. Now wilt thou yield thee, or shall I have to break thy pretty head?"

"An I must drink sour ale, I must," quoth Robin; "but never have I yielded me to man before, and that without wound or mark upon my body. Nor, when I bethink me, will I yield now. Ho, my merry men! come quickly!"

Then from out the forest leaped Little John and six stout yeomen clad in Lincoln green.

"How now, good master," cried Little John, "what need hast thou that thou dost wind thy horn so loudly?"

"There stands a tinker," quoth Robin, "that would fain take me to Nottingham, there to hang upon the gallows tree."

THEN the Sheriff was very wroth because of this failure to take jolly Robin, for it came to his ears, as ill news always does, that the people laughed at him and made a jest of his thinking to serve a warrant upon such a one as the bold outlaw; and a man hates nothing so much as being made a jest of; so he said: "Our gracious Lord and Sovereign King himself shall know of this, and how his laws are perverted and despised by this band of rebel outlaws. As for yon traitor Tinker, him will I hang, if I catch him, upon the very highest gallows tree in all Nottinghamshire."

Then he bade all his servants and retainers to make ready to go to London Town, to see and speak with the King.

At this there was bustling at the Sheriff's castle, and men ran hither and thither upon this business and upon that, while the forge fires of Nottingham glowed red far into the night like twinkling stars, for all the smiths of the town were busy making or mending armor for the Sheriff's troop of escort. For two days this labor lasted, then, on the third, all was ready for the journey. So forth they started in the bright sunlight, from Nottingham Town to Fosse Way and thence to Watling Street; and so they journeyed for two days, until they saw at last the spires and towers of great London Town; and many folks stopped, as they journeyed along, and gazed at the show they made riding along the highways with their flashing armor, and gay plumes and trappings.

In London King Henry and his fair Queen Eleanor held their court, gay with ladies in silks and satins and velvets and cloth of gold, and also brave knights and gallant courtiers.

Thither came the Sheriff and was shown into the King's presence.

"A boon, a boon," quoth he, as he knelt upon the ground.

"Now what wouldst thou have?" said the King. "Let us hear what may be thy desires."

"O good my Lord and Sovereign," spake the Sheriff, "in Sherwood Forest in our own good shire of Nottingham, liveth a bold outlaw whose name is Robin Hood."

"In good sooth," said the King, "his doings have reached even our own royal ears. He is a saucy, rebellious varlet, yet, I am fain to own, a right merry soul withal."

"But hearken, O my most gracious Sovereign," said the Sheriff. "I sent a warrant to him with thine own royal seal attached, by a right lusty knave, but he beat the messenger and stole the warrant. And he killeth thy deer and robbeth thine own liege subjects even upon the great highways."

"Why, how now," quoth the King, wrathfully. "What wouldst thou have me do? Comest thou not to me with a great array of men-at-arms and retainers, and yet art not able to take a single band of lusty knaves without armor on breast, in thine own county! What wouldst thou have me do? Art thou not my Sheriff? Are not my laws in force in Nottinghamshire? Canst thou not take thine own course against those that break the laws or do any injury to thee or thine? Go, get thee gone, and think well; devise some plan of thine own but trouble me no further. But look well to it, master Sheriff, for I will have my laws obeyed by all men within my kingdom, and if thou art not able to enforce them thou art no sheriff for me. So look well to thyself, I say, or ill may befall thee as well as all the thieving knaves in Nottinghamshire. When the flood cometh it sweepeth away grain as well as chaff."

Then the Sheriff turned away with a sore and troubled heart, and sadly he rued his fine show of retainers, for he saw that the King was angry because he had so many men about him and yet could not enforce the laws. So, as they all rode slowly back to Nottingham, the Sheriff was thoughtful and full of care. Not a word did he speak to any one, and no one of his men spoke to him, but all the time he was busy devising some plan to take Robin Hood.

"Aha!" cried he suddenly, smiting his hand upon his thigh, "I have it now! Ride on, my merry men all, and let us get back to Nottingham Town as speedily as we may. And mark well my words: before a fortnight is passed, that evil knave, Robin Hood, will be safely clapped into Nottingham gaol."

But what was the Sheriff's plan?

As a Jew takes each one of a bag of silver angels, feeling each coin to find whether it be clipped or not, so the Sheriff, as all rode slowly and sadly back toward Nottingham, took up thought after thought in turn, feeling around the edges of each but finding in every one some flaw. At last he thought of the daring soul of jolly Robin and how, as he the Sheriff knew, he often came even within the walls of Nottingham.

"Now," thought the Sheriff, "could I but persuade Robin nigh to Nottingham Town so that I could find him, I warrant I would lay hands upon him so stoutly that he would never get away again." Then of a sudden it came to him like a flash that were he to proclaim a great shooting-match and offer some grand prize, Robin Hood might be over-persuaded by his spirit to come to the butts; and it was this thought which caused him to cry "Aha!" and smite his palm upon his thigh.

So, as soon as he had returned safely to Nottingham, he sent messengers north and south, and east and west, to proclaim through town, hamlet, and countryside, this grand shooting-match, and every one was bidden that could draw a long bow, and the prize was to be an arrow of pure beaten gold.

When Robin Hood first heard the news of this he was in Lincoln Town, and hastening back to Sherwood Forest he soon called all his merry men about him and spoke to them thus:—

"Now hearken, my merry men all, to the news that I have brought from Lincoln Town to-day. Our friend the Sheriff of Nottingham hath proclaimed a shooting-match, and hath sent messengers to tell of it through all the countryside, and the prize is to be a bright golden arrow. Now I fain would have one of us win it, both because of the fairness of the prize and because our sweet friend the Sheriff hath offered it. So we will take our bows and shafts and go there to shoot, for I know right well that merriment will be a-going. What say ye, lads?"

Then young David of Doncaster spoke up and said: "Now listen, I pray thee, good master, unto what I say. I have come straight from our friend Eadom o' the Blue Boar, and there I heard the full news of this same match. But, master, I know from him, and he got it from the Sheriff's man Ralph o' the Scar, that this same knavish Sheriff hath but laid a trap for thee in this shooting-match and wishes nothing so much as to see thee there. So go not, good master, for I know right well he doth seek to beguile thee, but stay within the greenwood lest we all meet dole and woe."

"Now," quoth Robin, "thou art a wise lad and keepest thine ears open and thy mouth shut, as becometh a wise and crafty woodsman. But shall we let it be said that the Sheriff of Nottingham did cow bold Robin Hood and sevenscore as fair archers as are in all merry England? Nay, good David, what thou tellest me maketh me to desire the prize even more than I else should do. But what sayeth our good gossip Swanthold? is it not 'A hasty man burneth his mouth, and the fool that keepeth his eyes shut falleth into the pit'? Thus he says, truly, therefore we must meet guile with guile. Now some of you clothe yourselves as curtal friars, and some as rustic peasants, and some as tinkers, or as beggars, but see that each man taketh a good bow or broadsword, in case need should arise. As for myself, I will shoot for this same golden arrow, and should I win it, we will hang it to the branches of our good greenwood tree for the joy of all the band. How like you the plan, my merry men all?"

Then "good, good!" cried all the band right heartily.

A fair sight was Nottingham Town on the day of the shooting-match. All along upon the green meadow beneath the town wall stretched a row of benches, one above the other, which were for knight and lady, squire and dame, and rich burghers and their wives; for none but those of rank and quality were to sit there. At the end of the range, near the target, was a raised seat bedecked with ribbons and scarfs and garlands of flowers, for the Sheriff of Nottingham and his dame. The range was two-score paces broad. At one end stood the target, at the other a tent of striped canvas, from the pole of which fluttered many-colored flags and streamers. In this booth were casks of ale, free to be broached by any of the archers who might wish to quench their thirst.

Across the range from where the seats for the better folk were raised was a railing to keep the poorer people from crowding in front of the target. Already, while it was early, the benches were beginning to fill with people of quality, who kept constantly arriving in little carts, or upon palfreys that curveted gayly to the merry tinkle of silver bells at bridle reins; with these came also the poorer folk, who sat or lay upon the green grass near the railing that kept them from off the range. In the great tent the

archers were gathering by twos and threes; some talking loudly
of the fair shots each man had made in his day; some looking
well to their bows, drawing a string betwixt the fingers to see
that there was no fray upon it, or inspecting arrows, shutting one
eye and peering down a shaft to see that it was not warped, but
straight and true, for neither bow nor shaft should fail at such
a time and for such a prize. And never were such a company of
yeomen as were gathered at Nottingham Town that day, for the
very best archers of merry England had come to this shooting-
match. There was Gill o' the Red Cap, the Sheriff's own head
archer, and Diccon Cruikshank of Lincoln Town, and Adam
o' the Dell, a man of Tamworth, of threescore years and more,
yet hale and lusty still, who in his time had shot in the famous
match at Woodstock, and had there beaten that renowned
archer, Clym o' the Clough. And many more famous men of
the long bow were there, whose names have been handed down
to us in goodly ballads of the olden time.

But now all the benches were filled with guests, lord and lady,
burgher and dame, when at last the Sheriff himself came with
his lady, he riding with stately mien upon his milk-white horse
and she upon her brown filly. Upon his head he wore a purple
velvet cap, and purple velvet was his robe, all trimmed about
with rich ermine; his jerkin and hose were of sea-green silk, and
his shoes of black velvet, the pointed toes fastened to his garters
with golden chains. A golden chain hung about his neck, and
at his collar was a great carbuncle set in red gold. His lady was
dressed in blue velvet, all trimmed with swan's down. So they
made a gallant sight as they rode along side by side, and all
the people shouted from where they crowded across the space
from the gentlefolk; so the Sheriff and his lady came to their
place, where men-at-arms, with hauberk and spear, stood about,
waiting for them.

Then when the Sheriff and his dame had sat down, he bade
his herald wind upon his silver horn; who thereupon sounded
three blasts that came echoing cheerily back from the gray walls
of Nottingham. Then the archers stepped forth to their places,
while all the folks shouted with a mighty voice, each man calling upon his favorite yeoman. "Red Cap!" cried some; "Cruikshank!" cried others; "Hey for William o' Leslie!" shouted others

yet again; while ladies waved silken scarfs to urge each yeoman
to do his best.

Then the herald stood forth and loudly proclaimed the rules
of the game as follows:—

"Shoot each man from yon mark, which is sevenscore yards and
ten from the target. One arrow shooteth each man first, and
from all the archers shall the ten that shooteth the fairest shafts
be chosen for to shoot again. Two arrows shooteth each man
of these ten, then shall the three that shoot the fairest shafts
be chosen for to shoot again. Three arrows shooteth each man of
those three, and to him that shooteth the fairest shafts shall the
prize be given."

Then the Sheriff leaned forward, looking keenly among the
press of archers to find whether Robin Hood was amongst them;
but no one was there clad in Lincoln green, such as was worn
by Robin and his band. "Nevertheless," said the Sheriff to himself, "he may still be there, and I miss him among the crowd
of other men. But let me see when but ten men shoot, for I wot
he will be among the ten, or I know him not."

And now the archers shot, each man in turn, and the good
folk never saw such archery as was done that day. Six arrows
were within the clout, four within the black, and only two smote
the outer ring; so that when the last arrow sped and struck the
target, all the people shouted aloud, for it was noble shooting.

And now but ten men were left of all those that had shot before, and of these ten, six were famous throughout the land, and
most of the folk gathered there knew them. These six men were
Gilbert o' the Red Cap, Adam o' the Dell, Diccon Cruikshank,
William o' Leslie, Hubert o' Cloud, and Swithin, o' Hertford.
Two others were yeomen of merry Yorkshire, another was a tall
stranger in blue, who said he came from London Town, and the
last was a tattered stranger in scarlet, who wore a patch over
one eye.

"Now," quoth the Sheriff to a man-at-arms who stood near
him, "seest thou Robin Hood amongst those ten?"

"Nay, that do I not, your worship," answered the man. "Six of
them I know right well. Of those Yorkshire yeomen, one is too
tall and the other too short for that bold knave. Robin's beard
is as yellow as gold, while yon tattered beggar in scarlet hath

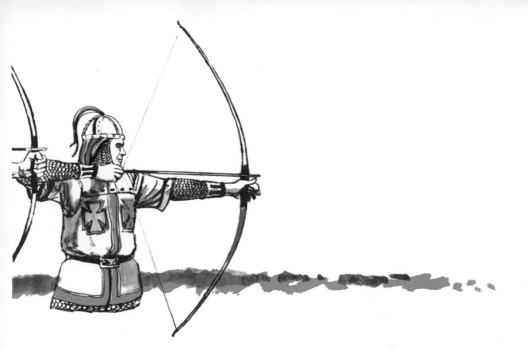

a beard of brown, besides being blind of one eye. As for the stranger in blue, Robin's shoulders, I ween, are three inches broader than his."

"Then," quoth the Sheriff, smiting his thigh angrily, "yon knave is a coward as well as a rogue, and dares not show his face among good men and true."

Then, after they had rested a short time, those ten stout men stepped forth to shoot again. Each man shot two arrows, and as they shot, not a word was spoken, but all the crowd watched with scarce a breath of sound; but when the last had shot his arrow another great shout arose, while many cast their caps aloft for joy of such marvellous shooting.

"Now by our gracious Lady fair," quoth old Sir Amyas o' the Dell, who, bowed with fourscore years and more, sat near the Sheriff, "ne'er saw I such archery in all my life before, yet have I seen the best hands at the long bow for threescore years and more."

And now but three men were left of all those that had shot before. One was Gill o' the Red Cap, one the tattered stranger in scarlet, and one Adam o' the Dell of Tamworth Town. Then all the people called aloud, some crying, "Ho for Gilbert o' the Red Cap!" and some, "Hey for stout Adam o' Tamworth!" but not a single man in the crowd called upon the stranger in scarlet.

"Now, shoot thou well, Gilbert," cried the Sheriff, "and if thine

be the best shaft, fivescore broad silver pennies will I give to thee beside the prize."

"Truly I will do my best," quoth Gilbert, right sturdily. "A man cannot do aught but his best, but that will I strive to do this day." So saying, he drew forth a fair smooth arrow with a broad feather and fitted it deftly to the string, then drawing his bow with care he sped the shaft. Straight flew the arrow and lit fairly in the clout, a finger breadth from the centre. "A Gilbert, a Gilbert!" shouted all the crowd; and, "Now, by my faith," cried the Sheriff, smiting his hands together, "that is a shrewd shot."

Then the tattered stranger stepped forth, and all the people laughed as they saw a yellow patch that showed beneath his arm when he raised his elbow to shoot, and also to see him aim with but one eye. He drew the good yew bow quickly, and quickly loosed a shaft; so short was the time that no man could draw a breath betwixt the drawing and the shooting; yet his arrow lodged nearer the centre than the other by twice the length of a barleycorn.

"Now by all the saints in Paradise!" cried the Sheriff, "that is a lovely shaft in very truth!"

Then Adam o' the Dell shot, carefully and cautiously, and his arrow lodged close beside the stranger's. Then after a short space they all three shot again, and once more each arrow lodged within the clout, but this time Adam o' the Dell's was farthest from the centre, and again the tattered stranger's shot was the best. Then, after another time of rest, they all shot for the third time. This time Gilbert took great heed to his aim, keenly measuring the distance and shooting with shrewdest care. Straight flew the arrow, and all shouted till the very flags that waved in the breeze shook with the sound, and the rooks and daws flew clamoring about the roofs of the old gray tower, for the shaft had lodged close beside the spot that marked the very centre.

"Well done, Gilbert!" cried the Sheriff, right joyously. "Fain am I to believe the prize is thine, and right fairly won. Now, thou ragged knave, let me see thee shoot a better shaft than that."

Naught spake the stranger but took his place, while all was hushed, and no one spoke or even seemed to breathe, so great was the silence for wonder what he would do. Meanwhile, also, quite still stood the stranger holding his bow in his hand, while one could count five; then he drew his trusty yew, holding it drawn but a moment, then loosed the string. Straight flew the arrow, and so true that it smote a gray goose feather from off Gilbert's shaft, which fell fluttering through the sunlit air as the stranger's arrow lodged close beside his of the Red Cap, and in the very centre. No one spoke a word for a while and no one shouted, but each man looked into his neighbor's face amazedly.

"Nay," quoth old Adam o' the Dell presently, drawing a long breath and shaking his head as he spoke; "twoscore years and more have I shot shaft, and maybe not all times bad, but I shoot no more this day, for no man can match with yon stranger, whosoe'er he may be." Then he thrust his shaft into his quiver, rattling, and unstrung his bow without another word.

Then the Sheriff came down from his dais and drew near, in all his silks and velvets, to where the tattered stranger stood leaning upon his stout bow, whilst the good folk crowded around to see the man who shot so wondrously well. "Here, good fellow," quoth the Sheriff, "take thou the prize, and well and fairly hast thou won it, I trow. What may be thy name, and whence comest thou?"

"Men do call be Jock o' Teviotdale, and thence am I come," said the stranger.

"Then, by Our Lady, Jock, thou art the fairest archer that e'er mine eyes beheld, and if thou wilt join my service I will clothe thee with a better coat than that thou hast upon thy back; thou shalt eat and drink of the best, and at every Christmas-tide fourscore marks shall be thy wage. I trow thou drawest better bow than that same coward knave, Robin Hood, that dared not show his face here this day. Say, good fellow, wilt thou join my service?"

"Nay, that will I not," quoth the stranger, roughly. "I will be mine own, and no man in all merry England shall be my master."

"Then get thee gone, and a murrain seize thee!" cried the Sheriff, and his voice trembled with anger. "And by my faith and troth I have a good part of a mind to have thee beaten for thine insolence!" Then he turned upon his heel and strode away.

It was a right motley company that gathered about the noble greenwood tree in Sherwood's depths that same day. A score and more of barefoot friars were there, and some that looked like tinkers, and some that seemed to be sturdy beggars and rustic hinds; and seated upon a mossy couch was one all clad in tattered scarlet, with a patch over one eye; and in his hand he held the golden arrow that was the prize of the great shooting-match. Then, amidst a noise of talking and laughter, he took the patch from off his eye and stripped away the scarlet rags from off his body and showed himself all clothed in fair Lincoln green, and quoth he: "Easy come these things away, but walnut stain cometh not so speedily from yellow hair." Then all laughed louder than before, for it was Robin Hood himself that had won the prize from the Sheriff's very hands.

Then all sat down to the woodland feast and talked amongst themselves of the merry jest that had been played upon the Sheriff, and of the adventures that had befallen each member of the band in his disguise. But when the feast was done, Robin Hood took Little John apart and said, "Truly am I vexed in my blood, for I heard the Sheriff say to-day, 'Thou shootest better than that coward knave, Robin Hood, that dared not show his face here this day.' I would fain let him know who it was who won the golden arrow from out his hand, and also that I am no coward such as he takes me to be."

Then Little John said, "Good master, take thou me and Will Stutely and we will send yon fat Sheriff news of all this by a messenger such as he doth not expect."

That day the Sheriff sat at meat in the great hall of his house at Nottingham Town. Long tables stood down the hall, at which sat men-at-arms and household servants and good stout villains,* in all fourscore and more. There they talked of the day's shooting as they ate their meat and quaffed their ale. The Sheriff sat at the head of the table upon a raised seat under a canopy, and beside him sat his dame.

"By my troth," said he, "I did reckon full roundly that that knave, Robin Hood, would be at the game to-day. I did not think that he was such a coward. But who could that saucy knave be

---

* Bond-servants.

who answered me to my beard so bravely? I wonder that I did not have him beaten; but there was something about him that spoke of other things than rags and tatters."

Then, even as he finished speaking, something fell rattling among the dishes on the table, while those that sat near started up wondering what it might be. After a while one of the men-at-arms gathered courage enough to pick it up and bring it to the Sheriff. Then every one saw that it was a blunted gray goose shaft, with a fine scroll, about the thickness of a goose quill, tied near to its head. The Sheriff opened the scroll and glanced at it, while the veins upon his forehead swelled and his cheeks grew ruddy with rage as he read, for this was what he saw:—

> "Now Heaven bless thy grace this day,
>   Say all in sweet Sherwood,
> For thou didst give the prize away
>   To merry Robin Hood."

"Whence came this?" cried the Sheriff in a mighty voice.

"Even through the window, your worship," quoth the man who had handed the shaft to him.

Now when the Sheriff found that neither law nor guile could overcome Robin Hood, he was much perplexed, and said to himself, "Fool that I am! Had I not told our King of Robin Hood, I would not have gotten myself into such a coil; but now I must either take him captive or have wrath visited upon my head from his most gracious Majesty. I have tried law, and I have tried guile, and I have failed in both; so I will try what may be done with might."

Thus communing within himself, he called his constables together and told them what was in his mind. "Now take ye each four men, all armed in proof," said he, "and get ye gone to the forest, at different points, and lie in wait for this same Robin Hood. But if any constable finds too many men against him, let him sound a horn, and then let each band within hearing come with all speed and join the party that calls them. Thus, I think, shall we take this green-clad knave. Furthermore, to him that first meeteth with Robin Hood shall one hundred pounds of silver money be given, if he be brought to me, dead or alive;

and to him that meeteth with any of his band shall twoscore pounds be given, if such be brought to me dead or alive. So, be ye bold and be ye crafty."

So thus they went in threescore companies of five to Sherwood Forest, to take Robin Hood, each constable wishing that he might be the one to find the bold outlaw, or at least one of his band. For seven days and nights they hunted through the forest glades, but never saw so much as a single man in Lincoln green; for tidings of all this had been brought to Robin Hood by trusty Eadom o' the Blue Boar.

When he first heard the news, Robin said, "If the Sheriff dare send force to meet force, woe will it be for him and many a better man beside, for blood will flow, and there will be great trouble for all. But fain would I shun blood and battle, and fain would I not deal sorrow to women folk and wives because good stout yeomen lose their lives. Once I slew a man, and never do I wish to slay a man again, for it is bitter for the soul to think thereon. So now we will abide silently in Sherwood Forest, so that it may be well for all; but should we be forced to defend ourselves, or any of our band, then let each man draw bow and brand with might and main."

At this speech many of the band shook their heads, and said to themselves, "Now the Sheriff will think that we are cowards, and folk will scoff throughout the countryside, saying that we fear to meet these men." But they said nothing aloud, swallowing their words, and doing as Robin bade them.

Thus they hid in the depths of Sherwood Forest for seven days and seven nights, and never showed their faces abroad in all that time; but early in the morning of the eighth day Robin Hood called the band together and said, "Now who will go and find what the Sheriff's men are at by this time? for I know right well they will not bide forever within Sherwood shades."

At this a great shout arose, and each man waved his bow aloft and cried that he might be the one to go. Then Robin Hood's heart was proud when he looked around on his stout, brave fellows, and he said, "Brave and true are ye all, my merry men, a right stout band of good fellows are ye; but ye cannot all go, so I will choose one from amongst you, and it shall be good Will Stutely, for he is as sly as e'er an old dog fox in Sherwood Forest."

Then Will Stutely leaped high aloft and laughed loudly, clapping his hands for pure joy that he should have been chosen from amongst them all. "Now thanks, good master," quoth he, "and if I bring not news of those knaves to thee, call me no more thy sly Will Stutely."

Then he clad himself in a friar's gown, and underneath the robe he hung a good broadsword in such a place that he could easily lay hands upon it. Thus clad, he set forth upon his quest, until he came to the verge of the forest, and so to the highway. He saw two bands of the Sheriff's men, yet he turned neither to the right nor the left, but only drew his cowl the closer over his face, folding his hands as if in meditation. So at last he came to the Sign of the Blue Boar. "For," quoth he to himself, "our good friend Eadom will tell me all the news."

At the Sign of the Blue Boar he found a band of the Sheriff's men drinking right lustily; so, without speaking to any one, he sat down upon a distant bench, his staff in his hand, and his head bowed forward as though he were meditating. Thus he sat waiting until he might see the landlord apart, and Eadom did not know him, but thought him to be some poor tired friar, so he let him sit without saying a word to him or molesting him, though he liked not the cloth; "for," said he to himself, "it is a hard heart that kicks the lame dog from off the sill."

As Stutely sat thus, there came a great house cat and rubbed against his knee, raising his robe a palm's breadth high. Stutely pushed his robe quickly down again, but the constable who commanded the Sheriff's men saw what had passed, and saw also fair Lincoln green beneath the friar's robe. He said nothing at the time, but communed within himself in this wise: "Yon is no friar of orders gray, and also, I wot, no honest yeoman goeth about in priest's garb, nor doth a thief go so for naught. Now I think in good sooth that is one of Robin Hood's own men." So, presently, he said aloud:—

"O holy father, wilt thou not take a good pot of March beer to slake thy thirsty soul withal?" But Stutely shook his head silently, for he said to himself, "Maybe there be those here who know my voice."

Then the constable said again, "Whither goest thou, holy friar, upon this hot summer's day?"

"I go a pilgrim to Canterbury Town," answered Will Stutely, speaking gruffly, so that none might know his voice.

Then the constable said, for the third time, "Now tell me, holy father, do pilgrims to Canterbury wear good Lincoln green beneath their robes? Ha! by my faith, I take thee to be some lusty thief, and perhaps one of Robin Hood's own band! Now, by Our Lady's grace, if thou movest hand or foot, I will run thee through the body with my sword!"

Then he flashed forth his bright sword and leaped upon Will Stutely, thinking he would take him unaware; but Stutely had his own sword tightly held in his hand, beneath his robe, so he drew it forth before the constable came upon him. Then the stout constable struck a mighty blow; but he struck no more in all that fight, for Stutely, parrying the blow right deftly, smote the constable back again with all his might. Then he would have escaped, but could not, for the other, all dizzy with the wound and with the flowing blood, seized him by the knees with his arms even as he reeled and fell. Then the others rushed upon him, and Stutely struck again at another of the Sheriff's men, but the steel cap glanced the blow, and though the blade bit deep, it did not kill. Meanwhile, the constable, fainting as he was, drew Stutely downward, and the others, seeing the yeoman hampered so, rushed upon him again, and one smote him a blow upon the crown so that the blood ran down his face and blinded him. Then, staggering, he fell, and all sprang upon him, though he struggled so manfully that they could hardly hold him fast. Then they bound him with stout hempen cords so that he could not move either hand or foot, and thus they overcame him. But it was a doleful day's doings for two of that band; for the constable was sorely wounded, and the other, that Stutely smote upon the crown, lay sick for many a day ere he was the stout man that he had been before this famous fight.

Robin Hood stood under the greenwood tree, thinking of Will Stutely and how he might be faring, when suddenly he saw two of his stout yeomen come running down the forest path, and betwixt them ran buxom Maken of the Blue Boar. Then Robin's heart fell, for he knew they were the bearers of ill tidings.

"Will Stutely hath been taken," cried they, when they had come to where he stood.

"And is it thou that hast brought such doleful news?" said Robin to the lass.

"Ay, marry, for I saw it all," cried she, panting as the hare pants when it has escaped the hounds; "and I fear he is wounded sore, for one smote him main shrewdly i' the crown. They have bound him and taken him to Nottingham Town, and ere I left the Blue Boar I heard that he should be hanged to-morrow day."

"He shall not be hanged to-morrow day," cried Robin; "or, if he be, full many a one shall gnaw the sod, and many shall have cause to cry Alack-a-day!"

Then he clapped his horn to his lips and blew three blasts right loudly, and presently his good yeomen came running through the greenwood until sevenscore bold blades were gathered around him.

"Now hark you all!" cried Robin. "Our dear companion, Will Stutely, hath been taken by the vile Sheriff's men, therefore doth it behoove us to take bow and brand in hand to bring him off again; for I wot that we ought to risk life and limb for him, as he hath risked life and limb for us. Is it not so, my merry men all?" Then all cried, "Ay!" with a great voice.

"Now," quoth Robin again, "if there be any here that care not to risk life and limb, let them bide within Sherwood shades, for I constrain no man to my will; but to-morrow I will bring Will Stutely back or I will die with him."

Then up spake stout Little John. "Thinkest thou, good master," he said, "that there be one among us all that would not risk life and limb for fellow in trouble? If such there be, then do not I know every man in this company of stout yeomen. And, moreover, if there be such, I wot he should be stripped and beaten from out our merry woodlands. Is it not so, good friends?"

Then all cried, "Ay!" again, for there was not one man amongst them all that would not venture everything for a friend in need.

So the next day they all wended their way from Sherwood Forest, but by different paths, for it behooved them to be very crafty; so the band separated into parties of twos and threes, which were all to meet again in a tangled dell that lay near to Nottingham Town. Then, when they had all gathered together at the place of meeting, Robin spoke to them thus:—

"Now we will lie here in ambush until we can get news, for it doth behoove us to be cunning and wary if we would bring our friend, Will Stutely, off from the Sheriff's clutches."

So they lay hidden a long time, until the sun stood high in the sky. The day was warm and the dusty road was bare of travellers, except an aged palmer who walked slowly along the highroad that led close beside the gray castle wall of Nottingham Town. When Robin saw that no other wayfarer was within sight, he called young David of Doncaster, who was a shrewd man for his years, and said to him, "Now get thee forth, young David, and speak to yonder palmer that walks beside the town wall, for he hath come but now from Nottingham Town, and may tell thee news of good Stutely, perchance."

So David strode forth, and when he came up to the pilgrim, he saluted him and said: "Good morrow, holy father, and canst thou tell me when Will Stutely will be hanged upon the gallows tree? I fain would not miss the sight, for I have come from afar to see so sturdy a rogue hanged."

"Now, out upon thee, young man," cried the Palmer, "that thou shouldst speak so when a good stout man is to be hanged for nothing but guarding his own life!" and he struck his staff upon the ground in anger. "Alas, say I, that this thing should be! for even this day, toward evening, when the sun falleth low, he shall be hanged, fourscore rods from the great town gate of Nottingham, where three roads meet; for there the Sheriff sweareth he shall die as a warning to all outlaws in Nottinghamshire. But yet, I say again, Alas! for, though Robin Hood and his band may be outlaws, yet he taketh only from the rich and the strong and the dishonest man, while there is not a poor widow nor a peasant with many children, nigh to Sherwood, but has barley-flour enough all the year long through him. It grieves my heart to see one as gallant as this Stutely die, for I have been a good Saxon yeoman in my day, ere I turned palmer, and well I know a stout hand and one that smiteth shrewdly at a cruel Norman or a proud abbot with fat money-bags. Had good Stutely's master but known how his man was compassed about with perils, perchance he might send succor to bring him out of the hand of his enemies."

"Ay, marry, that is true," cried the young man. "If Robin and his men be nigh this place, I wot right well they will strive to bring him forth from his peril. But fare thee well, thou good old man, and believe me, that, if Will Stutely die, he shall be right well avenged."

Then he turned and strode rapidly away; but the Palmer looked after him, muttering, "I wot that youth is no country hind that hath come to see a good man die. Well, well, perchance Robin Hood is not so far away but that there will be stout doings this day." So he went upon his way, muttering to himself.

When David of Doncaster told Robin Hood what the Palmer had said to him, Robin called the band around him and spoke to them thus: "Now let us get straightway into Nottingham Town, and mix ourselves with the people there; but keep ye one another in sight, pressing as near the prisoner and his guards as ye can, when they come outside the walls. Strike no man without need, for I would fain avoid bloodshed, but if ye do strike, strike hard, and see that there be no need to strike again. Then keep all together until we come again to Sherwood, and let no man leave his fellows."

The sun was low in the western sky when a bugle note sounded from the castle wall. Then all was bustle in Nottingham Town and crowds filled the streets, for all knew that the famous Will Stutely was to be hanged that day. Presently the castle gates opened wide and a great array of men-at-arms came forth with noise and clatter, the Sheriff, all clad in shining mail of linked chain, riding at their head. In the midst of all the guard, in a cart, with a halter about his neck, rode Will Stutely. His face was pale with his wound and with loss of blood, like the moon in broad daylight, and his fair hair was clotted in points upon his forehead, where the blood had hardened. When he came forth from the castle he looked up and he looked down, but though he saw some faces that showed pity and some that showed friendliness, he saw none that he knew. Then his heart sank within him like a plummet of lead, but nevertheless he spoke up boldly.

"Give a sword into my hand, Sir Sheriff," said he, "and wounded man though I be, I will fight thee and all thy men till life and strength be gone."

"Nay, thou naughty varlet," quoth the Sheriff, turning his head and looking right grimly upon Will Stutely, "thou shalt have no sword but shall die a mean death, as beseemeth a vile thief like thee."

"Then do but untie my hands and I will fight thee and thy men with no weapon but only my naked fists. I crave no weapon, but let me not be meanly hanged this day."

Then the Sheriff laughed aloud. "Why, how now," quoth he, "is thy proud stomach quailing? Shrive thyself, thou vile knave, for I mean that thou shalt hang this day, and that where three roads meet, so that all men shall see thee hang, for carrion crows and daws to peck at."

"O thou dastard heart!" cried Will Stutely, gnashing his teeth at the Sheriff. "Thou coward hind! If ever my good master meet thee thou shalt pay dearly for this day's work! He doth scorn thee, and so do all brave hearts. Knowest thou not that thou and thy name are jests upon the lips of every brave yeoman? Such a one as thou art, thou wretched craven, will never be able to subdue bold Robin Hood."

"Ha!" cried the Sheriff, in a rage, "is it even so? Am I a jest with thy master, as thou callest him? Now I will make a jest of thee and a sorry jest withal, for I will quarter thee limb from limb, after thou art hanged." Then he spurred his horse forward, and said no more to Stutely.

At last they came to the great town gate, through which Stutely saw the fair country beyond, with hills and dales all clothed in verdure, and far away the dusky line of Sherwood's skirts. Then when he saw the slanting sunlight lying on field and fallow, shining redly here and there on cot and farmhouse, and when he heard the sweet birds singing their vespers, and the sheep bleating upon the hillside, and beheld the swallows flying in the bright air, there came a great fulness to his heart so that all things blurred to his sight through salt tears, and he bowed his head lest the folk should think him unmanly when they saw the tears in his eyes. Thus he kept his head bowed till they had passed through the gate and were outside the walls of the town. But when he looked up again he felt his heart leap within him and then stand still for pure joy, for he saw the face of one of his own dear companions of merry Sherwood; then glancing quickly around he saw well-known faces upon all sides of him, crowding closely upon the men-at-arms who were guarding him. Then of a sudden the blood sprang to his cheeks, for he saw for a moment his own good master in the press, and, seeing him, knew that Robin Hood and all his band were there. Yet betwixt him and them was a line of men-at-arms.

"Now, stand back!" cried the Sheriff in a mighty voice, for the crowd pressed around on all sides. "What mean ye, varlets, that ye push upon us so? Stand back, I say!"

Then came a bustle and a noise, and one strove to push between the men-at-arms so as to reach the cart, and Stutely saw that it was Little John that made all that stir.

"Now stand thou back!" cried one of the men-at-arms whom Little John pushed with his elbows.

"Now stand thou back thine own self," quoth Little John, and straightway smote the man a buffet beside his head that felled him as a butcher fells an ox, and then he leaped to the cart where Stutely sat.

"I pray thee take leave of thy friends ere thou diest, Will,' quoth he, "or maybe I will die with thee if thou must die, for I could never have better company." Then with one stroke he cut the bonds that bound the other's arms and legs, and Stutely leaped straightway from the cart.

"Now as I live," cried the Sheriff, "yon varlet I know right well is a sturdy rebel! Take him, I bid you all, and let him not go!"

So saying he spurred his horse upon Little John, and rising in his stirrups smote with might and main, but Little John ducked quickly underneath the horse's belly and the blow whistled harmlessly over his head.

"Nay, good Sir Sheriff," cried he, leaping up again when the blow had passed, "I must e'en borrow thy most worshipful sword." Thereupon he twitched the weapon deftly from out the Sheriff's hand. "Here, Stutely," he cried, "the Sheriff hath lent thee his sword! Back to back with me, man, and defend thyself, for help is nigh!"

"Down with them!" bellowed the Sheriff in a voice like an angry bull; and he spurred his horse upon the two who now stood back to back, forgetting in his rage that he had no weapon with which to defend himself.

"Stand back, Sheriff!" cried Little John; and even as he spoke, a bugle-horn sounded shrilly, and a clothyard shaft whistled within an inch of the Sheriff's head. Then came a swaying hither and thither, and oaths, cries and groans and clashing of steel, and swords flashed in the setting sun, and a score of arrows whistled through the air: and some cried "Help, help!" and some, "A rescue, a rescue!"

"Treason!" cried the Sheriff in a loud voice. "Bear back! bear back! else we be all dead men!" Thereupon he reined his horse backward through the thickest of the crowd.

Now Robin Hood and his band might have slain half of the Sheriff's men had they desired to do so, but they let them push out of the press and get them gone, only sending a bunch of arrows after them to hurry them in their flight.

"Oh stay!" shouted Will Stutely after the Sheriff. "Thou wilt never catch bold Robin Hood if thou dost not stand to meet him face to face." But the Sheriff, bowing along his horse's back, made no answer but only spurred the faster.

Then Will Stutely turned to Little John and looked him in the face till the tears ran down from his eyes, and he wept aloud, and kissing his friend's cheeks, "O Little John!" quoth he, "mine own true friend, and he that I love better than man or woman in all the world beside! Little did I reckon to see thy face this day, or to meet thee this side Paradise." Little John could make no answer, but wept also.

Then Robin Hood gathered his band together in a close rank, with Will Stutely in the midst, and thus they moved slowly away toward Sherwood, and were gone, as a storm-cloud moves away from the spot where a tempest has swept the land. But they left ten of the Sheriff's men lying along the ground wounded—some more, some less—yet no one knew who smote them down.

Thus the Sheriff of Nottingham tried thrice to take Robin Hood and failed each time; and the last time he was frightened, for he felt how near he had come to losing his life; so he said: "These men fear neither God nor man, nor King nor king's officers. I would sooner lose mine office than my life, so I will trouble them no more." So he kept close within his castle for many a day and dared not show his face outside of his own household, and all the time he was gloomy and would speak to no one, for he was ashamed of what had happened that day.

The Beginning of King Arthur

BY SIDNEY LANIER

Illustrations by Emil Weiss

> In the land of King Arthur, knights stormed castles to rescue beautiful damsels from towers. They waged bloody tournaments, often to the death, to avenge insults. Proud of their exploits, the knights would hurry back to Arthur's court at Camelot to recount their chivalrous deeds at the Round Table. Legend tells us that some day Arthur will again rule over England and restore knightly honor.

IT befell in the days of the noble Utherpendragon, when he was King of England, [that there was born to him a son who in after time was King Arthur. Howbeit the boy knew not he was the king's son. For when he was but a babe] the king commanded two knights and two ladies to take the child bound in rich cloth of gold, "and deliver him to what poor man you meet at the postern gate of the castle." So the child was delivered unto Merlin, and so he bare it forth unto Sir Ector, and made an holy man to christen him, and named him Arthur; and so Sir Ector's wife nourished him. Then within two years King Uther fell sick of a great malady; [and thereof he died]. Then stood the realm in great [danger] a long while, for every lord made him strong, and many weened [*thought*] to have been king. [And so, by Merlin's counsel, all the lords of England came together in the great church of London on Christmas morn before it was day, to see if God would not show by some miracle

From *The Boy's King Arthur,* by Sidney Lanier.

who should be king.] And when the first mass was done there was seen in the church-yard, against the high altar, a great stone four-square, like to a marble stone, and in the midst thereof was an anvil of steel, a foot of height, and therein stuck a fair sword naked by the point, and letters of gold were written about the sword that said thus: WHO SO PULLETH OUT THIS SWORD OF THIS STONE AND ANVIL, IS RIGHTWISE KING BORN OF ENGLAND.

So when all the masses were done, all the [lords] went for to behold the stone and the sword. And when they saw the scripture, some assayed [*tried*] such as would have been king. But none might stir the sword nor move it.

"He is not yet here," said the archbishop, "that shall achieve the sword, but doubt not God will make him to be known. But this is my counsel," said the archbishop, "that we let purvey [*provide*] ten knights, men of good fame, and they to keep this sword."

And upon New Year's day the barons let make a tournament for to keep the lords together, for the archbishop trusted that God would make him known that should win the sword. So upon New Year's day when the service was done the barons rode to the field.

And so it happened that Sir Ector rode to the jousts, and with him rode Sir Kay, his son, and young Arthur that was his nourished brother. [But Sir] Kay had lost his sword, for he had left it at his father's lodging, and so he prayed young Arthur to ride for his sword. "I will with a good will," said Arthur, and rode fast after the sword; and when he came home, the lady and all were gone out to see the jousting. Then was Arthur wroth, and said to himself, "I will ride to the church-yard and take the sword with me that sticketh in the stone, for my brother Sir Kay shall not be without a sword this day." And so when he came to the church-yard Arthur alighted, and tied his horse to the stile, and so went to the tent, and found no knights there, for they were all at the jousting; and so he handled the sword by the handles, and lightly and fiercely he pulled it out of the stone, and took his horse and rode his way till he came to his brother Sir Kay, and delivered him the sword. And as soon as Sir Kay saw the sword, he wist [*knew*] well that it was the sword of the stone, and so he rode to his father, Sir Ector, and said:

"Sir, lo here is the sword of the stone; wherefore I must be king of this land." When Sir Ector beheld the sword, he returned again and came to the church, and there they alighted, all three, and went into the church, and anon he made Sir Kay to swear upon a book how he came to that sword.

"Sir," said Sir Kay, "by my brother Arthur, for he brought it to me."

"How gate [got] you this sword?" said Sir Ector to Arthur.

"Sir, I will tell you. When I came home for my brother's sword, I found nobody at home for to deliver me his sword, and so I thought my brother Sir Kay should not be swordless, and so I came thither eagerly and pulled it out of the stone without any pain."

"Found ye any knights about this sword?" said Sir Ector.

"Nay," said Arthur.

"Now," said Sir Ector to Arthur, "I understand that you must be king of this land."

"Wherefore I?" said Arthur.

"Sir," said Ector, "for there should never man have drawn out this sword but he that shall be rightwise king of this land. Now let me see whether ye can put the sword there as it was and pull it out again."

"That is no mastery," said Arthur; and so he put it in the stone. Therewith Sir Ector assayed to pull out the sword, and failed.

"Now assay," said Sir Ector to Sir Kay. And anon he pulled at the sword with all his might but it would not be. "Now shall ye assay," said Sir Ector to Arthur.

"I will well," said Arthur, and pulled it out easily. And therewithal Sir Ector kneeled down to the earth, and Sir Kay.

"Alas," said Arthur, "mine own dear father and brother, why kneel ye to me?"

"Nay, nay, my lord Arthur, it is not so: I was never your father nor of your blood, but I wote [know] well ye are of an higher blood than I weened [thought] ye were." And then Sir Ector told him all. Then Arthur made great moan when he understood that Sir Ector was not his father.

"Sir," said Ector unto Arthur, "will ye be my good and gracious lord when ye are king?"

"Else were I to blame," said Arthur, "for ye are the man in the world that I am most beholding [*obliged*] to, and my good lady and mother your wife, that as well as her own hath fostered and kept me. And if ever it be God's will that I be king, as ye say, ye shall desire of me what I may do, and I shall not fail you."

"Sir," said Sir Ector, "I will ask no more of you but that you will make my son, your fostered brother Sir Kay, seneschal of all your lands."

"That shall be done, sir," said Arthur, "and more by the faith of my body; and never man shall have that office but he while that he and I live."

Therewithal they went unto the archbishop, and told him how the sword was achieved, and by whom. And upon the twelfth day all the barons came thither for to assay to take the sword. But there afore them all, there might none take it out but only Arthur; wherefore there were many great lords wroth, and said, "It was great shame unto them all and the realm to be governed with a boy of no high blood born." And so they fell out at that time, that it was put off till Candlemas, and then all the barons should meet there again. But always the ten knights were ordained for to watch the sword both day and night; and so they set a pavilion over the stone and the sword, and five always watched. And at Candlemas many more great lords came thither for to have won the sword, but none of them might prevail. And right as Arthur did at Christmas he did at Candlemas, and pulled out the sword easily, whereof the barons were sore aggrieved, and put it in delay till the high feast of Easter. And as Arthur sped afore, so did he at Easter; and yet there were some of the great lords had indignation that Arthur should be their king, and put it off in delay till the feast of Pentecost.

And at the feast of Pentecost all manner of men assayed to pull at the sword that would assay, and none might prevail; but Arthur pulled it out afore all the lords and commons that were there, wherefore all the commons cried at once: "We will have Arthur unto our king; we will put him no more in delay for we all see that it is God's will that he shall be our king, and who that holdeth against it we will slay him." And therewithal they kneeled down all at once, both rich and poor, and cried Arthur

mercy, because they had delayed him so long. And Arthur for-
gave it them, and took the sword between both his hands, and
offered it upon the altar where the archbishop was, and so was
he made knight of* the best man that was there. And so anon
was the coronation made, and there was he sworn to the lords
and commons for to be a true king, to stand with true justice
from thenceforth all the days of this life. Also then he made all
lords that held of the crown to come in, and to do service as
they ought to do. And many complaints were made unto King
Arthur of great wrongs that were done since the death of King
Uther, of many lands that were bereaved of lords, knights, ladies
and gentlemen. Wherefore King Arthur made the lands to be
given again unto them that owned them. When this was done
that the king had stablished all the countries about London,
then he let make Sir Kay seneschal of England; and Sir Baudwin
of Britain was made constable; and Sir Ulfius was made chamberlain; and Sir Brastias was made warden to wait upon the
north from Trent forwards, for it was that time for the most part
enemy to the king.

Then on a day there came into the court a squire on horseback, leading a knight before him wounded to the death, and
told him there was a knight in the forest that had reared up a
pavilion by a well [*spring*] side, "and hath slain my master, a
good knight, and his name was Miles; wherefore I beseech you
that my master may be buried, and that some good knight may
revenge my master's death." Then was in the court great noise
of the knight's death, and every man said his advice. Then
came Griflet, that was but a squire, and he was but young, of
the age of King Arthur, so he besought the king, for all his
service that he had done, to give him the order of knighthood.

"Thou art full young and tender of age," said King Arthur, "for
to take so high an order upon thee."

"Sir," said Griflet, "I beseech you to make me a knight."

"Sir," said Merlin, "it were pity to leese [*lose*] Griflet, for he
will be a passing good man when he cometh to age, abiding

---

* "Of" was often used for the modern *by* in Sir Thomas Malory's time,
and is still so used upon occasion. "Made knight of the best man" thus
means *made knight by the best man.*

with you the term of his life; and if he adventure his body with yonder knight at the fountain, he shall be in great peril if* ever he come again, for he is one of the best knights of the world, and the strongest man of arms."

"Well," said King Arthur. So, at the desire of Griflet, the king made him knight.

"Now," said King Arthur to Sir Griflet, "sithen [*since*] that I have made thee knight, thou must grant me a gift."

"What ye will, my lord," said Sir Griflet.

"Thou shalt promise me, by the faith of thy body, that when thou hast jousted with the knight at the fountain, whether it fall [*happen*] that ye be on foot or on horseback, that in the same manner ye shall come again unto me without any question or making any more debate."

"I will promise you," said Griflet, "as ye desire." Then Sir Griflet took his horse in great haste, and dressed his shield, and took a great spear in his hand, and so he rode a great gallop till he came to the fountain, and thereby he saw a rich pavilion, and thereby under a cloth stood a fair horse well saddled and bridled, and on a tree a shield of divers colors, and a great spear. Then Sir Griflet smote upon the shield with the end of his spear, that the shield fell down to the ground.

With that came the knight out of the pavilion, and said, "Fair knight, why smote ye down my shield?"

"For I will joust with you," said Sir Griflet.

"It were better ye did not," said the knight, "for ye are but young and late made knight, and your might is nothing to mine."

"As for that," said Sir Griflet, "I will joust with you."

"That is me loth," said the knight, "but sith [*since*] I must needs, I will dress me thereto; but of whence be ye?" said the knight.

"Sir, I am of King Arthur's court." So they ran together that Sir Griflet's spear all to-shivered [*shivered all to pieces*], and therewithal he smote Sir Griflet through the shield and the left side, and brake the spear, that the truncheon stuck in his body, that horse and knight fell down.

---

* "If" here means *whether*. "In great peril if ever he come again," *in great danger of never getting back.*

When the knight saw him lie so on the ground he alighted, and was passing heavy, for he wend [*weened*] he had slain him, and then he unlaced his helm and got him wind, and so with the truncheon he set him on his horse, and betook him to God, and said he had a mighty heart, and if he might live he would prove a passing good knight. And so Sir Griflet rode to the court, whereas great moan was made for him. But through good leeches [*surgeons*] he was healed and his life saved.

And King Arthur was passing wroth for the hurt of Sir Griflet. And by and by he commanded a man of his chamber that his best horse and armor "be without the city or [*before*] tomorrow day." Right so in the morning he met with his man and his horse, and so mounted up and dressed his shield, and took his spear, and bade his chamberlain tarry there till he came again. And so King Arthur rode but a soft pace till it was day, and then was he ware of three churls which chased Merlin, and would have slain him. Then King Arthur rode unto them a good pace, and cried to them: "Flee, churls." Then were they afraid when they saw a knight, and fled away. "O Merlin," said King Arthur, "here hadst thou been slain for* all thy craft, had I not been."

"Nay," said Merlin, "not so, for I could save myself if I would,

* "For" here means *in spite of;* as still is used, in certain phrases.

and thou art more near thy death than I am, for thou goest towards thy death, and* God be not thy friend."

So, as they went thus talking, they came to the fountain, and
the rich pavilion by it. Then King Arthur was ware where a
knight sat all armed in a chair. "Sir knight," said King Arthur,
"for what cause abidest thou here? That there may no knight
ride this way but if he do joust with thee?" said the king. "I
rede [advise] thee leave that custom," said King Arthur.

"This custom," said the knight, "have I used and will use,
maugre [in spite of] who saith nay; and who is grieved with
my custom, let him amend it that will."

"I will amend it," said King Arthur.

"And I shall defend it," said the knight. Anon he took his
horse, and dressed his shield, and took a spear, and they met
so hard either on other's shield, that they all to-shivered [shiv-
ered all to pieces] their spears. Therewith King Arthur drew his
sword. "Nay, not so," said the knight, "it is fairer that we twain
run more together with sharp spears."

"I will well," said King Arthur, "and [if] I had any mo [more]
spears."

"I have spears enough," said the knight. So there came a squire,
and brought two good spears, and King Arthur took one and
he another. So they spurred their horses, and came together
with all their mights, that either brake their spears to their
hands. Then Arthur set hand on his sword. "Nay," said the
knight, "ye shall do better; ye are a passing good jouster as ever
I met withal, and for the love of the high order of knighthood
let us joust once again."

"I assent me," said King Arthur. Anon there were brought two
great spears, and every knight gat a spear, and therewith they
ran together that Arthur's spear all to-shivered. But the other
knight hit him so hard in midst of the shield that horse and man
fell to the earth, and therewith Arthur was eager, and pulled out
his sword, and said, "I will assay thee, Sir knight, on foot, for I
have lost the honor on horseback."

"I will be on horseback," said the knight. Then was Arthur

---

* "And" means *if*, here. In later times it becomes contracted into "an,"
when used in this sense.

wroth, and dressed his shield towards him with his sword drawn. When the knight saw that, he alight, for him thought no worship to have a knight at such avail, he to be on horseback, and he on foot, and so he alight and dressed his shield unto Arthur. And there began a strong battle with many great strokes, and so hewed with their swords that the cantels [*pieces, of armor or of flesh*] flew in the fields, and much blood they bled both, that all the place there as they fought was over-bled with blood, and thus they fought long, and rested them, and then they went to the battle again, and so hurtled together like two rams that either fell to the earth. So at the last they smote together, that both their swords met even together. But the sword of the knight smote King Arthur's sword in two pieces, wherefore he was heavy. Then said the knight unto Arthur, "Thou art in my danger whether me list to save thee or slay thee, and but thou yield thee as overcome and recreant thou shalt die."

"As for death," said King Arthur, "welcome be it when it cometh, but as to yield me to thee as recreant, I had liever die than to be so shamed." And there withal the king leapt unto Pellinore, and took him by the middle, and threw him down, and raced* off his helm. When the knight felt that, he was adread, for he was a passing big man of might, and anon he brought King Arthur under him, and raced off his helm, and would have smitten off his head.

Therewithal came Merlin, and said: "Knight, hold thy hand, for and [*if*] thou slay that knight, thou puttest this realm in the greatest damage that ever realm was in, for this knight is a man of more worship than thou wottest of."

"Why, who is he?" said the knight.

"It is King Arthur."

Then would he have slain him for dread of his wrath, and heaved up his sword, and therewith Merlin cast an enchantment on the knight, that he fell to the earth in a great sleep. Then Merlin took up King Arthur, and rode forth upon the knight's horse. "Alas," said King Arthur, "what hast thou done, Merlin? hast thou slain this good knight by thy crafts? There lived not so worshipful a knight as he was; I had liever than the stint [*loss*] of my land a year, that he were on† live."

"Care ye not," said Merlin, "for he is wholer than ye, for he is but on‡ sleep, and will awake within three hours. I told you," said Merlin, "what a knight he was; here had ye been slain had I not been. Also, there liveth not a better knight than he is, and he shall do you hereafter right good service, and his name is Pellinore, and he shall have two sons, that shall be passing good men."

Right so the king and he departed, and went unto an hermit that was a good man and a great leech. So the hermit searched all his wounds and gave him good salves; and the king was there three days, and then were his wounds well amended that he

---

* "Raced" off: *violently tore off.*
† "On live:" old form of *alive.*
‡ "On sleep," *asleep:* as just above "on live," *alive.*

might ride and go. So Merlin and he departed, and as they rode, Arthur said, "I have no sword."

"No force,"* said Merlin, "hereby is a sword that shall be yours, and [if] I may." So they rode till they came to a lake, which was a fair water and a broad, and in the middest of the lake King Arthur was ware of an arm clothed in white samite, that held a fair sword in the hand. "Lo," said Merlin, "yonder is that sword that I spake of." With that they saw a damsel going upon the lake.

"What damsel is that?" said Arthur.

"That is the Lady of the Lake," said Merlin; "and this damsel will come to you anon, and then speak ye fair to her that she will give you that sword." Anon withal came the damsel unto Arthur and saluted him, and he her again.

"Damsel," said Arthur, "what sword is that, that yonder the arm holdeth above the water? I would it were mine, for I have no sword."

"Sir king," said the damsel, "that sword is mine, and if ye will give me a gift when I ask it you, ye shall have it."

"By my faith," said Arthur, "I will give you what gift ye will ask."

"Well," said the damsel, "go ye into yonder barge and row yourself to the sword, and take it and the scabbard with you, and I will ask my gift when I see my time."

So King Arthur and Merlin alighted and tied their horses to two trees, and so they went into the ship, and when they came to the sword that the hand held, King Arthur took it up by the handles, and took it with him. And the arm and the hand went under the water; and so they came unto the land and rode forth. And then King Arthur saw a rich pavilion: "What signifieth yonder pavilion?"

"It is the knight's pavilion," said Merlin, "that ye fought with last, Sir Pellinore, but he is out, he is not there; he hath ado with a knight of yours, that hight [was named] Egglame, and they have fought together, but at the last Egglame fled, and else he had been dead, and he hath chased him to Caerleon, and we shall anon meet with him in the high way."

* "No force," *no matter.*

"It is well said," quoth King Arthur, "now have I a sword, and now will I wage battle with him and be avenged on him."

"Sir, ye shall not do so," said Merlin, "for the knight is weary of fighting and chasing, so that ye shall have no worship to have ado with him, also he will not lightly be matched of one knight living; and therefore my counsel is that ye let him pass, for he shall do you good service in short time, and his sons after his days. Also ye shall see that day in short space, that ye shall be right glad to give him your sister to wife."

"When I see him," said King Arthur, "I will do as ye advise me."

Then King Arthur looked upon the sword and liked it passing well.

"Whether liketh you better," said Merlin, "the sword or the scabbard?"

"Me liketh better the sword," said King Arthur.

"Ye are more unwise," said Merlin, "for the scabbard is worth ten of the sword, for while ye have the scabbard upon you ye

shall leese [*lose*] no blood be ye never so sore wounded, therefore keep well the scabbard alway with you."

So they rode on to Caerleon, and by the way they met with
Sir Pellinore. But Merlin had done such a craft that Pellinore
saw not Arthur, and so he passed by without any words.

"I marvel," said the king, "that the knight would not speak."

"Sir," said Merlin, "he saw you not, for and [*if*] he had seen
you he had not lightly departed."

So they came unto Caerleon, whereof the knights were passing glad; and when they heard of his adventures, they marvelled
that he would jeopard his person so alone. But all men of worship said it was merry to be under such a chieftain that would
put his person in adventure as other poor knights did.

It befell on a time that King Arthur said to Merlin: "My
barons will let me have no rest, but needs they will have that I
take a wife, and I will none take but by thy counsel and by thine
advice."

"It is well done," said Merlin, "that ye take a wife, for a man
of your bounty and nobleness should not be without a wife. Now
is there any fair lady that ye love better than another?"

"Yea," said King Arthur, "I love Guenever, the king's daughter
Leodegrance* of the land of Cameliard, which Leodegrance
holdeth in his house the Table Round that ye told he had of my
father Uther. And this damsel is the most gentlest and fairest
lady that I know living, or yet that ever I could find."

And Merlin went forth to King Leodegrance of Cameliard,
and told him of the desire of the king, that he would have to his
wife Guenever his daughter.

"That is to me," said King Leodegrance, "the best tidings that
ever I heard, that so worthy a king of prowess and of nobleness
will wed my daughter. And as for my lands I will give him,
wished I that it might please him, but he hath lands enough, he
needeth none; but I shall send him a gift that shall please him
much more, for I shall give him the Table Round, the which
Utherpendragon gave me; and when it is full complete, there
is an hundred knights and fifty, and as for an hundred good

* "The king's daughter Leodegrance," *King Leodegrance's daughter*.

knights I have myself, but I lack fifty, for so many have been slain in my days."

And so King Leodegrance delivered his daughter Guenever unto Merlin, and the Table Round with the hundred knights; and so they rode freshly with great royalty, what by water and what by land, till they came that night unto London.

When King Arthur heard of the coming of Guenever and the hundred knights with the Table Round, he made great joy for their coming, and said openly, "This fair lady is passing welcome to me, for I loved her long, and therefore there is nothing so pleasing to me. And these knights with the Round Table please me more than right great riches."

Then in all haste the king did ordain for the marriage and the coronation in the most honorablest wise that could be devised.

"Now Merlin," said King Arthur, "go thou and espy me in all this land fifty knights which be of most prowess and worship."

Within short time Merlin had found such knights that should fulfil twenty and eight knights, but no more he could find. Then the bishop of Canterbury was fetched, and he blessed the sieges [*seats*] with great royalty and devotion, and there set the eight and twenty knights in their sieges.

And when this was done Merlin said, "Fair sirs, ye must all arise and come to King Arthur for to do him homage; he will have the better will to maintain you."

And so they arose and did their homage. And when they were gone Merlin found in every siege letters of gold that told the knights' names that had sitten therein. But two sieges were void.

"What is the cause," said King Arthur, "that there be two places void in the sieges?"

"Sir," said Merlin, "there shall no man sit in those places but they that shall be of most worship. But in the Siege Perilous there shall no man sit therein but one, and if there be any so hardy to do it he shall be destroyed, and he that shall sit there shall have no fellow."

And therewith Merlin took King Pellinore by the hand, and, in the one hand next the two sieges and the Siege Perilous, he said in open audience, "This is your place, and best ye be worthy to sit therein of any that is here."

AMERICAN TALL TALES

Americans have always enjoyed "tall tales" and "yarns" filled with humor and exaggeration. When tales, yarns, and jokes are retold from generation to generation, they become folklore—stories that tell the common experiences of a group of people.

Most of the tall tales that grew up in the United States were born during the 1800's when America was a young, new nation bursting with energy, trying to carve a place for itself out of a vast wilderness.

Almost every region in the country has its own

ILLUSTRATION BY ESTELLE HOLLINGWORTH

legendary heroes, and every occupation that played an important part in building the nation created its own giant characters who boasted and laughed while they tried to solve the hardships facing them. The created characters were usually bigger, stronger, and smarter than ten men put together, and they were always able to do impossible feats. Very often, real people were put into stories, but everyone exaggerated their adventures.

Sailors told about the heroic Captain Stormalong and his great ship, the *Courser;* railroad men sang of Casey Jones, engineer on the Cannonball Express; steel-workers invented Joe Magarac, who could stir molten steel with his bare hands; and cowboys praised Pecos Bill who "made" the Grand Canyon.

The eastern part of the country loved to tell stories of Ethan Allen, a real person who actually fought in the Revolutionary War with the Green Mountain boys. By fun-filled exaggeration, Ethan grew into a man as high as a maple, strong as an ox, fast as a deer.

In the South, the lumberjacks spoke of Tony Beaver who lived on his lumber camp "up Eel River." His right-hand man, Big Henry, had an axe that cried "boo" whenever it was swung.

The loggers in the northern lumber camps invented the giant lumberjack, Paul Bunyan. Paul ate enough food to feed the people of a good-sized city. Babe, Paul's giant blue ox, created ten thousand lakes in Minnesota with his footprints.

The West also told hundreds of stories about super-cowboys like Pecos Bill who roped and saddled a mountain lion. Stories circulated of desperados like Jesse James and Billy the Kid and their exciting gunfights with sheriffs like Wyatt Earp and Bat Masterson. Again, even though stories about these outlaws are based on fact, we cannot believe all that is said about them.

The Black Duck Dinner

BY JAMES STEVENS

Illustrations by Dell J. McCormick

> Paul Bunyan was born with a glossy black beard and a mustache. The gigantic legendary lumberjack created the Great Lakes with his footprints as he tramped across the country. With the help of his blue ox Babe who measured forty-two ax handles and a plug of tobacco between the eyes, Paul Bunyan operated a logging camp in the days when logging was heroic.

EXCEPT in the spring, when the log drives were being made down the rivers, Sunday was a day of rest in Paul Bunyan's camp. It was a day of earnest thought, and of cleanliness and pleasure also. For on Sunday Paul Bunyan planned the next week's work, thought out his orations, imagined new inventions, and dreamed of historical exploits for the future. And on Sunday his loggers made their beds, cleaned their clothes, and shaved their faces. The pleasures of this day were the pleasures of the table, for Paul Bunyan, after building his second cookhouse, and developing his famous kitchen organization around Hot Biscuit Slim, the chief cook, originated the custom of grand Sunday dinners.

Every Sunday dinner was a feast; but some of them, of course, were nobler and more enjoyable than others. His roast pork and plum pudding dinners always delighted the loggers when they were served on winter Sundays; they shouted over the baked trout and cherry pie Sunday dinners that he gave them in the spring; in the summer a vegetable and strawberry shortcake Sunday dinner made them happy every time; and in the fall the Sunday dinners of fried chicken and peach cobbler made them

prance and roar with pleasure. And the Thanksgiving and
Christmas dinners of roasted webfooted turkeys, cranberries and
chocolate cake—the loggers were always speechless when they
thought about them.

Every Sunday morning would see the loggers performing the
ceremonies of cleanliness as soon as their after-breakfast pipes
were smoked. First, the beds were made; and this was a more
trying job than you would think, especially for the loggers who
had poor eyesight. These unfortunates would throw their blankets into a pile, then shake them out one at a time, and attempt
to replace them in the bunks. Here difficulties beset them, for
Paul Bunyan's blankets had small square checks; and it took a
sharp eye to detect which was the long way of a blanket, and
which was the wide way. Even the most sharp-eyed loggers
would sometimes lose confidence in their vision when replacing
these perplexing blankets; and they would remove them time
and again before deciding that they were spread correctly. As
for the cross-eyed and nearsighted men, it was sometimes pitiful
to behold the most troubled of them stretching out blankets in
their extended hands, turning them in slow revolutions, doubt-
fully placing them on the bunks, and then wearily lifting them
again. These unfortunate men never quitted their Sunday bed-
making until they were worn out; and all the following week
they were sure that they had the long way of their blankets on
the wide way of their bunks. They would swear to have them
right next time; but every Sunday their attempts at bed-making
would end in as unsatisfying a manner.

Everyone in the West knows that sheepherders of our time
often worry themselves into insanity in their lonely camps, trying to discover the wide way and the long way of their quilts
and blankets. Fortunately, Paul Bunyan's loggers were all
strong-minded men, and their blankets did no more than bedevil
them.

After bed-making the loggers heated cans of water over small
fires built out in the timber, and they washed their clothes. Shaving, boot-greasing, sole-calking, hair-cutting, beard-trimming,
button-sewing, and rip-mending followed; and he was an expert
in these Sunday morning chores who had time to stretch out on

his smooth blankets for a smoke before the dinner gong rang at twelve.

At the ringing of this gong the inexpressible pleasures of Paul Bunyan's Sundays began. First, the loggers enjoyed the ecstasy of eating; and it was an ecstasy they were fitted to enjoy gloriously. After dinner the loggers would lie on their bunks and dream drowsily all afternoon of a loggers' paradise; and the paradise they dreamed about was none other than Paul Bunyan's camp; but a camp whose life began each day with a Sunday dinner, and whose days were all like the warm drowsy hours of these Sunday afternoons.

But most of the loggers would be awake and hungry again at suppertime, ready to enjoy the Sunday supper of cold meat, potato salad, doughnuts, jelly rolls and coffee. Then in the twilight, and for a long time after the bunkhouse lamps were lit, they would smoke, and talk contentedly of the delight they got from Paul Bunyan's cookhouse; and they would prophesy about the Sunday dinners of the future. There were no bunkhouse pastimes on Sunday nights. After some hours of low-voiced contented talk, the loggers would change their underclothes and get into their newly made beds, rested and inspired for Monday's labor.

The great cookhouse which so ennobled and cheered Paul Bunyan's loggers on their Sundays was the grandest and best planned affair of its kind ever heard of. The dining hall was so commodious and had so much room between the tables that four-horse teams hauled wagonloads of salt, pepper and sugar down the aisles when the shakers and bowls were to be filled. Conveyor belts carried clean dishes to the tables and returned the dirty ones to the wash room. The long-legged flunkies wore roller skates at mealtime, and the fastest among them could sometimes traverse the dining hall in forty-seven minutes.

But it was the kitchen, the powerhouse of this vast establishment, which had the most interest. This domain, ruled by the temperamental culinary genius, Hot Biscuit Slim, was as large as ten Ford plants and as noisy as the Battle of Gettysburg. The utensils that hung on its walls, from the steam-drive potato mashers and sleeve-valve, air-cooled egg beaters to the big armorplate potato kettles, the bigger force-feed batter mixers and the grandiose stew kettles, in which carcasses of cattle floated about like chips in a mill pond when beef dinners were being prepared—these polished utensils glittered even when the ranges were smoking their worst at hot cake time.

Paul Bunyan had devised the monorail system for this kitchen, and overhead cranes rattled about at all hours, carrying loads of dishes from the Dishwashing Department to the Serving Department, loads of vegetables and meats from the Supply Department to the Preparations Department, and loads of dressed food from the Preparations Department to the Finishing Department. The dishes were washed on a carriage like the log carriages of modern sawmills. The head dishwashers jerked levers that threw heaps of dirty dishes from the conveyor belts to the carriage, then the carriage was shot forward until the dishes struck a sharp-edged stream of soapy water that had dropped one hundred feet. The clean dishes were bucked off on live rolls, and the head dishwasher shot the carriage back for another load. Some of the clean dishes were run through dry kilns, and others were piled for air-drying by Swede dish-pilers, who wore leather aprons and mittens and could pile sixty thousand dishes per pair in twelve hours.

A list of the marvels of Paul Bunyan's kitchen would fill a book as large as a dictionary. Elevators whirred between the kitchen and the vegetable bins, and a wide subway held four tracks that led to the fruit and vinegar cellars. A concrete chute carried the coffee grounds, eggshells and other waste to the kitchen yard, and from morning till night it roared like a mill-race. Billy Puget, boss over the scraper gang, often had to work his mules and men fourteen hours a day in order to keep the kitchen yard cleaned of coffee grounds and eggshells.

Paul Bunyan's loggers had little understanding of the tremendous organization that was required for the operation of such an establishment as the cookhouse. They thanked old Paul for feeding them so well, and they agreed that Hot Biscuit Slim was a powerful good cook. Less fortunate loggers of to-day think of Paul Bunyan's camp life as a dream of bliss, and they are sure that if they had been there they would have worshiped Paul

Bunyan. His own loggers, however, took the cookhouse glories as a matter of course, and they never realized what inventiveness, thought and effort were needed to give them such Sunday dinners and such Sunday afternoon dreams and content.

Nor did Paul Bunyan expect shouted praises and thanks from his loggers. He gave so much to them because he expected much from them. He worked his men twelve hours a day, and, had they thought about it, they would have been astounded by any idea of working less. And they would have been perplexed by any other scheme to ease their lot. If there were not to be great exertions, they would have asked, why their sturdy frames, their eager muscular force? If they were not meant to face hazards, why was daring in their hearts? A noble breed, those loggers of Paul Bunyan's, greatly worthy of their captain! He himself told them in a speech he made at the finishing of the Onion River Drive that they were "a good band of bullies, a fine bunch of savages." I should like to quote this speech in its entirety, for it celebrated the accomplishment of a historical logging enterprise, and it was a master oration which showed the full range and force of Paul Bunyan's oratorical powers. But as nine days and eight nights were required for its delivery, it is obvious that no publication save the *Congressional Record* could give all of it. It was at this time that Paul Bunyan served his great black duck dinner.

The speech ended on a Tuesday, and until the following Saturday morning there were no sounds save the snores of weary men and the scratching of the sleepless Johnny Inkslinger's fountain pen. By Saturday noon he had a time check and a written copy of the oration for every man in camp. After dinner the Big Swede, using a fire hose, a ton of soap, and a tank of hair tonic began to give the blue ox his spring cleaning, and Johnny Inkslinger turned in for the three hours of sleep which he required each week. Paul Bunyan was arranging his personal belongings for the move to a new job and musing on his recent accomplishment. He had never driven logs down a rougher or more treacherous stream than Onion River. And the hills over which the timber had been skidded were so rocky and steep that they tried even the strength of the blue ox. Worst of all was the rank growth of

wild onions that had covered the ground. They baffled all attempts to fell the trees at first, for they brought blinding floods
of tears to the loggers' eyes and made their efforts not only futile
but dangerous. When the Big Swede was standing on a hillside
one day, dreaming of the old country, he failed to observe a
blinded logger come staggering up the slope, and he did not
hear him mumble, "This looks like a good stick." Not until the
logger had chopped a notch in the leg of his boot had the Big
Swede realized his peril. Paul Bunyan, baffled by such incidents,
was about to abandon the whole operation when the alert Johnny Inkslinger heard of the failure of the Italian garlic crop. He
quickly made a contract with the Italian government, which
sent over shiploads of laborers to dig up the wild onions and take
them home as a substitute for the national relish. When this had
been accomplished it was possible to log off the country.

There had been other difficulties to overcome, too, and as
Paul Bunyan spread out a tarpaulin and prepared to roll up his

boots and workclothes, he remembered them and praised the
saints that they were ended. The next job offered the best
promise of easy and simple logging of any he had ever en-
countered. For miles the land rose in gentle slopes from a wide
and smoothly flowing river; there was no brush or noxious vege-
tation among the clean, straight trees; and, best of all, the timber was of a species now extinct, the Leaning Pine. The trees of
this variety all leaned in the same direction, and it was thus
possible to fell them accurately without the use of wedges. Paul
Bunyan was sure of a season's record on this new job. He thought
of the fresh brilliancy it would give his fame, and like a row of
snowy peaks glimpsed through the spaces of a forest, his teeth
glittered through his beard in a magnificent smile. But another
thought quickly sobered his countenance. "Those good bullies
of mine!" The words came in a gusty murmur. He dropped the
tarpaulin and strode over to the cookhouse. Hot Biscuit Slim,
the kitchen chief, came forth to meet him. There was a knowing
look in the cook's eyes.

"It's to be a great Sunday dinner to-morrer?" he asked, before
Paul Bunyan could speak.

"The greatest Sunday dinner ever heard of," said Paul Bunyan.
"I want this to be remembered as the noblest meal ever served
in a logging camp. My loggers shall feast like the victorious sol-
diers of old time. It is a natural privilege of heroes to revel after
conquest. Remember, as you prepare this feast, that you may
also be making immortal glory for yourself."

"You jest leave it to me, Mr. Bunyan!" answered Slim. "If the
baker'll do his part with the cream puffs, cakes and pies, I promise you I'll make 'em a meal to remember. First, oyscher stew,
an' then for vegytables, cream' cabbage, of course, mash' potatoes an' potato cakes, lettuce an' onions——"

"No onions!" thundered Paul Bunyan. There was a terrific
crash in the kitchen as hundreds of skillets and kettles were
shaken to the floor.

"Uh—I forgot," stammered Hot Biscuit Slim. "Well, anyway,
they'll be oyscher soup, vegytables, sauces, puddin's, hot biscuits, an' meat in dumplin' stew, an' mulligan stew, an' they'll
be drippin' roasts, all tender an' rich-seasoned—oh, the meat
that I'll give 'em! the meat—" he paused sharply, shivered as

though from physical shock, and misery glistened in his eyes—
"only-uh-only—"

"Only you have no meat," said Paul Bunyan gently.

"I'm admittin' it," said Slim wretchedly. "Honest, Mr. Bunyan,
no matter how I try I jest *can't* remember to order meat, 'spe-
cially for Sunday dinner. I can remember vegytables, fruits an'
greens easy as pie, but, by doggy, I always forget meat. I ain't
pertendin' a cook's worth keepin' who can't remember meat,
no matter how good he is at fixin' it. I wouldn't blame you if you
fired me right off, Mr. Bunyan."

Hot Biscuit Slim leaned against the toe of the hero's boot and
wept.

"That means I must rustle deer and bear," said Paul Bunyan
patiently. "Well, bear meat and venison will make a royal feast
when they have passed through your kettles and ovens. Light
the fires, go ahead with your plans; you may yet make history
tomorrow!"

He turned away, and Hot Biscuit Slim watched him worship-
fully until he was a dim figure on distant hills.

"The best friend me an' my pap ever had," he said. "I'd do
anything for a boss like that. I'll learn to remember meat, by
doggy, I will!"

Rumors of the marvelous dinner that was being planned
reached the bunkhouses, and the loggers indulged in greedy
imagining of the promised delights. The day went slowly; the
sun seemed to labor down the western sky. Before it sank soft
clouds obscured its light, bringing showers and early shadows.

At the approach of darkness Paul Bunyan began his return
march to the camp. He was vastly disappointed by the meager
results of his hunt. Although he had gone as far as the Turtle
River country, he had snared but two deer and three small bears.
These only filled a corner of one pocket of his mackinaw, and
they would provide but a mere shred of meat apiece for his men.
Paul Bunyan did not feel that he had done his best; he was not
one to rest on feeble consolations. As he journeyed on he was
devising other means to carry out his plans for a memorable and
stupendous feast. And ere he was within an hour of the camp
the Big Swede was unconsciously outlining the solution of the
problem for him.

The Big Swede went to the stable some time after supper to see that Babe was at ease for the night. The clouds were thinning now, and when he opened the stable door soft light poured in on the blue ox, making lustrous spots and streaks on his sleek sides. He turned his head, his bulging blue eyes shining with gentleness and good-will, and his tongue covered the foreman's face in a luscious caress.

"Har noo," remonstrated the Big Swede.

As he solemnly wiped his drenched face he sniffed the fragrance of Babe's breath and stared with a feeling of envy at the clean, glowing hair. When he had finished his inspection and left the stable, it was evident that he was wrestling with some laborious problem. His whole face was tense with a terrific frown; his memory groped among the shadows of some distant happening; he scratched his sides vigorously and breathed deeply of the air, sweet with the odors of washed earth. The purity of the spring weather, the fresh cleanliness it gave the world, and the aroma and sleekness of the blue ox, had brought the Big Swede to face his own sore need of a washing. He dreaded it as an ordeal, an exceptional and hazardous undertaking, and for that reason he wished that he might accomplish it immediately. He wandered aimlessly on, tormented by an unaccustomed conflict of the soul and the flesh, and at last he came to the edge of a cliff. He stared in surprise at the appearance of a lake below. He could not remember so large a body of water near the camp. But the Big Swede had no room for more than one emotion at a time, and a violent resolve now smothered his surprise.

"Yah, aye do him noo," he muttered.

He disrobed swiftly and ran to a rock that jutted from the cliff. Swinging his fists he leaped twice into the air; the second time he flung himself outward in a magnificent dive, his body made a great curve, and then, head first, he plunged downward. But there was no tumultuous surge and splash of waters as a climax of this splendid dive. Instead, the Big Swede's head struck white canvas with a dull, rending impact. For he had mistaken Paul Bunyan's tarpaulin for a lake! The force of his plunge drove him through the canvas and half-buried him in the soft earth underneath. His arms were imprisoned, but his legs waved wildly, and his muffled bellows shook the earth. A prowling log-

ger saw what seemed to be shining marble columns dancing in
the moonlight and felt the ground trembling under his feet.

"It can't be," he thought bravely.

Just then the Big Swede made another heroic effort to yell for
help, and the logger was shaken from his feet. He jumped up
and ran to Johnny Inkslinger with an alarming tale of dancing
ghosts that shook the earth. The timekeeper, after sharpening
twenty-seven lead pencils to use in case it was necessary to make
a report on the spot, started with his medicine case for the
place where the logger had directed him. When nearly there
he remembered that he had failed to bring his ten gallon carboy
of alcohol, which, next to Epsom salts, he considered the most
important medicine in his chest. He ran back for it, and by the
time he finally reached the Big Swede, that unfortunate's bellows had diminished to groans, and his legs waved with less
and less gusto. After thoroughly examining and measuring the
legs, Johnny deemed the proof positive that they belonged to
the Big Swede. Then he got busy with paper and pencil and
figured for half an hour. "According to the strictest mathemati-
cal calculations," he announced, "the Big Swede cannot continue
to exist in his present interred, or, to be exact, half-interred condition; consequently he must be extricated. I have considered
all known means by which this may be accomplished, I have
figured, proved, and compared results, and I have arrived at a
scientific conclusion. I direct that the blue ox and a cable be
brought here at once."

When the loggers had obeyed this command, Johnny made
a half-hitch with the cable around the Big Swede's legs, which
were waving very feebly now, and in two seconds, amid a monstrous upheaval of dirt and a further rending of the canvas, the
Big Swede was dragged out. For a few moments he spat mud
like a river dredge; then the timekeeper proffered him the ten
gallon carboy of alcohol. It was drained at a gulp, and then, with
aid from Johnny Inkslinger, he was able to stagger to the camp
office. When Paul Bunyan reached the camp, the Big Swede
was lying on his bunk, bundled in bandages from head to foot.
Johnny Inkslinger was still busily attending him; bottles of medicine, boxes of pills, a keg of Epsom salts, rolls of bandages, and
surgical implements were heaped about the room. The time-

keeper gave a detailed account of what had happened, and then
Paul Bunyan questioned the victim, who answered briefly, "Aye
yoomped, an' aye yoomped, an'—*yeeminy!*"

Johnny Inkslinger gave his chief a voluminous report of the
Big Swede's fractures, sprains and contusions.

"He is also suffering from melancholia because he is still un-
washed," said Johnny. "But I think I'll restore him. I've dosed
him with all my medicines and smeared him with all my salves.
I'd have manipulated his spine, but, confound him, he strained
his back, and he threatens violence when I touch it. But I have
many formulae and systems. He shall live."

"Surely," said Paul Bunyan. "A man is the hardest thing to kill
there is."

Knowing that the Big Swede's wounds were nothing in com-
parison with the ones which he had received in the Dakota battle, Paul Bunyan worried no more about his foreman. He
stepped from the camp office, plucked up a young pine tree and
brushed his beard, thinking again of his unrealized plan. He
remembered the wordless dejection of Hot Biscuit Slim on re-
ceiving the scanty supply of deer and bear meat. He determined
that the Sunday dinner should yet be as he had planned it;
otherwise it would be a bad augury for great achievements in
his new enterprise. He thrust the tree into his shirt pocket and
walked slowly towards his outdoor headquarters, pondering
various schemes that came to mind.

When he reached the white sheet of water he was astonished
by its deceptive appearance. It had a silvery glitter in the moonlight, for its surface still held the moisture of the showers. Small
wonder, thought Paul Bunyan, that the Big Swede had dived
into it; never was a lake more temptingly beautiful or seemingly
more deep. He was gazing at the torn canvas and the huge
cavity made in the ground by the Big Swede, when he heard
a great chorus of shrill and doleful voices in the sky. He looked
up and saw an enormous host of black ducks in swerving flight.
They had lost their way in the low-hanging clouds at dusk, and
now they were seeking a resting place.

Here, thought Paul Bunyan, is a noble offering of chance. Was
a black duck more acute than the Big Swede, that the bright,
moist canvas would not deceive him also? And once deceived,

would not the ensuing dive be fatal? Wasn't a black duck's neck of more delicate structure than the Big Swede's, and wouldn't it surely break when it struck the tarpaulin? This variety of black duck grew as big as a buzzard, and here they were so numerous that clouds of them darkened the moon. Now to deceive them. Paul Bunyan could mimic the voices of all the birds of the air and all the beasts of the fields and woods, save only that of the blue ox, who always replied with a jocular wink when his master attempted to simulate his mellow moo. In his moments of humor Paul Bunyan declared that he could mimic fish, and one Sunday when he imitated a mother whale bawling for her calf the loggers roared with merriment for seventeen hours, and were only sobered then by exhaustion. His voice had such power that he could not counterfeit the cry of a single small creature, but only the united cries of flocks and droves. So he now mimicked perfectly the chorus that rang mournfully in the sky, and at the same time he grasped the edge of the tarpaulin and fluttered it gently.

The effect was marvelous. Now indeed was the canvas a perfect imitation of water. Had you been standing by the sole of Paul Bunyan's boot and seen the gentle flutter you would have been sure that you were watching a breeze make pleasant ripples on the surface of a lake. Ere long the black ducks were enchanted by the sight and sound, and Paul Bunyan heard a violent rush of air above him as of a hurricane sweeping a forest. A vast dark cloud seemed to plunge out of the sky. Another instant and the canvas was black with feathered forms. Paul Bunyan grasped the four corners of the tarpaulin, swung the bundle over his shoulder and strode home to the cookhouse. Hot Biscuit Slim was called forth, and when he saw the mountainous pile of black ducks that filled the kitchen yard he became hysterical with delight. He called out the assistant cooks, the flunkies and dishwashers, and, led by Cream Puff Fatty, the baker, the white-clad underlings streamed for eleven minutes from the kitchen door. The chief cook then made them a short but inspiring speech and fired them with his own fierce purpose to make culinary history.

Paul Bunyan listened for a moment, and then sought repose, with peace in his benevolent heart.

All night fires roared in the ranges as preparations went on for the great dinner. The elevators brought a load of vegetables every minute from the deep bins, potatoes were pared and washed, kettles and roasting pans were made ready, and sauces and dressings were devised. The black ducks were scalded, plucked and cleaned by the Preparations Department, and by morning the cranemen were bringing them by the hundreds to the Finishing Department, where the kettles and pans were waiting for them.

Most of the loggers stayed in their bunks this morning, and those who did come to breakfast ate sparingly, saving their appetites. Time passed quietly in the camp. The loggers washed and mended their clothes and greased their boots, but they did not worry themselves with bed-making. The other Sunday morning chores finished, they stretched out on their unmade bunks and smoked. They were silent and preoccupied, but now and again a breeze blowing from the direction of the cookhouse would cause them to sigh. What enchantment was in the air, so redolent with the aroma of roasting duck and stewing cabbages, so sharply sweet with the fragrance of hot ginger and cinnamon from the bakery where Cream Puff Fatty fashioned his creations! A logger who was shaving would take a deep breath of this incense, and the blood would trickle unnoticed from a slash in his cheek; another, in his bunk would let his pipe slip from his hand and enjoy ardent inhalations, blissfully unaware of his burning shirt; yet another, engaged in greasing his boots, would halt his task and sit in motionless beatitude, his head thrown back, his eyes closed, quite unconscious of the grease that poured from a tilted can into a prized boot.

At half past eleven the hungriest of the loggers began to mass before the cookhouse door, and as the minutes passed the throng swiftly increased. At five minutes to noon all the bunkhouses were empty and the furthest fringe of the crowd was far up Onion River valley. The ground shook under a restless trampling, and the faces of the loggers were glowing and eager as they hearkened to the clatter and rumble inside the cookhouse, as four-horse teams hauled in loads of salt, pepper and sugar for the shakers and bowls. Then the loggers began to stamp and shout as they heard the flunkies, led by the Galloping Kid on his

white horse, rushing the platters and bowls of food to the tables. Tantalizing smells wafted forth from the steaming dishes. The loggers grew more restless and eager; they surged to and fro in a tidal movement; jests and glad oaths made a joyous clamor over the throng. This was softened into a universal sigh as the doors swung open and Hot Biscuit Slim, in spotless cap and apron, appeared wearing the impressive mien of a conquering general. He lifted an iron bar with a majestic gesture, paused for dramatic effect amid a breathless hush, and then struck a resounding note from the steel triangle that hung from the wall.

At the sound a heaving torrent of men began to pour through
the doors in a rush that was like the roaring plunge of water
when the gate of a dam is lifted. The chief cook continued to
pound out clanging rhythms until the last impatient logger was
inside.

Then Hot Biscuit Slim reëntered the cookhouse. He was reminded of a forested plain veiled in thin fog as he surveyed the
assemblage of darkly clad figures, wreathed with white and
fragrant blooms of steam. His impression was made the more
vivid when the loggers plunged their spoons into the deep bowls
of oyster soup, for the ensuing sounds seemed like the soughing
of wind in the woods. The chief cook marched to the kitchen
with dignity and pride, glancing to the right and left at the
tables that held his masterwork. He asked for no praise or ac-
claim; the ecstasy that now transfigured the plainest face was
a sufficient light of glory for him.

The soup bowls pushed aside, the loggers began to fill their
plates, which were of such circumference that even a long-
armed man could hardly reach across one. The black ducks, of
course, received first attention. And great as the plates were, by
the time one was heaped with a brown fried drumstick, a ladle
of duck dumplings, several large fragments of duck fricassee, a
slab of duck baked gumbo style, a rich portion of stewed duck,
and a mound of crisp brown dressing, all immersed in golden
duck gravy, a formidable space was covered. Yet there was room
for tender leaves of odorous cabbage beaded and streaked with
creamy sauce; for mashed potatoes which seemed like fluffs of
snow beside the darkness of duck and gravy; for brittle and
savory potato cakes, marvelously right as to texture and thickness; for stewed tomatoes of a sultry ruddiness, pungent and
ticklish with mysterious spices; for a hot cob of corn as long as
a man's forearm, golden with sirupy kernels as big as buns; for
fat and juicy baked beans, plump peas, sunny applesauce and
buttered lettuce, not to mention various condiments. Squares of
cornbread and hot biscuits were buttered and leaned against the
plate; a pot-bellied coffee-pot was tilted over a gaping cup, into
which it gushed an aromatic beverage of drowsy charm; a kingly
pleasure was prepared. More than one logger swooned with
delight this day when his plate was filled and, red-faced, hot-

eyed, wet-lipped, he bent over it for the first mouthful with the joy of a lover claiming a first embrace.

In the kitchen the chief cook, the baker and their helpers watched and listened. At first the volume of sounds that filled the vast room was like the roar and crash of an avalanche, as dishes were rattled and banged about. Then the duck bones crackled like the limbs of falling trees. At last came a steady sound of eating, a sound of seventy threshing machines devouring bundles of wheat. It persisted far beyond the usual length of time, and Hot Biscuit Slim brought out his field glasses and surveyed the tables. The loggers were still bent tensely over their plates, and their elbows rose and fell with an energetic movement as they scooped up the food with undiminished vigor.

"Still eatin' duck," marveled Hot Biscuit Slim.

"They won't be more'n able to *smell* my cream puffs," said the baker enviously.

The loggers ate on. They had now spent twice their usual length of time at the table. Each plate was in a dark shadow from tall rows of slick black duck bones and heaps of corn cobs. But——

"Still eatin' duck," reported Hot Biscuit Slim.

That no one might see his grief Cream Puff Fatty moved to a dark corner. He was now certain that none of the loggers could have room for his pastries. They ate on. They had now spent three times their usual length of time at the table. The baker was sweating and weeping; he was soaked with despair. Then, suddenly:

"They're eatin' cream puffs!" cried Hot Biscuit Slim.

Cream Puff Fatty could not believe it, but a thrill of hope urged him to see for himself. True enough, the loggers were tackling the pastries at last. On each plate cream puffs the size of squashes lay in golden mounds. As the spoons struck them their creamy contents oozed forth from breaks and crevices. Stimulated by their rich flavor, the loggers ate on with renewed gusto. They had now stayed four times as long as usual at the table. Other enchantments still kept them in their seats: lemon pies with airy frostings, yellow pumpkin pies strewn with brown spice specks, cherry pies with cracks in their flaky crusts through which the red fruit winked, custard pies with russet freckles on their golden faces, fat apple pies all odorous with cinnamon, cool, snowy cream pies, peach cobblers, chocolate puddings, glittering cakes of many colors, slabs of gingerbread, sugar-powdered jelly rolls, doughnuts as large around as saucers and as thick through as cups, and so soft and toothsome that a morsel from one melted on the tongue like cream. So endearing were the flavors of these pastries that the loggers consumed them all.

Cream Puff Fatty and Hot Biscuit Slim solemnly shook hands. There was glory enough for both of them.

At last there were no sounds at the tables save those of heavy breathing. The loggers arose in a body and moved sluggishly and wordlessly from the cookhouse. They labored over the ground towards the bunkhouses as wearily as though they had just finished a day of deadening toil. Soon Onion River valley resounded with their snores and groans. . . .

At supper time, when Hot Biscuit Slim rang the gong, Cream Puff Fatty stood by his side. This was to be the supreme test of their achievement. For five minutes the chief cook beat the triangle, and then a solitary logger appeared in the door of a bunkhouse. He stared at them dully for a moment and then staggered back into the darkness. This was indeed a triumph! Great as other feasts in the cookhouse had been, never before had *all* the loggers been unable to appear for supper. This was a historic day. Cream Puff Fatty and Hot Biscuit Slim embraced and mingled rapturous tears. It was their high moment. They would not have traded it for all the glory that was Greece and the grandeur that was Rome. . . . They had intimations of immortality. . . .

For five weeks the loggers lay in a delicious torpor, and then Johnny Inkslinger brought them from their bunks with doses of alcohol and Epsom salts. By this time the Big Swede had recovered from his injuries, and Paul Bunyan waited no longer to move his camp. The buildings, which rested on skids, were chained and cabled together, and the blue ox hauled them over the hills to the new job.

Nothing marred the beauty of that summer; stirring breezes blew all the days over the loggers as they felled the Leaning Pine trees in perfect lines on the grassy slopes. The blue ox waxed fat with the ease of his labor. Weeks passed without the

Big Swede having a serious accident. Dust gathered on Johnny Inkslinger's medicine case. Hot Biscuit Slim never once failed to remember meat. And a record number of logs were piled above the rollways. Paul Bunyan planned a great drive with prideful confidence that it would be the glorious climax of a historic season. But here fortune deserted him, for, after driving the logs for nine days, and seeing an exact repetition of scenery three times, he had Johnny Inkslinger survey the placid river. The river was round; it flowed in a perfect circle; and Paul Bunyan had driven the logs three times over the same course!

Nothing daunted, he thereupon determined to saw the logs and transport the lumber overland, and he erected his famed sawmill, which was nineteen stories high, with each bandsaw and each circular saw running through all the floors. A description of the original machines and devices used in this mill would fill the pages of a mail order catalogue. It is needless to say that it operated perfectly. The only great difficulty Paul Bunyan had to overcome originated from the smokestacks. He was compelled to equip them with hinges and drawbridge machinery so that they could be lowered to let the clouds go by.

Joe Magarac, Pittsburgh Steel Man

BY WALTER BLAIR

Illustrations by Glen Rounds

THERE are more fool stories about the way Joe Magarac was born than you can shake a stick at, more, as a matter of fact, than there are about the birth of any hero who's turned up in this history so far. There's no doubt *where* he was born: it was some place in the iron and coal country, probably in Pennsylvania. All of the following theories, though, have been offered as to *how* he was born:

1. He was born down in the center of an iron ore mountain —a hematite mountain, so they say—several thousand years ago (three or four, nobody knows which). And because that mountain was more or less on top of him, the poor man had to lie there until a miner came to him one day and told him they needed help in the steel mills. Then he traveled to Pittsburgh in an ore car.

2. He didn't just travel in the ore car; he was born in the thing. Then, before he could say "Boo," he was run through Bessemer furnaces and then open-hearth furnaces, until he came out as A-1 steel.

3. He wasn't born in an ore car at all, but in a coal mine— at Nanty Glo, not far from Johnstown. (Those that claim this say they could prove it by sticking a pin into Joe and showing there was coal dust in his veins instead of blood. Only time anyone used a pin that way, though, the pin bent double before it had a chance to stick him.) Well, these people claim that he rode to Pittsburgh in a coal car.

From *Tall Tale America*, by Walter Blair, copyright 1944 by Walter Blair. Published by Coward-McCann Inc.

4. He didn't just ride in the coal car; he was born in the thing. Then, when a breaker who was sorting out the bad pieces from the good came upon him, the breaker pulled him out and talked him into being a helper.

To sum this up, Joe was either born in a mine (iron or coal) or in a car (coal or iron ore)—so far as anybody has been able to figure out definitely.

However he was born, he did turn up, in time, in Pittsburgh, a great center of the steel making business.

Pittsburgh had changed plenty since Mike Fink had been born there. When Mike was born, the place was a huddle of a few cabins, sawmills, limekilns and stores, with a stockade to keep the Indians from dropping around and scalping the settlers. But going into Pittsburgh in Joe's day, along about the time of World War I, or a little before, first you'd see a dark smudge against the sky, then you'd ride along a boulevard by the slums, and then you'd find yourself on streets lined by skyscrapers so high that their top stories were lost up there in the murky sky.

If you went out to the steel mill district, you'd ride on a street car across an oily river. After a while, you'd come to a place where there were a good many old two-story brick houses without front porches or front yards—with their front doors opening right onto the sidewalks.

This would be Hunkietown, so called because the Hungarian steel workers lived there, in the rows and rows of brick houses.

A day the people of Hunkietown never will forget was the day when Steve Mestrovic had the contest to see who'd marry his daughter Mary. The week before, he'd sent out news to the newspapers about this contest, and now a whole crowd of men had come around to try to win the girl's hand.

Mary Mestrovic was a prize worth trying for. Her eyes were as blue as the flames of a blowtorch; her cheeks were as red as a hunk of red-hot iron, and her hair was the color of melted steel. All the boys in Hunkietown that weren't engaged or married had been calling Saturday nights at the Mestrovic house since Mary had reached the age of fourteen. And she was eighteen now, an age when her father thought it was proper for her to marry.

"The man that wins my Mary," says Steve, "will have to be, of course, a steel man. More than that and in addition on top of it, he will have to be the strongest steel man there is."

Besides the contest, there was to be a party, with as much stuff to eat and drink as you'd ordinarily have at a Hunkie wedding. What with that as an attraction, and the contest as another attraction, a crowd turned up that was a regular whopper. Among those that came that Sunday were steel workers from everywhere, from Homestead, for instance, and Monessen and Duquesne and just about everywhere along the river. They were great strong square men, with muscles stretching tight their Sunday clothes.

Steve Mestrovic climbed on a chair and spoke so everybody could hear. "I am not a speech maker," he said. "But I wish to tell you what this contest is like. From the mill, I have brought to the house three dolly bars, and each one is bigger than the other. One of these, it weighs three hundred and fifty pounds; another, it weighs five hundred pounds; and another, it weighs so much as the other two put together. You can tell which one it weighs the most by seeing which is the biggest. Now, we start with the little one; and the man that is the best lifter is to win my beautiful Mary. I thank you."

So the contest started, and everybody in the contest lifted the little bar over his head without so much as a grunt—everybody, that is, except a couple of fellows from Homestead. They explained the fact that they couldn't lift the bar by saying they hadn't had time to eat any breakfast. But everybody laughed at them anyhow.

Steve climbed up on a chair again, told everybody he wasn't a speech maker again, and made a speech again. "Everybody has lifted the little dolly bar with the utmost of ease," he said, "everybody, I mean, except those two loafers from Homestead, and the men and women that aren't trying to win my Mary's hand in wedded marriage, though they are still most welcome to the party. The next dolly bar is still heavier, so next you try to lift it. I thank you."

The way the men's faces got red when the men tried, and the way they grunted, made clear that the second bar, just as Steve had said, was a heavier one. Only three men, for all the wrestling and grunting that went on, managed to hoist it above their heads. Pete Pussick and Eli Stanoski and a fellow from Johnstown were the three that made it.

"Well," says Steve, back on top of the chair again, "you can see how it goes, and you can see with your own eyes that there aren't so many left to try to lift that biggest and heaviest bar of all. Now this contest is fair and square and on the upright, and I wish the best man to win without prejudice or anything. But I wish to say one little thing. The little thing I wish to say is that I hope either Pete or Eli does it and the fellow from Johnstown doesn't do it. Because the mills in Johnstown, they are coffee mills when you compare them to our mills, as who would? They make only two hundred tons of steel a day, which we here would scorn to do. Now go ahead, and may the best man win, so long as he isn't from Johnstown."

While everybody watched, Eli took hold, grunted, and started to come up with his body, lifting the bar. Of a sudden, though, his body stopped, because he'd come to the end of his arms, and the bar didn't budge any more than if Eli had been trying to lift the world.

Then it was Pete's turn. Pete rolled up his sleeves, rubbed his hands together, and took hold. Then he started up, and this time at any rate, the bar did start to come up too. Of a sudden, though, when it was about an inch and three-quarters up in the air, it started down. And when it hit the floor, the walls of the house sort of trembled and shook, as if an earthquake had come along.

"Ho! Ho!" the fellow from Johnstown yelled. "I show you now what mills are like coffee grinders. You don't know Johnstown, I see. In Johnstown, the steel men are so strong that each man can take hold of his belt, lift, and hold himself out at arm's length. In Johnstown the steel men are so tough that they tear down the mills each night and each day put them up again, just to keep their muscles working. In Johnstown, we take the engines off the ore trains and pull the ore trains ourselves. In Johnstown—"

"You are not in Johnstown now," Steve broke in, "so what you have to tell us about that coffee mill place is without interest to us. You are now in front of that dolly bar. And we will be most grateful to you if instead of trying to talk that dolly bar off the floor, you try to lift it off, which I hope you cannot."

"I will lift it," the Johnstown man said. And he stooped to lift the dolly bar.

Then he lifted a little, and his face got red, as red as the skies above the steel mills at night.

He lifted some more, and his mouth got white, as white as the limestone that's used in making steel.

He lifted some more, and the sweat dripped off his forehead and off his cheeks, like the sweat of three men that're tending open hearth furnaces on a hot day.

But the dolly bar didn't budge.

"Oh, Tuckett!" he said, letting go. And he stood up, swabbed his face, and looked fiercely at everybody, as if he was daring anybody even to snicker. Some of the men took their bandannas out, and held them up to their mouths, and their shoulders shook—but they made coughing noises instead of laughing ones.

The Johnstown fellow half closed his eyes, and looked at them very carefully. His look said that he dared anybody to take his bandanna away from his mouth and laugh out loud.

And then somebody in the back of the crowd *did* laugh— "HO-O-O! HO-O-O!"

(The laugh sounded like somebody that had stuck his head into a big empty iron barrel and was laughing and echoing in there.)

"Who was that that laughed?" the Johnstown man asked, quick as a blast in a blast furnace, and fairly close to as loud. "I call you up here, if you dare to come!"

The crowd parted. Then there was some clicking, as if a machine was running with an electric current. Then the crowd saw that the clicks were coming from a great huge fellow that was striding up to the Johnstown man. This fellow was so big that he had to walk with his head bent so he wouldn't bump it on the ceiling. His wrists were as big as another man's waist, and the rest of him, from the top of his pate to his toes, was in proportion.

"I don't care how big you are!" the Johnstown man yelled. Then he started a haymaker down at his shoestrings, and brought his fist up to hit the man on the chest, which was high as he could reach.

There was a "Ping!" like the sort that you'd hear if your fist hit the top of an oil car that had been covered with canvas, and that echoing "HO-O-O! HO-O-O!" laugh again. Then the Johnstown man was dancing around, shaking his fingers and saying, "They're busted! They're busted!"

This big fellow took the Johnstown man in one hand, and the biggest dolly bar in the other, and lifted them over his head as easy as a giant would lift a butterfly and a fountain pen. He stooped down about three feet, but both of them hit the ceiling, just the same. (The dolly bar knocked a bit of plaster off, and Steve Mestrovic shows the place to people to this day.)

Then the big man put the Johnstown man, who was still shaking his fingers, down on the floor. Then he took the biggest dolly bar and bent it until it was in the shape of a figure eight, and he eased it down to the floor.

After he'd watched what the big man did with the dolly bar, the Johnstown fellow sort of oozed out of the crowd, like running steel, and disappeared.

When it was as plain as an ingot mold on a flat car that the big man had won the contest, Steve came bustling up to him. "You win," he said, shaking the big man's hand. "You win fairly and squarely and on the upright. All I hope is that you are a man of Pittsburgh, where the mills they are bigger than coffee grinders. Your name, what is is?"

"My name," the stranger said, "is Joe Magarac."

"Joe Magarac!" says Mary Mestovic, in a voice that showed she was horrified. "Why, in Hungarian, 'magarac' means 'jackass!'"

"Sure," Joe said. "Jackass, that's me—my name and my nature. I eat like a jackass and work like a jackass, so they call me Joe Magarac."

The crowd laughed, and Steve frowned. "Mrs. Magarac!" he said. "What a name for my beautiful girl to have—what a name to exchange to from a fine name like Mary Mestrovic! I hope you are not a steel man, Joe Magarac. Because if you are not, then you cannot have my girl's hand in wedded marriage, in line with the rules of the contest."

"Oh, I'm a steel man all right," Joe said. "Look!" With that, he unbuttoned his shirt, so everybody could have a look at his chest.

A ray of sunlight hit his chest, and it sparkled.

Then Mary Mestrovic screamed, and somebody said, "He's a steel man all right—made out of solid steel!"

Steve Mestrovic's face puckered up, and it was plain that he was puzzled. "You are *made* of steel," he said. "That I agree. But in the sense I used the word, a steel man is only a man that works in a steel mill—helps make the steel, you see, in the open hearth furnace. Do you do that, Joe Magarac?"

"Sure," says Joe. "I been living in the ore pile by the blast furnace ever since I came here. I work all day and all night without stopping. Sure, I work with the steel."

"Well," says Steve, "it looks as if you met the needs of the contest, and I am pleased to hear that you work in Pittsburgh anyhow. I am most sorry, however, about your name."

Mary started to cry. "I don't want to m-m-marry a m-m-man that w-w-works all the time," she blubbered.

"Wait!" says Joe. "What's this m-m-marry stuff? I never heard of it before."

When they told him that marriage meant staying home at night or in the daytime, depending which shift you were on— "Oh," says Joe. "I didn't want that. I want to work all the time, except when I eat like a jackass. Can't I get out of it?"

Steve and Mary both spoke up at once to say of course he could, and somebody in the crowd said that anybody that worked all the time certainly was a jackass.

So Pete Pussick, who'd done better in the contest than anybody else except Joe Magarac, won Mary's hand, and not long afterward they were married. They tried to get Joe to be best man (since he was the best man, anyhow)—but he said he didn't want to stop work for foolishness of that sort. At the wedding supper, Steve made seven speeches, each of which sounded very good to him.

By the time the wedding came along, Joe was as happy as he could be. For one thing, he'd arranged for board at Mrs. Horkey's boarding house, the best in Hunkietown—and she made five meals a day for him, each about the size of a jackass' meal. For another thing, he'd been put to work at number seven furnace at the open hearth—and he worked there all day and all night, stopping only to eat.

Joe made steel his own way, of course.

First he'd collect the charge—scrap steel, scrap iron, coke, limestone, melted pig iron or blown Bessemer steel. Others used cars to carry the charge to the furnace, and others used the charging machine to dump it into the furnace, but not Joe. He just lugged in all this stuff by the armful, and then chucked it into the door.

You know how it is outside the furnaces in one of those Pittsburgh steel mills. The air is all choked up with heat, and most people find it tolerably warm. But Joe Magarac would go and sit right in the door of the furnace, sticking his hands in now and then, to see if the heat was right or to scoop out some brew to see if the mixture was right—for all the world like a cook tasting soup. If the mixture didn't have the right proportions, he'd heave in whatever was needed—a little coke, or limestone, or whatever would make it right for the best steel.

Finally he'd say, "The mixture's right, and the heat's just right—thirty-two hundred degrees. Guess it's time to pour out."

Then he'd go down to the back of the long row of furnaces, and get in back of number seven. At a time like that, other workers would pick at the clay and sand in the vent hole very carefully and they'd take off the last thin layer with a blow torch.

Not Joe, though. Joe'd put the ladle in place—which was quite a job in itself, since the ladle was a giant bucket that would take twenty-four tons of melted steel without stretching. Then he'd put the slag catcher in place. And then, he'd take his forefinger and tap the vent hole. Then the molten steel would come pouring out in a white rush.

When the ladle was full, others had to use cranes to pick up the ladles and dump the liquid steel into the ingot molds. Not Joe, though. Joe would cup his hands, dip up the stuff, and throw it into the molds himself.

And when the stuff was cooled enough, instead of taking it over to the rolling mill, the way others did, Joe would take the stuff in his hands and squeeze it, hard and slow.

It would come rolling out between his fingers in the prettiest rails you ever laid eyes on.

Well, you can imagine that a fellow that worked like that in the steel mills was pretty much of a sensation. The big boss was so proud that he had a big sign painted and nailed outside the mill. What it said was:

THIS IS THE HOME OF JOE MAGARAC

Bosses from all over the country—from Youngstown and Johnstown and even Gary—came to Joe and tried to hire him at wages that were terrific. But, "Not on your life I work for you," says Joe. "Your furnaces, they look like cookstove in Mrs. Horkey's boarding house. Your finishing mill rolls, they look like toothpicks. Besides, if I went to another mill, I'd miss work, and I work like a jackass, you know—all the time."

The men were downright proud to have Joe work with them. A good many were so interested in the way Joe made steel that they'd stay on after they'd finished their shifts just to watch him. And quite a few fellows from other places heard about him, got jealous, came around, and had contests with him.

Joe Magarac always won, though, naturally. Best race he ever had was with a fellow from Gary, who raced Joe for three days and was only three thousand tons behind him at the end. That was mighty close for a race with Joe Magarac.

When times were good, back there in the days of World War I, Joe was most useful, and hardly a week would go by without some government official turning up and trying to pin a medal on Joe, and bending the pin. But after a while, hard times came, and the workers were working only part time, and then some weren't working at all.

When this happened, a committee made up of Steve Mestrovic and Steve's son-in-law, Pete Pussick, and a fellow from Johnstown came around to see Joe.

Steve cleared his throat and made a little speech. "Look," he said, "I'm not much of a speech maker, but I can tell you how things are, and you can for yourself decide what you are to do. The point is that you work so much that you keep other men from working. It isn't fair. You ought to work just eight hours or maybe four hours, like the rest of us, that have families to feed."

"You're right," Joe answered him back. "Even a jackass can see that when there's not work enough to go around, the right thing is to divide up. But I'm not happy unless I work all the time, except when I eat like a jackass. What can I do?"

"Well," Steve said, "before you started to work, you lay around somewhere, didn't you? It has been told to me, see, that you lay in a mine or a car or some such place. Maybe perhaps you might do that once more again until the times they get better."

"Good idea," says Joe. "Come to think of it, I haven't got around to doing any sleeping for fifteen or twenty years. It is high time, therefore, that I did."

So he went out and slept and slept in some secluded place or other, nobody knew where.

And since nobody thought to wake him up when things got better again, I suppose he's still there.

Stormalong

BY ANNE MALCOLMSON

Illustrations by Robert McCloskey

> *Stormy's gone, that good old man,*
> *To my way, hay, storm along, John!*
> *Stormy's gone, that good old man,*
> *To my aye, aye, aye, Mister Stormalong.*

STORMY'S gone, of course. He died before the last Yankee clipper furled her silver sails. But stories about "that good old man" are told still wherever old sailors gather. Just where Old Stormalong was born isn't important. He first appeared on a wharf in Boston Harbor. The captain of the *Lady of the Sea*, the largest clipper ship in the China trade, was signing on men. Stormy gave his full name, Alfred Bullrod Stormalong. Without looking up from his ledger, the captain wrote down the initials, "A. B."

A. B. Stormalong stood five fathoms tall, which is the same as thirty feet. The captain glanced up at his new man. He whistled with surprise. "Phew!" he said. "There's an able-bodied seaman for you, boys."

Someone noticed that the giant's initials stood for just that. From that day to this sailors have tacked A. B. after their names. This shows that they are able-bodied seamen like Stormy.

Old Stormalong's size and strength helped him a lot on the sea. He didn't have to climb the rigging to furl the topsails. He just reached up from the deck and did it. He could hold the pilot's wheel with his little finger even in the worst weather. In less than a week he'd been promoted from common sailor to bos'n.

The cook didn't care much for his company, however. He made too much work in the galley. He had a weakness for food. He knew a good deal about cooking and wanted everything prepared just so. Besides, he wanted lots of it.

From *Yankee Doodle's Cousins*, by Anne Malcolmson, copyright 1941 by Anne Malcolmson. Published by Houghton Mifflin Company.

He liked a couple of ostrich eggs fried sunny-side-up for breakfast. For lunch he expected a dory full of soup. After his meals he used to lie out on deck in the sun and pick his teeth with an oar.

But Old Stormy was too valuable a man to dismiss because of the cook's grumbling. There were many occasions on which the *Lady of the Sea* would have become the *Lady on the Bottom of the Sea,* had it not been for her bos'n.

Once, for instance, in the warm waters of the tropical Atlantic, the captain gave orders to hoist sail and weigh anchor after a morning of deep-sea fishing. The crew heaved and strained at the capstan bars. The anchor refused to budge. Something was holding it fast to the bottom. Not even when Stormalong heaved along with the crew would the iron stir.

So Old Stormy stuck a knife into his belt and dove overboard to have a "look-see." Hand over hand he climbed down the anchor chain. Suddenly great waves arose. A commotion began on the ocean floor. The surface frothed and churned. From below came sounds of battle. The crew could see dimly two dark forms struggling in the water's depths. Then the long, black, slimy arm of a giant octopus slapped into the air.

At the sight of it the crew gave up their bos'n for lost. No human being could possibly fight single-handed one of those great devils of the sea and come out alive. But before they had a chance to arrange a funeral service for him, Old Stormalong climbed slowly up the chain and pulled himself on deck.

"Phew!" he sighed. "That old squid was a tough one. Had hold of the anchor with fifty arms and grabbed the bottom with the other fifty. He won't trouble us now, though. Tied him tighter than a schoolboy's shoe-lace. Tied every one of his arms in a double knot."

A year or so after this adventure Old Stormy lost his taste for the sailor's life. He said it was the food. He was tired of hardtack and dried fish. He had a hankering for some tender, fresh green vegetables.

His shipmates, however, guessed that the real trouble was lack of space. The *Lady of the Sea* was the biggest clipper afloat, but even so she cramped her bos'n. He couldn't sleep stretched out anywhere on board.

After a last voyage around Cape Horn, Stormalong left the wharf at Boston with his pay in his pocket and an eighteen-foot oar over his shoulder. He bade his friends good-bye. He said he was going to walk west, due west. He would stop and settle down as soon as someone asked what the long pole might be. He figured that any county whose inhabitants didn't recognize an oar was far enough from the coast for him.

The *Lady's* crew heard nothing from their shipmate for several years. Then in the San Francisco gold rush the mate had news. Stormy had bought a township and was one of the best farmers in the whole U.S.A. Stormy a farmer? The mate couldn't believe his ears. But when he was told of Farmer Stormalong's miracles, he knew it was his man, without a doubt!

Stormalong specialized in potatoes. During his first growing season the whole countryside dried up. It didn't rain for six weeks. The little spring that fed the horse trough gave only enough water for the stock. There was not an extra drop with which to irrigate the crops.

Then Old Stormalong went to work. He labored over those drooping, dying plants until the perspiration ran from him in rivers. He sprinkled those potatoes with the sweat of his brow. At the end of the season, when other farmers were moaning over their burnt acres, he drove to market with a bumper crop of the largest, tastiest spuds ever to be mashed with cream and butter.

In spite of this success, Stormy wearied of farm life. He was a restless fellow. Often at night when he had milked the cows and locked the hen roost, he sat in front of his stove and dreamed about the old days on the ocean. At last he couldn't deny to himself that the sea was calling him back.

Word spread through the countryside about a new ship, the *Courser*. It was so huge that it couldn't enter Boston Harbor. The inlanders thought it was just another Yankee yarn. They laughed about it as they sat on the front porch of the country store. But to Stormalong the *Courser* was more than a fable. It was a dream come true.

He sold his farm and returned to the East. For several days he hung around the waterfront, looking like the ghost of his former self. His ruddy salt-sea color was gone, his eyes had lost their shine, and the "shellbacks," or sailors, who had known

him in the old days realized that he was a sick man, yearning
for the feel of the spray.

They couldn't tell him much about the whereabouts of the
big ship he was seeking. It was a real boat, all right. It had
anchored outside of Cape Cod some time before with a cargo
of elephants for Mr. Barnum's circus. The *Lady of the Sea* had
been pressed into service as a tender to bring the freight to
shore.

The more the old bos'n heard about the *Courser* the more
his mouth watered to see her and join her crew. At last, when
a whaler brought word that she was cruising along the Grand
Banks off Nova Scotia, Stormy couldn't stand it any longer. He
dove off T Wharf and swam out to sea.

The next time his old friends saw him, he was the captain
of the big vessel. The old fire was back in his eyes, his cheeks
were brown as mahogany, and his spirit was dancing. For the
Courser was the only ship in all the world which suited him.
He was the only skipper in all the world to do her justice.

She was so long from stem to stern that it took a man on
horseback a good twenty-four hours to make the trip. A string
of Arab ponies were stabled in front of the fore-bitts for the
use of the officers on duty. The masts were hinged to let the
sun and moon go by. The mainsail had been cut and hemmed
in the Sahara Desert, the only expanse of land large enough
for the operation. When a storm blew up from the horizon, the
skipper had to give the order to man the topsails a good week
in advance. It took the men that long to climb the rigging.

This last fact had its disadvantages, of course. Until the
United States Weather Bureau caught on to the trick of send-
ing out weather reports in advance, the *Courser* was often
caught in a hurricane without notice enough to furl in her cloth.
She was large enough to ride out any storm, even in full sail,
without much damage. But there was no way of telling how
far off her course she'd be blown in the process.

One time, for instance, during a North Atlantic winter gale,
the *Courser* was pushed this way and that until she ended up
in the North Sea. As you know, the North Sea is just a little sea,
and not in the same class with an honest-to-goodness ocean. In
fact, it was so small and crowded with islands that the *Courser*
couldn't turn around.

There to port lay Norway and Denmark. Straight ahead lay the continent of Europe, and to starboard the British Isles. Stormy roared with anguish. He feared lest his clipper, his lovely queen of the five oceans, would have to join the lowly North Sea fishing fleet for the rest of time.

There was a way out, however. When Stormalong and the mate measured the English Channel they found that at high tide it was an inch or two wider than the *Courser*. With luck they might squeeze through it and out into the Atlantic again.

So the skipper sent the officers to Holland to buy up all the soap in sight. Then he put his crew to work, soaping the sides of the big boat. They slapped the greasy stuff on thick until the *Courser* was as slippery as an eel.

Captain A. B. Stormalong himself took the pilot's wheel and steered. Just at the turn of tide, with her full sails set, the *Courser* glided through into the broad Atlantic Ocean. But she had a close call. The headlands on the English coast scraped most of the soap off the starboard side of the vessel. To this day the cliffs at Dover have been white.

After this adventure Old Stormy was talked about in every port in the world. No sailor could deny that his highest ambition was to ship on the *Courser* under "that good old man."

Great was the mourning from Portsmouth to Hongkong when news of Stormalong's death finally came. Several reports of it were spread around. One version had it that he was drowned in a storm off Cape Hope. But most of the tales agreed that he died of indigestion. His magnificent appetite had finished him.

His old shipmates gathered for the funeral. They made him a shroud of the finest China silk. They dug his grave with a silver spade. They lowered his coffin into the ground with a silver chain, the color of his sails. And the tears that fell from the eyes of those hard old salts drenched the earth like the rain of a nor'easter.

> *Old Stormy has heard an angel call,*
> *To my way, hay, storm along, John.*
> *So sing his dirge now, one and all,*
> *To my aye, aye, aye, Mister Stormalong.*

Johnny Appleseed, Planter of Orchards

BY WALTER BLAIR

Illustrations by Glen Rounds

BACK there in Massachusetts on the day Johnny was born, there was one of those Massachusetts May storms that rain cats and a fair number of dogs. But along about when Baby Johnny had polished off his first big cry, the sun came out and made a handsome rainbow.

One end of this rainbow was hitched to Monadnock Hill, where the great carbuncle sparkled in the sunshine. From here the rainbow arched up in the gray-blue sky until the other end swooped down right smack into the Chapman dooryard near Ipswich. There, this end of the rainbow got all tangled up in a big Spitzenberger apple tree which was so loaded with blossoms that it looked more or less like a big snowball. Result was the rainbow colored up the blossoms with all the colors you can think of, off hand, at any rate.

The nurse that was taking care of Johnny and his mother claimed that she picked him up and carried him over to the window for a look at the tree.

"You'll never believe the way he carried on," she said. "Why, he humped and gurgled and stuck out his little white paws as if he wanted to pick all those blossoms! And he was only forty minutes old, too!"

Well, frankly, some of us historians *don't* believe this story—sounds fishy to us. But it's a known fact that as long as Johnny was a baby, each spring he'd whoop and squall and holler around, not giving the family a lick of peace, until they handed him a branch of apple blossoms to hang onto. Then he wouldn't bang the petals off, or eat them, like other babies would. Instead,

From *Tall Tale America*, by Walter Blair, copyright 1944 by Walter Blair. Published by Coward-McCann Inc.

he'd just lie there in his crib, looking at those apple blossoms, sniffing at them now and then, and smiling as happy as an angel plumb full of ice cream.

When Johnny ended his babyhood and started in being a boy, his mother got to feeling that he was concentrating a little too much on apple trees. "Sonny," she said, "you've got to branch out a little. Apple blossoms are fine things, I agree. But you can't depend on them for all the joy you get out of life. Wild flowers and animals, in some ways, are more or less like apple blossoms, and you might come to like them, too. Come on and see."

So she'd take the little fellow and meander around in the woods with him, introducing him to plants and squirrels and such. Since she was part Indian (Pequod, I believe), Mrs. Chapman knew many of these things almost as well as she knew her kinfolk. And after a while, when Johnny had caught on, there wasn't anything that gave him as much pleasure as taking a stance in front of a wild flower or forest animal and just standing there to admire it until dinner time.

If a flower or weed had a name for making a body well, he'd just about go wild the minute he set eyes on it. Hoarhound, catnip, pennyroyal, ginseng, dog fennel—these were the growing things he favored above all others. Some of these things were ugly as sin and smelled to high heaven, too, but he didn't seem to care a hang. And if the family didn't keep a close watch over him, dear little Johnny would haul whole messes of these herbs home and come close to stuffing the house with them.

He was keen about birds and animals, too. He'd rather listen to a wild bird tuning up his pipes—even if the bird was a hoarse old crow—than eat a piece of pumpkin pie with blackberry jam on it. He was never happier than when he was lugging around some little animal or other, even if, say, it was a skunk, an animal many people sort of tried to avoid. And whenever an animal in the neighborhood was sick or had a broken leg, the neighbors would say:

"Take the brute over to Johnny Chapman; he'll fix him up for you."

Any time he got hold of an animal in a fix like that, he'd wrap bandages around scratched places or put splints around broken legs. Or if a dog or cat was sick, he'd feed the beast some of the bad-tasting medicine he'd made out of herbs.

Before long, the animal would perk up and go kiting it for home, as fast as four legs and a tail would carry it. So it appears that this cure worked pretty well.

When he wasn't doctoring helpless little animals, Johnny would be reading. The book he liked best, for some years, was the one by Aesop, the old Greek slave, that told about animals who kept doing human things—such as lying, cheating, or stealing from one another. Naturally, an animal lover like Johnny was tickled no end by a book that flattered dumb brutes that way.

But in time Johnny's father, a preacher, began to call his attention to the Bible. "There are animals in the Bible, sonny," his father pointed out, "all those animals in the Garden of Eden that were friendly, for instance, and didn't eat one another up, and those animals that took the excursion on Noah's ark, and Balaam's ass, and the four horses of the Apocalypse. Matter of fact, the Bible swarms with animals."

Result was Johnny started to read the Bible for the animals in it. When he found that this book also had a good many parts about apples, that made him think the book was just about perfect. And after a while, when he could catch on to the ideas, they were as much to his taste as the animals and the apples.

They say that Johnny got to be so fond of these two books, *Aesop's Fables* and the Bible, that even after he'd gone to Harvard College and got highly educated, he still couldn't find any books that came within twenty yards of giving him so much pleasure.

It was shortly after Johnny got thoroughly educated that the Chapman family picked up and went to Pittsburgh. And it was in Pittsburgh that something happened to Johnny that made him behave the way he did the rest of his days.

He didn't change, mind you—just got to be more so.

Just what happened isn't clear. Some say that a woman somehow found she couldn't keep her promise to marry Johnny, and that affected him. Some say Johnny got malaria, and it did things to him he didn't get over. Some claim that he got kicked in the head by a horse he was trying to doctor. Still others incline to the idea that it wasn't any one of these things, but all three working together. And if all three of these things did happen to him within the space of a short time, you can understand that there'd be likely to be some noticeable results.

Whatever the cause was, Johnny hit on the idea of getting into this business—or "mission," as he called it—of spreading apple trees all over the Middle West.

His idea was that there ought to be more apple trees in the pioneer parts of Pennsylvania and Ohio and Indiana, and he was the fellow to see to it that there were. So each fall, in cider making time, he'd get around to the sweet-smelling cider presses in Pennsylvania. There he'd collect the pomace, the mashed up stuff that was left after the juice had been squoze out of the apples. Then he'd wash the seeds out, and let them dry in the sun. There were only a few things he liked better than rubbing his finger tips over the slick seeds.

The next spring, he'd bag these seeds, some in old coffee sacks or flour sacks, some in little deerskin pouches. Then he'd start tromping westward, carrying seed packets of one kind and another along with him. He'd hand out the little pouches to the movers West, one to each family. The big bundles he'd tote along to use himself, stopping here and there to plant the seeds all along rivers, in meadows, wherever people would let him or there weren't any people. Even after the seedlings got a good start in some of the orchards, Johnny Appleseed (as he was called by now) would drop around every so often to tend them.

What Johnny would do, in short, was to go traipsing all over the country, sleeping out in the open, eating whatever was handy, stumbling through the trackless forest or tramping through mud and snow, to get these apple orchards started. As the years passed, he covered plenty of ground, too—made it as far south as Tennessee and as far west as the Rocky Mountains.

Some people claimed it was pretty silly.

Maybe you'll ask what people thought was foolish about it. The answer they'd give would be that he wouldn't take any money for going to all this trouble—not a red cent. And it's well known, these people point out, that the only reason that makes sense for doing things is to make money.

"Money?" Johnny Appleseed would say, "*that* for money!" And he'd snap his horny fingers. "I've got a mission, that's what

I've got. What do you do with money? Just spend it for clothes or houses or food, I understand, and a saint doesn't care a snippet for any of these. Fact is, he sneers at them, every time he gets a chance. Only thing I want is to get these apples, and herbs that're good for folks, scattered all over the Middle West."

So he'd give those pioneer families appleseeds—free. And if they'd let him have a little ground for his tree nurseries, he'd plant whole orchards for them, and tend the seedlings, too— free. In the course of a few years, he had nurseries all along the shores of Lake Erie, along Elk Creek, Walnut Creek, French Creek, along the Grand River, the Muskingum, the Tuscarawas, the Mohican, and hundreds of other lakes, rivers and creeks. And instead of selling the seedlings from these nurseries (as he easily could have done), he'd heel them in and wrap them in wet straw and give them to the movers—free.

People that held Johnny was on the queer side said that if these facts didn't prove their point, they had other facts about the way he'd go wandering around in the Indian country, even when the redskins were on a rampage, without a gun or even a knife on him.

"Indians?" the little cuss would say. "*That* for Indians!" And he'd snap his bony fingers. "What'll Indians do to you if you go along peaceful-like and don't hurt them? Nothing—that's what they'll do. A saint gets onto some facts that other people don't, and one of them is that Indians are our brothers."

Well, there is some reason for saying that this was a cracked idea—one that, on the face of it, was plumb crazy. But there's one little detail that keeps it from being a clincher—the fact that, somehow, the Indians *didn't* hurt him—just the way he'd said they wouldn't. Whether the redmen were scared off by his strange looks, or whether they thought he was a heap big medicine man, or what it was, is hard to say. Anyhow, he got along with Indians better than a good many white people got along with white people.

When anybody brought up the matter of animals, Appleseed was likely to go through that finger-snapping business again. "Leave animals alone," he'd say, "and they'll do the same by you. They're brothers and sisters to you, sort of, only they don't borrow clothes and other truck and they don't misunderstand you the way human brothers and sisters do."

And he'd do the strangest things about varmints you ever heard tell of. One night some of those Ohio mosquitoes came along—some of those pests that are so big that, to set them apart from the common little ones, some people call them gallinippers. Well, Johnny had a fire out there in the woods, and considerable smoke was coming out with the flames. He noticed that these gallinippers kept getting into the smoke and choking to death, or maybe flying into the flames and getting cremated.

At a time like that, most people would just say, "Yaah, serves the brutes right," and chuck more wood on the fire.

But Johnny said, "Poor things! Guess I'll have to put out that fire." Then he sloshed water over the blaze, and lay there shivering in the dark—and being et by gallinippers, the rest of the night.

Then there was the time that Johnny was going from Mansfield to Mt. Vernon one cold winter's day, slushing through the snow in those bark sandals of his. Night came, no cabin was near, and he looked around for some big hollow log to sleep in. He found a dandy, built a fire near by, cooked his mush, slupped the stuff up, and started to crawl into the hollow log,

When he'd got in about to his hips, though, he heard a groaning grunt. Peeking in, helped by the light of the fire, he saw a big bear lying in there with his paws crossed on his chest, enjoying his winter snooze.

Johnny backed out, inch by inch, slow as a snail, being quiet so as not to interrupt the bear's sleep. "Beg your pardon, Brother Bear," he whispered. "I didn't mean to bother your sleep. Saints love bears too much to disturb them any."

Then he yawned, stretched, and curled up in the snow.

People that claimed Johnny was touched said that if all these facts didn't show it, they could mention at least three more. One was that he never ate meat, because of this liking he had for varmints. A second was that he kept planting dog fennel, as well as appleseeds, all over the country. "Dog fennel," he said, "keeps away malaria and typhoid, and heaven knows what all." (He was wrong, of course: all it does is smell bad and choke up vegetable gardens.) A third was that, though he never exactly came out and said it, he kept hinting all the time that he was a saint.

But some people kept arguing against anybody that tried to

run down Johnny Appleseed in any way. "He was a hero and a saint," they'd say. "He had something he believed in, enough to suffer for—and he went to a lot of trouble to bring it about. Talk about overcoming hardships! Why he'd go traipsing around without any shoes, in his bare feet, dressed up in a gunny sack, in the coldest weather. He didn't even have a decent hat: either he'd wear that pan he cooked mush in or he'd wear that cardboard affair he'd made that looked like a conductor's cap. And why? Simply because he was sweet and good and he wanted to get orchards scattered all over the countryside to look pretty and grow apples for folks."

Well, you can see there are arguments for both sides.

If you want to figure which side you want to take, it might help for you to have a look at Johnny when he was paying one of those hundreds of calls he paid on the farmers scattered through the Middle West.

This particular call was one he made back in 1839 when Mr. Martin Van Buren was president. Mr. Van Buren was a little plump bald-headed man, chiefly famous, at the time, because he perfumed his sidewhiskers and ate his White House vittles out of silver dishes.

The Merritt family, out there in a clearing near Perrysville, Ohio, was a powerful long way from anything as elegant as perfume or silver dishes. Whatever perfume there was around the Merritt place came from the flower garden and the farmyard, and the dishes they ate out of had been whittled out of wood. They had this farm, this big house and this big barn, and they worked from dawn to sundown—Mr. and Mrs. Merritt and the three children—Paul, Rose and little Phyllis.

When bedtime came, because they'd worked so hard, the Merritts usually just fell into bed and slept like logs. But this May night, Mrs. Merritt woke up, listened a while, then poked her husband.

He stopped snoring and said, "Huh?"—the way husbands do at a time like that.

"Henry," she said, "those night birds out there are making so much noise they went and woke me up with all their singing."

"Well," says Mr. Merritt, "I'll go to the window and politely ask the nasty old things to shut up. That what you want me to do?"

"Listen," Mrs. Merritt told him.

When he stopped grumbling long enough to listen, it was clear that the nightbirds really were having a jamboree out there. They were near the barn, just whooping it up, singing their best and loudest—even letting go with a cadenza or two every now and then.

"They are noisy, for a fact," Mr. Merritt said.

Mrs. Merritt by now had got out of bed and had gone over to the window. Mr. Merritt could see her there in the moonlight, in her long white nightgown.

"Come back to bed," Mr. Merritt told her. "You'll catch your death."

"Henry," Mrs. Merritt said, "they're out in that apple tree near the barn. You can see dozens of them, black against the apple blossoms."

"Thank you," Mr. Merritt said. "I'm glad to know where they are—didn't have a ghost of an idea where they were before. But you're catching your death. And you and those dratted birds, between you, are keeping me awake. Come back to bed."

After Mrs. Merritt had listened a while longer, she said: "Henry, there's somebody snoring out there in the barn! I can hear him snore!"

"He's probably asleep," Mr. Merritt figured. "Don't worry. I expect it's just some old tramp, asleep in the haymow."

"But why didn't the dogs bark?" Mrs. Merritt wanted to know.

"That *is* a puzzle," Mr. Merritt said. He got a hand out from under the covers and scratched his head. Then he said, "I've got it. It's probably that no account Johnny Appleseed out there, Dogs never bark at him. And wild animals and snakes and such, as a rule, don't think he's worth the trouble of hurting. And that would explain those blasted nightbirds in the apple tree, too. Now come on back to bed."

"We should have figured it out before," says Mrs. Merritt. "I'm a-coming."

Well, the next day, just before breakfast, Johnny came marching from the barn to the house. The three Merritt children stood there in the kitchen window and goggled at the man with all their might and main as he crossed the barnyard. He was a sight, for fair.

First thing the children noticed was his gray hair and gray

whiskers. He had more of both of them than a mountain man coming in for rendezvous, because he'd let them go longer—for a matter of a good many years. The hair was down over his shoulders and down over his chest, and it waved every which way in the breeze. Next thing they noticed was the way he was dressed. He had a pasteboard cap with the wide bill on it. Instead of a shirt, he had an old sugar sack with holes chopped out of it for his head and arms to go through. His pants were old and short and shredded at the bottom of each leg. One suspender had the job of holding them up, and it was worn until it looked a mite insecure. One foot had a boot on it, and the other was bare. Next the children noticed his bright gray eyes, shining from under bushy eyebrows and through tangles of hair.

Last thing they noticed was that Johnny was marching at the head of sort of a parade. Behind him, in line, more or less in step too, and looking proud as peacocks, marched the Merritt dogs Spotty and Snip, then a ewe, and finally a white hen. They were all talking to Johnny, passing the time of day so to speak, as they marched along.

When the parade got close enough, Mrs. Merritt called out: "Good morning, Johnny. We thought you'd be along one of these days, to tend the orchard. Come right in, and find a chair."

"Good morning, everybody," Johnny said, taking off that pasteboard cap. "Shall I bring in my brothers and sisters to breakfast with us?"

"We won't have any of those animals in the house, except Spot and Snip, if that's what you mean," Mr. Merritt told him.

Johnny, looking sad, turned to the animals. "It's just the way I feared," he said. "They're narrow-minded—won't let you in. Well, I'll join you later." The animals looked sad too, complained a bit, then marched back toward the barnyard, looking dignified as a squad of judges.

After Johnny came into the house, he sat down in the kitchen. The children made kind of a circle around him, and stared and stared, their mouths wide open—didn't stop even when he stroked their hair.

"Sleep well?" Mrs. Merritt asked Johnny, while she busied herself around the stove.

"Yes and no," he answered her. "Of course I wanted to lie down on the nice hard floor out there—sleep better on the floor, you know. But that dear old horse asked me to leave—said it was his stable. So I had to sleep on that soft hay in the hayloft, which rather bothered me. But I was all fagged out, I could smell the sweet apple blossoms, and there were nightbirds singing—so I got some sleep in anyhow."

"Those confounded birds woke us up with their cluttering and clattering," says Mr. Merritt. "We'd rather you'd slept on the floor in the parlor."

"Oh, no, Mr. Merritt. I didn't want to wake you up so late at night," says Johnny, smiling sweetly. "Saints with missions are thoughtful of people, you know."

With the same sweet smile spread all over the lower end of his leathery face (so far as you could see through the whiskers), Johnny turned to Mrs. Merritt. "And how," he asked her, "have the big Merritts and the three little angels been since I last broke bread with them?"

"Well," Mrs. Merritt told him, "all three of those little angels went and caught themselves the whooping cough in January, and I had lumbago in February, and Mr. Merritt had the miseries in March. Aside from that, we've been fine and well."

"I still have the miseries now and then," Mr. Merritt said.

"I never have the miseries," Johnny said. "I live in the great out-of-doors, think high thoughts and such, and eat up all my mush. That way, I never have miseries."

Mr. Merritt got middling red and started to say something, but by now little Phyllis had taken her thumb out of her mouth to ask a question: "Why do you wear only just one boot, Mr. Appleseed?"

"Well, I'll tell you, little Phyllis. This bare foot here, he went and stumbled his big toe the other day, so I'm punishing him for a while."

"Oh, I see," nods Phyllis.

The last few minutes, Mrs. Merritt had been taking hot things from the stove and sailing into the dining room with them. Now, hanging up her apron, she said: "Well, I guess everything's ready. Henry, will you bring in an extra chair?"

Mr. Merritt grunted while he carried the kitchen chair into the dining room. "The trouble isn't that there aren't enough chairs," he said. "It's that there are too many people."

When they all were sitting around the table, Johnny asked a question: "Is there enough for all the animals and for the three little angels?"

"Of course there is!" Mr. Merritt said, getting reddish again, this time with a touch or two of purple.

"Good," Johnny said. "Make it a point never to eat a bite till I've made sure. Saints are thoughtful of others that way."

"We're lucky to be fixed so you can eat with us," says Mr. Merritt. "Now, can I have the pleasure of giving you a big helping of sausage?"

"Dear me, no," says Johnny, holding up his hands as if something scary was coming at him. "Never eat a four-footed friend, as I've told you before; it'd make me feel like a cannibal. Just give me a little mush and a few pancakes. Saints are never very heavy feeders."

So Johnny ate his little meal of two bowls of mush and eight pancakes, and then leaned back in his chair. "That was perfect, Mrs. Merritt, just perfect," he said. "Only thing that might just possibly make it a smidgeon better would be some apple sauce or maybe a piece of apple pie."

"Apples?" says Mr. Merritt. "I think they disagree with me— give me the miseries."

If Mr. Merritt had whacked the Appleseed Man over the head with a plow, Johnny wouldn't have looked more astonished. He blinked his gray eyes, back of all that hair, and stood up in a daze, like a fellow setting out to do a little sleep-walking. He put his napkin down on the red-checkered tablecloth, cleared his throat, took a stance, and made one of those speeches of his about apples.

"Apples," he started out, "never, from the beginning of time, disagreed with anybody. They were in all the great countries of the earth; they were in the Hanging Gardens of Babylon that were one of the Seven Wonders; they were in the Garden of Eden; they—"

"Seems to me," Mr. Merritt interrupted him, "they caused some trouble in the Garden of Eden."

"That's wrong!" Johnny said, excited-like. "I don't know who started that story, but he was a bad man. Look in the Good Book, and you'll see that all it says is, they ate of 'the fruit of the tree.' Now that could be anything—a peach, a plum, a persimmon, a lemon—anything, in short, except an apple. Be sure the Lord wouldn't keep anyone from eating an apple. How many times is the apple spoken of in the Good Book in a favorable way? Eleven times, that's how many.

"Now you take an apple tree, and put it alongside of any other, and what do you find? Well, you find there isn't any fruit tree that lives so long and still gives fruit. An apple tree will bring good fruit a hundred and fifty years without even getting stooped over. Apple trees have got the handsomest blossoms, too, that smell the best of any fruit blossoms. Apple trees grow anywhere—north, south, east or west. Then take the fruit itself —how long does it last? Well, it'll last a sight longer than any other fruit you can name. Keep an apple, and a tomato, and a peach, and an orange in the same cellar, and after all the rest are squashed and nasty looking, the apple will be firm and crunchy and good to gnaw on. Then think of the things you can't make without apples. There's cider—"

"How about cherry cider, Mr. Appleseed?" asked Paul, who took after his father and liked to argue.

"That's not cider," Johnny answered, speaking very quickly. "That's just cherry juice. They pay it a high compliment when they call it cider. Only way to make real cider is out of apples. There are other things you can't make without apples, too—prime things—vinegar, apple butter, apple dumplings, apple sauce, even apple pies. Where'd the world be today if it wasn't for apples? In a horrible fix, that's where!"

Then Johnny got ready to wind up his speech. He stood up very straight, brushed a hank of hair out of his eye, and stared at something in the distance. "I see America," he said, using his quivery deep voice, "a nation of apple orchards. The apple trees bloom in the spring, and the men and women and children love the blossoms. The birds sing, the sun ripens the fruit, and the pickers carry the fruit to the cool cellars. Then men and women and children everywhere become strong and good and healthy, like me, because they eat apple pies."

Johnny sat down, wiping his forehead with the table napkin.

"I'm sure," says Mrs. Merritt, starting to rid up the table, "that Mr. Merritt will try some of those apples some time. Sounds to me as if they might cure those miseries of his. Won't you, Henry dear?"

Mr. Merritt sort of grunted.

"What are you going to do today, Mr. Appleseed?" Paul wanted to know.

"I'm going to get some nice herbs planted, so you won't be ailing around here so much. I'll plant some hoarhound, to take for a cold, and some dog fennel, that'll keep away malaria, and pennyroyal and catnip and rattlesnake weed. Then I'm going to put some new Russet appleseeds into the moist brown earth, and tromp them down just right. And I'm going to tend the seedlings in the nursery and the orchard. Guess I'd better get started."

"Can Paul give you a hand?" Mr. Merritt wanted to know. Mrs. Merritt gave him a quick look, and then traded a smile with Johnny.

"Of course he can—and the other angels, too," says the Apple-seed Man. "Come on, angels!" And he started out of the door.

"Psst!" whispers Mr. Merritt to Paul, pulling him aside. "You watch where he puts those dratted dog fennel seeds. They don't do any more for malaria than hay does, they choke the vege-tables, and they smell to high heaven. Run along, and keep your eyes peeled."

So Paul went out to the barn, along with the girls, and got there just as Johnny was picking up his seeds. He couldn't find one bag, however, even after he'd hunted all over for it. Finally Rose, who was helping, said:

"Here it is, in Nanny's stall! Nanny ate all the seeds! Oh, you naughty, naughty goat!"

But Johnny just said, "I don't mind, Nanny. I don't care, Rose, if animals eat all my seeds. And rattlesnake weeds won't hurt a goat. Nothing hurts a goat, you know. So come on, brothers and sisters, to work."

With the dogs, the ewe, the hen and the Merritt children trailing behind, Johnny set to work. For all he was such a skinny little runt, he could work like a horse. So, though he took time out to set a squirrel's broken leg and to make a willow whistle for Paul, by supper time he'd finished all the work he'd laid out for himself.

After supper, he was at his best. He'd reach a knotty fist into his knapsack and pull out presents for all the children. Rose got cloth for a doll dress, little Phyllis a sparkling string of beads, Paul a brace and bit. Then he told them stories—about the people he'd visited, about the heavenly angels who came calling while he sat alone by his campfire, about the way he saved the settlers from the Indian attack.

"When I was visiting in this tepee and learned what they were up to, I lit out. I'd stop at all the settlements, and holler: 'The tribes of the heathen are upon your doors and devouring flames followeth after them!' That way people were warned—"

"Well," Paul said, "I don't see why you didn't just say, 'The Indians are coming.'"

"Prophets don't talk that way," Johnny answered him back, and he went on and finished his story.

After the children had gone to bed, Johnny played his fiddle a while. Then he said, "Let me read you some news fresh from heaven." He read out of the Bible then, until Mr. Merritt started to snore. After the Merritts had gone upstairs, Johnny stretched out on the floor—slept fine there, too.

The next morning, after the Appleseed Man had waved good-by, Mrs. Merritt said, "Henry, don't you think he's wonderful? Isn't he just a saint on earth?"

Mr. Merritt sort of grunted, and asked Paul to show him where that dratted dog fennel had been planted, before he forgot.

So for years and weary years, Johnny Appleseed went on his saintly way, planting appleseeds and bad-smelling herbs. Through good weather and bad he traipsed, and his bags of seeds were a weight on his scrawny shoulders.

When many years had passed and he was old and stiff in his joints as seven new hinges, one stormy day he caught his death of cold tending an orchard he'd planted.

As soon as Senator Sam Houston of Texas, back in Washington, D.C., heard Johnny had died, he stood up and made a speech. Along toward the end, "This old man," he said, "was a great citizen. His was a work of love, and in time to come people will call him blessed." This was a good guess: though some people run him down, the way I've mentioned, others still speak highly of Johnny Appleseed.

And it's claimed by some that, even today, if you

1. Go to a certain part of Ohio in apple blossom time;
2. Get up before sunrise;
3. Go to a certain old apple tree—

you'll see the smoke from Johnny's fire as it dies out. Maybe you'll even catch a glimpse of Johnny's spirit as it moves along westward with the spring, on his mission of waking up the blossoms and tending the orchards.

I haven't looked into this, never having been in the right place at the right time. But quite a few people say that Johnny Appleseed was a queer one, of course, and they wouldn't be at all surprised if it turned out he really was carrying on that way.

Pecos Bill Invents Modern Cowpunching

BY JAMES CLOYD BOWMAN

Illustrations by Laura Bannon

ALL the men of the I. X. L. were eating out of Pecos Bill's hand within less than a week after he arrived. He took to the life of a cowboy like a duck to water. He learned their best tricks, then went on to do better. Gun Smith and Chuck and the rest were very soon like children before him. Among themselves, they bragged about their noble deeds; but when Pecos was around, they couldn't help thinking that they were mere bridled cayuses.

He could stand on the ground beside a broncho, turn an air flop, and land astride the pony before it had time to tighten a muscle. He could ride bareback without a bridle. He could urge his pony at top speed over ground so rough and uneven that Gun Smith and the others were afraid even to attempt it with bit and saddle. And he was so casual and modest about everything he did that they thought Pecos the eighth wonder of the world. Almost at once he was full of ideas. And what ideas!

Up to Pecos Bill's day, when a man wanted to capture a horse or a steer, he would lay a piece of rope down on the ground, make a loop in one end of it, sit down behind a tree or a blind, and by laying a bait, try to coax the wild critter to step within the loop. He would then jerk sharply on the rope, and perhaps one time in a dozen, if he was lucky, he would succeed in making a catch. It was no uncommon thing for a man to wait around and lose an entire month's time without laying hold of a single animal.

"Well, this sort of thing has got to be changed," said Pecos Bill to himself when no one was near to hear him. "A man can't be expected to waste his entire lifetime catching a single horse or cow."

Without further delay, Pecos got hold of the longest piece of rope he could find around the ranch, and began to throw it through the air. Next he rode off alone where the others could not see what he was doing. After three days of constant practice, he found that he could lasso almost anything. He was limited only by the reach of his line.

Pecos Bill would just make a large loop in one end of his rope, swing it wildly about his head three or four times, and then, with a quick flip of his forearm and wrist, send it flying like a bullet. And as he grew more and more skilled, he added rapidly to the length of his rope.

As soon as he was entirely sure of himself, Pecos asked the boys to come out and let him show them his new invention.

"See that roan steer across there? That's Old Crook-horn, our wildest critter, ain't it?" Pecos asked quietly.

Before anyone was aware of what he was doing, Pecos had whirled his loop about his head and had sent it so fast in the direction of the four-year-old, that the eye could scarcely follow it.

In an instant the old steer began to jump and bellow, and Pecos Bill to tow in the rope. Soon the astonished steer stood with lowered head before the even more surprised cowboys.

Not content with this great skill, Pecos began practicing from horseback.

In another week, he again called his cowboys out to see what he could do. They watched, with popping eyes, as he gave his rope a double turn around his saddle-bow. He then started his broncho at a hard gallop. They saw him quickly approach a rather tall, scraggly mesquite tree, whirl his loop wildly about his head and then fling it into the air. When he dragged a great hawk down from the topmost branch with the noose about its neck, the men were unable to believe their eyes.

"What sort o' wonder worker is this anyway?" they asked each other. "No human could ever throw the rope like that!"

Then Pecos Bill showed the men how it was done, and after

two or three months of hard practice, each of them was able
to make frequent catches at a distance of from ten to not more
than twenty feet.

In the meantime, Pecos Bill had become dissatisfied with
the fact that he couldn't find a longer rope. So he began to
braid himself a cowhide lariat. This is how he went to work.
First he looked up some old horned steers that had lived so
many years within the depths of the trees that there were green
algae on their backs—moss-backs, sure enough. What's more,
these steers were so old their faces were gray and wrinkled.

Whenever Pecos Bill got hold of one of these old fellows, he
first loosened the hide behind the ears. He then grasped the
steer by the tail and with a flip of his wrist and forearm and a
wild yowl, he frightened the animal so that it jumped out of
its skin. The tough hides of these old moss-backs were just
what Pecos needed.

Three or four years later when he had it finished, his loyal
ranchers declared on all sides that the lariat was as long as the
equator, and that Pecos could lasso anything this side of China.

It was thus that Pecos Bill solved one of the problems that
had worried cowhands and their bosses for years.

Another thing that Pecos very soon learned was that every
ranch outfit was a bitter enemy of every other outfit. When
two neighboring ranchers happened to meet anywhere near the
supposed boundary of their pasture lands, they would begin
to complain about missing cattle. Soon one would accuse the
other of rustling—a polite word for stealing—his stock. Then
there would be a sudden flashing of pistols, and one or the
other, and often both men would bite the dust.

"Why do they all make such fools of themselves?" Pecos Bill
asked. "Why don't they invent some way of marking their horses
and cattle so that they will know them wherever they happen
to meet them? All this fighting and killing is sheer nonsense.
The spirit of the Coyote pack is entirely lacking."

While Pecos Bill was trying to invent a plan for marking the
animals, a deer fly gave him just the right suggestion when it
nipped him sharply on the arm. In chasing the fly away, he just
naturally happened to notice the tattooed star that was his own

mark of identification. "Mother was wiser than all these cowmen put together," Pecos declared, laughing at himself for having been so slow in finding the right idea! "Why of course cattle and horses can be tattooed the same way. Then they'll be marked for life."

That very evening Pecos Bill explained his plans to Bean Hole. The cook listened, then shook his head. "But tattooin' is too infernal slow," declared Bean Hole, looking at the purple markings up and down the backs of his own arms. "It wasted more'n a whole week of my time to do these pictures. It'd be quicker to burn the mark on. I ain't been cookin' all these years for nothin'. I know that if you burn the skin deep enough, it'll leave an everlastin' scar. Look at this mark now—I've been carryin' it on my wrist for more'n twenty-seven years, and it's just as plain now as ever it was."

"You're right," shouted Pecos. "Together we're invented a new system of bookkeeping for every cowhand in the world."

That evening Pecos explained the new invention to the cowboys, who were open-mouthed at the cleverness of the plan. Rusty Peters, who was a blacksmith by trade, was set immediately to make the brands. He bent the iron so that it would read I X L when burnt upon the side of a horse or a cow.

The next morning all the men were as excited as boys. They herded and roped the cattle, dragging them near the heated irons and throwing them on their side to apply the stinging brand. All day long the smoke curled. All day long the cattle bellowed.

"Keep that iron a cherry red, I'm a-tellin' you," shouted Bean Hole, as he gave directions. "Hold it on long enough to do more'n singe the hair. Wait till it smells like the Devil's own stithy, and looks like the whole critter was burned to a cracklin'. That's not near long enough. She'll shed that mark before the snow flies. There, that's about right. Let her bawl her fill. The loss of a few mouthfuls of hot air ain't going to hurt her any."

"Keep quiet, you old bag o' wind," shouted Rusty Peters, hard at work. "I ain't a blacksmith for nothin'! I'll burn a brand across your mouth in a minute if you don't keep quiet."

By evening the entire job was completed. It was found that

the I. X. L. outfit possessed fifty-seven steers of various ages, forty-one cows, some fat and sleek, some spindly and thin, and twenty-four calves.

"This small herd ain't really enough to bother with," Pecos Bill observed in disappointment. "I thought you cowmen said you had a real ranch. Why, the woods are full of wild cattle that belong to nobody in particular. I'll just go out and drive in a few thousand of them. We'll put our trademark on them, and then they'll be ours."

"But how in tarnation will we ever keep these longhorns from runnin' straight away again?" asked Gun Smith with doubting stare. "What's the use of goin' through all this trouble disfigurin' the sides of all these cattle with our silly I. X. L. advertisement, if we're goin' to turn 'em back to the wild prairies again?"

Pecos Bill had not thought of this. The general custom among the cowmen had been to allow all the cattle to go and come whenever they liked. The ranch shack was nearly always built beside running water, and naturally, a few of the timid and lazy cows and steers would make this their home. The more ambitious stock would just as naturally wander off across the prairies and mesa and take refuge within the mesquite woods. Soon they would be as wild as deer and as diffcult to catch.

This careless way of doing things meant that each ranch had a mere handful of shifting population, as far as the cattle were concerned. When the pasture and the water elsewhere were scarce, the cattle would flock to the ranch; but most of the time they would not even trouble themselves to take a French leave.

"It's dead wrong," said Pecos Bill to himself as he squatted on his haunches. "The problem to be solved is this: How are the cattle to be kept together in a herd after they are branded?"

While he was trying to work out the answer, he loped off alone to the top of a small mountain one morning before the others were awake. Far over the rolling prairies he could see many small wandering herds of cows and steers.

"Of course, if bad should come to worse, I could just round the herd up every night and throw my noose about them, and tie the cattle up till morning," he smiled. "But that ain't a good solution, for I can't bind myself that close to the ranch. I've got to reserve my energy for bigger work. All kinds of things are waiting to be invented."

At first as he sat and thought, his mind was just one grazing herd after another. He saw cattle scattered all over the prairies; he saw cattle stampeded, and he saw cattle leaving the herd to get lost in the wild mesa. But after a little, things cleared up and he knew what he was going to do.

He got up, stretched the kinks out of his muscles and started at a brisk gallop for the ranch house. As soon as he arrived he called out for everybody to come.

"Here's the plan," he said excitedly. "The way to keep the herd together is for you men to ride out with the cattle every day. By waking up the drags and by holding back the leaders, the herd can be kept together and can be made to go to the best feeding grounds every day."

"You mean," said Gun Smith, with an ironical smile, "that us cowpunchers has got to be ordinary bovine critters the rest of our lives?"

"And stay with the herd all night and sleep with the hootowl?" asked Moon Hennessey sourly.

"Oh, yes," and the musical Mushmouth sang with a pretense of tears in his voice:

> "The centipede runs 'cross my head,
> The vinegaroon crawls in my bed,
> Tarantulas jump and scorpions play,
> The bronchs are grazin' far away,
> The rattlesnake sounds his noisy cry,
> And the Coyotes sing their lullaby,
> While I *sleep* soundly beneath the sky."

"It don't appeal to me," complained Moon Hennessey.

"Oh, well, you'll be just crazy about it when you've tried it —especially if the herd stampedes in your direction," suggested Gun Smith with irony. "It's goin' to be a regular picnic, Sundays and week days together, an' there's no doubt about it."

"And if the herd gets stampeded you'll be on hand to turn the leaders and start them milling until they are bitterly disappointed in trying to run away," added Pecos Bill quietly. "Besides, sleeping out under the stars is wonderful, once you've acquired the knack. I know from long experience."

"It'll all be easier than handlin' a month-old heifer calf," laughed Gun Smith bitterly.

"Well, now that we have decided what to do, I'll go out and drive in the cattle to be branded. And while I'm away Gun Smith will be your foreman. He'll keep you out of mischief. We can't get started too soon. So, with your permission, I'll be going right away. I'll have a herd ready to be branded first thing in the morning."

As soon as Pecos Bill had darted out into the night, the men began to wonder whether his coming to them had been a blessing or a curse.

"Chuck, before this monstrosity of yours arrived," began Moon Hennessey, "we was leadin' a peaceful and easy life. All we was expected to do was swap lies, and eat juicy tobacco. Now, it seems, we're goin' to be set at hard labor!"

"To my way of thinkin', the change will be all to the good," answered Chuck. "And who knows—it may bring us glory and honor—and gold!"

"Well, then, since I'm the appointed foreman of this outfit until Pecos returns," Gun Smith drawled as he put his hands on his guns, "I'm goin' to give you, Chuck, the place of highest honor. While the rest of us turn in for the night, you, Chuck, will take your Old Pepper and make contact with our branded herd. If they object to your presence and attempt to trample you and your noble steed to smithereens by startin' a wild stampede, you'll simply turn the leaders and set the herd millin'. If they show signs of thirst, you will lead them beside the still water!"

"Thank you very much for the honor," answered Chuck, as he rose promptly to carry out the assigned task.

"The rest of us motherless mavericks," Gun Smith continued, "will remain here, so's to be on hand with the ropes and the brandin' irons when Old Pecos returns any minute with his promised herd of wild cattle."

"Well," added Moon Hennessey with a bored yawn, "Old

Pecos will be doin' splendid if he shows up by the end of next week. There'll be no herd here tomorrow mornin', I can promise you that."

"Don't fool yourself," replied Chuck spiritedly as he turned on his heel. "You evidently ain't yet acquainted with my brother."

"Brother!" fairly hissed Moon Hennessey in a rage. "Cut out your star identification talk and go on about your business!"

Next morning the men were awakened at early dawn by the dull thud, thud, thud of innumerable hoofs, and by the monotonous bawling of the weary cattle. As the men rubbed the sleep out of their eyes and looked about, they discovered, to their astonishment, that Pecos Bill had actually returned with a herd so large that they couldn't begin to see either its beginning or end.

"What, aren't you boys up yet?" Pecos called with a smile. "I've been having a wonderful night. And I've got enough cattle here to keep all of us busy for a while, anyway."

"Enough wild critters to keep the brandin' irons sizzlin' and the smoke risin' for a month of Sundays, I'd say," conceded Gun Smith, none too happily.

But Pecos Bill had no use for conversation just then. Breakfast was gulped down, cattle struggling and bellowing; the alkali dust flying mountain high; Bean Hole rushing about like a chicken with its head off, shouting his directions amid the din and waving his kettles and pans, and Rusty Peters keeping the smoking brands busy. This was the way it went all day long. By the time the sun had set, the tired men had added three hundred and thirty-eight cattle to their herd. Three hundred and thirty-eight—hurrah for Pecos Bill!

Pecos Bill himself was so happy over the results that frequently during the following months he would go out for an evening adventure, returning promptly the following morning with hundreds more bawling wild cattle. By the end of the season the I. X. L. ranch was one living sea of four-footed beasts.

As soon as his men had finished branding the incoming herd with the I. X. L. trademark, Pecos Bill at once began looking around to find other worlds to conquer. He instructed the men

how to live in the saddle, and how to take cat naps astride their
grazing ponies. He showed them how to soothe the cattle by
crooning songs to them, and how to keep the herd together
without annoying even the leaders.

When the herd stampeded, as it was sure to do at times,
Pecos taught the men how to turn the leaders, and thus start
the entire herd milling in a circle until the cattle finally winded
themselves, and stopped through sheer weariness in the very
spot from which they had started in the first place.

During these days, Bean Hole was the busiest man this side
of Mars. After trying for a week to feed the men by carrying
food out to them from the ranch shack, he finally gave up. On
four or five different occasions, as he was starting out with his
kettles and pans, he actually met himself on the trail coming
back with the empty dishes of the previous afternoon. If he
hadn't stopped his foolishness of trying to work twenty-seven
hours a day just when he did, most likely his ghost would still
be wandering on the wind over the same trails.

In the despair of complete exhaustion, Bean Hole finally
hitched two spans of mules to the chuck wagon, loaded it down
with enough food to last a fortnight, and left the ranch shack
to take care of itself. He hadn't been gone half an hour before
the place looked as deserted as the ruins of Pompeii.

Very soon the entire life of the ranch was going along according to the new plan. Everything was clicking like clock work
and Pecos Bill was so pleased, for the present at least, that he
couldn't think of anything left to invent. So he decided to go
out and tell the world about what he had been doing, not for
the sake of his own fame, but for the benefit of the cowmen
of the entire range country.

One evening, after the cattle had settled down for the first
sleep of the night, Pecos Bill announced to Gun Smith, his foreman, that it would be necessary for him to go away from the
ranch for a few days. "If anybody asks where I am," he whispered, "just tell them that I'll be back for breakfast, like as not."

Pecos then took his boots under his arm, threw his coiled
rope over his shoulder, and went bounding off across the rolling
prairie. When he came to a strange ranch, he would quickly

put on his boots and walk in great dignity, with jangling spurs, up to the boss of the outfit. Very soon he would be telling the wide-eyed cowman his story. In this way he easily covered forty or fifty miles in an hour and a half or two hours.

Pecos Bill thus visited all the ranches of the entire Southwest within two or three months. Not forgetting a single detail, he told the men everywhere what he had done. At first they thought him the biggest liar that had ever been invented in the whole world of cowmen. But when he had limbered up his lariat, and when they had witnessed his performance, they were quite willing to believe everything he told them.

What they saw was even more wonderful than what he had said. For with perfect ease, he would lasso any animal within reach of their vision. He could lasso a grazing or galloping steer, or lay his flying noose around the neck of a bald eagle in full flight.

The flying visits led later to many heated disputes among the puzzled ranchers: "You say this Pecos Bill left Hub's Ferry at nine o'clock? But he was at Slippery Mike's by eleven, and that's a good forty miles as the crow flies, ain't it? And he was alone and on foot, wasn't he? Who is this Pecos Bill, anyway?" Every rancher seemed to have a bigger yarn to tell than his neighbor.

But they were all true—certainly! And through the efforts of Pecos Bill, ranchmen began to have a spring roundup and fall roundup. Pecos persuaded the ranchers of a given range section or river valley to drive together all the cattle of their entire district. They then sorted them into individual herds according to the particular brand of each owner. After this work was completed, each owner branded all of his calves. The strays, with no brand, and the orphan mavericks were then distributed equally and branded so that they could never again go astray. And every bit of the plan was Pecos Bill's.

In the fall the roundup was repeated so that the stray cattle could be located and given back to their rightful owners. After all the exchanges were made, the cowmen, as they took their herds back to their individual feeding grounds, found it easy to count the number of steers that were in condition for the market and the number that they would have to pasture during the coming winter.

Thus it was that each owner was given what belonged to him, according to the laws of reason, and not in accordance with the earlier outlawry of the pistol.

And so it came about very naturally, through the organization of all the scattered cowmen, that the fame of Pecos Bill rapidly spread to the four corners of the range country. From the valley of the Rio Grande, through Texas and New Mexico, Arizona and Colorado, Kansas and Nebraska, and far into the wilderness of Montana and Wyoming, cowboys, when they met, would carelessly throw one foot free from its stirrup and in a resting position shout to their nearest companion: "Say, have you heard about the rope Uncle Bill is still braidin' down on the Pecos? Why, it's already twice as long as the equator! You know, if Old Pecos Bill could only get a toe hold on the moon, he'd turn in and lasso this wanderin' planet of ours and bring it back into the Milky Way, where it belongs! Yes, and Pecos could do it easier than you or I could lasso a year-old heifer calf!"

Tony Beaver

BY ANNE MALCOLMSON

Illustrations by Robert McCloskey

TONY Beaver, the great lumberjack of the South, lived "up Eel River." You won't find Eel River on any maps. The geographers haven't decided where to put it. The people of Louisiana and Arkansas are sure that it's in the cypress swamps. Georgians are just as sure that it's in the turpentine hills. North Carolinians insist that it's in the Smoky Mountains. But West Virginians, who know most about Tony, say that Eel River is high up in their own Alleghenies.

It's not hard to visit the camp, however, if you really wish to see it. Just send word to the lumberjack himself by the next jay bird you see, and Tony will send his path after you.

By the way, this path has an interesting story. One autumn day long ago, as Tony Beaver walked through the woods, something tickled his legs. It felt smooth and ribbony, like a snake. He tried to brush it off, but it clung to his boots and licked at his laces. Glancing down, he saw a baby path, dancing, frisking, romping around him. Tony searched the bushes, expecting to find a mother road near-by. But the path was all alone.

From the way the little fellow wagged its tail and jumped up and down, Tony guessed that it must be lonely. From the looks of its stones and weeds, which hadn't been brushed in a long time, he knew it lacked a mother's care. It was obviously an orphan, just a poor little orphan path that led from Somewhere to Nowhere.

Tony took a fancy to it and carried it gently back to Eel River. Here he gave it food and brushed the cockle-burrs out of its grasses. He let it sleep in front of the fire. In time it became the camp pet. The boys were fond of the clever little thing and taught it a number of tricks. When it became old enough and strong enough, Tony made it his special messenger.

The path still has one bad habit which Tony has never been able to cure. It likes speed. It skims over the hills and down the valleys like a runaway roller-coaster. Some timid people who have visited Eel River say they'd rather spend the rest of their lives at camp than ride home on that streak of greased lightning.

If you aren't too shaken up when you get there, you will find Eel River an unusual logging camp. It's very large, in the first place. After all, Tony and his jacks are big men. In the second place, the bunkhouses look like overgrown watermelons. Instead of the square log buildings you find in Minnesota and Maine, these are shaped like footballs. Their outer walls are smooth and green, their inner walls soft and pink. The bunks and chairs are carved from the same hard black stone as the fireplaces. In case you think your eyes are spoofing you, the bunkhouses really are watermelons.

Before Tony became interested in logging, he had a melon farm. He grew fruit so huge that the hands had to use bucksaws to cut them from the vines. The only trouble with them was they were too big to haul to market. Tony had to think about that problem for several days. While he was thinking he sat by his fire and smoked his pipe. The clouds of black smoke rising from his corncob made the people of Arkansas hide in their cellars. They thought a tornado was blowing up.

Finally Tony figured it out. He built a railroad right up to the melon patch. Three flatcars were hitched together. The smallest melon was rolled aboard. The engine chugged off with Tony Beaver sitting on top of his prize, as proud as you please.

Unfortunately, the tracks ran up a steep grade and down again in a hairpin turn. The engineer, who wasn't used to hauling a load of one watermelon, forgot to be careful. The car lurched against the hillside. The cargo wobbled unsteadily. Then, whang! The melon, Tony and all, rolled off the flatcars, down the hill, and splashed into Eel River with a kerplunk that caused a flood as far away as New Orleans.

The force with which it hit the water broke the melon into a thousand pieces. For hours the river churned red. It looked

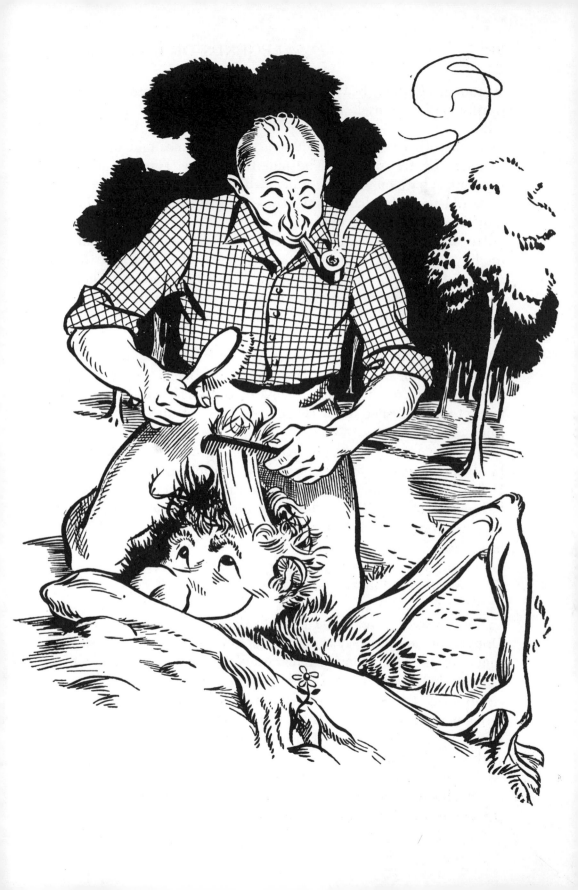

as though Farmer Beaver had been drowned. But, no! He simply pulled himself up on one of the seeds and paddled ashore.

As the other seeds floated downstream they caught against the dam by the sawmill. The jam there gave Tony an idea. He made a bargain with the miller, who cut them up into planks and sold them for hardwood. Thus Tony Beaver became interested in the logging business.

He didn't want to waste the rest of those melons. He had his boys roll them to the edge of the field. They dug out the red meat, cut doors and windows, and put in chimneys. Then they built fireplaces of some seeds and carved others into furniture. Lo and behold! There stood as fine a set of bunkhouses as ever was!

The most interesting person at the Eel River Camp is, of course, Tony Beaver himself. He's too great a person to describe. You'll have to see him for yourselves. And until you do, you'll have to be satisfied with stories of some of the wonderful things he's done.

Some years after he'd given up farming and gone into the lumber business, Tony was brought again into the public eye. He still kept a small garden of a few thousand acres on which he raised peanuts. His "goobers," as he called them, were sold at circuses and baseball games all over the United States. He had also a stand of molasses maple trees, which produced the sweetest, most delicious syrup you ever poured over a flapjack. They say Paul Bunyan used to send for a small ocean of it every year.

Tony Beaver never could learn to do things in a small way. One season he produced so many goobers and so much molasses that even he was swamped. The circus people complained that peanut shells were heaped so high in the tents the audiences couldn't see the rings. Negro mammies from Richmond to New Orleans moaned that they couldn't fry cakes fast enough to sop up the 'lasses. Even so, the Eel River warehouses were bursting with unsold goods.

To add to Tony's troubles it began to rain. It rained for days and nights without stopping, until the hill country above Tony's private town of Eel River Landing was flooded. At first the

townsfolk didn't mind. They found it entertaining to be able
to sit on their own front porches and watch henhouses and
church steeples sweeping past them downstream.

Still it poured. They began to be alarmed. Their own levees
were about to break. It looked as though Eel River Landing
itself might be washed out into the Gulf of Mexico.

A committee was elected and sent to ask Tony if he could
do something to stop the flood. He shook hands with all the
members and sat down in front of the bunkhouse fire to smoke
his pipe and think. Soon a Big Idea came to him.

The members were sent home to collect all their friends and
relations at the peanut warehouses. The loggers were sent to
the molasses stores. Big Henry and Sawdust Sam, his foreman,
hitched the big oxen to the vinegar cruet and the salt box, and
drove them to the riverside. The big logger himself borrowed
a wooden spoon from the cookhouse and followed after.

As soon as everyone had met, Tony gave his directions. The
townsfolk shelled the peanuts as fast as they could and tossed
the nuts into the river. The lumberjacks emptied the molasses
barrels into the water from the other side. Sam dumped in the
salt. Big Henry poured in the vinegar. Great Tony Beaver
straddled the flood, one foot on one side, one on the other, and
stirred that river for all he was worth.

The goobers and 'lasses stuck to the reeds. They clogged the
river bed. The current began to slacken. Eel River was oozing,
not racing, toward the town.

Then the sun came out, the hot noonday sun. A sweet-
smelling mist arose as its rays heated the mixture. Still Tony
swished his spoon from bank to bank. Bubbles appeared gradually along the shores, little pearl bubbles at first, then big
balloon bubbles. Finally the whole river boiled up. The steam
rose higher than the mountains. The odor was delicious!

Tony's spoon churned faster and faster. As the river bubbled
and hissed and spouted, its brown speckled waters thickened.
From time to time the big lumberjack lifted his ladle and let
it drip. Each time the drops fell more slowly, until at last one
spun out into a fine hard thread.

With that, Tony Beaver tossed the spoon aside and jumped
to the bank. With a jerk he yanked a cloud across the sun. Im-

mediately the river cooled. The thick, sticky mass stopped seething and began to harden. The current had stopped completely. There above Eel River Landing stretched a dam and a broad lake, as brown and quiet and hard as a rock. Except for the white pebbly specks made by the goobers, it was as smooth as a skating rink.

The townsfolk cheered. A holiday was declared and the committee gave Tony a vote of thanks for saving the village. The kids ran home for their ice skates. Soon everyone was gliding in and out among the peanut bumps. People for miles around came to help celebrate.

It was the best party West Virginia ever had, except that there were no refreshments. These were easily supplied, however.

"Break yourself off a piece of the dam," Tony suggested to a hungry-looking youngster. "It tastes mighty good."

The boy thought Tony was joking. But when the big logger reached down and broke off a hunk, he agreed to try it. M-m-m-m! It certainly did taste good. One or two other brave fellows tried it. Soon there was a scramble for the sweet nutty stuff.

Tony had not only saved the town. He had invented peanut brittle.

INDEX of Authors and Titles

ACKNOWLEDGMENTS

The publishers wish to express their appreciation to the following publishers, agents, authors, and artists who have granted permission to use material appearing in this book. Any errors or omissions are unintentional and will be corrected in future printings if notice is sent to The Crowell-Collier Publishing Company.

THE CAXTON PRINTERS, LTD.   Illustrations by Dell J. McCormick for "Black Duck Dinner" from *Paul Bunyan Swings His Axe*, published by The Caxton Printers, Ltd., Caldwell, Idaho; used by special permission of the copyright owners.

COWARD-McCANN, INC.   "Joe Magarac, Pittsburgh Steel Man" and "Johnny Appleseed, Planter of Orchards," from *Tall Tale America*, by Walter Blair, illustrated by Glen Rounds, copyright 1944 by Walter Blair; used by permission of Coward-McCann, Inc., publishers.

THE DIAL PRESS   "Pandora, the First Woman," "The Golden Touch of King Midas," "Perseus Slays the Gorgon," "The Golden Fleece," and "The Flight of Icarus," from *Stories of the Gods and Heroes*, by Sally Benson, illustrated by Steele Savage, copyright 1940 by Sally Benson; used with permission of the publishers, The Dial Press.

HOLT, RINEHART AND WINSTON, INC.   "Thor Gains His Hammer," "How Odin Brought the Mead to Asgard," "The Death of Balder," "The Punishment of Loki," and "The New Day," from *Thunder of the Gods*, by Dorothy Hosford, illustrated by Claire and George Louden, copyright 1952 by Dorothy Hosford; reprinted by permission of Holt, Rinehart and Winston, Inc., New York, publishers.

HOUGHTON MIFFLIN COMPANY   "The Chimaera" and "The Miraculous Pitcher," from *The Wonder Book for Boys and Girls*, by Nathaniel Hawthorne, illustrated by Walter Crane and Hammatt Billings; "Stormalong" and "Tony Beaver," from *Yankee Doodle's Cousins*, by Anne Malcolmson, illustrated by Robert McCloskey, copyright 1941 by Anne Malcolmson; reprinted by permission of and arrangement with Houghton Mifflin Company, the authorized publishers.

ALFRED A. KNOPF, INC.   "The Black Duck Dinner," reprinted from *Paul Bunyan*, by James Stevens, copyright 1925, 1947 by Alfred A. Knopf, Inc.; by permission of Alfred A. Knopf, Inc.

LITTLE, BROWN & COMPANY   "Orpheus and Eurydice," "Pygmalion and Galatea," and "Pyramus and Thisbe," from *Mythology*, by Edith Hamilton, illustrated by Steele Savage, copyright 1940 by Edith Hamilton; by permission of Little, Brown & Co.

LONGMANS, GREEN AND COMPANY, INC.   "The Death of Roland," from *The Song of Roland*, translated by Merriam Sherwood, copyright 1938 by Longmans, Green and Company.

THE MACMILLAN COMPANY   "Phaeton" from *The Age of Fable* by Thomas Bullfinch, illustrated by Boris Artzybasheff. "Aladdin; or, The Wonderful Lamp" and "Ali Baba and the Forty Thieves" from *The Arabian Nights* by Padraic Colum, copyright 1923, 1951, 1953 by The Macmillan Company; "Odysseus at the Palace of King Alcinoüs" from *The Adventures of Odysseus and the Tale of Troy* by Padraic Colum, copyright 1918 by The Macmillan Company, 1946 by Padraic Colum; used by permission of The Macmillan Company.

JULIAN MESSNER, INC.   "The Last Adventure," reprinted by permission of Julian Messner, Inc., from *Heroes of the Kalevala, Finland's Saga*, by Babette Deutsch, illustrated by Fritz Eichenberg, copyright 1940 by Babette Deutsch.

ALBERT WHITMAN & COMPANY   "Pecos Bill Invents Modern Cowpunching," from *Pecos Bill*, by James Cloyd Bowman, illustrated by Laura Bannon, copyright 1937 by Albert Whitman & Co.; reprinted by permission of Albert Whitman & Co., Publishers.